MW00975237

Andie Beth

Steps

Jan Shearouse Alexuk

Copyright © 2011 by Jan Shearouse Alexuk

Andie Beth
Steps
by Jan Shearouse Alexuk

Printed in the United States of America

ISBN 9781613791615

All rights reserved solely by the author. The author guarantees all contents are original and do not infringe upon the legal rights of any other person or work. No part of this book may be reproduced in any form without the permission of the author. The views expressed in this book are not necessarily those of the publisher.

www.xulonpress.com

Chapter One

Election Night

"Rachel, are you out there?"

I'm not getting an answer. Let me try again.

"Rachel, ARE YOU OUT THERE?"

When I type in caps, I get her attention. Rachel is my best friend, and I'm checking to see if she is on facebook®. Rachel's photo says she|s online. Come on, Rachel answer me before I get caught.

It is election night, and I'm stuck studying for a world history mid-term tomorrow. My parents could have gotten me out of it, but not Mr. and Mrs. Perfect. After all, Andie Beth, how would it look if you skipped the test when all your friends had to take it after I preached education, education, education throughout my campaign?

Oh, by the way, did I mention his campaign was for President of the United States. I hope he loses. Publicly, I smile a lot for the press while hissing under my breath every time he gives a speech. It is election night and instead of being downstairs watching election returns, I'm stuck in my third floor bedroom supposedly studying for the history test.

I HATE HISTORY! Who cares about ancient civilizations? I don't care what the Romans did. All these Caesars' have me confused. Names and dates, names and dates is all Mrs. Morgan, my world history teacher, cares about.

Before you think I'm weird or something, let me tell you, I don't want to be downstairs with all the "La De Da" people involved in Daddy's campaign. If one more person asks me how I feel about the possibility of Daddy becoming President, I will strangle them. If Mama whispers in my ear one more time to remember my manners, I may strangle her.

I can see the headline now: *Future First Lady Murdered by Daughter.* How would dear old

Daddy would react then? Please, God, let the man lose. Surely, people out there aren't fooled by this guy.

"Rachel, where are YOU?"

She's with her parents watching the returns. Her dad is running for senator again. He's been in the senate since she was four years old, and we became friends when Daddy was elected when I was eight. She lives in Washington, D.C., but her family has an apartment in Baton Rouge.

We have to go to family political events like parades, parish fairs, and fundraisers together, and became friends that way. We text on the phone and facebook® and see each other whenever she is in town. Baton Rouge is only an hour and a half away so she stays here a lot. We are sort of like sisters. Mama calls her, her other daughter. If the truth be known, Mama would rather have Rachel as a daughter. Around adults Rachel is everything I'm not. She plays the game well, and is the perfect example of what a young lady should be. Behind closed doors she cuts loose like the rest of us. She even had her belly button pierced without her parents knowing about it, and sticks a band aid on it sometimes to cover it up. Of course, Rachel would never expose her belly button in public. Not prim and proper Rachel.

Mama thinks that Rachel is a good influence on me, which is why she lets her stay here.

"Rachel is a straight A student, Andie Beth. You could be too if you would just apply yourself. Mrs. Le Brun says that Rachel comes home from school and dives into her homework. You could learn a lot from your friend."

I roll my eyes and answer the required "Yes, Mama."

Again Mama is clueless. Rachel hangs out with me because I live my life the way I want to live it.

"A.B. what is it about your mother?"

"What do you mean?"

"My mom thinks your mother is Superwoman."

"Earth to Rachel. It's because Mama is a guidance counselor. Everyone at school thinks it must be great to have such an understanding Mother. All I hear all day is how your mother can really relate to us, and how she is so cool. In other words Rach old buddy, old pal, your mom has fallen under the Lynn Nettles Spell."

"Well, if it means we can hang out together what difference does it make?"

Our family didn't move to Washington when Daddy was elected to the Senate. Mama liked her job as a guidance counselor at my high school, and didn't want to quit work. She didn't resign until school ended last year to campaign with Daddy. I had to put up with being in the same school with her for my freshman year. Then my brother Trey graduated.

He is a basketball player. Daddy wanted him to play for Louisiana State University in Baton Rouge, where Daddy played football a long time ago. Mama said she was staying here for the good of the children. I think it was her routine she was worried about, but it sounded better to everyone the other way. It makes her appear like the martyr that she pretends to be.

Daddy has a small apartment that he rents in Washington, and comes home almost every weekend. When Congress isn't in session, he's here all the time, and that's when the sparks fly. My parents are hard enough to take one-on-one, but when it is both of them against you, forget it.

"Andie Beth did you do your homework? Andie Beth clean up your room. Andie Beth you know the rules."

Andie Beth this and Andie Beth that, that's all I hear with both of them around. Now it's not that easy. My best tactic is avoidance. I avoid talking to both of them. This has been pretty easy the last few months of the campaign.

Since Trey is at LSU, my grandmother Josie has stayed here since school started.

My parents check in every night with the obligatory phone call.

"Andie B. how was school today?"

"Fine."

"What did you get on your biology test?"

"B-. Where do you go tomorrow?"

"Georgia and Florida."

"When will you be home again?"

"Monday afternoon. Come home right after school. We have to leave again on Tuesday. Be good. We love you."

"Love you too."

Click and the conversation ends. Grandma Josie asks me how they are, and I tell her fine. I grumble about having homework to do, and trudge to my room while tripping over the tacky green rug in the hall and fall on my bed.

"Why can't I have a normal family?" I scream into my pillow.

"I want my mama and daddy. It's not fair. My life sucks. I want my life back. I cry out to the world and no one hears me. Just like when I was a little kid and no one saw me.

Grandma Josie cannot hear me. She's in the kitchen on the opposite side of the house. It is a good thing too, because she thinks it's great that we're probably going to live in the White House.

"All that fancy food and people waiting on you, Andie Beth you'll be spoiled rotten."

Yeah, right. Like Mama will allow that. She'll want me to clean my own room. I can hear her now talking to the maids.

"Oh, no, there's no need to clean Andie Beth's room. She is quite capable of doing that herself. Save yourself some time and energy for the important people who live here."

Then she'll turn on me, and remind me of my status as First Daughter.

It's not fair. My life sucks.

Why am I crying so much? Because I know it is happening. I'm going to end up as First Daughter. I grab the box of Kleenex from my headboard, but it is empty. I cannot stop crying. I reach down to the floor to grab the first thing I can find to wipe my face, my basketball practice jersey. I wipe my tears with it gagging myself in the process. Man I stink. I stumble into the bathroom to wash my face, throwing the jersey in the hamper on the way. Might as well take a shower while I'm here. Grandma Josie will be up to check on me in a while.

That's how my life has been for the last three months. Mama and Daddy came home late last night after I was asleep. I knew they had been here because when I woke up in the middle of the night. I could smell Mama's perfume. She still wears Chanel # 5 after all these years. Daddy must have been here too, because there was a baseball cap with Nettles 2012 stuck on my head. I know Daddy had to put it there because Mama does not have a sense of humor.

But why didn't they wake me up? Don't they realize how much I've missed them? If they hugged me, I would have woken up. These people are totally clueless. I have not seen them in over two weeks. HELLO EARTH TO

PARENTS. Your daughter has missed you. I'd never admit it. Andie Beth Nettle's Rule Number 3: never let your family know how much you love them. Only use the word love when making a response where not using it could get you in trouble.

They left to vote before I got up this morning. You'd think they would at least have breakfast with me. Yeah, right, seeing me wasn't very high on their priority list. Grandma Josie said that Daddy felt it was important for him and Mama to be the first ones in their precinct at the polls. I threw on a pair of jeans, an LSU tee shirt and my Nikes®. When I came downstairs, Grandma Josie greeted me with a scowl on her face.

"Andie Beth, are you wearing that to school today?"

"Ma'am, no uniforms this week. It's Homecoming Week, and we can wear whatever we want."

"Well, normally I don't say anything, you know. I know you young people do your own thing these days. But don't you think you might want to dress up today?"

"Nope, today is just another day as far as I'm concerned."

"Andie Beth Nettles, you know better than that. Today is one of the most important days in your family's life. There's going to be photographers all over the place. What will people think if they see you on the news dressed like a bum?"

"Did Mama or Daddy say I had to dress up? Ma'am, all my friends will think I've lost my mind if I dress up when I don't have to. They're already making fun of me, and the election isn't over. As for the reporters, they will say that Senator Nettles has a regular kid for a daughter who isn't trying to be someone she's not."

"No, your parents didn't say a word. But Andie Beth, your life is going to change over the next few weeks, and you better get rid of that attitude."

"Not if he doesn't win, ma'am. I'm going to be late for school. Gotta fly."

"Come straight home from school."

"Can't Gram. Basketball practice, remember?"

"Okay, then, right after practice. And Andie Beth?"

"Yes, ma'am."

"Lose the attitude or otherwise you're going to be grounded until Christmas. You know how your parents hate it."

"Yes, ma'am."

"And have a good day and study hard."

I finally escaped the house glad that Gram didn't push the clothes thing. I was surprised there wasn't a note from

Mama telling me what to wear, but I guess she was too tired to write it. I made it to the corner just as the school bus was coming to a stop.

There wasn't a lot of talk among the kids at school about the election. One or two asked me if I was packed for the White House. I made a face at them. Everyone was more concerned with mid-terms and homecoming. I had Latin and biology tests. St. Martins is one of the few schools that still teach Latin, and Mama insisted I take it. This is my second year, and the tests are translation and open book. She told me I have to take two years of French starting next year. The biology test was another story. We're studying anatomy, and there are too many muscle groups. I blew it.

My world history teacher asked me if I was going to be in school tomorrow, and offered to let me take a make-up test. I assured him that I would be in class no matter what the outcome is tonight.

Lunch, my favorite subject, was spent discussing the basketball season. Most of the team eats together, and we talk strategy. A lot of the time is spent razzing each other when one of us starts bragging about how good we think we are. It sure beats eating the mystery meat they feed us every day. Just the smell of it makes me want to puke.

Our first game is next week, and I made varsity. If Daddy wins the election I'll miss most of the season, so I don't know how much playing time I'll get. My parents might as well have stamped LOSER on my forehead. My teammates think our team may be pretty good this year, but we're a young team with only three seniors.

We have a lot of speed with our guards who can really move the ball down the court. The transition game is our specialty. Brooks rebounds the ball and throws it inside to Walker who passes it off to Bordeaux who passes to Comeaux who shoots and scores. Or at least that's the way it's supposed to work. If Daddy wins the election, I'll be in some school with strange kids, and it will be too late to join the team.

But of course, Mama and Daddy keep saying there's softball. I've always been able to play any position, and they keep reassuring me that with my skill I'll make the softball team at the new school. But who knows what I'll get into. The team could be full of superstars, and I'll be a transfer student. They may not even let me try out. Quit worrying Andie Beth. he hasn't won yet. O please, God, let him lose.

The way they talk I think that they already have the school picked out. It's probably the same private school that Rachel attends. Most of the government kids go to it because of the security.

But, maybe he'll lose and I won't have to go. Wouldn't it be awesome if this is a bad dream, and I wake up tomorrow and Daddy's Nettles Construction truck is parked in the driveway? My life could be normal again. God, I'll make a deal with you. You let Daddy lose the election, and I'll clean up my room until graduation without complaining. Come on, God. That's a good deal. I can stay out of trouble, and you don't have to hear my whining.

School is over, and I head to the gym for basketball practice. Coach starts us off with running drills. We run until we're falling over. First we run two miles around the track, and then more drills. Coach Perry believes in running. He constantly yells "Run, Run, Run."

When practice ends I am beat, and when I jerk the sweatband off my head all the sweat drenches my eyes and they burn from the salt. Making a mad dash for the water fountain, I gulp down water as if it is the first drink I've ever taken. Rivers of water run down the back of my legs filling my socks making a squishing sound. My jersey is soaked and sticking to my body, and my shorts feel like they are Crazy Glued to my rear. I slide the scrunchies out of my hair, and wring them out on the gym floor. I need a shower. The rest of the team heads for the locker room, and I lag behind. I don't want to go.

The basketball court is my special place. I am the queen, and the spectators are my servants who have come to watch the mistress at work. Here I have to prove myself to play. It is the one place in the world where I feel powerful. Special privileges on the court are reserved for seniors. The rest of us earn the right to play. Peasants cheer us when we do well, but dare not boo us when we do poorly. We are the elite. I am one of the chosen. The gym is my sanctuary. Here I am free.

Most of the team has left the locker room. Heather, one of the few left, says "Hurry up, Andie B. the bus is leaving. Do you still want a ride?"

"Sure, hold your horses. Where's the fire?"

Peeling off my uniform I make a mad dash for the shower. I'm glad no one else is around.

There's no hot water, and I forgot the soap. Have to take a longer one later. Getting dressed quickly I shove my uniform in my gym bag and head out the door. Heather and Sandi are still talking about some guy.

Heather, a junior, has her own car. I figure no one in my family will remember I'm still at school so I'd better take advantage of it.

I can't wait until I turn sixteen in exactly four months and five days and can finally get my license. I know just the car I want. It has to be a gray Jeep that I can take to the mountains for skiing and the beach for surfing. It will be Andie B.'s freedom machine. Mama and Daddy bought Trey a car when he turned sixteen, so they have to buy me one too. It's only fair.

As we start walking out to the parking lot, I see Mama's Black Blazer with her in the driver's seat reading from a stack of papers.

"Heather thanks for the offer, but it looks like my mom is here after all. See you tomorrow."

Andie Beth

"Sure A.B. and good luck in the election tonight. I bet your dad wins."

Opening the back door, I throw my backpack and gym bag on the seat. I get in the front seat beside Mama. As if not to acknowledge my existence, she doesn't even look up. Does she even know I'm in the car? I don't say anything. Eventually she looks over at me giving me a half-hug in the process.

"Hey, Andie B. how are you? I've missed you."

"Fine, Mama. I didn't think you'd remember to pick me up today being Election Day."

"You didn't think we'd leave you stranded at school did you? Your daddy wanted to come pick you up himself, but he figured with all the photographers following him around today, it would only embarrass you."

"So, how did you manage to escape?"

26

"Went out the back door, and jumped in the car. Almost took out a couple of local news vans in the process. She laughs the familiar laugh I've heard so seldom lately. How are your mid-terms going, and basketball practice? I just realized I haven't seen you in two weeks, and we've got to get you some new Nikes ®. Those look like you've been running around in the bayou."

"School is a drag. I think I bombed the biology mid-term. There were too many muscle groups to memorize. I think I reversed the arm and leg muscles. Tomorrow is my last mid-term, world history. Mrs. Morgan said I could take a make-up test if I wanted to because of election night, but I told her you said I had to take the test with everybody else. Basketball practice is fine. The first game is next week. Is Daddy going to be able to come to it? And as for my Nikes®, I like them this way. They're

27

just getting comfortable. Besides you said I could buy my own clothes from now on. You know if you'd stay home more often, you wouldn't have to ask so many questions. You might just get to know me. "

"We're trying to keep your life as normal as possible. That's why you haven't been on the campaign trail. We thought you would be happier that way."

"The only way I could be happy is if this election wasn't happening. It hasn't been the same since Daddy was elected to the Senate, and now he may be President. Mama are you really as happy about all this as you are acting?"

Mama slaps me across the face with her right hand. I recoil in shock at the pain.

"I can't believe I just did that."

Mama looks down at her hand surprised at what she did. She has not hit me since I was a little girl, and I am stunned. The full impact of what has happened has not yet registered for either of us.

She slams on the brakes and pulls over to the curb on a side street three blocks from home. Mama is furious, and has that you've messed with Lynn Nettles and you're going to pay for it look on her face which means my life is over. She turns off the ignition, unfastens her seatbelt, and faces me. Her face is beet red, and I quickly realize that I should have followed Grandma Josie's advice and lost the attitude. If only I had kept my big mouth shut. Andie B. you are such an idiot. You can forget the ski trip now. You can forget your life. Mama's never been this mad not even when I almost killed my brother. If it wasn't for that stupid sign, I would never have grabbed the matches. Daddy said it was my clubhouse too. I only wanted to scare him a little bit. He told me I couldn't play because I wasn't big enough.

I want to take back the words that I just said, but know it is too late. Having a heart attack would be a welcome relief right now, because I have a feeling that I might not live to move to Washington after Mama gets finished with me.

"Andie Beth Nettles I have had it with you. Your daddy and I have done everything we could possibly do to make you happy, and yet you still continue to act like a spoiled brat. We could have moved to Washington eight years ago when your daddy was elected to the Senate. Most people thought we were crazy for not doing it. But no, he and I thought we were doing what was best for our children by staying here in Kenner and giving you a more stable environment.

Do you have any idea of how lonely I have been for the last eight years? How every time he got on that plane to return to Washington I wanted to run after him, and tell him to find a house so we could move?

When he decided to run for President, the first thing I thought was that we would be together as a family. Your brother would be in college, and it would be the three of us again. We would be in the same house, and we would have him at home every night. His office would be three floors away from us. I could feel like a wife again.

You're right. We didn't ask you how you felt about him becoming President. Maybe we should have, but it's too late now. Any other kid would be thrilled; living in the White House; going to school with Rachel; having all the privileges of being the First Kid; taking trips with your daddy and me. But no, not you. Andie Beth wants it her way or not at all. Well, guess what young lady, it's too late. According to the exit polls, he is going to win the election.

Whether you like it or not, you're moving to Washington in January.

I'm starting the car. We're going home. You are to march in the house; give your daddy a hug, and go straight to your room. Tell him you have to study for your test. I'll tell Mama you want to have dinner in your room, because you have so much homework. I don't want to see your face again tonight. You are grounded until I tell you differently. That means no telephone, no television, no music, and no computer."

It's probably a good idea if I don't say anything. We pull into the driveway, and I grab my gear out of the back seat and try to dodge the reporters and photographers who have set up camp in front of the house. Mama shadows me with a phony smile plastered on her face. Reporters are shouting questions at her about how she feels about the election. She smiles and waves at the photographers while hissing at me to smile and wave.

I'm in the house. Daddy is in the living room surrounded by a group of men and women who I recognize from the campaign. I head for the stairs, but he sees me.

"Buzzie, you weren't going upstairs without saying hello to me were you?

"Hi Daddy."

I drop my things on the stairs, and rub my face. No sense arousing suspicion. I sneak a glance at Mama who is talking with Grandma Josie. All these people around, and they're clueless. None of them would ever guess what Mama did to me. I wish they'd notice. They all think she's wonderful. They don't see how mean she really is. They didn't see her hit me. I'm hurting you idiots. But none of you get it. I don't think any of you ever will.

"What's wrong with your face? It looks red."

"Nothing Daddy. I got elbowed in practice. I'll be okay. I've missed you too Daddy.

"Well, act like it and give the old man a hug"

I hug Daddy tight. I want him to get the message about what has just happened, but I can't talk to him. Not today. Not with her on the other side of the room. I want my daddy, but Daddy doesn't get it. He hasn't gotten it for a long time.

"I've got to go study, Daddy. Glad you're home."

"Thanks Andie B. I'm glad I'm home too."

I grab my backpack and gym bag and run up the stairs taking them two at a time but not before glancing over my shoulder to see if Mama is looking. She isn't. Nothing has changed.

My room looks the same as it did this morning. Guess I'm going to have to clean it up, because I'll be spending a lot of time here over the next few months. I drag the hamper out of the bathroom and start picking up dirty clothes, and shooting baskets with them. Some of these clothes smell like they have been here since the summer.

I see my face in the mirror, and the red mark is still there. I can't believe Mama did that. She hit me hard. I grab a washcloth and drench it in cold water. It helps a little but my salty tears make the pain worse. Tripping over my basketball I land head first on my bed and the flood of tears gush out like a dam bursting from the pressure. I can't stop crying.

I hear footsteps on the stairs. The top step creaks alerting me that someone is coming. Since Trey left for college, the third floor is now mine.

Jumping off the bed, I head to the bathroom and close the door grabbing a wet washcloth to wipe my face. Maybe, it's Daddy coming to rescue me, my knight in shining armor. No, Gary Nettles is too caught up in practicing his acceptance speech to be bothered with me. More likely it's the wicked Mama of the south coming to inflict more punishment on me. No, Lynn Nettles is too busy playing the perfect candidate's wife to waste her time with me. It's probably Grandma Josie with supper.

I come out of the bathroom, and toss the basketball in the rocking chair so I won't trip over it again. Grabbing my backpack I sit at my desk and dig for my world history book and notebook. I roll the chair over to the bed, and bury my feet under the blanket folded on the end of it. The blanket feels fuzzy, and smells like fabric softener. Grandma Josie must have washed it today. There is a knock on the door. It is Grandma Josie.

"Your mama says you're not eating with us tonight. Said you're studying. Just as well. I don't know when your parents will get around to eating. Too many people in this house for me right now."

"Is that all she said Gram?"

"Well, I know she seemed a little upset when she first came home. Said she didn't want to talk - something about road rage. You didn't do anything to make her mad did you?"

"No, not me Gram. It must have happened before she picked me up. She was upset then."

"What happened to your face? It looks red."

"Got elbowed in practice. I'll be okay."

"Andie Beth, is something bothering you? You look sort of teary-eyed."

"No, ma'am I'm fine. My face is sore from Heather's elbow."

"Well, you tell Heather to go easy on you. After all, you're going to be the President's Kid."

"Okay Gram"

"Now eat your dinner before it gets cold. I'll be up to check on you later and get the dishes."

"Gram you know I love you, don't you?"

She winks, and I see Mama's smile.

I want to jump up and hug Gram. Part of me wants to tell her the story, but I check my mouth. I can't tell her that her precious daughter Lynn hates me. I would look bad. I hate lying to Gram, but I can't tell her what happened like I couldn't tell Daddy. No one understands. Lynn Nettles is the queen. They both worship her. Tomorrow, she will be the First Lady, and the country will worship her, minus one.

I take one look at dinner, and want to throw up. Eating is the last thing I want to do tonight. When I'm uptight, my emotions go straight to my stomach and I can't eat. But I have to get rid of the food. If I don't eat, Gram will tell Mama, and it will be another charge added to my rap sheet. After sticking the brownies in a desk drawer for later, I flush the rest of the food down the toilet, leaving the green beans since Gram knows I hate them. Guess I'd better study but I don't really want to. This subject always puts me to sleep, but I better get it over with. The knock at the door wakes me up. It is Grandma Josie coming to pick up the dishes.

"What's wrong Gram all the noise get to you? Has he won yet?"

"Just wanted to come get these dishes out of the way. Lord knows if it was up to you, you'd have every dish in the house up here."

"I'd leave one plate for you Gram, couldn't let you go hungry."

"It's so noisy down there a woman can't hear herself think. How your mama and Daddy stand it is beyond me. Well, guess I'll say goodnight. Now stand up and give your Gram a hug."

I stand up before I realize that my foot has fallen asleep, and almost fall on the floor. Grandma Josie catches me in her frail arms, and holds tight.

"Andie B. you are the clumsiest kid I have ever seen. How you manage to play all those sports without killing yourself is beyond me."

"Practice, Gram practice."

"Goodnight Andie B."

I shuffle through my notes. None of them make sense. Some of the papers are under my bed. I spend the next hour on the floor crawling around trying to get organized. I give up. This isn't working. I'm not studying anymore. It doesn't matter anyway. Who cares if I pass history? Do you hear me world? I don't care. I'm not studying any more tonight, and no one can make me.

Let me turn on the computer, and see if Rachel's out there.

"Rachel, are you out there?"

She finally comes on line with a greeting: CONGRATULATIONS! START PACKING FOR THE WHITE HOUSE!

"Rachel, are you telling me what I think you're telling me?"

"Yeppers, your daddy has just been projected as the next President of the United States even without the western states. You're moving to D.C."

"Your dad won too, right?"

"Sure did, so we'll be there together. But you knew already, right? What did your parents say? Is there a big party going on? What are you doing in your room?"

"I didn't know he'd won until you told me just now. Nobody's been upstairs. I'm grounded. I had a major argument with Mama. But we'll talk about it tomorrow. I'm not even supposed to be on the computer."

"Well, I guess now I get to call you First Kid, and tell everyone that my best friend is the President's Kid. I can hardly wait for your first big White House party. Let's see should you host it in the solarium or the south lawn"

"I don't have a clue what you're talking about, but I better get off the computer before I get busted again."

"A.B. I know you wanted him to lose, but try to be happy. We can have a blast being together in D.C. I can hardly wait."

"Glad you're happy. I'm not. Bye Rach."

"See you A.B."

I turn off the computer to avoid getting caught. Where do I go from here? My life as I know it has just ended. Daddy has been elected President, and Mama is the First Lady. My worst nightmare has come true.

I tiptoe downstairs making sure I jump creaky stairs. On the second floor landing, I hear laughter and celebrating. I creep down a few stairs, and peek around the corner. The living room is crowded with a bunch of strangers. A bunch of old fuddy duddies dancing around like idiots in some old movie. They're gulping champagne. They think it's great. I think it's nasty. In the middle are Mama and Daddy. They are both shaking hands and hugging everyone in sight. The phone is ringing, and the room gets quiet.

Someone hands Daddy the phone, and he says three words: yes, thank you.

"That was Governor Cox. He has just conceded the election. Folks, it looks like we've won. Now why don't y'all head down to the Sheraton, and Lynn and I will be down there in a few minutes to celebrate with you."

A loud cheer erupts and for a minute I think the roof is going to come off the house. I take advantage of the noise to crawl back to my room unnoticed. I jump into bed. while turning off all the lights but the bedside one.

In a few minutes I hear footsteps in the hall outside my door then a light knock. It's Mama and Daddy. They enter the room, and I don't look up from my book. Mama sits on the side of the bed, and Daddy stands behind her.

"Andie B. we have something to tell you. Your daddy was just elected President. We're going to the White House."

I start to cry. Daddy assumes it is tears of happiness. Mama knows better.

"Well, little girl what do you have to say to him?" Mama says.

"Congratulations, Daddy. I knew you would win. You too, Mama you will be a perfect First Lady."

Daddy leans over and kisses me on the forehead, and Mama gives me a hug.

"Goodnight, Buzzie, and don't stay up too late studying."

"Goodnight Daddy and congratulations Mr. President."

"We love you, Andie B."

"I love you Mama, and you too Daddy."

They leave the room, and my fate is sealed. I am now the daughter of the President of the United States. I close my book and notebook, and turn off the light, wrapping myself in a cocoon of the sheets where no one can touch me. You're on your own now Andie B.

Election night is over, and I have lost.

Chapter 2

Transition

"**R**achel, are you out there?"

Here we go again. Just once I wish she would stay at her computer more than five minutes at a time.

Christmas is only two weeks away. Our family has been in a state of organized chaos since election night, in spite of Mama and Daddy's efforts to keep things normal.

The day after the election I went to school. Instead of riding the school bus I was accompanied by two secret service agents. One drove the car, and sat in it all day, and the other one sat in a chair outside each of my classes. She was a hall monitor. Even though I didn't study much, I salvaged a B- on the world history test.

Basketball season started the next week. At half-time the score was tied. I didn't get to play very much the first half, but scored two points with free throws after I was fouled.

When we headed into the locker room, I looked in the bleachers. Mama was buried in her usual stack of papers, bulging briefcase right beside her; Grandma Josie on one side of her; and Grandpa Webb and Grandma Elizabeth on the other. All three grandparents waved at me. Mama didn't look up. I kept looking for Daddy. When he called last night, he said he would try to attend the game. He was working with his Transition Team trying to nominate people for his cabinet. Every day he was on television announcing another name to a staff position. None of the names sounded familiar to me.

The second half of the game started, and still no Daddy. I ought to be used to him not showing up by now.

By the fourth quarter we were ten points ahead, and Coach Perry began substituting. He put me in the game, and I took a shot. After I watched the ball go through the net, I looked up and no one was watching me. I ran down the court, and I heard the gym door slam open. I realized that the President Elect was in the building. My teammates passed me the ball a couple of more times, and I shot and scored. As the final buzzer sounded I was fouled again. Time had run out on the clock, but I shot two more free throws ending up with ten points for the night. We won the game 64-48.

When I came out of the gym, the whole family was waiting for me as well as some of my friends including my boyfriend Matt.

"A.B., you coming with us? We're heading for pizza at King Louie's. The whole team is going. The guys are going too." one of my teammates shouted.

I glanced at my parents and grandparents surrounded by the secret service agents leaning against the cars. They expected me to come home with them.

"Are you two coming or not?" she shouted again.

Matt gave me this look that said he really wanted us to go.

"Are you going or not A.B.? "

"I don't know, Matt. Let me go ask my parents. There's the hassle with the Secret Service agents hanging with us.

And I'm still grounded, remember? I'm not even sure if my parents will let me go."

"Yeah, but you'll be with your parents for the rest of your life. Two more months, and I won't see you again. Your mom needs to lighten up."

"Let me go talk to them. Maybe I can convince them."

"You want me to come with you?"

"No, because if she says no, that will just make it worse. Go stall Heather for a few minutes, so I can talk to them."

Dashing over to where my family is I trip in a pothole, and twist my knee. Pain surges through it, but I grit my teeth, and stay upright. I arrive out of breath.

"Mama all the gang is going for pizza to celebrate. Can I go too? It's the first game of the season, and I scored ten points. It's important. Can I Mama just this once?

"Andie B. have you forgotten?"

"Please. I promise I'll be home by curfew. "

"You know the rules. Last time I checked you were grounded."

"Aw, c'mon Mama this is different. Just this once can't you bend the rules? Please, Mama." I look to Daddy for support, but he's not saying anything.

"Daddy, tell her. You played basketball. You understand even if she doesn't.

"This is between you and your mama, Andie B. You know the rules. If your mama says you can't go, then you can't go."

"I never get to have any fun. It's not fair. I'm always the one left out."

"Young lady, get in the car NOW."

"Can't I at least tell Matt I can't go?"

"I said NOW Andie Beth Nettles, and I mean NOW."

"Aw Jeez, it's not fair. It's just not fair. Nobody in this family cares about what I think anymore."

I pick up my gym bag and run to Daddy's car and fling myself on the back seat. I want to cry, but I refuse to give in to the tears. Crying means they win. But I won't let them.

Daddy gets in the car, and we start our convoy home. Everyone else is riding with Mama.

"Just what do you think you're doing young lady?"

I curl into a ball wrapping my arms around my knees. No way am I going to look at him. If anyone would under-stand, I thought it would be Daddy. He's supposed to be on my side. I bite my lip to keep from crying. I'm in shock. I stare straight ahead. I won't look at him.

"Are you listening to me Andie Beth? Because if you aren't you had better be. Do you hear me?"

"Yes, sir," I mumble.

"Good, because I'm only going to say this once. I have had it with you. I'm giving you two choices, and you better make up your mind right now. You can get with the program, straighten up, and accept the fact that you're moving to the White House, or you can go to boarding school and they can deal with you and your attitude. There's no middle ground."

Daddy's face is so red I can see the vein popping out on his forehead. I've never seen him this mad. He doesn't say anything the rest of the way home. When we pull in the driveway, he hops out of the car, and sprints over to open Mama's car door.

They walk up the sidewalk like two lovesick teenagers. They act like nothing has happened. Well, it hasn't. At least not to them. No way am I going in that house now. I drop my gym bag on the back steps, and wander to the back yard. The fragrance of freshly cut grass greets me as I round the corner of the house. Motion sensor lights flash on, and immediately three Secret Service agents appear out of the shadows like trees that have come to life.

"Is everything okay Miss Nettles?"

"Yeah, I'm going to stay out here for a while."

The back yard is lit, and I flip the power switch on the worn electrical box near the basketball court. Daddy had the lights installed last Christmas as a special present for Trey and I so we could shoot baskets at night. Sometimes if I can't sleep, I sneak out here in the middle of the night to shoot free throws. Mama and Daddy can't see the light from their room.

Grabbing the basketball from the bench I stand at the free throw line and shoot adding my own commentary as I release the ball. It's Nettles at the line in triple overtime.

If she makes this basket, her team will win the national championship. It is all up to her. She shoots, she scores. Nettles has taken the Naval Academy women to their first national championship. And ladies and gentlemen, she is only a freshman. Ouch, there goes my knee again. Man it hurts. Let me go see if the pool guy has covered the pool. Taking off my shoes I ease myself down to the edge of the pool being careful not to put too much weight on my knee. Then I consider a better idea. I walk out the edge of the diving board and lie down staring at the stars.

When I was a little girl I wanted to be an astronaut, and visit all the planets. I convinced my parents to send me to space camp in Alabama the summer I was ten. Camp was awesome. We studied science, and did all these really neat experiments. I was having a great time until we went on a machine called the centrifuge. It spun you around faster and faster in circles like some of the carnival rides. I wasn't scared. It was a lot of fun. When I climbed down I threw up in front of everybody. All the kids started teasing me, and calling me names. They said I'd never be an astronaut if I couldn't even ride that ride.

The next day I came home from camp. I told Mama what had happened, and I didn't feel good. She took me to the doctor. It turned out I had an ear infection. On the ride all the fluid was bouncing around inside my ear and that's what made me throw up.

The next summer when Mama and Daddy asked me if I wanted to go to camp I told them no. I said I didn't like science any more. The real reason was I didn't want to face those kids again.

Trey was playing basketball all the time. Daddy put in the court for him, and I used to make Kool Aid and sell it to all his friends when they would come over. One day when they were standing around, I picked up the basketball, and stood at the free throw line. The ball was heavy, and I traced the outline of the word Wilson® with my fingers as I stood there. Bounce, bounce, bounce. The sound of the ball against the concrete had a ring. It was a special sound all its' own. I looked up at the basket and lofted the ball as hard as I could. The ball arced and went through the basket without ever touching the backboard. One of Trey's friends came over.

"Hey, Nettles you better watch it. Your little sister can shoot free throws better than you."

"Andie B. where did you learn to shoot so well? Can you do it again?"

I put on an exhibition for Trey's friends that afternoon shooting ten free throws in a row. After that he and his friends let me hang around more. Sometimes they even acted like they liked me. I still brought them Kool Aid, but I had moved up a notch. I was now their mascot. From that day on I knew that basketball was going to play an important part in my life.

I am startled from my daydream by a sound in the bushes. I hear footsteps and heavy breathing and almost fall in the pool. All I see are two dark eyes glowing in the dark. Crawling off the diving board I see Cajun, the mutt, bringing me his slobbery tennis ball. I grab the ball, and throw it. Cajun races after his favorite treasure. After strolling to the back steps, I sit down. I'm not ready to go inside.

Looking up I see the red lights of a plane taking off from New Orleans International. We live in the flight path of one of the runways. I wonder where all those people are going so late at night. Are they flying off on some exotic vacation? Are they tourists returning home? Or maybe they're just people like me wanting to escape? I wish I could go with them. Right now I'd rather be anywhere but here. It's not fun here anymore.

Cajun comes back with his ball again, and sits beside me licking the salt off my cheeks with his wet tongue. Caj' this is a situation not even you can fix. The breeze feels cold against my face. The temperature is dropping. Hearing a car stop, I hope it's not my parents. Their car was gone when I came around the corner. The glow of the pizza sign on top of the car means food has arrived. The pizza guy strolls up the driveway.

"Is this the Nettles house?"

"Yes."

"I got two pizzas here."

"Let me get some money."

"They're already paid for. Here you want 'em."

"Yeah, thanks."

The pizzas are still warm, and the grumbling in my stomach reminds me of how hungry I am. The strong scent of the pepperoni and cheese rises through the box to blast my nose. I curl my arm under the boxes, and grab my gym bag with my other hand opening the door with my little finger. Caj rushes into the kitchen, and takes his spot under the table hoping for handouts.

"Well Bumble that walk from the car sure took you long enough. What did you do go to Houston first?"

"Grandpa."

"I knew you'd come in when the pizza came. Never known you to turn down pizza."

"We're eating off paper plates tonight. No dishes for anyone to wash."

"Now sit down child before the pizza gets cold."

"Who ordered pizza? At least you didn't get one with those nasty mushrooms on it. They taste like Cajun's tennis ball."

"You been eating Cajun's tennis ball? I thought it looked smaller."

"Your Grandpa did. He figured you couldn't go out with your friends; we'd have our little party. Just the four of us. Of course it means you have to hang out with us old folks."

"Where did Mama and Daddy go?"

"Some awards banquet downtown. We tried to get them to stay here with us. Told them we were a lot more fun. But the group gave a lot of money to your daddy's campaign, and he thought they needed to put in an appearance."

"They said they'd be really late, so your Grandpa and I are staying over. No since in fighting that traffic just to get across the lake."

"Awesome. I like it when you guys are here

"Well, what am I chopped liver?"

Everyone bursts out laughing.

"No Grandma Josie it's just that you. . ."

"I'm always here. Is that what you mean?"

"Watch it Bumble your grandmas are ganging up on you."

"I think I better shut up, and eat my pizza. I've been in enough trouble for one day."

"Good idea, Andie B. You remind me of your daddy when you do that."

"Now Elizabeth don't be boring the child with old stories. Kids today don't want to hear about the old days."

"I do. C'mon Grandma Elizabeth. What did Daddy do?"

"Same thing you just did. Be talking away without even thinking. He loved to tease people. Then he'd start to get himself in trouble, and he'd get quiet like he was hoping that no one had noticed. That's why it's a good thing he's got speechwriters. Lord knows what would happen if they let him talk on his own. But he's that way because of your grandpa. Nobody on my side of the family acts like that."

"She's right Bumble. Her side of the family hits people and hits them hard. One time I was trying to steal a good-night kiss from your grandma, and her two big old brothers came and beat me up. Told me I'd better never lay a hand on their little sister again. They were a mean bunch. I had to bring her to Louisiana to get away from them."

"Webb, quit filling that child's head with your nonsense. Don't believe a word he says Andie B."

"Before I forget, Andie B., Trey called while you were outside. He asked how the game went, and said to tell you congratulations. Said he'll text you later. We all talked to him. I don't know why that boy can't come home once in a while."

"Thanks Grandma Josie. Trey's busy. I miss him too. Daddy said he and I are going to one of Trey's games before Christmas. I can hardly wait to see Trey in his LSU uniform. "

I sneak Cajun a piece of crust under the table. He sticks his head on my knee begging for more. His wet breath soaks my leg. Gross.

"Pizza is great. Thanks Grandpa."

I get up from my seat, and walk around the table, and put my arms around Grandpa's neck.

"You're the greatest."

"Thanks Bumble. I think you're pretty great too. I can't wait to tell the guys at the airport about that shot you took from the corner. That girl was on top of you."

"Can we go flying again soon Grandpa? I need to practice on my takeoffs and landings."

"That can be arranged. Let me check with the guys, and see if they fixed that part. As soon as it's fixed we'll go up. Maybe, we'll go to Mobile. Just the two of us. There's some land over there I want to see."

"All right."

"Andie B. how's your knee?"

"It's throbbing Grandma Josie."

Grandma Josie fixes an ice pack for my knee, and hands me two Tylenol and a glass of water.

"Okay, Andie B. now you're all set. You go put this on your knee, and by tomorrow morning you should be as good as new. Here take these two Tylenol now. "

"Thanks, Gram. I guess that's my hint that it's time to go to bed."

"Well, it is getting late Andie Beth. And you've had a busy week. In fact, we all have. Now scoot. "

"Yes, ma'am. Goodnight everybody."

I walk around the table and hug both women. Each of them, in their own unique way, teaches me about life. They have done it by sharing their life's stories with me. This is the way I remember them.

Grandma Elizabeth is the stoic aristocrat, whose family felt that she had married below herself when she married the Navy pilot just as World War II was winding down. When he announced to her family that he was moving her from southern Maryland where her family had lived for over 200 years, to Louisiana, they were outraged and almost disowned her. But the birth of a daughter, followed in rapid succession by another daughter and two sons drew the family back together. Elizabeth Johnson Nettles never forgot her roots traveling north each summer, children in tow, to escape the oppressive Louisiana heat and humidity, to spend the summers with her family.

It was a heritage that she would pass down to her children, and then to her fourteen grandchildren. Her motto: *Never Forget Where You Came From* was firmly embedded in their brains from early childhood. Each summer she would head to the beach house on the Maryland shore where the children and grandchildren would gather; sometimes as individuals; sometimes in groups; for lessons in living.

To the grandchildren if often seemed like boot camp. Grandma Elizabeth had very strict rules. The most important one was if an adult other than an older cousin calls you by your complete name you are always to answer yes ma'am or yes sir as opposed to yes Mama or yes Mr. Smith. Familiarity is only allowed when a shorter version or nickname is used in referring to you. This lesson was ingrained in the grandchildren from the time that they were three years old. And there were frequent quizzes. Pity the grandchild who flunked one of Grandma Elizabeth's quizzes. That grandchild received no dessert at supper that night.

She taught them manners, and how to set a proper table. This went for the boys as well as the girls. Grandma even went so far as to teach her grandchildren how to ballroom dance. This class was the most dreaded of them all, because no girl wants to dance with her pimply faced boy cousin. But you weren't given a choice. If Grandma Elizabeth said do it, you did it.

From Grandma Elizabeth I learned how to act like a lady.

Grandma Josie was the exact opposite of Grandma Elizabeth in a grassroots sort of way. Christened Eleanor Josephine at birth, she grew up in Corpus Christi, Texas. Her father worked at the Naval Station repairing aircraft engines, and it was he who introduced her to a young pilot just starting out his career as World War II was ending. James Wallace was a striking figure in his Navy uniform, and it didn't take long for Josie Marston to fall in love. The next twenty two years of her life would be spent as a Navy wife traveling all over the world until early in 1967 when she would hear the dreaded knock at the door, and receive the message that CMDR James Frederick Wallace's plane had been shot down off the coast of Viet Nam less than ninety days before he was scheduled to retire.

When her only child Lynn decided to attend Tulane University in New Orleans, Josie moved there too. She couldn't bear to be apart from her. She had already lost her husband, and the thought of losing her daughter was too much to take. After living all over the world, it felt good to finally put down roots. When Lynn married Gary Nettles, Josie was unsure of what her role would be in the family, but she soon found out. Mama and Daddy were both attending law school, when Mama dropped out shortly before the birth of my brother and decided to go back to work when school started later that year, Grandma Josie became his babysitter, and then mine four years later. She found her place in this family. Grandma is our caretaker.

From Grandma Josie I learned compassion.

The woman missing from the table, Lynn Nettles, a.k.a. Mama, is the hardest one to figure out. Maybe Daddy is right. Maybe it is because I'm so much like her. All I know is she is a fake and a phony. She comes across as Superwoman to the whole world. She can hold her own with an audience as well as Daddy. The way she's always carrying that briefcase around I think she forgets that she's going to be First Lady, not President. I know one thing she'll never get the Mother of the Year trophy from me no matter how she fools the country. The sweet syrup can continue to drip off her mouth all she wants it to, but I know the truth.

From Mama I learned I do not want to be like her. I just want to be me.

I go to my room and change clothes for bed. I trip over the corner of my desk hurting my knee even more. Stopping to turn on the computer, I change my mind. Daddy's warning runs through my brain. I grab a book from my backpack and throw it on the bed. We're reading *The Red Badge of Courage* for English class. If I have it in front of me, at least I'll stay out of trouble temporarily.

Turning out the overhead light, I get into bed and try to adjust the ice pack on my knee which has begun to throb. I find the bottle of Dr. Pepper® that I keep stashed under my bed. Two gulps of Dr. Pepper® are the instant solution for any pain. I put the top back on the Dr. Pepper® bottle, and there it is the familiar Lynn Nettles knock at the door.

"Just thought I'd come up to check on you, and see how your knee was doing."

"You're back early. My knee hurts some Mama, but I'll be okay. Like you tell me, I'm Lynn Nettles' daughter. I can take anything."

"But, you're still my baby girl and whether you believe it or not I still care about you."

"It's like you say Mama, we can't go backwards. You and Daddy aren't the only ones making lots of adjustments. My life will never be the same again, and no one has bothered to ask me how I feel about it. So, I guess it doesn't matter."

"Andie B., it matters. It's just that you can't change history. Good night, I love you."

"I love you too Mama."

She kisses me on the forehead, and leaves the room not looking back. I turn off the light and go to sleep.

Three weeks have passed since that night. Mama and Daddy have made several trips to Washington together. They have been spending a lot of time with each other. Daddy even took Mama on a cruise to celebrate their twenty fifth wedding anniversary and Mama's fiftieth birthday. Years ago when they were married, it was on the day before her birthday. This year it coincided with Thanksgiving so they were gone all Thanksgiving week.

Thanksgiving was strange this year. I thought my brother would come home but since Mama and Daddy weren't going to be here, he went home with his roommate. For a while I thought it was just going to be Grandma Josie and me at the house by ourselves. But it turned out okay. One of Daddy's sisters, Ellie, decided to have a big

Thanksgiving dinner at her house for the family, and when she heard we were by ourselves she invited us.

It was neat getting to see my aunts and uncle and most of my cousins. There are five of us who are in middle and high school, and we have a good time together. I haven't laughed that hard in a long time. We all had our CD's, and one of my cousins had a Playstation hooked up so we had our own tournament going. If Gram hadn't made me wear a dress, I could have played basketball or touch football with the guys.

Everyone was talking about the inauguration. Everyone in Daddy's family including his two sisters, one brother, all the cousins, and even some of Grandpa Webb and Grandma Elizabeth's brothers and sisters will be coming to the festivities. Most of them will spend the night of the inauguration in the White House with us. It will be wall to wall Nettles and Johnsons. Grandma Josie only has one sister, and she will come too along with her two grown children. It will be one big family reunion.

"Wow, Andie B., you're the President's Kid now. Do we have to bow down to you, your majesty?"

"Only, if you want me to beat you up, Glenn. I'm no different than I was last summer when we hung out together in Maryland."

"Yes, you are. You get to live in the White House and everything. That is so cool. I read all about the White House in school. It's got gazillion bathrooms."

"Give me a break. It's not that big a deal. And besides you can come visit me any time you want."

"Just think my cousin is the President's kid. I brought some paper for you to write your autograph on. I'm gonna be rich when I sell these."

"You're going to be dead when you sell them, because your mom is going to kill you."

I wish I could be as excited about this as the rest of the family is. My aunts and uncles were pretty cool about it. They didn't pressure me for opinions about how I felt about what had happened, and I didn't offer any opinions about how I felt. Grandma Josie, with her usual insight, noticed how I acted on our way home Thanksgiving night.

"Andie B. I'm really proud of you."

"What do you mean Gram?"

"You never let on to anyone today how you really feel about what's happening. I don't think your other grand-parents even know do they?"

"Nope."

"Is that all you have to say? I've never known you not to express your opinion."

"I just took the safe way out. Figured if I didn't say anything, I couldn't get myself in trouble. As for Grandpa Webb and Grandma Elizabeth, they think this move is so great I hate to burst their bubble. If Daddy thinks they need to know how I really feel, let him tell them. Gram why are you the only person who understands me?"

"I raised your Mama didn't I? Does that answer your question?"

"Am I that much like her?"

"Afraid so. Except in one area. Your mama was shy when she was a child and teenager. She didn't start expressing her opinions until she went to Tulane. She was angry about the Viet Nam War and became an active feminist."

"How do you put up with me?"

"The same way I put up with your mama, lots and lots of love."

I lean over and hug her and fall asleep with my head on her shoulder. The next sound I hear is the car door opening when we pull in the driveway two hours later.

"Guess, I wasn't much company Gram."

"You're okay, but did you know you snore?"

"No, I don't."

"Sure, do, and if you don't believe me ask one of the agents."

My parents came back from their trip on Monday with big smiles on their faces, and sunburned. Both of them seemed more relaxed than I had seen them in a long time. But they quickly jumped back into the action, and left for Washington the next day. They were going to meet with the President and First Lady and tour the White House.

Mama promised to bring me back pictures of different rooms that I could choose from for my room.

They were also going to see the Le Brun's, and enroll me in Rachel's school, Brockton Academy. Rachel was excited about it. I wasn't.

Mama and Daddy came home last night. Mama was very excited about the White House and the school.

"Andie Beth, you will just love it. The White House is huge, and we have two floors to ourselves. We have our own den, called a sitting room, a private kitchen and dining room.

There's a solarium on the floor above us that you can use for parties with your friends. I picked out these two adjoining rooms you can have for your own near the solarium; one can be your study, and the other one your bedroom. There is a bedroom nearby for your brother when he visits."

"And the best news of all. Can I tell her Lynn?"

"Go ahead Mama, I was saving it for last, but you go ahead and tell her."

"I'll be there too full time. I'm giving up my apartment here. I've spent so much time with you over the last few months I'm not about to let you go off to Washington and leave me behind."

"Really, Gram?"

"Really, Andie B."

"Who came up with that idea? It's awesome."

I run over and hug Grandma Josie harder than I can remember hugging her in ages. Having Grandma Josie with me will make the move more tolerable.

"Well, actually your mama suggested it. There may be times when she and your daddy are gone, and someone will need to be around to keep an eye on you. Plus, I'd get awfully lonely here in New Orleans with both my girls way up north in Washington. So, I think you ought to give your mama a thank you hug."

I hug Mama. It is one of the few times I have hugged her lately and really meant it.

"Thanks Mama."

I say this with realness that I haven't felt in a long time, and I can tell she feels it.

"Well, what about me? Am I the only one around here that doesn't get a hug?"

"I don't know Daddy. What have YOU done for me lately?"

"Well, how about convincing your Mama to let you go on the ski trip to Colorado and convincing Senator and Mrs. Le Brun to let Rachel go with you."

"You did that, you really did that Daddy?"

"Hey, did you forget who I am? I'm the President Elect. I have power."

Mama, Grandma Josie, and I burst out laughing.

"Listen to you three, you even laugh alike. I'm out-numbered. I surrender."

We laugh even louder. Then I go over and give Daddy a hug whispering thanks in his ear.

Mama's other news was about school. She had managed to get me in the same classes with Rachel. The school said my test scores were high, and I was placed in one of the highest groups.

"Andie Beth, you are going to have to study harder at Brockton. They said after looking at your test scores."

"I know Mama. You don't even have to say it. After looking at my test scores, they have determined that I'm not working up to my potential."

"You got it. So, if want to stay in the same classes with Rachel, you are really going to have to study. Just remember, it's up to you. Your Daddy and I can't do it for you. It all depends what your priorities are."

"Yes, Mama."

"And your daddy has convinced me that you've been grounded long enough. As of now, you're not grounded anymore. But let me remind you."

"Let me remind you that if you get into trouble again, you will be grounded again, and we will cancel the skiing trip."

"Andie Beth Nettles are you mocking me?"

"No ma'am. I just know you. Remember me? I'm Lynn Nettles' daughter."

This time Daddy and Grandma Josie burst out laughing, and even Mama can't help herself and she starts laughing too.

"Goodnight Andie B. Now go tell Rachel you two are going skiing. But don't stay up too late on the computer. You still have school tomorrow."

"Goodnight everybody."

I run up to my room and find a message from Rachel on the computer.

"A. B. we're going skiing. My Mom just told me. Isn't it great?"

"Rachel, you did it to me again. Why do you always know what's going on in my life before I do?"

"As your best friend that's what I'm supposed to do."

"Yeah, right. Good night Rachel."

"Good night A.B."

I change clothes, turn off the lights and get in bed. A slight smile, Mama's smile, creeps across my face as I fall asleep.

Chapter 3

Christmas

"**R**achel, are you out there?"

"You know I can't go anywhere."

I'm stuck here in my room. Ten days and counting to the move. It's early January, and my life has taken a turn from chaotic to tragic.

My brother Trey came home for vacation a week before Christmas. He's going to LSU on a basketball scholarship, but he's only a freshman, and he's warming the bench. Daddy has gone to two of the games, but they were on school nights, so of course Mama wouldn't let me go. His team will be playing University of Maryland and George Washington University, so she says we can watch him play after we move.

I was sitting in the den watching my favorite movie.

"Are you watching *Amelia*™ again? You ought to have it memorized by now."

"What did you do buy out the mall? Hope all of those are for me."

"In your dreams Buzzard. In your dreams."

"You want some cookies? Grandma Josie just baked them."

"I see you're still addicted to Dr. Pepper™. How bad is your addiction these days A.B.? Still hiding it under your bed?"

"How did you know that? I don't remember telling you."

"Andie B. the whole family knows. Mom blamed me for taking the bottles when she kept noticing that they were disappearing from the kitchen. I never told her it was you, but when I left for college she was bound to have figured it out."

"I doubt it. She's not around much. She's been too busy campaigning for Daddy."

"Look, I've always been honest with you, right?"

"That's what I admire the most about you oh honored big brother."

"Then I've got one thing to tell you: lighten up on Mom."

"But my question for you is: when is she going to lighten up on me? You have it so easy. She doesn't stay on your case like she does mine."

"She only stays on your case because she's trying to keep you out of trouble, and she loves you."

"Do you know you sound more and more like Daddy every day?"

"Not likely. Just try to cut them some slack. They're trying Buzzard. Listen, some of my old friends from school and I are going to *The Eight Ball* to play pool later if you want to tag along."

"You sure you want your little sister to come with you? I mean I wouldn't want to cramp your style with some hot babe."

"Of course you're invited; besides somebody has to pay the bill. I just blew all my money on Christmas presents."

"Well, then, my purse and I would be honored to join you. But you better clear it with Mama. She'll probably have some reason why I can't go."

"You leave Mom up to me. Remember I'm her first-born. I have her right where I want her."

Mama and Daddy walk in.

"Trey, did I hear you say you have me right where you want me? And where would that be?"

I burst out laughing, and left the room. It has been a good afternoon. For once I am not the only Nettles off-spring who is in trouble. My brother has been nailed by Mama and Daddy. Life is good.

Trey works his charm on Mama, and convinces her that he'll keep an eye on me if she lets me go out with him and his friends. At first she's not so sure. He even manages to get my curfew extended to 12:30 a.m. so he won't have to rush home by 11:00 p.m. It's not like I could get in trouble. The Secret Service agents are tagging along, but because I'm with Trey they stay in the background more than usual.

Trey and his friends make me feel like I'm one of them, and not a little kid. I wish I could feel this way all the time. The most awesome part of the whole night; Mama and Daddy aren't waiting up for us at the door when we come home. I see their light on under their bedroom door but even that doesn't bother me.

I wake up on Christmas Eve morning to hear rain pounding on the roof. It is a gray windy day, and is raining so hard that it reminds me of the hurricanes that we experience here on the Gulf Coast during the summer.

I spend most of the day in my room packing for the ski trip to Colorado. We leave the day after Christmas. Even though you don't go to my school, Mama has convinced the principal to let you go with me on the trip.

The majority of the kids going are juniors and seniors. It is a rite of passage among the students. My brother went during his junior and senior years, and I had been looking forward to going next year.

When school started, and it became obvious Daddy might win the election, I asked Mama and Daddy if I could go this year. They told me after the election when they returned from a trip to Washington.

It rained all day today. I finished my packing leaving a little room for any clothes I might get for Christmas and want to take with me. When I wandered downstairs, I noticed that the furniture store was making a delivery. They brought in two chairs covered in black plastic. Mama and Daddy must be getting new chairs as Christmas presents to take to the White House.

All of the furniture in our house is going in storage. I'm taking some items from my room like my desk, computer, television, stereo, and posters. I have to wake up with the New Orleans Saints football team looking down at me. Mama said I could put posters up in my new room - as long as they were tasteful. Every morning I see the Saints and Derek Jeter, a New York Yankee, smiling at me. Who knows? Maybe I can get Daddy to invite them to the White House.

A Tulane professor and his family are buying our house. Daddy said that once he leaves the White House he and Mama won't need a big house like this anymore. It is sad. This is the only home that any of us have ever known. What scares me though is where will we stay we come back to New Orleans to visit? It will be hard to visit my friends in Kenner if I'm staying with my grandparents in Mandeville. But does the President even get a vacation?

My brother has a fire going in the fireplace, and I can smell Daddy's gumbo cooking in the kitchen. Christmas Eve is the one holiday that we spend together as a family without anyone else. Everyone is expected to be home by late afternoon for family time. Supper consists of Daddy's gumbo with salad made by my brother and French bread from one of the local bakeries. It is the one night of the year that the men cook.

After supper we get dressed up and go to Christmas Eve Services at St. John's Episcopal Church. Because of the Secret Service we have to leave early, and travel in two limos. Additional agents are at the church. I recognize them.

Our family has always gone to St. John's. Trey and I were baptized there. Now we even have a certain way we have to get out of the car. It's always Daddy and Mama first then I and whoever else is around. I'm now a second class citizen. I have to walk behind Mama and Daddy when we go anywhere together. Except when there are photographers around wanting to take family pictures. Then I'm always beside Mama with this smile pasted on my face. I hate having my picture taken. Yuck. Mama even told me what dress to wear to church tonight so I wouldn't clash with hers. Who cares?

When we arrived at St. John's, the photographers and news vans were there. We had to stop several times and have our picture taken as a family. Trey was beside Daddy, and I was beside Mama. Grandma Josie was even in some of the pictures. I thought we'd never get inside the church.

We found our spot in the third pew on the right. The church is small and the five of us plus the secret service agents took up three pews. It was jammed packed. All the lights in the church were turned off, and candles on the window ledges flickered in the stained glass windows. Instead of the usual musty smell, the church smelled like apples and pine. The organist played Christmas carols before the service began. It was quiet and peaceful.

When we came out of St. John's there were more photographers and reporters around. It's Christmas Eve. Don't these people have anything better to do? Don't they have families? Daddy shuffled us to the car. He and Mama held hands again as they walked to the house. Enough already. These two never stop.

Mama and Daddy headed for the den. I headed for the stairs.

"Where are you going Buzzie?"

"Upstairs to change clothes. This dress itches."

"Aw, c'mon in here Buzzie. You look so pretty tonight. I like looking at my girls all dressed up."

"DADDY."

"By the way, where did Trey run off to?"

"He said in the car he wanted to call Sam when he came home."

"Sam?"

"Samantha, Daddy. His new girlfriend. He showed me a picture of her."

"What have I missed?"

"You're out of touch Daddy."

Mama laughs.

"She has a point dear."

"Now that it's finally stopped raining, I'm going to change clothes, and shoot some baskets."

I go up to my room, and take off the dress. Then I hear the rain again. Well, there goes that idea. Might as well put on my pj's, and perform my Christmas Eve vigil.

"What are you doing here big brother?"

"What do you think?"

"Looking for Santa?"

"Nope, just for you."

"How you know I'd be here?"

"You haven't missed a year since you were three."

"I didn't think you'd remember this year."

"Why? We do this every year."

"But we're grown up now."

"Buzzard, we'll still be doing this when we're old."

"You really think so?"

"Yep. And our kids will think we're crazy."

"We are."

"Trey, do you realize this will be our last Christmas here?"

"Yep."

"Am I the only one in the family that is bugged by this?"

"It bugs me too, only in a different way."

"What do you mean, Trey?"

"It means that next year we'll be hanging out on the White House steps. And I think it's bothering Mom and Dad too."

"What do you mean?"

"Well, they've been in this house a lot longer than us. It's got to mean something to them."

"Then, why did they sell it?"

"It's too big."

"But now we're homeless."

Trey laughs. We look up and standing at the bottom of the stairs are Mama and Daddy.

"If you two are looking for Santa Claus, he said to tell you he was skipping our house this year."

"Why Daddy?"

"Something about Trey's grades and your pig sty room."

Mama and Daddy come upstairs. Daddy puts his arm around me and drags me to my room. It's like the old days when we were little kids, and he would scoop me up off the stairs. I turn out the lights and crawl into bed.

Yuk. Cajun plants a big wet kiss on my face.

"What's wrong with you dog?"

He runs back and forth to the door scratching to get out.

"Caj, what gives? What's the rush? We're not kids anymore. There's no rush to head downstairs. I want to go back to sleep. Lie down boy."

I close my eyes hoping that Cajun will get the hint. Maybe he'll settle down for a little while. The glow of the alarm clock tells me it's only 6:00. It's too early to get up even on Christmas morning. I'm almost back to sleep when Cajun jumps on the bed again.

"Look dog, you better hope the house is on fire when I get out of this bed. Because if it isn't your Christmas present goes back to the pet store. Do you hear me?"

Cajun cocks his head compliantly as if to say "just try and get away with it".

I open the door and Cajun bounds down the stairs like he's on a rescue mission. Diving for the bed and burying my head in my pillow, I try to shut out the world. The door is open just in case Caj decides to come back. I hear the thunder and rain and notice the lightning flashes. Great. More rain. Just what I wanted on Christmas morning. Rolling over on my back I stare at the ceiling, how many hours of my life have I spent staring at this same ceiling. The smell of cinnamon winds its way up the stairs. Gram must be baking cinnamon buns for breakfast. That's what got Cajun so excited. I lie in bed and breathe in the scent. My mouth waters and my stomach growls like a bear coming out of hibernation. I'm starved. Grabbing my robe off the chair I bolt down the stairs to the kitchen.

"Hi Gram."

"I knew you'd be the first one up. Have you been in the den yet to see what Santa brought you?"

"Aw, Gram you know I'm too old for that stuff."

"You want a glass of milk?"

"How about a cup of coffee instead? It smells great."

"Didn't think you liked the stuff. Tell you what how about half coffee and half milk. That way I stay out of trouble."

"You must have made it strong."

"Just the way your Daddy likes it."

"Is it ever going to stop raining? This is driving me nuts. I'm not used to being cooped up like this."

"I think it's kind of nice myself. Besides you'll be outdoors plenty over the next few days."

"Yep, I can hardly wait. I'm more excited about the ski trip than I am about Christmas."

"Funny. I didn't notice."

"Gram."

"Um. Cinnamon buns. I can smell them all the way upstairs."

"Hey Daddy."

"Merry Christmas Buzzie. Should have known you'd be the first one here."

"Always."

"Here's your coffee Gary, and the buns should be ready in about five more minutes. I'm going to get something out of my room. Don't let the buns burn Andie B."

"So, Buzz. You excited about your trip?"

"You know it Daddy."

"Just remember, take it easy and never ski alone."

"I won't Daddy. Besides I'll have Rach along."

"Just think before you act and you'll be okay."

"Yes, Daddy."

The oven timer rings, and I get up from the table and take the buns out of the oven just as Trey walks in.

"Oh no, if you baked those I'm not touching them."

"Slaved over a hot stove just for you big brother."

Gram comes back in the kitchen.

"Andie B. did you get my cinnamon buns out of the oven?"

"Gram you baked them not Buzzard right?"

"Of course, Trey."

"Whew. My stomach couldn't take Buzzard's cooking; especially on Christmas morning."

Trey opens the door and lets Cajun back in. He grabs him by the collar.

"Buzzard, grab a towel to wipe off your dog. He's soaking wet."

"Don't you let him on my clean kitchen floor with those muddy paws. Cajun look at you. You're a mess."

I throw Trey a towel. Cajun shakes spraying muddy water all over Trey.

"Thanks a lot dog. Andie B. get down here and help me. He's your dog not mine."

"All right. What's wrong Caj? Big brother just doesn't know how to treat you does he?"

I wipe the mud off Cajun's paws and tail trying to dry him off. Trey and I throw the towels behind the kitchen door. Maybe Gram won't notice them for a while. Cajun slinks down to his place by my stool at the end of the counter.

"Now you two wash your hands. You're almost as dirty as that dog."

"Yes Gram".

"C'mon Trey quit hogging the hot water."

"Me? Since when do you care about being clean?"

"Since you left town and there's enough hot water to go around. Couldn't get clean before. No hot water."

The clicking of heels on the tile floor interrupts our argument. We turn and see Mama as she enters the room.

"Cut it out you two. I could hear you all the way upstairs. But evidently your father and grandmother couldn't, and they were right here in the room with you."

Daddy looks up from his newspaper. Even on Christmas morning he's absorbed in world events.

"What? Cut it out kids. Whatever you were doing stop it now."

"Gary they could be killing each other, and you wouldn't notice. I can understand Mama. She lets them get away with everything. But you, you're their father."

"Lighten up sweetie, it's Christmas. They're both still alive. They remind me of the way Joan and I used to pick at each other. Now relax."

He walks over and gives her a kiss.

"Here have one of your mom's cinnamon buns. They're delicious."

Trey and I slip over to our stools at the end of the island. As I pass Mama I see she's wearing makeup, and is dressed in one of her designer outfits. She looks like she's going to the opera instead of Christmas with her family. The rest of us are still in our pajamas or sweats. I mean the woman can't even open Christmas presents with her family without putting on a show. If she's this dressed up already, I know it means I'll have to wear a dress to Grandma Elizabeth's and Grandpa Webb's. I was hoping

I could get away with jeans because of the rain. Daddy walks over and gives her a kiss.

"Lynn you look beautiful this morning."

"Why thank you Mr. President. I didn't think anyone noticed. Why aren't you all in the den? Figured you'd be in there by now Andie B."

"Nope, waiting for Gram's cinnamon buns."

"Yeah, Mom food first this year. Decided to start a new tradition. Eat first then presents."

"You two are growing up. I remember when nothing would keep you from that den first thing in the morning."

"Oh no Trey, we're becoming one of them."

"No, little sister, I promise you we will never become one of them."

"Are you sure Trey?"

"I guarantee it."

"They seem awful sure of themselves don't they Lynn?"

"Definitely. We'll check back with them in a few years when they have kids of their own."

"Never happen Mom. Don't plan on any grandkids from me for a long time."

"Me neither."

"That's what I wanted to hear. Especially from you young lady. You're entirely too young to be thinking about those kinds of things."

I roll my eyes. The woman can't relax even on Christmas morning. We go in the den where there is a fire in the fireplace, and all the lights are turned out except the ones on the Christmas tree.

"Remember the rules everybody, stockings first then presents."

"Aw Mama".

As soon as I grab my stocking and dump it on the couch, Cajun comes sniffing around looking for food.

"Andie Beth do something with your dog. He's in the way. Look in his stocking. Maybe there's a rawhide bone."

"Come here Caj let's see what Santa left for you."

I pull out a bone; Cajun snatches it from my hand, and plops down on the rug in front of the fireplace and starts gnawing. He's not moving.

I go back to my stocking. There's a pair of LSU socks, a Justin Bieber cd, a couple of bags of peanut M&M's, scrunchies, a toothbrush and toothpaste. We have a family tradition of each of us putting items in each other's stockings. It's fun to guess who gives what things.

"Lynn thanks for the tie. It's so stylish I may wear it today."

"No thanks needed I didn't give it to you."

"Well, Josie, I apologize. I forgot my wife inherited her good taste from her mother."

"Not me Gary. I confess. I gave everyone M&M's. My impractical side came out this year."

"Don't look this way Dad. I did my stocking shopping at the campus bookstore."

"Andie B., you bought your brother and I ties? When did you start noticing men's fashions?

"Don't. The Dollar Store had a Buy One Get One Free Sale, couldn't resist."

Mama and Daddy laugh.

"I want to open presents?"

"Now that's the Andie B. I'm used to."

"What's this one? To: Andie B. From: Cajun. Cajun have you been stealing some of my allowance? "

"Open it Buzzard, let's see what your dog bought you. Probably some flea shampoo. I've seen you scratching a lot lately."

I make a face at Trey, and tear off the wrapping paper.

"Aw, Caj. You bought me a new I Pod to replace the one you trashed."

I go over and put my arms around Cajun's neck, but he is oblivious to the attention and continues to gnaw on his bone.

The next gift I open has Mama's distinctive handwriting on the tag. The size and shape of the box tells me it is clothes. I'm careful not to tear into this one. I lift the top off to discover layer upon layer of fabric.

"What is this?"

I pull the clothes out of the box.

"Whatever it is, it sure is long."

"It's your dress for the inaugural balls, Andie B. I saw it at Neiman Marcus, and had to get it for you. You'll be the belle of the ball."

"I don't think so. I mean thanks Mama, I guess."

"Now run upstairs and hang it up before it gets all wrinkled."

"Now, but there are still more presents to unwrap."

"Yes, now. The presents will still be here when you get back. Now be careful with it."

I take the dress upstairs and hang it on the back of my closet door. Once I hang it up I take a good look at it. She bought me a turquoise dress. I hate turquoise. No way am I wearing this monstrosity to the inaugural balls. It even smells frilly. Like they put some sort of deodorizer on it. No way am I going to any dumb dance with my parents. I'll have to figure some way to get out of going even if it means getting grounded in the process. Andie Beth Nettles can only be pushed so far. I close the closet door to escape having to look at the dress. I fly downstairs again.

"Did you hang the dress up?"

"Yes, Mama."

"Where?"

"On the back of my closet door."

"That will do for now, but we may have to find a better place for it. I'll figure something out later."

Everyone has opened their presents. Mama and Daddy are sitting in their new chairs they bought to take to the White House.

"Boy this back massager feels good. I could fall asleep right here."

"Don't get too comfortable Gary; you and Trey have a lot of trash to take out."

"Andie B. I think Santa left you two more presents back here in the corner."

Leaning against the wall is the sleekest pair of skis I have ever seen.

"You bought me my own set of skis? I don't believe it."

"We thought you'd need them for your trip. Plus you'll be able to use them at Camp David once we move."

I run my hand along the polished edges, and inhale the deep aroma of the wax.

"My own skis. Wait until Rachel sees them."

"There's another gift in the box beside them."

"Oh yeah, I didn't see it."

"Well open it."

Inside the box is a basketball. Not just any basketball, but the Wilson® Supreme Collegiate Indoor Outdoor basketball. It's the one I've been dreaming about all my life.

"How did you know?"

"Know what?"

"Know I wanted this."

"Buzzie, we're not as out of it as you think. Your mama and I do pay attention to what you say."

"But I've wanted one of these forever."

"And now we think you're responsible enough to take care of a basketball this expensive."

"Truth is Buzzard they didn't want you taking that old raggedy one to the White House".

"Trey."

"Is that true Daddy? Is that the only reason?"

"Don't listen to your brother, Andie B. After the way you've been playing this season, your mama and I wanted to reward you".

"Thanks Daddy."

"Now let's clean up this wrapping paper and the rest of you can go dress to go over to Mandeville."

"I'm wearing jeans, okay, Mama?"

"No way. If I have to wear a tie, you at least have to wear a dress."

"Mama? Come on it's raining and yucky outside. Who's going to care what I have on?"

"Sorry, Andie B., but no jeans. Come upstairs. Maybe we can find something in your closet that we both agree on."

"Told you Buzzard."

I stick out my tongue at Trey.

"Cut it out you two. Now take your gifts up to your rooms. Now. Andie B. I'll be up in a minute."

"Thought you could get away with it didn't you?"

"Trey, you're not too old to get your car keys taken away. Quit picking on your sister."

"See college boy, you can still get into trouble."

"Gary, talk to your children. They're not listening to me. I'm going in the kitchen. I need another cup of coffee."

"Look you two. Can't you agree to a 24 hour cease fire? It's Christmas. Andie B. leaves tomorrow morning. Try to get along until then. Otherwise, you're on your own. If you get grounded, just remember I told you so. Do I make myself clear?"

"Yes, Daddy."

"Yes, Dad."

I grab my presents and take them to my room and throw them on my bed .When I come out of the shower; Mama is rummaging through my closet.

"How about the gray wool skirt, Andie B.?"

"It itches too much Mama. How about navy slacks and a sweater?"

"Sorry kiddo, I said you have to wear a dress. The photographers are camped outside waiting to take our picture. Any other suggestions before I make one?"

"The red jumper. At least I can move around in it."

"The red jumper with pantyhose and we have a deal."

"Mama, why do I have to wear pantyhose? You never used to make me wear them. What's the big deal now?"

"Because you're growing up. You're almost sixteen. It's time you started wearing pantyhose and makeup."

"Makeup too?"

"You better get used to it. It's part of becoming a woman. You're the President's kid now. And do something with your hair. Pull it back. I don't want to see it in your face all day."

"Yes Mama."

Mama leaves and I turn up the music. Dancing around the room I throw a few more cds in my backpack for the trip. I'm not ready to join the family downstairs yet. I'm going to stay up here as long as I can. There is a knock at the door. Gram peeks in.

"Andie B. do you know what time it is? Everyone is waiting downstairs."

"Guess I wasn't paying attention Gram."

"Caught up in your own little world again weren't you? What was it this time? Basketball, skiing, or Matt?"

"Gram."

"Well, hurry up. Everyone's waiting."

I get dressed making sure to do what Mama has told me. I don't need to get in trouble on Christmas. Pulling my hair into a tight ponytail, I take careful steps to insure there aren't any strands around my face. A couple of dots of Covergirl and some lip gloss and I'm set. My appearance ought to satisfy the First Lady. I find a pair of black flats in the back of the closet. I'm not wearing heels. Maybe Mama won't notice. I walk downstairs just as Gram is coming back up.

"Let me look at you girl."

"Gotta pass inspection, huh, Gram?"

"Just trying to protect you. You look good except go back and find your black heels. I bet you thought your mama wouldn't notice."

"Gram."

"Hurry now Andie B."

I go back in my room, dig the heels out of the closet, and put them on. Ouch. They pinch my toes. My Nikes® would feel so much better. I don't see how Mama wears these torture chambers every day. Gram is still waiting halfway down the steps. She looks me up and down.

"Okay, that's better. I think you're ready."

"Wow, look at you. Okay, who are you and what have you done with my tomboy daughter?"

"Daddy."

"That's funny. The voice sounds like Andie B. But it sure doesn't look like her. I've got to get a closer look."

"Daddy. Puhlease. Enough already."

"You look beautiful Buzzie. I may have to change your name. Let's see what can I call you?"

"Let's go Gary. The agents are waiting."

We leave the house and cameras go off everywhere. Mama was right. All the photographers are there with reporters. They try to ask Daddy questions as we walk toward the car and wave. I don't get the waving bit. I wouldn't do it if Mama wasn't so insistent about it. My heels sink into the soft grass, and I almost trip. I hate these shoes. At least the rain has stopped.

When we arrive at Grandma Elizabeth's and Grandpa Webb's, Daddy's two sisters and brother and their kids are there. The scent of turkey, crawfish pies, and pumpkin pies baking greet us at the door.

"Bumble look at you. You're so dressed up I didn't recognize you."

"Hi Grandpa."

"Your Grandma and aunts are in the kitchen putting the finishing touches on dinner, and the cousins are in the den."

"No, I'm right behind you Webb. Merry Christmas Presidential family. My that sounds good. Just think I'm the President's mother."

"Merry Christmas Gram."

Gram gives me a hug.

"Now Andie Beth you and Trey run along to the den with the young folks."

Trey and I head for the den where the cousins are hanging out. There are two televisions going. One has a college all star football game on with the mute button on, and the other one is being used for video games. A Black-eyed Peas cd is blasting away. I look around and see that all twelve of us are here.

"Andie B. come here."

"Lauren, I was looking for you and Michelle."

"Come on let's go upstairs and talk to get away from these guys."

We go to one of the guest bedrooms. It's the one I stay in when I spend the night. I like it because it smells like lavender, and the hardwood floor has so much wax on it that you can see your reflection. The first thing I do is kick off my shoes.

"Nobody's going to get mad at us for skipping out will they?"

"Are you kidding? In that mob I doubt if we'll be noticed."

"Weird isn't it? Twelve cousins and only three girls."

"Yeah, but what's even weirder is that we're all the same age."

"I never thought about that. All of our moms were preggers at the same time."

"Yep. They couldn't even get close to the dinner table that year."

Lauren walks across the floor with her back tilted like she's pregnant. Michelle and I start laughing.

"I never thought about it."

"So, are you excited about living in the White House?"

"Truth?"

"Truth."

"Nope. I really don't want to leave Kenner."

"You're kidding. Man I hate my school. I'd give any-thing to leave."

"Not me. If I could figure out a way to stay I would."

"What do your mom and dad say about it?"

"There's nothing to say. And listen you guys Gram and Grandpa don't know how I feel so keep your mouths shut okay?"

"My parents think it's great. Mama keeps saying just think my big brother is the President."

"My dad too. He keeps talking about how he always knew your dad was smart, but never that smart. Keeps saying stuff like I'm the little brother of the President. Like he's trying to make sense of it."

"Too weird."

"Yep. too weird."

"Well at least I'll have you guys around at the inauguration."

"Yeah, but you'll be up there on the front row."

"Ladies and gentlemen the First Daughter. Say a few words to your adoring fans Ms. Nettles."

"I'm sorry. No comment."

We all burst out laughing.

Gram Elizabeth comes in the room.

"Wondered where you three wandered off to? Went to count heads in the den, and was missing three."

"Can we hang here Gram? It's easier to talk away from the boys."

"Sure, I don't see why not. Just keep an eye on the clock. We'll be eating in around thirty minutes. Don't want to have to come looking for you again."

"Thanks Gram."

"So has your mom taken you shopping for your inauguration ball dress?"

"No, she gave it to me as a Christmas present."

"She didn't even let you pick it out?"

"Nope."

"What color is it?"

"Turquoise."

"Ew. You hate turquoise. Are you going to wear it?"

"Do I have a choice? Unless something happens to it."

"Andie B. do you have a plan?"

"Let's just say I'm working on one."

"You are going to tell us about it."

"Not yet."

"We better get downstairs."

I start to leave the room.

"Andie B. your shoes."

"Oh yeah."

We go downstairs and eat Christmas Dinner. My grandparents have two huge dining room tables which they put together for special occasions. That way everyone gets to sit together. All twenty three of us. Grandpa is at one end of the table and Daddy, the eldest son, is at the other end which seems like a mile away. Grandma has carefully positioned place cards at each chair so everyone knows where to sit. She mixes up kids and adults and families. I think she puts the names in a hat and draws them out. After we eat, we open presents. Each of us gets a present from Gram and Grandpa. The adults draw names and so do the kids.

"Gram, you got me a running suit from the Naval Academy?"

"Just like the plebes wear. Special ordered it from the school."

"Thanks Gram."

"Now my gift is little Bumble but don't let the size fool you."

I tear in to the box. Inside is a little book. Engraved on the front is: Flight Log Andie Beth Nettles 2011-.

"My own flight log. That means."

"That means if you're going to get your pilot's license this year, you're going to be flying back and forth between Washington D.C. and here with me, and you need your own log book for your hours."

I rub my fingers over the engraving again. My own log book. I jump up and hug Grandpa.

"Thanks Grandpa."

"Speaking of flying. We better head back home. It's getting late, and Andie B. has an early flight to Colorado tomorrow morning."

"Goodnight everybody."

Gram and Grandpa give us all hugs, and we pile into the car for the return trip across the causeway. The lights of the city glisten in the night, and a strong cold wind is blowing across the lake.

We come in the house, and Trey heads upstairs to call Sam.

I linger at the bottom of the stairs as Mama and Daddy come in the house.

"Andie Beth are you packed and ready to go tomorrow?"

"Yes Ma'am."

"Good then off to bed. You've got a busy day ahead of you."

"Mama, it's not even 10 yet. Can't I stay up for a while? I'm not even tired. Come on Mama."

"Tell you what. Go upstairs and get ready for bed. If you want to read or listen to music for a little while, that's okay. But no telephone calls or computer tonight. I'll be in to say goodnight in a few minutes."

"Thanks Mama."

"Now how about giving the old man a hug?"

"Goodnight Daddy. I love you."

"I love you too Buzzie. Now get upstairs before your mama changes her mind."

I go upstairs and change clothes. Glad to finally be rid of the pantyhose and heels. Cajun comes in and takes his place on the soft woven rug beside my bed. Turning on the radio to my favorite jazz station I crawl into bed with the new book about Fighter Planes that Lauren gave me for Christmas. Mama walks in the room. She nudges Cajun out of the way and he runs downstairs. She comes over to the bed and I scoot over to give her room to sit down. She has changed into her robe, and looks comfortable for the first time today. After sitting down, she pushes my hair out of my face.

"Did you have a good Christmas Little B.?"

"Yes Mama. You haven't called me that name since I was a kid."

"I know, but when I looked at you today across the dinner table I realized how grown up you were."

"I don't feel grown up most of the time Mama."

"Well, you are. And it makes me feel old."

"You're not old Mama. You can't be."

I yawn.

"See I told you you were sleepy. I know my Andie B. I can tell when you're tired. You always get that sad look in your eyes."

"I guess so. Goodnight Mama."

"Goodnight Little B. I love you."

"I love you too Mama."

Mama kisses me on the forehead, and turns out the light. Cajun comes in the room and plops down on the rug. I turn over and fall asleep. Christmas is over.

Chapter 4

The Accident Part I

"**R**achel, are you out there?"

This is my last time on facebook® for a few days. It's also my last night in my room. The movers pack us for Washington tomorrow. Grandma Josie took my posters and signs off the wall today. I had to sit and watch from a chair. It seems weird knowing I'll never go sliding across this floor again in my socks, or open the door to catch a whiff of what's cooking downstairs. Man it's hard to roll this chair when I can't use my feet. I'm out of breath, and I only traveled four or five feet. I start to open the window, and then remember the security system. I still don't see how someone could break in three stories up. The roar of the plane engines alerts me that the airport is busy tonight. I want to watch the planes take off. The best view is from the back yard. Mama told me not to come back downstairs. She said I needed to rest. I don't care I'm going. Who wants to stay in this dumb old room anyway? After today this room belongs to a twelve year old boy. It won't be my room ever again. It's not fair.

Mama says my room at the White House is larger than this one. I hope so. I haven't seen it. She and I picked out the paint during Christmas. She wanted pink. I wanted navy and gold, the colors of the Naval Academy. We compromised on light blue for my room, and yellow for the study. I'll have the whole top floor of the White House to myself with the solarium next door for parties. Trey will have a room up there too.

I hope Trey comes home a lot. Even though he gets on my last nerve most of the time I like having him around. He even convinced Daddy to get a pool table for the solarium. Told him he'd stay home more when he visited if he agreed to it. Maybe Daddy will come upstairs and play 8-ball with me when he's not too busy being President. Trey promised me he would come to Washington for his spring break; unless LSU gets in the NCAA tournament. If they do I hope Daddy and I can go to the games. Mama and Daddy give me more privileges when Trey is around. Mama doesn't treat me like a baby. He's coming home in a couple of days, so we can fly to Washington together.

"C'mon Rachel where are you?"

Tomorrow is my last day at St. Martins. It seems weird. I've been with some of the kids since kindergarten. We figured we'd be together until graduation. I never thought I'd be the one to leave. Matt's dad is an airline pilot, and he's never been transferred. Why did Daddy have to go and win the stupid election? There's a basketball game tomorrow night, but I can't play. What started out as a great plan may end up costing me my athletic career. No more sports for me this year and maybe forever. All because of that stupid turquoise dress. I'm going downstairs I want to look at the planes one last time.

Whoops there go the crutches. Guess they'll hear me coming. Grandma Josie really overdosed the stair railing on Lemon Pledge. I'm having trouble holding on to it. My hand hurts from gripping it so hard. It's so slippery, and now my hand stinks like moldy lemons.

"Andie B. what are you doing coming downstairs?"

"I'm going outside to watch the planes."

"No you're not young lady. You get back up to your room."

"What's going on?"

"Daddy, all I want to do is go watch the planes for a while. It will be my last chance. Can I Daddy? Please Daddy. Mama says no."

"I don't see any problem. C'mon Buzzie. Let me help you."

Daddy lets me lean on him down the stairs. He smells like Brut. Sure is better than the lemons. At the bottom of the stairs he hands me my crutches.

"Lynn, what's the problem? It's her last night here. Let her do what she wants."

"And suppose she falls again. You know how wet the grass gets at night. Are you going to risk her getting hurt again?"

"Andie B. I was just bringing you a snack. You shouldn't be going up and down those stairs."

"I tried to tell her Mama, but nobody listens to me around here."

"Tell you what Buzzie I need a break from my paper-work. Can I join you just to put your mama's mind at ease? "

"Sure Daddy."

"Well, I see I'm not going to win this one. But only fifteen minutes. It's cold and damp outside and all we need is for both of you to catch pneumonia before the inauguration. And where's Cajun? Take him with you."

Daddy grabs his jacket, and we go outside with Cajun trotting behind us. We stop at the rusty old bench by the basketball court. It's the only piece of lawn furniture still around, and is anchored into the concrete. Daddy throws Cajun's tennis ball, and I lower myself to the bench.

"You're getting pretty good at getting up and down."

"Yeah. Thanks for talking Mama into letting me come out here."

"It didn't take much. Guess you were getting pretty bored up there up in your room."

"Sorta."

"Well Buzzie tomorrow's your last day of school at St. Martins. You scared?"

"Sorta."

"Is this going to be a one word conversation or you going to talk to me?"

"Sorry, Daddy, I was watching the planes."

"Next time we take off it will be for Washington."

"You scared Daddy?"

"Sorta."

Daddy pulls me close to him. His muscular arm envelopes me like a glove. Putting my head on his immense chest I feel it moving up and down with every breath he takes. We stare at the sky as the planes magically dart across the sky like fireworks on the Fourth of July. Words aren't necessary. I feel closer to Daddy than I have in ages. I look up at him and start to say something. But I don't. Daddy appears hypnotized. Maybe he is remembering. I know I am.

"We better go in Andie B. You're shaking like a leaf. Why didn't you tell me you were cold?"

"Cause I wanted to stay out here with you Daddy."

"Tell you what let's go in and have some hot chocolate before your mama gets mad at us."

Snatching my crutches off the ground, I pull myself up. Daddy helps me, and we head for the house. Cajun barks when Daddy opens the storm door. Mama and Grandma Josie are sitting at the kitchen island drinking coffee.

"I was about to send Cajun out on a search and rescue mission. That was a long fifteen minutes."

"We were watching the planes. Any of Josie's cookies still left? I'm starved. Buzzie, you want some hot chocolate to warm you up."

"Sure Daddy."

"Sit down Gary. I'll fix it."

"Why don't you go in the den? The three of us will be in there in a minute."

"Need some help Andie B.?"

"No, Mama, I'm fine."

I hobble into the den and stretch out on the couch. A stabbing pain shoots through my left knee. It reminds me of the skiing accident that ruined my trip, and I start thinking about it all over again.

We left the day after Christmas. When we arrived at the airport, almost all the kids were there. Rachel's mom and dad drove her down from Baton Rouge. The three of them were waiting for us.

"Rach."

"A.B. It's about time. Where have you been? You only live ten minutes from here."

"Waiting to make my grand entrance. Have you checked in yet?"

"No, figured I'd better wait for you."

"Here's your boarding passes Ms. Nettles and yours too Ms. LeBrun."

"Who's that?"

"One of the agents who is traveling with us. There will be more in Breckenridge. Get used to it."

"Do they always call you Ms. Nettles?"

"Most of the time. Don't worry about them. Most of the time they're invisible."

"St. Martin's kids. Everybody over here."

"C'mon Rach."

"Andie B. When did you get here? I didn't see you."

"Hey Matt."

"Okay, kids. It's time to board."

Rachel and I run over to tell our parents goodbye. The way everyone is hugging us you'd think we were never going to see each other again.

"Listen, you two remember to never ski alone, and to think. Andie Beth if you run into any problems tell one of the agents. Remember, they're there to protect you."

"Yes ma'am."

"Rachel, that goes for you too. You two look out for each other."

"Yes ma'am."

"Now get going, and have fun."

"C'mon A.B."

Rachel and I run to catch up with the group. Breckenridge here we come.

"Wonder if there will be any cute guys out in Colorado? Oh, I forgot. You're not looking. You've got Matt."

"Got Matt? I doubt it. Look at him. He's too busy with the football team to pay any attention to me."

"So does that mean you're looking?"

"No, it means I don't care. Like any guy is going to want to have anything to do with me?"

"Are you kidding? You're the talk of the school. Every guy at Brockton wants to date you."

"Yeah right."

"Andie B. I'm not kidding. I've had guys ask me out so we could double with my best friend."

"Meaning me?"

"Yep."

"What did you tell them?"

"Well, a couple of the offers were tempting. But I told them no. Said you'd have to make up your own mind when you get to D.C."

"Too weird."

"You're the President's kid. Your stock just went up."

"Give me a break."

"Just wait and see. Every guy in the world will want to dance with you at the inaugural balls."

"It won't happen."

"What do you mean? Of course they will."

"I mean I'm not going to the inaugural balls."

"Yeah right. You know your parents are going to make you go. I've been begging mine to let me. It'll be cool."

"Well, quit wasting your energy because I'm not going."

"How are you going to get out of it?"

"You'll see."

"Have you gone dress shopping, or is your mom having a famous designer make your dress?"

"Oh, yeah. I didn't tell you. She gave me this grotesque turquoise dress for Christmas. Said she saw it at Neiman Marcus and fell in love with it."

"But doesn't she know you hate turquoise?"

"Evidently not. The whole world knows but not her. But I'm not wearing it because I'm not going."

"Sounds like you've got a plan."

"All I can tell you is if you see me fall on Thursday don't panic."

"You're going to hurt yourself aren't you?"

"Just a little bit."

"But won't that mess you up for softball?"

"Nope. Just means I'll be on crutches for the inauguration."

"I hope you know what you're doing."

"Trust me Rach, I do."

"Look, we're landing."

"It's about time."

"Okay kids grab your stuff and head for the bus."

"A.B. you've got your own skis?"

"Yep. Got them for Christmas."

"Cool."

"Are we going to have time to make a run when we get there?"

"Hope so."

"Miss Nettles just to let you know we're next door. You know the drill. Let us know if you need anything."

"I know. Daddy told me before we left. Are you guys going to be skiing with us too?"

"Some of us will. We'll try and stay out of your way as much as possible."

"I don't have to tell you every time I go downstairs do I?"

"Miss Nettles you don't even have to talk to us. Just remember we're around in case of an emergency. We'll try to be invisible. Have fun."

"Thanks."

"The agents seem pretty cool."

"They are. It's just weird feeling like I'm always being watched."

"Does that mean they'll go on dates with you?"

"Guess so. Now you see why I tell you no guy is going to want to go out with me. Can you imagine kissing a guy while an agent watches? "

"Ew."

"Let's go. I want to get in at least one run today. Race ya."

Another busload of kids is arriving as we run out the door. I don't even notice. But Rachel does. We're on the chair lift, and she's jabbering away.

"Did you see him?"

"Him who?"

"That tall blond guy getting off the bus?"

"Our bus? We don't have any tall blond guys at St. Martins."

"No dummy, the bus that was pulling up as we left. Looked like some boys school. Didn't see any girls."

"No wonder I beat you to the lift. You were checking out some guy."

"I do not check out A.B. I gaze."

"Means the same thing. I told you Rach I came here to ski."

"Each to his own. But you'll be sorry when I take home the prize. That guy is a stud."

After one quick run down the mountain, the sky turns dark and dreary and snowflakes come down like swarms of bees searching for the hive. Fog rolls into the valley, and we tramp to the lodge slowly putting one foot in front of the other over the icy glaze which coats the landscape. Pulling my hat off, my damp hair escapes the binding of the scrunchie and flies in every direction then freezes to the side of my face. It is the same feeling I have when I come off the basketball court. The feeling of victory in achieving yet another goal. I have conquered the mountain. Only in athletics do I get that feeling. Only then am I fully in control.

The bright lights of the lodge beckon us to safety like a lighthouse in a sea of snow. Inside, music blares and kids are dancing and talking as if time has stopped. Shoving open the monstrous oak door, we sneak upstairs in a cat-like trance before anyone notices us.

"Made it."

"Did anyone see us?"

"Don't think so. Good let's get changed and check out the action. I'm going on a search mission."

"Looking for the blond guy?"

"You bet. I'll know his name by this time tomorrow."

We spend the next four days skiing and hanging out with our friends. Rachel sees the blond guy several times, but never gets close enough to him or any of his friends to find out his name. Somehow, I'm never around for these sightings, and start to believe that he is a figment of her imagination. Matt spends most of his time with his football buddies.

"A.B. I notice Matt is either hanging out with Heather or the football team. You two breaking up?"

"I don't know. Why, what's he saying?"

"Just that now that you're the President's kid, and you're moving you aren't the same."

"C'mon on Clay I haven't changed. Have I?"

"Not to me, but Matt thinks so. I've wanted to ask you out for a long time, but Matt's my best friend and guys don't do that."

"Well Matt doesn't get it. I was grounded until after Thanksgiving. I can't help it if my parents are strict."

"Yeah. But then you brought Rachel on this trip. Our school trip."

"She's my best friend. That's why I brought her. I like hanging out with her.

If you're the messenger, then tell Matt that I'm here and I've been here all along. He knows where to find me."

"I will."

"And Clay?"

"Yeah?"

"You're a good friend. If you had asked me out, I would have said yes."

The Thursday sun blinds me as I roll over. A bright blue cloudless sky greets me as I peek out of the curtains. All night long I was tossing and turning and waking up. Today is the day I put my plan into action. I hope I'm doing the right thing. But I don't have a choice. There is no other alternative. It's either do it or wear the awful dress.

Throwing on a pair of jeans and Annapolis sweatshirt I head downstairs for breakfast. Rachel is still asleep. She spent all last night mingling with other lodges in search of her mystery man. She is determined to find him.

"Andie B. over here."

"Hey Matt."

"Where's Rachel?"

"Still crashed. She partied late last night. Pass the muffins down here I'm starved."

"Isn't this great? I'm going to hate to go home on Saturday."

"Then school starts on Monday."

"You had to bring that up. But only three weeks for you then the big move."

"Now who's bringing up bad news? But you guys are coming to the inauguration?"

"Yep. My dad has reservations for us. Since the school band is in the parade, we'll have almost a plane load of people from St. Martins. That's not even counting the rest of Kenner, Metairie and New Orleans."

"The only difference is you guys get to come home. I'm stuck."

"But you'll be back for the state playoffs?"

"Grandpa says he'll come get me in *The Bee*, so I can come watch."

"Are your parents still going to let you fly it?"

"Why not, Grandpa will be with me."

"Yeah and secret service agents."

"I'm going upstairs and grabbing my skis. Anybody want to race?"

"I'm in."

"Me too."

"Downstairs in fifteen minutes."

Running in the room I plop down on my bed. The shower is running, and I can hear Rachel singing. I decide to wait for her. The water finally stops.

"Hurry up Rach I'm ready to ski. The gang is waiting."

"Go ahead without me. I'll catch you on the second run."

Grabbing my gear I head downstairs. Everyone is waiting by the front door.

"For someone in such a big hurry, what took you so long?"

"Talking to Rachel."

"So, now we're going to hang around and wait for her?"

"Nope, she'll catch up with us on the second run."

"Good."

"Matt, she's a nice person. Give her a chance. Please."

"I guess so."

"Now let's go ski."

"You heard it everybody. The First Kid has spoken."

We head for the chair lift. Matt even sits by me for a change.

"Are we breaking up?"

"Yeah."

"We can talk on the phone and e-mail each other."

"Guess so."

"D.C. is a long way from Kenner. I guess it wouldn't work."

"Yep."

"But we've still got the big New Year's Eve Party tomorrow night, and three more weeks at home."

"For sure."

"And I'll be back to visit my grandparents."

"That's right."

"So we can still be friends?"

"If that's what you want."

"Yes."

"Okay."

"Let's race."

The icy wind buffets me as I soar down the mountain. A somber grimace is plastered on my face as I remember all the good times Matt and I have had together. He has always been a part of my life. We shared the same playpen at our mother's Junior League meetings when we were toddlers. Mama says it was Matt who gave me the nickname A.B. because he couldn't pronounce Andie Beth. She would bring me to the meetings, and he cried out "A.B., A.B." as she carried me into the room. Now it was over. Faster Andie B., faster. Go for the win. I'm at the bottom of the mountain. The tears running down my face dampen the joy of winning the race. I have lost someone very important to me, and my life will never be the same.

My goggles are all fogged up so I jerk them off. Wiping the tears from my eyes with an icy mitten, I head for the chair lift again. I want to get in several runs before I put my plan into action. The timing has to be just right. I can't let what just happened with Matt overshadow what is going to happen today. Andie B. how can you be so stupid? Why did you even bring up the subject?

"What took you so long?"

"Matt and I broke up."

"What? Here? Why now?"

"It just seemed like the right time."

"You broke up with him?"

"No. I asked him if we were breaking up, and he said yes."

"Why did you go and do something dumb like that?"

"I don't know. I guess I saw it coming. Wanted to get it out in the open."

"What did he say?"

"Nothing much. Just agreed with me."

"Well, at least you're free."

"That I am. But it's a weird feeling."

"What do you mean?"

"Matt and I have been together forever."

"Yeah, but you knew it would happen when you moved."

"Knowing and liking are two different animals."

"Well, if you ask me he has the hots for Heather."

"He does spend a lot of time with her. Anyway, I came here to ski."

"Let's go."

Again, the air pummels my face like a boxer in a championship fight. I want to cry more; but, more than that, I want to be comforted. There is no one around to comfort me. I need Mama. She and Daddy are in New York City with friends. Their plane left right after ours, and they won't be home until Sunday. I could call her but it wouldn't

help. Grandma Josie is visiting her sister in Houston, and is

flying home this morning. Besides, grownups don't under-

stand. They're too old to remember what fifteen is like.

Once again I beat Rachel to the bottom of the hill. The

swish, swish, swish of the new skis on the fresh snow helps

me soar faster and faster. After lunch I will make a run

down the expert slope to see where I want to fall. I have to

ski the toughest course, or no one will believe what hap-

pens. They know I would never fall on a less challenging

trail. The world must never know it is an accident. Rachel

is the only person I've told, and that's because she's my best

friend. I could get her in plenty of trouble if she decides

to squeal. Her parents would die if they knew all the wild

things she does.

Roaring like an angry lion, my stomach alerts me that it is time for lunch. My mittens drip both inside and out with a hot and cold combination of sweat and snow. Pulling them off my soggy hands I stuff them in the pocket of my parka. Out of the corner of my eye I spot one of the agents whom I hadn't noticed before. Rachel finally catches up with me, and we tramp back to the lodge. We don't speak until we get to our room.

"Are you okay A. B.?"

"I don't know. But I know I'm starved."

"Do you think all the kids know by now?"

"Depends on how much Matt has said. Besides it's not official until I move."

"Yeah. But are you really going to dance with him tomorrow night at the party?"

"I won't be dancing with anyone."

"You're not still planning on going through with that plan are you?"

"Why not?"

"A.B. you're liable to hurt yourself."

"That's the idea."

"I hope you know what you're doing."

By the time we make it to the dining room most of the other kids are already there. Rachel has her eyes peeled for the blonde guy, but doesn't see him. Matt is sitting at a corner table surrounded by his football buddies with his arm around Heather. It didn't take him long to move on. Neither of them sees me. There are a couple of empty chairs at a table where the basketball team is sitting.

"Andie B. is it true? Is it true?"

"Is what true Ashley?"

"Did you and Matt really break up? Heather was strutting around bragging saying you thought you were too good for him."

"Yeah, we broke up."

"Well, Heather has already moved in. But you knew she was putting her tiger claws in him a long time ago. Even before the election."

"Guess so. Can we talk about something else?"

"Clay wants to ask you out."

"No thanks I'm through with guys for a while. Think I'll be a nun."

"Boy that would freak your parents out. Did you call your mom?"

"No. They're on a trip. I'll tell them when we get back."

"You sure aren't upset about this."

"Look, Ashley, enough already. I knew it was coming. Long distance relationships never work. Now shut up or I'm moving to another table."

"Oh, there he is. No. It's not him. If I could just find out the name of his school."

"I give up. Between Ashley talking about Matt, and you looking for mystery guy I can't win. I'm going skiing."

"A.B.?"

"Yeah."

"Take it easy, okay. I'll catch up with you later."

I race up the stairs two at a time slamming the door as I enter the room. Rachel's pursuit of mystery guy will keep her busy for an hour or two. Staring out the window I observe the skiers heading for the chair lift. My plan bounces around in my head like a ping pong ball. Maybe breaking up with Matt will give more standing to the accident. Rachel will tell people I must have lost my concentration because I was upset about the breakup.

Two voices are arguing inside my brain. Mama's voice shouts don't do it. How immature can you be? If you don't want to go, just tell me. But the other voice, the wiser, experienced voice of Andie B. says do it. If you don't, your picture will be splattered on the front page of newspapers around the world in that tacky turquoise dress. Your parents will not expect you to go if you're on crutches.

Staring out the window I see Matt and Heather walk to the chairlift. They will not risk going down the expert slope. Neither of them are daredevils like me. I wait a few more minutes to allow them time to get on the chairlift before I head out. Rachel is still downstairs. If I leave now, I can escape her disapproving stare. My mind is made up.

Chapter 5

The Accident Part II

My first run is rather uneventful. I take it slow and easy in order to spot the perfect place for my fall. Timing and location are everything. The time has to be late in the day on the last run. Today is the last day we can ski because the slopes will be closed tomorrow because it is New Year's Eve. Our plane leaves early on New Year's Day.

I have to fall close to the bottom of the run so it will be easy for me to hobble out under my own power without calling too much attention to myself. My only goal is to be on crutches for the next three weeks.

On the second run, I find the perfect spot. It's on the side of the trail. I don't see Rachel, but I told her I wouldn't start my final run until 4 p.m. At the bottom of the hill I flop down on a bench and watch other skiers. Some of the kids are heading for the lodge. A light snow is starting to fall and the skies look like gray elephant hide that stretches for miles on end. Pushing up my bright purple parka sleeve I see that it is now 3:45. Time to make my ascent up the mountain. I head for the chairlift. This is one ride I will make alone.

Just remember Andie B. You can do anything you put your mind to do. Relax. Take a deep breath. A blast of frigid air hits me in the face at the top of the mountain. Pausing for a moment to survey the scene, I am conscious that the sky is darker. The clouds have blended together in one colossal mass of gray as if a giant brain has spilled from the heavens. A thick cover of ice casts a glaring shadow on the snow like finely polished silver in a fancy restaurant. A solitary beam of sunlight peeks out of the mass like a searchlight pointing me in the only direction I can go - down. I take another deep breath, and look around. Other skiers mingle around but I don't recognize them. The time is now. I must go down the mountain. I push off. I'm on my way.

In the distance I see the spot where I have elected to fall. Glancing up I realize that I am almost there. Bend your knee, Andie B. Bend your knee. It will only hurt for a little while. As I lean into my fall, bending my left knee as a cushion for my right one I realize something is wrong. Without warning my boot has come out of my left ski, and I hit the ground hard. Out of control I propel down the mountain. I hurtle towards a cluster of trees on the edge of the trail. This isn't the way it was supposed to happen. My legs are split like an open pair of scissors. What's happening to me? Hitting the ground like a ton of bricks I begin to slide. My legs are still spread apart. The world is a blur. My goggles are covered in snow. After what seems like hours my body comes to a stop. Grabbing my goggles the strap breaks in my hand. Looking up I see the most handsome set of blue eyes I have ever imagined.

"Are you okay? Here take my bandanna. Your chin is bleeding."

"Go on kid. We'll take it from here."

As blue eyes skis away, I notice the tuft of blond hair peeking out the back of his cap. I try to sit up but fall back down.

"Miss Nettles just lie down. You're going to be fine. It's agent Landry."

"My knees."

"You're fine. The ski patrol will be here in a minute, and we'll get you out of here. Hold that bandanna tight on your chin."

I glance up and see Rachel's bright orange parka as she zooms down the mountain. Remembering my instructions she doesn't stop.

"Miss Nettles, are you still with us? Try and stay awake."

Using every ounce of energy I can muster, I pull myself up only to fall back down.

"Miss Nettles don't try to sit up. Where is that ski patrol? Don't they know who this is?"

My knees are throbbing like two buoys in the Gulf of Mexico during a hurricane. It's not supposed to hurt this much. What went wrong? It was just supposed to be a simple fall. Mama's going to kill me. Now I may never get into the Naval Academy. I hear more voices around me.

"Miss Nettles we're going to put you on a stretcher and down the mountain to a hospital. Try and stay awake."

"Get Rachel too."

"Slide the backboard under her and a neck brace too. We don't want to take any chances. And someone get find Miss Le Brun and tell her to meet us at the ambulance."

I feel the cold foam collar being wrapped around my neck. But there's nothing wrong with my neck or back. Don't these people realize it's my knees that hurt? Two sets of gloved hands gently slide a stiff board under my back. In the background I hear an agent talking on a two-way radio. I am on a stretcher strapped on a snowmobile. The engine roars, and we take off in a cloud of snow followed by another snowmobile right behind us. In a matter of minutes we are at the bottom of the mountain. I want to sit up, but the ski patrol still has me strapped on the grimy canvas stretcher. It smells like an old tent.

Two different sets of hands lift the stretcher into a waiting ambulance where they unstrap me and slide me on a gurney. Rachel is sitting there next to a guy who I recognize as one of the other agents.

"A.B. you okay?"

"I'm fine Rach. It's just my knees. They hurt."

One of the paramedics in the ambulance takes the bandanna from my hand, and cleans off my chin.

"Looks like you're going to need a few stitches there. You hit something hard going down."

"Great."

"Here hold this against it until we get to the hospital."

We race through traffic, and I can hear the radio from the front seat where one of the chaperones is sitting with the driver.

"Can't I sit up? Nothing hurts but my knees."

"Sorry Miss Nettles. Not until you're at the hospital."

"But there's nothing wrong with my neck or back."

"They're going to take x-rays to make sure. From what the agents said you took a pretty hard fall."

"Yeah too hard."

"What did you say?"

"I said yeah too bad. My boot came out of my ski."

Rachel looks like she has just seen a ghost. It dawns on her I am hurt worse than I intended. We arrive at Memorial Hospital in Colorado Springs. The doors open, and I am wheeled in to a room with bright lights. Rachel is running behind me to keep up.

"Sorry Miss. You can't go in with her while the doctor is examining her."

"Where's Agent Landry? Agent Landry, tell the nurse it's okay. I want Rachel with me."

Agent Landry nods his head, and Rach is allowed in the room.

"Miss Nettles. I'm going to call your parents."

"Agent Landry tell them it's just my knees. Trust me. See. I can wiggle my fingers and toes."

"Okay. I'll be right outside."

Meanwhile, one of the chaperones calls Grandma Josie to get permission for treatment. Since my parents are out of town, she is the family contact on my permission slip.

"Miss Nettles, my name is Dr. Sears. What hurts?"

"Just my knees. One of my boots came out."

"Okay, let's get some x-rays just to make sure. Let me take a look at your chin. Looks like you're going to need three or four stitches."

"Miss Nettles I talked with one of your parent's aides, and he'll relay the message to them. Dr. Sears you might want to check for a concussion. She hit the ground hard, and was unconscious for a couple of minutes."

"Do we have permission for treatment yet?"

"Yes, Mrs. Wallace, Miss Nettle's grandmother, just okayed it."

"Then let's get this young lady down to x-ray."

Two guys wheel me to x-ray with Agent Landry and Rachel beside me. Rachel looks bewildered as if the reality of the whole situation hasn't sunken in yet. All I know is my knees feel awful. If I'm hurt anywhere else, I don't know it. Instead of taking individual x-rays the radiologist decides to do a full body scan. The two guys move me to a metal table which slides into a tunnel open at both ends. After a few minutes it is all over, and I am back on the gurney on my way back to the Emergency Room.

"Let's get your chin stitched up while we're waiting for the scan results."

"Can I sit up now? I'm feeling fine. I really need to call my grandmother and tell her I'm okay."

"Slow down Miss Nettles. You can't sit up until I get the test results. Just relax. Let me do my sewing."

"Ouch. It burns. It feels like my face is on fire."

"Good. Then I'm doing my job right. There I'm finished. Let me cover it up, and you'll be all set. I'll be right back."

"Rach, do I look awful?"

"A.B. what you said in the ambulance. This was an accident?"

"Shh. Rach. Keep quiet. I was getting ready to put my plan into action, and my boot came out. Trust me. I never meant for it to turn out this way."

"Well, Miss Nettles you're right. You've got severely sprained MCL ligaments in your knees, but you survived well. I guess being fifteen and an athlete really helps."

"Great. Can I go back to the lodge now?"

"Not so fast. I want to keep you hospitalized until you fly home on Saturday. According to Agent Landry your head made a pretty good dent in the landscape. To be on the safe side I want to keep you here."

"But that means I'll miss the New Year's Eve party."

"Well, look at it this way. You can't dance."

"Yeah right."

"I've got you a private room in the pediatric ward. Rachel can stay with you if she'd like. One of the agents is waiting to take her to the lodge and pick up your things."

"Will you Rach?"

"Why not? I probably wouldn't have any fun by myself."

"Dr. Sears, this just means crutches right?"

"Yes and physical therapy for the next two months."

"But I will be able to play basketball and softball again."

"You want the truth Miss Nettles?"

"Yes ma'am."

"Well the truth is I don't know. Both Tulane Medical Center and Bethesda in Maryland have some of the best orthopedists in the country. That's a decision they'll have to make."

"Great. That's all I need now."

"You've got a lot of healing to do, and a great deal of physical therapy ahead of you. Somehow Miss Nettles I think you can do anything you put your mind to. Now let's get this collar off your neck, and get you in your own room."

Once again I take a gurney ride through the hospital corridors. My knees are still throbbing, and I have a headache. I don't remember my head hitting the ground but it must have. My eyes burn from the bright lights in the hospital. I would close my eyes, but I'm not ready to sleep. I don't realize the sun has gone down until I reach my room. A doctor comes in and identifies himself as the orthopedic resident. He wraps a silvery mesh cast around each of my knees. Rigid metal strips run down each side so I can't bend them. The casts are shiny like aluminum foil. My legs make me look like some sort of creature from outer space. A young nurse brings me a couple of pain pills.

"Ma'am, could you give me something for this head-ache too?"

"Miss Nettles I'm one step ahead of you. This pill will also help your head. Just relax."

"Everyone keeps telling me to relax. Based on these contraptions on my knees it doesn't look like I have any choice. I need to call my grandmother."

"Gram. It's me. Andie B."

"Child are you all right? I was just watching a news conference on television about you. Some doctor says you sprained your knees really bad, but it could have been a lot worse. Something about you hitting your head on a tree stump."

"Relax Gram I'm fine. They put braces on both knees. I'll be on crutches for a while. That's all. Have you heard from Mama and Daddy?"

"Not yet. But are you sure you're okay. I can fly out there."

"Gram I'm fine. My knees hurt, and I've got a head-ache. The nurse just gave me pain pills. Rachel should be back any minute. Just tell Mama and Daddy I'm a little sore. I don't want them to make a big deal out of this."

"Andie B. it is a big deal."

"But not to me. Please Gram. They'll be home Sunday. Then they can find out."

"Now get some rest."

"Yes, ma'am."

Rachel comes in followed by two agents. She has brought our things from the lodge.

"Boy, A.B. you're the talk of the ski resort."

"Great. Just what I need everyone's pity."

"They're all talking about how only you would have enough guts to try skiing down a double black diamond slope. But I told them you've skied black diamond slopes since you were twelve."

"Thanks for defending me."

"Ladies, what will it be pizza or burgers? Figured you two don't want hospital food."

"Pepperoni pizza double cheese and no mushrooms. Right A.B.?"

"Right."

"Okay. I'll be back in a few minutes. There's an agent right outside the door if you need anything."

"Agent Landry?"

"Yes Miss Nettles?"

"Thanks for everything. I mean it."

"You're welcome. Now I've got to get that pizza."

"A.B. you trashed your knees. I heard the agents talking about it."

"Well I guess I'm lucky. Believe me, Rach I didn't intend for it to turn out this way. All I was trying to do was get out of wearing that tacky dress."

"Your parents are going to freak out. Have they called yet?"

"Nope. I talked with Grandma Josie. She said I made the evening news."

"Agent Landry and I saw the news vans outside the hospital. There's a soda machine down the hall. You want a Dr. Pepper®?"

"Yes. I'm dying of thirst."

"I'll be right back."

As soon as Rachel left a nurse came in.

"Miss Nettles, how is the pain now?"

"It hurts but not as bad."

"I'm packing your knees in ice. That will help the swelling. Do you hurt anywhere else?"

"Just my head."

"Sorry, can't pack it in ice. I'm afraid you may be sore all over tomorrow, but we'll do whatever we can to help."

"Thanks."

The pizza arrives and Rach and I pig out. I didn't realize how hungry I was. We watch television for a while, and I fall asleep.

The next time I wake up it's morning. At first I forget where I am, and start to jump out of bed. But my legs won't move. I feel like I have been run over by a truck. My entire body feels tender and bruised. As I wipe the sleep out of my eyes, the previous day's events come back to me, and I remember the accident. I glance over at the bed next to me where Rachel is sleeping. She's on her side. Once again I try to move, but can't turn on my side. Raising the bed I'm determined to sit up. That's better. Rachel starts to stir.

"A.B. you okay?"

"Yeah, why?"

"You moaned and groaned a lot last night. One time I called the nurse for you."

"That's weird. I don't remember anything after we started watching television. I didn't say anything embarrassing did I?"

"No, it was mostly moaning and groaning, although one time you did cry out for your mom."

"Not my dad?"

"I don't think so. But it was the middle of the night so I don't remember a whole lot."

"What time is it Rach?"

"Almost 8:30. Why?"

"My stomach is growling. I think it is the only part of my body that isn't sore."

"I'll take a shower and get dressed. This hospital has to have some doughnuts somewhere."

"How did you know I wanted doughnuts?"

"Best friend intuition. I'd better take my clothes in the bathroom with me just in case one of the agents or a doctor comes in to check on you."

"Good idea."

Rachel was right. While she was in the shower, Agent Landry came in followed by two doctors: Dr. Byrnes, an orthopedist and Dr. Foley, a pediatrician, and a nurse.

"Miss Nettles how do you feel today?"

"Like I've been run over by a truck, and the truck is still on top of me."

"Let me examine you, and you tell us where it hurts."

"It would be easier to tell you where it doesn't hurt."

"Okay, tell us where it doesn't hurt?"

"My hands and stomach feel pretty good, but the rest of me aches."

"Describe the pain."

"Like a bad case of the flu. I'm achy all over."

"Is it worse in some places?"

"I guess so. My knees, head and shoulders hurt the most."

"You pulled through your fall in a lot better shape than most people. I've seen skiers in full body casts after enduring similar accidents. Haven't you Dr. Byrnes?"

"Yes, now I'm going to take the braces partially off so I can take a closer look at your knees. Don't worry Miss

Nettles; I'll try to touch them as little as possible. Okay. I'm all finished."

"Do I have to stay in bed all day? I'm used to moving around."

"Well, I think you can try out your crutches. In fact, the younger patients are having a New Year's Party later today if you want to attend. You're our only teenager here now."

"Did I hear New Year's Eve Party?"

"Rachel, these are my two doctors. I told them I wanted out of this bed, and they told me about a kid's party. I think we're a little old for it."

"I don't know A.B. I think you should put in an appearance. Besides, the kids might want to meet the future First Kid."

"Miss Nettles I agree with your friend. The children would enjoy it."

"Okay. Besides if it means I can move around, I'm all for it. But right now don't you and Agent Landry have a mission?"

"She's feeling better all right. A.B. is back to her bossy self. Agent Landry can you help me find doughnuts for my starving best friend?"

"I'll do my best."

Rachel and Agent Landry go in search of food. While they are gone, a couple of nurse's aides come in and help me with my crutches and into the bathroom. I manage to take a shower. Standing up is a struggle, and the nurses tell me it will probably be four weeks before I'll be off crutches full time I hope that doesn't mean I have to sleep in the den when I get home. I want my own bed.

When Rachel and Agent Landry get back I'm lying on top of the bed propped up by several pillows. I feel better just by being dressed in sweatpants and a sweatshirt.

"Well look at her. Miss Le Brun we must have the wrong room. When we were here before there was an injured teenager."

"Oh no you don't. Bring me a doughnut or I'll be forced to get off this bed and run after you."

"We'd better feed her Agent Landry. I don't know if you know it or not but she's prone to violence."

"I didn't read that in her biography."

"It's a well kept secret. The President Elect and First Lady don't even know."

"Are we going to talk or eat?"

"Agent Landry stay with us. I want you to tell me more about what a pain my best friend is to guard."

"Well, Miss Le Brun I was hoping you would tell me more about her habits."

"I'm not invisible you know? You two just keep on talking about me. I'll feed my face."

"Ladies, I have to go make a few calls. I'll be back before the party starts just to make sure everybody is where they're supposed to be."

"So, A. B. that means we are going."

"Why not? It's right down the hall. From what one of the aides told me they have it at dinner and have games for the kids. She told me that the parents come too."

"But what about the press?"

"Agent Landry and the hospital won't allow it. Daddy is really strict about anyone taking Trey or my picture when he and Mama aren't around. That's why there weren't any photographers at the ski resort. That we knew of anyway."

Rachel and I spend the day playing cards and watching sports on television. I keep hoping that maybe Mama or Daddy will call but they don't.

"Andie B. how are you today?"

"Grandma Josie I was just thinking about you. I'm better."

"It was hard getting through the phone lines. CNN gave several health updates about you today. Said two doctors examined you this morning."

"Yes, Gram. They were nice. Did you talk to Mama and Daddy?"

"No, I figured they would call you."

"They didn't but maybe it's just as well. Mama will probably ground me again."

"Why on earth child?"

"For going down a double black diamond."

"I don't think so. You quit worrying about such things."

"Rach and I are going to a New Year's Eve Party with the kids who are stuck here in pediatrics."

"Sounds like fun."

"The nurses invited us. Seems like I'm the only teen-ager here right now."

"You're still coming home tomorrow?"

"Yes ma'am. You'll be at the airport to meet us right. Rach is staying with us until her parents come back with Mama and Daddy."

"I'll be there."

My first experience on crutches is awkward. Rachel and I walk down the hall to a playroom where a dozen children are gathered with their parents and staff members. I see a couple of agents blending in with the group.

"Miss Nettles, I'm glad you and your friend decided to join us."

"Thanks, but call me Andie B. Miss Nettles sounds so stuffy, like an old maid schoolteacher. And this is Rachel."

I look down and see a blonde girl who looks like she is about six years old. She is pulling an IV pole with her as she comes toward me. She stops directly in front of me.

"My name is Molly. Is your daddy going to be the President?"

"Sure is. Did you vote for him?"

"I'm too little to vote."

"Are you sure? You look pretty old to me."

"No silly, I'm only six and a half. How old are you?"

"Fifteen and three quarters."

"Why are you on crutches?"

"I hurt my knees skiing. What happened to you?"

"I had to have an operation, but I'm going home tomorrow."

"Me too."

Molly and her parents walk away. Before they do her parents shake my hand.

"A.B. you're as good a politician as your parents. It must be in the genes."

"Thanks Rach."

I spend the next hour hobbling around the room. Several of the children stop and ask me questions. I autograph casts, and books. Most of the parents stay in the background, although a few shake my hand. I flinch when one well intended lady puts her hand on my shoulder. She quickly backs off and apologizes. Several of the agents talk to me. They make an effort to blend in the group.

"Miss Nettles I was skiing behind you when you fell. I surprised you're able to sit up today."

"Was it that bad? It all happened so fast."

"I've skied for a long time, and I'm surprised you weren't injured worse."

"Please tell me there's not a videotape of the crash floating around."

"I don't think so. Cameras were supposed to be banned from the slopes while you and your friends skied."

"I hope so. If my parents saw what happened, they would kill me."

After a supper of burgers and fries, the nurses gave out noisemakers and party hats to everyone. They did a countdown, and had one of the kids pull a string which unleashed a blanket of balloons from above. Everyone shouted "Happy New Year" even though it was only 7 p.m. We all said our goodbyes, and headed for our rooms. Molly and her parents waved to me as they walked to the opposite end of the hallway. When we got back to our room, Rachel and one of the aides helped me change clothes. It took forever because of the knee braces and tenderness of my skin. A nurse brought me a couple of pills for pain, and Rach and I watched a football game on television. I don't remember who was playing and fell asleep before midnight.

Our plane was scheduled to leave at 10 a.m. Agent Landry drove Rach and I to the airport. When we arrived, Rach pushed me in a wheelchair since it was a long walk.

"Rach let me do it. I need to show everybody I'm okay."

"Are you sure? You're still hurting. I can tell."

"Yeah. I'll be fine, but stand by in case I need you."

"A.B. are you okay? We missed you."

"I'm fine Tori. Just have to use crutches for a while."

"You missed a great party last night. The band was first-class. We danced until 2 a.m."

"Sorry I wasn't there, but as you can see I can't dance."

"Okay St. Martin's kids. Let's board. Andie Beth you get to go first."

"Coming through."

I roll my wheelchair toward the ramp with Rachel and Agent Landry close behind me. Agent Landry helps me to my seat, folds the wheelchair in half and gives it to a flight attendant. Rach slides in the seat next to me.

After we are in the air for a while, she asks me the question that I know is on her mind.

"Did you see Matt and Heather holding hands?"

"Yes."

"And right in front of you. C'mon A.B. that has to bug you."

"We broke up, remember?"

"But it's only been three days."

"Thanks for reminding me. Look Rach, you told me it was coming. I knew it was coming. Now it's happened. Trust me I'll get over it."

"I figured you would take it harder."

"What's there to take? We broke up. I 've got other problems now, or maybe you didn't notice my metallic legs."

"I'm sorry A.B. I just hate to see you hurt by that two-timer."

"What can I tell you? He found himself a hobby while I was grounded. Only his hobby was named Heather."

"At least you haven't lost your sense of humor."

"The only thing I've lost is the temporary use of my legs, and maybe my sports career. I just want to get home."

I lean my head against the window and close my eyes. Rachel takes this as a signal that I don't want to talk and leaves me alone. The pain medication they gave me before we left makes me sleepy. Soon, Rach is shaking my arm.

"A.B. we're landing soon."

"Already, we just took off."

"You fell asleep."

"Sorry, Rach. Guess I haven't been much company."

"It's okay. I bet it's the pain pills."

"You're probably right. Listen, I want to get off the plane last not first. Can you tell Agent Landry for me?"

"Sure, be right back."

The plane lands and everyone races to get off. Some of them yell goodbye to me, but most are just in a hurry to leave. The flight attendant brings the wheelchair and once again Agent Landry helps me into it. This time I let Rachel push me until we get to the entrance. As I roll myself into the airport, I see Mama, Daddy, Grandma Josie and Rachel's parents. Mama gasps. Daddy grabs her hand and sprints to me. Rach runs to her parents.

"Buzzie look at you."

"It's nothing Daddy I fell when I was skiing."

"It doesn't look like nothing. Why didn't you call us?"

"Agent Landry said he did, and Gram too. What are you guys doing back? I didn't think you were coming home until tomorrow."

"We figured we'd better get home. Our plane arrived a few minutes ago."

"You came home early because of me."

"Andie Beth you're our child. If we had known you were hurt this bad, we would have flown to Colorado."

"There's nothing you could have done. All I did was hang around the hospital for a day and practice using the crutches."

"Well, let's get you home and in bed. You need to rest."

"Mama. I'm not tired."

"Andie Beth."

"Ma'am?"

"Just do what I say."

"Let's get out of here. Ready Buzzie. Let me push."

"A.B. see you in three weeks."

"Yep. I'll be standing tall on my crutches Rach."

As we exit the airport, we are met by a group of reporters and photographers. I can't escape this time because I'm stuck in the wheelchair.

"Mr. President, how was your vacation?"

"Very relaxing."

"Miss Nettles how are you feeling?"

"Much better now that I'm home."

Agent Landry opens the door to the limo. Protocol says that Daddy always gets in first. Mama and Grandma Josie go to the other side. Only this time instead of getting in first Daddy helps me out of the wheelchair and then sits beside me.

We arrive at home, and once we're inside I receive more bad news.

"Don't even think about going upstairs Andie B."

"What do you mean Gram?"

"For the next few weeks you're sleeping in the down-stairs guest room. Some doctor named Byrnes called me yesterday, and said you told him your room was on the third floor. He asked if there was any place for you to sleep on the first floor, and I told him about the guest room."

"Good thinking Mama. I see you've got everything under control."

"Now don't fret Andie B. I had Trey bring down your computer and television. All the comforts of home. Now let me go see how my soup is coming along."

"You, young lady need to get some rest."

"Please Mama not until after supper. I slept on the plane. I'm not lying Mama. I really did."

"C'mon Buzzie let's go in the den and see what bowl game is on."

"Before you two get involved in a football game I think the three of us need to talk."

"Okay Daddy what did you do? I can't be in trouble I've been gone."

"That's what you think. But let's go in the den."

Mama kicks off her shoes and Daddy helps me on to the couch.

"You're not off the hook yet Andie Beth."

"Ma'am?"

"First of all, why didn't you call us after the accident?"

"Because Agent Landry said he was going to. When I talked with Grandma Josie, she said she had called you and left a message."

"Okay next question. Were you skiing alone?"

"Not exactly. Rachel was supposed to meet me at the top of the mountain, but she was late as usual. I took off slow figuring she'd catch up with me."

"Why were you skiing on an expert slope so late in the day?"

"C'mon Lynn, quit interrogating her. This is our daughter not a criminal on the witness stand."

"Because it was the last run of the day. The slopes were going to be closed on New Year's Eve. I didn't know when I'd get to ski again."

"Fine now that's enough questions. Are you satisfied Lynn?"

The vein on Daddy's head is starting to bulge. I can tell he's getting angry. I keep my mouth shut. Mama is not happy about what has happened. If I weren't in the room, I have a feeling my parents would be in a heated argument. If I could get out of the room, I would. I can't do it without help so I'm stuck. Once again I have messed with her perfect little world. Now she has a injured teenager to deal with.

"I'm sorry Mama. I didn't mean to get hurt. It was an accident. My boot came out of my ski. I guess some ice got wedged under it or something."

Mama comes over and sits beside me on the couch. She puts her arm around me and I flinch.

"Andie B. are you okay?"

"Yes Mama it's just that my shoulders still hurt."

"I thought it was just your knees that were injured."

"My knees, head and shoulders got the worst of it."

"So no hugs for a few days?"

"It's okay Mama. It just hurts. Where's Cajun? I figured he'd be in my face by now."

"Mama said Trey took him jogging. They should be home any minute."

"Hey Buzzard I hear you messed yourself up good this time. As for your mutt, I'm glad you're back. I'm tired of taking care of him. Gram told me to leave him outside so we could eat in peace."

"Tell the truth big brother you missed me."

"Like a sore on my. . ."

"Trey."

"Soup's on. Trey get the t.v. tables. We'll eat in here. Figured you'd all be watching the bowl games? Doesn't this family watch football anymore?"

"Toss me the remote Daddy. Let's see who's winning."

During dinner everyone seems to calm down. Grandma Josie's homemade vegetable soup seems to relax everyone. I catch Mama staring at my knee braces several times, but she doesn't bring up the accident again. She and Trey take the dishes into the kitchen, and Daddy puts up the t.v. trays.

"Where is the pain medication the doctor prescribed?"

"In my backpack."

"How often do you take it?"

"Twice a day if I need it. Morning and night. It says so on the bottles. But it makes me sleepy. I don't think I can take it and go to school."

"Well, I'll keep it in the kitchen. Are you sure you're going to be ready to go to school Monday? Dr. Byrnes said you're supposed to see a Dr. Starling at Tulane next week. I'm thinking you might want to take an extra few days, but we'll see what your mother has to say?"

"About what?"

"Andie B. was talking about school, and I told her she might want to take a few extra days off. At least until after she sees the orthopedic specialist on Wednesday."

"That might not be such a bad idea. But now I'm going to insist that you go to bed."

"Mama. It's not even 8 p.m. Daddy tell her please."

"Sorry, Buzzie. She's right. You need to get some rest. C'mon, let me help you with your crutches."

"Yes Daddy. Thanks."

"I'll bring your pills in a minute Andie B."

"Thanks Mama. Goodnight Trey, goodnight Daddy. C'mon Caj."

Mama brings me the pills. I reach over and find my jazz station on the radio. Gram has even gone to the trouble of bringing Cajun's woven rug and placed it beside the bed. He settles down, and Mama tucks me in.

The accident occurred three weeks ago, and today was the first time I was allowed back in my room.

"Andie B. wake up."

"What happened?"

"You fell asleep on the couch. Sorry you missed the hot chocolate, but we didn't want to wake you. C'mon I'll help you up the stairs."

"Thanks Daddy."

"I'll be up in a minute to say goodnight."

"Okay Mama."

"Well Buzzie this is your last night in your old room. And tomorrow is your last day at St. Martins. I'm going to miss this house."

"Me too Daddy, me too."

Chapter 6

Last Day at St. Martins Part I

♣

"Rachel are you out there?"

I'm at Grandpa Webb's and Grandma Elizabeth's house in Mandeville. We leave for Washington tomorrow. Yesterday was my last day at St. Martins.

Since we came home, the agents take me to school. St. Martin's upper school layout resembles a big spider with the commons area as the body and the classrooms as legs. Each leg represents a different subject area such as math,

English, and science. The spider's head is the cafeteria. At least I don't have to worry about going up and down stairs.

I'm afraid I'll be on crutches forever. Four days a week Agent Landry drives me directly from school to Tulane Medical Center for physical therapy. Dr. Starling, the orthopedist, is cool. She keeps telling me she is cautiously optimistic about my chances for playing softball in April. When I ask her about next year, she is more encouraging. Daddy asked Dr. Walker, the orthopedist from Bethesda in Maryland, to fly down and meet us last week. I guess when you're the incoming President all you have to do is snap your fingers and people do what you want.

Physical therapy is hard and frustrating. There are a couple of doctors, and a bunch of student interns from the Sports Medicine Department at Tulane. They all want to be trainers for professional sports teams, so they push and push. After an hour of therapy, I'm as tired as I was after basketball practice. Daddy says the White House has its' own physical therapy room, so I'll go there right after school. Two therapists will be assigned just to me plus one student intern.

Anyway, back to school. Mama and Daddy let me spend my last night in the house in my own room. On Friday I got up and was almost ready to go downstairs when Mama came in.

"Take it easy today, Andie Beth. You know if you get tired Agent Landry has a wheelchair in the van you can use. Use it if you need it."

"I won't need it."

"Let me put it to you another way Andie Beth. Either do it my way, or forget about going to the basketball game tonight. I'm not going to argue with you about this."

"Yeah. It's always your way or no way."

"That's about the size of it young lady."

"Daddy would let me."

"Well, it's too late to ask him. He's already headed to Chalmette for a farewell breakfast with The Chamber of Commerce."

"Why didn't you go with him?"

"Because I have to be here for the movers. Now if you're ready I'll help you downstairs. You did remember to pack a suitcase for Washington didn't you?"

"Yes ma'am. It's over there by the chair. But our stuff will be there by Inauguration Day, right?"

"Don't worry I'll take a quick run through your room to make sure you have what you need."

"You don't need to. I'm pretty sure Gram packed everything. The garment bag is inside my closet door."

"Let's go. Your breakfast is getting cold."

I hobble to the door and hesitate for just a minute. Stopping and turning around, I want to take one last look at my room. It is the only place I have ever slept. By the time I come home from school this afternoon, it will have been reduced to a maze of boxes and cartons. A swarm of butterflies surges through my stomach. It's happening. We really are moving. I want to cry, but can't. It's too late for tears. I remember Grandma Elizabeth's advice: Hold your head high Andie Beth. Remember you're a Nettles. I turn around and head downstairs with Mama at my side. For the last time in my life, the smell of Grandma Josie's pancakes wafts up the stairs.

"Thought you might like blueberry pancakes for your last day at school."

"I wish it was my last day forever. I'm tired of going to school."

"Well, get used to it. You've got at least six and a half more years; even more if you go to law school."

"Don't remind me. I may not survive this next semester if Brockton is as hard as I've heard it is."

"You'll make it. You just have to make up your mind and get your priorities straight."

"Easy for you to say Mama. School was a lot easier for you. I don't think either Trey or I inherited your brains."

"It will do you good to concentrate on your grades for a while since you can't participate in athletics."

"Dr. Starling says my knees may be okay by softball season."

"I wouldn't count on it. It might be a good idea to wait until next fall."

"I'll go crazy Mama."

"I think you'll survive."

"Yeah right."

"Look Andie Beth I know you're sad about leaving your friends, your school, and this house. I also know you've had a rough time the last few weeks with your knees. But you're not the only one in this family making adjustments. Quit your pity party, and let's go to school."

"You're going with me?"

"Afraid so. I signed you in eleven years ago for kindergarten. Now I'm going to sign you out for Washington."

"Does that mean I don't have to stay once you sign me out?"

"No, it means I don't have to come back later while the movers are here."

"Great just when I thought it couldn't get any worse; my mommy is going to school with me. I'll be the laughing stock of the sophomore class."

"Unless you're trying to get grounded, I'd advise you to stop talking right now. I've had about all of your mouth I can handle for one day. Do you understand me Andie Beth?"

"Yes, ma'am, but."

"No buts Andie Beth. Now let's go."

Gram hands me my backpack, and I walk out to the van with Mama beside me. Agent Landry is waiting for us with another agent who will give Mama a ride home. Mama and other agents sit around me.

As we ride to school, I look around at the gray winter day. The sky reminds me of the sky in Colorado on the day of my accident. That means it will probably rain this afternoon. We're too close to the water for it to snow very often. I have made this commute from Kenner to Metairie millions of times over the last eleven years especially if you count all the times I've gone back to school for basketball games and other events at night. Mama and the agents are talking about upcoming events. I stare out the window taking mental photographs of the scenery around me. These memories will grow in significance as I grow older. The trip, which takes fifteen minutes, seems longer today; as if the world is in slow motion.

At the end of my second period American Literature class, an announcement came over the intercom.

"This is Headmaster Jordan. All upper school students are to report to the auditorium at the beginning of third period for an assembly. Any tests scheduled for this period will be postponed until Monday."

A loud cheer erupts in our class. Mrs. Morgan, our world history teacher scheduled a test. Now I wouldn't have to take it. As we leave class and head to the auditorium, Clay comes up behind me and takes my backpack. In assemblies we sit in alphabetical order according to grade. Since kindergarten the seating arrangement has been: Nester, Nettles, and Newton, Clay, Andie B., and Matt. When we were in the lower grades Clay and Matt didn't like it. Why did they get stuck with a girl between them? Most of the girls in our class have names at the beginning of the alphabet. I used to wish that Mama had married a guy named Brown, so I could sit near the girls instead of boys. Sometimes after the lights went out, I would trade places with one of them so they could sit next to each other. After today, they won't have me in the middle.

The curtains opened and sitting on the stage were Daddy, Mama, and Trey plus our current and past teachers. I can't believe no one told me about this. I thought Daddy was in meetings all day, and Mama was home with the movers.

"Andie Beth will you please join your family on stage?"

Clay hands me my crutches, and I shuffle to the front of the auditorium. Headmaster Jordan helps me up the steps. I sit next to Trey.

"We have a few presentations to make to the First Family, but before I call on the presenters, I would like to ask the President Elect to say a few words."

Everyone stood up and clapped as Daddy walked to the podium. Reaching into his pocket he took out several index cards. This was all planned. None of my family had told me.

"Today is an extremely sad day for the Nettles' family. Lynn and I have been associated with St. Martin's since she began teaching here in 1975 her first year in New Orleans. Long before Trey and Andie Beth were born, we attended sporting events and other school functions. Both of our children attended St. Martins from kindergarten. We are excited about the opportunities that lie ahead for our family in Washington. Yet with every door opening to the future comes one closing to the past. St. Martins will always have a very special place in our hearts. Thank you."

Everyone stood up and clapped again and Headmaster Jordan and Daddy shook hands. The rest of the assembly was comprised of different teachers talking about how much they would miss Mama, Trey, and I. Coach Perry was the last person to speak.

"When the headmaster asked me to speak, I told him I wasn't used to speaking in public. When he told me why he wanted me to speak, I changed my mind. I have had the privilege of coaching Andie Beth in basketball and softball since eighth grade. Most of you know freshmen seldom letter in varsity sports. Although Andie Beth did not start as a freshman or sophomore, she came off the bench as the sixth man for the last two years in basketball. As a softball player, she was the only freshman starting pitcher in the conference. Normally we do not give athletic letters to players who don't finish the season. However, the headmaster and I decided to make an exception this year. Congratulations Andie Beth."

I hobbled to the podium. Headmaster Jordan asked me if I would like to say anything.

"I don't have a speech prepared because the assembly was a total surprise to me. I thought today was just another day at school. As my father said, St. Martins is the only school I've known. Some of us sophomores have been together since kindergarten. Late next week I start a new school in Washington where I only know one person. Not only will I be the new kid, but I'll be the President's kid. It's too weird, and I don't think it has sunk in yet."

Rach you wouldn't have believed it. The whole auditorium rocked in applause, a whole lot more than Daddy, Mama, or Trey received. It was awesome. Then a group started singing the Alma Mater and everyone joined in.

"Students, the assembly is dismissed. Resume your regular schedule."

"Andie Beth I'm going to the office, sign you out, and pick up your transcripts. You need to get moving to class."

"Yes, Mama."

"Buzzie, were you surprised at the assembly?"

"Major surprised Daddy, major surprised."

Clay was waiting for me at the bottom of the stairs with my backpack which he carried to class for me. I wonder if he and I would have ever dated. Not as long as Matt was around, I guess.

Lunch with the basketball team was rowdy as usual. No one brought up the subject of my leaving. While the rest of us were joking around, Matt and Heather sat at the end of the table making goo- goo eyes at one another. Clay sat by me. He had appointed himself my escort for the day.

After lunch I met up with Agent Landry so I could clean out my locker. I have had the same locker since eighth grade. Any one on an athletic team has phys ed sixth period. Our lockers are located in a hallway close to the gym so we can dump books before class and pick them up before we go home.

Agent Landry brought me a box. He's seen the inside of my locker so he also brought me a trash bag to throw garbage in. The inside of my locker door has pictures on it: a picture of Matt in his football uniform, Matt and Clay together, the three of us together, and newspaper clippings from my first varsity basketball and softball games where my name was mentioned. There's also a jacket, a couple of bottles of Dr. Pepper ®, and a Butterfinger® candy bar. I find a couple of old scrunchies and some stray bobby pins under my jacket. There are tons of school papers I throw away. I even find a note I started to write to Matt. It must have been important at the time. Don't need it any more. In the very back I find a bag that looks like it contains rotten fruit. So that's where the awful smell has been coming from. I don't remember where the bag came from, or when I put it in there, but it's grotesque. I leave my locker door open to air it out, and toss the lock in my backpack. Since it has an easy combination to remember, I'll use it at Brockton.

I'll clean out my gym locker during phys ed. I tell Agent Landry I'll need another bag and box for it too. He motions to another agent who takes the box to the van and the bag to the dumpster.

After another boring biology class, Clay and I headed to the gym. No one is practicing today since there are games tonight. Instead we have a health lecture on nutrition and various vitamins. I see one of the agents entering the gym with another box and bag. Grabbing my crutches I head for the locker room. This is my final task at St. Martins-cleaning out my gym locker.

The musty smell of sweat and wet towels blasts me when I hit the door. I ease my way over the damp floor dodging the puddles. My locker is in the back corner on the end away from the showers. It is the most private place in the room. Dropping the box I ease myself down to the bench.

I sit and stare at Nettles 45 and the blue basketball and softball emblems on my locker. I rub my fingers over them as if reading them in Braille. I hear the announcer as he says: "Coming into the game at guard for St. Martins, Nettles number 45."

A few months later another announcer says: "St. Martin's starting pitcher for today's game is Nettles number 45 with a record of two wins and one loss." It dawns on me I won't hear those words here again. It's not fair. I pound my fist on the bench. It's just not fair. I never received senior privileges. I never played on a championship team.

I'm leaving just as the teams have a chance. But nobody cares.

You play basketball and softball at Brockton. You act like sports are a game to you, not a way of life like they are to me. You play so you can meet boys. I play to win. Your head is in a different place when you play my way. You have to be able to taste victory, and accept nothing less. If everyone on Rachel's team thinks like she does, I dread the next two years. I must win in order to be successful. Second place isn't good enough. I pound my fists in to the locker. I start to kick it, but I look down at my feet and change my mind. Instead I pound my fists in to my locker again. The locker noise echoes off the walls. Agent Landry dashes around the corner.

"Miss Nettles, are you okay?"

"I'm fine."

"Do you need some help?"

"No, I'm okay."

"I'll stand here just in case."

Jerking the lock off it only takes a couple of minutes to pull stuff out of the bottom of my locker. First there are my game Nike™ high tops. I keep them here and only wear them on the court during games. Mama said if she saw them on my feet anywhere else she would never buy me another pair. Can't have Lynn Nettles' daughter playing in worn out shoes. There are my practice shoes, jersey, shorts and yuck some smelly old socks. I stand up using one crutch and take my shampoo, soap, and deodorant off the top shelf. I find several scrunchies. Tonight I'll wear my uniform jersey and warm up for the last time. I can't wear the shoes because of my knee braces. They attach two low for me to wear high tops. I'll dress at home. It will be too hard to change here with these monstrosities on my knees. Everything will be different from now on.

I glance down the aisle at Agent Landry. He has his back to me. I don't know if this is to give me privacy or he is looking for something. C'mon Andie B. you can't sit here all day. Face it your life at St. Martins is over. Snatching my crutches I stand up again and walk toward him. He jumps and turns around.

"Guess that's everything. The warm up suit and the game jersey need to go in the house with me so I can change for the game."

"No problem. I'll take care of it."

"Agent Landry, can I ask you something?"

"Sure Miss Nettles, what can I do for you?"

"How did you get stuck with the job of following me around?"

"Hey, following you around is a promotion."

"From what?"

"I used to guard an old senator. He lost his primary election and the agency promoted me to your father's campaign when they added more agents to guard you and your brother."

"But isn't it boring?"

"Miss Nettles with you every day is an adventure."

"Funny. I can't get used to being Miss Nettles all the time. Can't you call me Andie Beth?"

"The agency has pretty strict rules about that. I could get in trouble with your parents for being too familiar."

"But most of the time I never even see the other agents, just you."

"That's the way it is supposed to be. How about I call you by your secret service code name?"

"Which is?"

"Hyper One."

"Anything is better than Miss Nettles. It makes me feel so old."

"I'll see what I can do. You better get back in the gym. Your class is almost over."

I slither back to the bleachers next to Clay. The coach is still rambling on about vitamins. As I sit down the final bell rings. For most of St. Martins school is out for the week. For me it is out for ever.

My teammates don't say goodbye, because I will see them at the game. Clay grabs my backpack, and we head for the van. Some of the kids from the other classes come up and talk to me. It's strange. My life as I know it is ending. Nothing will ever be the same. I stop and turn around.

"A.B. stop a minute."

"Why Alicia?"

"I want to take a picture of you and Clay. Stand in front of the van."

"Hey, can I get in this too?"

"Yeah, c'mon Matt."

Heather doesn't join Matt. She stands off to the side with her arms folded in defiance across her chest with steam coming out of her ears. How dare Matt want to be in a picture with me?"

"C'mon guys smile. Your best friend is going to Washington."

We all laugh. This is the end. The last of the Three Musketeers. I glance at Heather. She is scowling. After today she will have them all to herself. Clay is the one I feel sorry for. But who knows? Alicia might be a possibility. I just wish I had paid more attention to him instead of Matt and all his moods. Clay never seems down. Agent Landry

opens the door to the van, and Clay helps me in.

"See you tonight at the game."

"I'll be there."

We make the ride home in silence. Just me and the

agents. I want to cry, but I can't in front of them. At least

the photographers left me alone. I was afraid they would

be hanging around the school. I hate having my picture

taken. They're probably all following Daddy around.

Two blue and white moving vans greet me when we

round the corner into our subdivision. The side doors are

open, and boxes are scattered all the front yard and side-

walk. Agent Landry pulls the van in the driveway.

Mama and Grandma Josie are sitting at the island

drinking coffee as if it is a normal Friday afternoon.

"There's our girl. Right on time. I told your mama I can set my watch by you."

"Hi Gram, hi Mama."

"I saved you a Dr. Pepper® and the last of the sugar cookies. Had to hide them from Trey. That boy can eat you out of house and home. Sure glad I don't have to feed him all the time."

"Thanks Gram."

"So, what did you think of the assembly today?"

"Big surprise. Mama when did they tell you about it?"

"When the election was over. Headmaster Jordan wanted to be sure your daddy and I would be there."

"You kept it a secret all this time. I didn't suspect a thing."

Grandma Josie laughs.

"Andie B. seems like you've had quite a few surprises the last few months."

"That's for sure. What other secrets do you have up your sleeve Mama?'

"How about your final report card from St. Martins?"

"I'm afraid to look. Tell me the bad news. How long am I grounded?"

"Andie Beth Nettles why do you always assume the worst?"

"Because Grandma, I mean ma'am it's safer that way."

"You must get that from your daddy's side of the family. Your mama isn't like that."

"Thank you Mama. Andie B. this is the best report card you've received in a long time. I told you if you would concentrate you could make good grades. Look at it."

Mama slides the computer printout across the island. Taking a deep breath I close my eyes tight for a second. I open them and scan the page. Straight As. Mama is right. I haven't made straight As since I was in the lower school.

"See I told you you could do it. Andie B. look at me."

I'm still staring at my report card. A.B. now you've gone and done it. The woman has been on your case for years about your potential, and now you've made straight As. She's going to expect these grades from now on. At least when you threw two or three Bs, you had something to work towards. Lynn Nettles never understood it was okay to be smart, you just didn't want to be too smart. That mentality was totally unacceptable. Good grief.

"Lynn, I think your daughter is in shock."

"I think so too Mama. Andie B. are you listening to me? I said look at me."

"Huh, what Mama? Okay. I'm looking at you."

Mama is smiling from ear-to-ear. I haven't seen her this happy in a long time. I'm sure she thinks my grades are due to her genes finally kicking in. The next words out of her mouth will be: I told you you could do it if you would put your mind to it. What she doesn't realize is the biology grade was a mercy grade. Mrs. Whittle is glad to see me go. Her class was the hardest one to concentrate in because it was near the end of the day before phys ed. My guess is she saw the other As in the computer and figured who cared what my final grade was. Mama is not going to do the math, and I'm not going to protest getting an A instead of a B. Mrs. Whittle hated our class, because most of us spent the hour looking at the clock waiting to get out. We knew we had to take the class, but we didn't like taking it. She would tell us that some day we would appreciate the details we learned in her class. I have to admit when the doctors talked about the damage in my mcl ligament at least I knew it was more than the top of my knee.

"Well, Andie B. I guess your daddy and I will have to come up with a suitable reward for these grades. Is there anything special you want? It's been a long time since you made straight As. I think the last time was in Mrs. Brenner's class in fifth grade."

"I can't think of anything off the top of my head. Do I have to decide right now?"

"Take your time. Look at me Andie Beth. I'm so proud of you."

Mama comes around the island and hugs me so tight I almost fall off the stool. Why is she only proud of me when I perform? Why can't she love me for just being me?

I slide off the stool and grab my crutches and the Dr. Pepper®. I start to leave the room.

"I'm going outside to watch the movers load the trucks."

Mama and Gram exchange looks. As I open the door, I hear them talking.

Chapter 7

Last Day at St. Martins Part II

♣

"She's going to the steps to think, isn't she Lynn?"

"It's been a big day for her Mama. You know Andie B. When she needs time alone she heads for the steps.

"Been that way since she was a toddler."

I head for the steps on the side of the house. Concentrating as I start to ease myself down, I don't notice Trey is home and is sprinting towards me. Before I realize it, his outstretched hands are helping me gain my balance.

"It's a long way to the ground Buzzard. All you need is to do is to hurt yourself again."

"Thanks big brother. Where have you been? Out giving the ladies of New Orleans your forwarding address?"

"I had a few stops to make. But I'm not going as far as you. I can always come to Mandeville for a weekend and stay with Grandma and Grandpa."

"Lucky dog."

"What about you? Have you broken all your ties at St. Martins?"

"Let's see. Matt and I broke up on the ski trip. Clay has been hanging around, but I think he feels sorry for me. You should have seen Matt and Heather at lunch today. He never looked at me that way. So, yeah I guess I'm free."

"And all the guys at Brockton anxiously await your arrival."

"Yeah right."

I punch Trey in the arm, and he punches me back."

"Yeah go ahead and hurt me. As long as I'm on these crutches I'm no good to anybody."

"C'mon Buzzard. That's not like you. If you want to be on the pitcher's mound in April, you've got to fight. I know you're a fighter, because I've been your victim plenty of times."

As Trey spoke I noticed he was scratching his shin above his ankle. I caught a glimpse of the white scar he took careful measures to cover up. That scar and the one on the back of his neck where the board hit him were the only visible reminders of the clubhouse fire. Every time I saw them I was reminded of that day.

I was four and he was seven. Daddy had built us a clubhouse in the backyard out of scraps of lumber he had salvaged from one of his nearby construction projects. He wanted it to be perfect even going so far as pouring a concrete slab for a foundation. All of us worked on building it: Grandpa Webb, Daddy, Trey and I. I carried the nails and the hammers. Daddy even let me hammer a couple of nails. Then I smashed my thumb and started crying. Trey called me a baby, and said I needed to go in the house with the girls. Daddy told me to go get some ice from Mama for my thumb and to hurry back. He said I was his good helper. I ran in the house where Mama, Grandma Elizabeth, and Grandma Josie were. Mama made an ice pack for my thumb. She said it would turn blue because I hit it so hard. Grandma Elizabeth wanted me to stay inside, but I ran out the door. As I came around the corner, I heard the guys laughing. I thought they were laughing at me. I stopped and went back to the steps. Daddy and Grandpa didn't come looking for me. Nobody ever did. They were all too busy.

When we finished the clubhouse, it was beautiful. I got to help slap the bright purple paint on it. By the time we were finished, my overalls were covered from head-to-toe. There was as much paint on me as there was the clubhouse. Daddy picked me up by my overall straps and carried me the kitchen door. I spread out my arms.

"I'm flying Daddy. Look I'm an airplane."

Daddy laughed. When we arrived at the kitchen, he hollered.

"Lynn, come get your daughter. I don't think you want her in the house like this."

But I thought I was his daughter. Now he was turning me over to her. She was no fun. Mama stayed dressed up all the time. She never even came to look at the clubhouse much less help us build it. When Mama came to the door, she started laughing.

"Andie Beth, you stay right there. Don't move. Take off your shoes and socks. Do you understand me young lady? Don't move."

"Yes, ma'am."

"Buzzie, you do what your mama says. I'm going back to the clubhouse and help your grandpa and Trey finish. You did a great job."

"Okay Daddy."

Daddy searches my face for a clean spot, pulls back my hair and kisses me on the forehead. As he walks away, Mama comes back with an old towel. She is trying hard not to laugh.

"Andie B. take off your overalls and put this towel around you. Then march upstairs to the bathtub."

"Mama why do I have to take a bath? It's not even night time yet. I'm not that dirty. Please Mama."

"Do as I say. If you keep talking back to me, you'll have stay in your room for the rest of the day. Do you understand me?"

"Yes Mama."

A few days later the clubhouse was finished and ready for occupancy. For the first few weeks everything was fine. When Trey was at soccer practice, I played in it. When his friends came over, they played in it. If no one was around, we would play together.

I thought boys had the better life. They worked outside and played sports. Girls had to dress up all the time. Even at Pre-K Mama the girls wore skirts almost every day. I hated it. Skirts itched. I was always getting them dirty when we played outside. Mama hates dirt. I love it.

Everything was going fine until one day Trey and his friends were playing, and I wanted to play too. Daddy had put a door, roof, and one window in the clubhouse so our toys wouldn't get wet. The door was supposed to stay open when we played, but the boys had closed it. I walked in and they were playing a game.

"I want to play."

"You can't Andie B. You have to read what is on the cards, and you can't read yet."

"I still want to play."

"Trey tell your sister to get lost."

"Go away Andie B."

"Don't wanna."

"If you don't, I'm going to tell Mom you're bugging us."

"Okay, but it's not fair."

I went to the steps and watched the airplanes for awhile. Daddy came home from work, and I went inside with him.

"Lynn look what I found on the steps."

"I thought you were playing with Trey, Andie B?."

"Dumb old boys wouldn't let me. But don't worry I'll show them."

"I bet you will."

Mama laughs.

"Go in the den and watch cartoons while your daddy and I talk a few minutes before supper."

"Okay."

"She was sitting on the steps by herself again Lynn."

"I saw her through the window. Gary that's where she goes when she wants to be alone. I kept an eye on her, and made sure she didn't head for the street. But she never comes in or leaves the yard. She just stops and sits on the steps. It's like it's her private sanctuary."

"Well whatever works."

The next day Trey put a sign on the clubhouse. It said: NO GIRLS. Even though I couldn't read, I knew what certain words were. I knew the word girl from the restrooms at school. It wasn't fair. Daddy said the clubhouse was supposed to be for both of us. Trey wasn't keeping me out. I'd show him. I went back in the house. I looked in the kitchen and didn't see Mama. I went in the den, and she wasn't there either. There was a bucket by the fireplace with newspapers and a box of long matches. Daddy and Mama told Trey and I never to touch the matches. They were only used to start fires in the fireplace. Until now I never even thought about touching them. But I was so mad at Trey I wanted to scare him. The matches were long so

I would burn a newspaper near the clubhouse. This would scare Trey and his friends. When they smelled the smoke, they would run out of the clubhouse, and while they were putting out my little fire I would go in the clubhouse and play. I looked around and still didn't see Mama. I snatched the box of matches and a couple of newspapers and headed outside. I wadded up the newspapers like Daddy does when he starts the fire and carried them to the backyard. I had to be close enough to the clubhouse so the boys would smell the smoke. I peeked in the window, and they were playing a game at the table. It took several times to light a match. Once the papers caught fire I ran to the corner of the house to watch.

What happened next scared me. A wind gust blew the burning newspapers on to the roof of the clubhouse. Trey's two friends ran from the building, but Trey didn't come with them. He was trying to grab toys and bring them. He tripped over a chair and had a hard time getting up. By now his friends were running home. There was nothing I could do to help him. I opened the kitchen door and screamed for Mama. She came running out. Trey stumbled out of the clubhouse, but I could tell he was hurt. I jerked him by the arm away from the fire. I was so scared. One of the neighbors called the fire department. By now the clubhouse was a pile of ashes on a concrete slab.

An ambulance came, and they put Trey on a stretcher. Once Mama was sure he was okay, she looked around and saw the box of matches on the ground.

"Do you know how this happened Andie Beth?'

"No ma'am."

"Andie Beth are you lying to me? Do you know how this happened?"

x

"Yes ma'am."

For the first time in my life I felt the intensity of Lynn Nettles' anger. The feel of the sting of her hand against my face left a permanent impression in my brain.

"I didn't mean to hurt him Mama. I just set some trash on fire so he'd leave the clubhouse. Is he going to die Mama? I didn't mean to hurt him."

Trey suffered burns to his neck, shin, and hands. They were not as serious as everyone first feared. He was treated in the emergency room and stayed home for a couple of days. Daddy never rebuilt the clubhouse. Another concrete slab was added to form the basketball court.

Trey and I never talk about the fire. It is a part of our past we'd both like to forget. Mama has never brought up the subject. The only evidence left are the physical scars on Trey and the emotional scars on me. Part of me knows Mama quit loving me a little on that day.

"Earth to Buzzard. Come in Buzzard. Where are you?"

"What Trey? What's going on?"

"Have you been paying attention to anything I've been saying for the last thirty minutes?"

"Yeah, something about your calculus professor and Sam is going to fly to D.C. with us."

"Where have you been?"

"Thinking about leaving this house. Just sitting on the steps thinking. Here comes Daddy."

"Mama said he was bringing home muffalettas from Pierres for dinner. Let me help you up, and then I'll go help him."

"Thanks."

Daddy jumps out of the car and walks toward us. Trey takes the bags of muffalettas from the agents and heads inside.

"Still sitting on the steps Buzzie?"

"Yes Daddy. This is where I used to wait for you to come home from work."

"I remember. I'd drive up and there you were."

"When I saw you coming around the corner, I'd get so excited. Can I tell you a secret Daddy? You may think it's dumb though."

"Sure Buzzie."

"Just now when you came around the corner, I forgot you were the President Elect. In my heart it was Daddy's home, Daddy's home like when I was a little kid."

"Buzzie that's sweet. I hope you always feel that way. Of course at the White House, I'll be walking home across the lawn. Let's go inside before Trey eats our sandwiches."

Daddy opens the door and we go in.

"Lynn look who I found on the steps."

"Some things never change Gary."

After dinner I changed into my basketball warm-ups. Cajun and our suitcases had already been taken to Grandpa Webb and Grandma Elizabeth's house in Mandeville. The movers were loading the last of the boxes in the vans as we headed to St. Martins one final time. At the gym I headed to the locker room. Tonight would be my final entrance with the team.

"Ladies and gentlemen presenting your Lady Saints."

The bleachers were alive as everyone stood and cheered. My teammates ran out on the court and began to warm up. I stood under the backboard clutching a basket-ball, and watched as they shot lay-ups, free throws, and jump shots. I slapped the basketball with my hands. The adrenaline rushed through my system. My heart beat faster, and I felt it pounding in my chest. I started to run out on the court. Then I looked down at the metallic knee braces on both legs and felt the pressure of the crutches under my arms. Not today Andie B. Not today.

The team finished warm-ups and headed for the bench. I followed them and found my spot on the end. We stood as the introductions were made.

"Introducing your Lady Saints. Tonight is the last game for one of our sophomores, Andie Beth Nettles. Due to injuries she will be unable to play. But let's all stand and give her a hand, number 45 Nettles, guard."

Everyone stood and clapped. I looked in the stands and there was Mama, Daddy, Trey, Grandpa Webb, Grandma Elizabeth, and Grandma Josie. Everyone looked so proud of me, even Mama. I came back to the bench and found my spot. I called this my ready spot-ready to go in the game at a moment's notice. Even though I couldn't play, I still sat there.

The boy's team was sitting on the front row of the bleachers right behind the bench. They stayed there through the first three quarters of the game. I glanced over my shoulder to see them talking and horsing around.

We won the game 70-60. Heather scored fifteen points. After the game I followed my teammates into the locker room for one last time. Agent Landry handed me backpack so I could change from my warm-up suit and jersey to jeans and a sweatshirt. Coach Perry entered the locker room.

"Ladies, before you start changing clothes, I have one more presentation to make to Andie B. The team decided you needed something to remember us by, so we autographed this basketball. Also, you don't need to change clothes. We want you to keep your jersey and warm-up suit and wear them in the White House so you won't forget where you came from."

"Thanks everyone. I'll miss you guys. You better go to state so I can come back and watch you win it. Good luck everyone."

Everyone clapped, and each girl hugged me. Even Heather. I left the locker room, gave my backpack to Agent Landry and headed to the bleachers. The girls sat where the boys had sat during our game. The boy's game had started. Matt and Clay were in the starting five. Last year's team was mostly seniors with only two juniors. Matt and Clay were the best junior varsity players so now they started as sophomores.

The rest of the team came out of the locker room and sat around me. Oddly enough Heather sat beside me.

"Andie B. you're not mad because Matt and I are dating are you?"

"Mad no. Irritated because you couldn't wait for me to leave town yes."

"What do you mean?"

"I mean I knew we would split when I moved. I didn't know he was already interested in someone else. I was blind. Even when people tried to tell me differently."

"It wasn't like that."

"Then how was it?"

"When you were grounded for so long, Matt was lonely. You couldn't talk on the phone or facebook ®, and your mom wouldn't let you hang out with us."

"And you had a car which made it nice and convenient for Matt."

"Yeah, sort of."

"Heather, it's okay. It's just Matt and I have been together forever. It seems weird not having him around."

"Andie B. I know you still care about him, and I can see the way he looks at you. He will always care about you."

"He looks at me like an old friend. He looks at you like a girlfriend. There's a difference."

The boys won their game too. The score was much closer: 60-58. Matt and Clay came over before they headed to the locker room.

"This is it guys. The next time I see you will be at the inauguration."

"Yep, you'll officially be the first kid."

"That's Ms. First Kid to you."

The three of us hugged each other with a group hug.

"Heather come here."

She had a puzzled look on her face.

"Just come here please."

I took Matt's hand and Clay's hand and put them in Heather's hand.

"They're all yours Heather. Take care of them for me. I've got to go. My family is waiting."

"See ya A.B."

"Later guys."

I headed for the gym doors where my family was standing.

"Ready to go Buzzie?"

"Yes Daddy."

A cold blast of air hit us in the face as we left the gym. One limo was parked outside along with Grandpa Webb's car and Trey's Charger. As the agent opened the door, I took one last look at the gym where kids were hanging out. This chapter of my life was over.

I climbed in the car, and an agent took my crutches from Mama. She eased on to the seat beside me. I rested my head on Mama's shoulder for the hour's drive to Mandeville. She put her arm around me and held me tight. I started to cry, and Mama pushed my hair out of my eyes. Daddy started to say something, but didn't.

"It's okay, Little B. It's okay. Mama's here."

"I'm scared Mama."

"Mama's here. Don't be afraid."

"But all my friends are here. I only have one friend in Washington. I don't want to go Mama."

"I know baby but we have to. Mama's going to take care of her Andie B. Mama's not going to let anything happen to her little girl."

"Promise Mama."

"Promise Andie B. Now just relax. Close your eyes and rest. We'll be at Gram's soon."

"I'm sorry I'm such a baby, Mama."

"It's okay Andie B. You're my baby, and that's all that matters."

Mama and Daddy exchange concerned looks. Daddy reaches over, takes Mama's hand, and squeezes it.

The sound of the tires hitting the gravel on the circular driveway at Grandpa Webb's jolts me out of my sleep. Embarrassed I wipe the sleep out of my eyes and sit up straight. As soon as the car came to a stop, an agent opened the doors for Daddy and Mama. I eased over to the edge of the seat and Agent Landry handed me my crutches.

When we entered the house, Trey headed for the kitchen. I started to follow but I stopped. Both Grandmothers follow him and soon the sound of dishes rattling in the cabinet echoes through the house as they take out cups for coffee for the adults. Daddy and Grandpa settle in easy chairs in front of the fireplace, and Mama goes to the couch. I'm still standing. I don't want to be around anyone.

"C'mon Buzzie. Sit down. Your arms have to be tired from holding up those crutches all day."

"No Daddy. I think I'm going to bed.

"This early on a Friday night. You're not getting sick are you Bumble?"

"No Grandpa. I'm just tired."

"C'mon Andie B. I'll help you up the stairs."

"You don't need to Mama. I can do it."

"I know you can, but let me help you anyway."

"Okay Mama. Goodnight Daddy. Goodnight Grandpa."

"Goodnight Buzzie."

"Love you Bumble."

Mama took off her heels and carried them in her hand. I went up the stairs with one hand on the railing and Mama beside me. When we opened the door, Cajun jumped off the bed, out the door, and down the steps.

"I can take it from here Mama."

"I know you can, but let me help you Andie B. It's okay to ask for help once in a while you know."

"Mama did you mean what you said in the car about taking care of me?"

"Of course I did. Why?"

"I don't know. It's just you're going to be so busy."

"You go ahead and change clothes. I'll be back in a minute."

When Mama comes back in the room, I'm in bed. She has changed too and has on her robe.

"Scoot over."

"What?"

"Scoot over. I want to show you something."

I scoot over and Mama lies down beside me. She pulls a picture out of the pocket of her robe. It is a picture of Mama holding a baby, and Daddy sitting with a little boy on his lap.

"I found this yesterday when I was sorting through some boxes. I thought I would have it enlarged for your daddy's office. Do you know when this was taken?"

"Don't have a clue."

"Mama took it the day you came home from the hospital. It's the first picture we have of you."

"Can't believe I was ever that small."

"You were. But you were tall even then. According to the back of the picture: 24 inches long weighing six pounds one ounce. Just think Andie B. you were two feet tall when you were born."

"Wow Mama."

"I promised you that day I would always take care of you. Tonight I'm promising you again. Andie B. your daddy and I love you very much, and we want the best for you."

"She's right Buzzie."

I didn't hear Daddy come in the room. Mama slipped the picture back in her robe pocket.

"Buzzie, we're all nervous about the future. I want you to promise me when you get scared you'll come to one of us. You've quite a few adjustments ahead of you over the next few weeks. You'll make it Buzzie. Your mama and I will be right there with you. Remember that and you'll be fine."

"Yes Daddy."

Mama gave me a hug and stood up. Daddy leaned over and gave me a kiss on the forehead.

"Andie B. remember one thing."

"What's that Mama?"

"Your daddy and I love you very much. You're our Andie B."

"I love you too."

Somehow I almost believed them. They turned off the light and left as Cajun raced in and almost knocked them down. He flopped down on the rug, and we both fell asleep.

Chapter 8

The Inauguration Part 1

♣

"**R**achel are you out there?" It seems weird talking to you on the internet, and knowing that you are close by. Daddy and Mama wanted to check out Camp David so the three of us plus Cajun flew here for the weekend. It was our first time to ride in Marine One, the President's Helicopter. After everything else that has happened this week, it was just one more adventure.

Wow what a week! We spent Saturday at Grandpa Webb's and Grandma Elizabeth's house in Mandeville. Their house is on Lake Ponchartrain, and the dining room has a huge picture window which looks out over the lake. Grandpa has a dock where he keeps his boat anchored. You can see it from the dining room. When I came downstairs, all the grandparents were sitting at the dining room table drinking coffee.

"Bumble, I thought we might have to send the National Guard after you. Never known you to sleep this late even on a Saturday."

"What time is it?"

"Almost 9:30. We came back to the table for a second round of coffee."

"You went to bed so quick last night Josie and I didn't even get to say good night. You okay?"

"I was tired. Dr. Starling said I could walk more, and I guess I overdid it Where is everybody else?"

"Your Daddy and Mama will be gone until late tonight. Seems every organization in five parishes wants them to put in an appearance today. Trey went back to Baton Rouge to pick up Samantha. She couldn't come with him yesterday because she had a late class. So you're stuck with us old folks unless you want to go hang out with your friends somewhere."

"No I told them goodbye last night. Most of them are leaving today for Washington. The band and some of the kids will be in the inaugural parade."

"Well, could I interest you in a trip to the airport? The weather is great all along the coastline."

"Webb, she can't fly the plane with those knee braces on."

"No, but I can be a passenger if Grandpa flies. Can I Gram please, please? It will be my last chance for a long time. I haven't been up in *The Bee* since before the holidays."

"Josie, what do you think? Gary and Lynn didn't tell me anything about what Andie B. could or couldn't do today."

"They didn't mention anything to me either. I don't see why not. Beats having her sit around here all day moping and whining."

"Great. So that means I can go."

"As long as you and your grandpa behave. And Webb if she starts getting tired, I expect you to bring her home."

"Okay, Bumble you heard the lady. Go grab your jacket and hat, and let's go. I'll go tell the agents what our plans are."

"Thanks Gram."

Grandpa and I headed for Lakefront Airport where he kept *The Bee.* A car with two agents followed us. After several months of this, I was beginning to know most of the agents by name. Agents Landry and Tobias were the main two assigned to me. I had gotten to know them pretty well. Grandpa had called ahead and when we arrived at the airport *The Bee* was parked in front of the hangar where Grandpa and his friends hung out. He parked his old beat up pick-up truck, and helped me out.

"Webb, you old codger what are you doing here today? Thought you were on your way to Washington."

"Bumble and I are going to take up *The Bee.* Thought we'd head to Pensacola and get some of that good Florida fruit."

"Andie B., we didn't even see you. How are your knees?"

"Doing pretty good Colonel Ballard. How's Jessica?"

"Off shopping with her grandma. Something about needing a dress for a Valentine Dance in a few weeks."

"Well, tell her I said hi."

"Will do. If your Grandpa starts giving you a hard time just whack him a couple of times with the crutches."

"Nah. Grandpa is great."

"Be back later Cliff."

"Have a good time you two."

Grandpa helped me up the two stairs to the plane. I read off the checklist as he tested all the equipment. The agents waited for us at the hangar. He had given them our flight plan, and we could contact them by radio. Turning the switch he fired the twin engines and the little Cessna slowly taxied down the runway.

Takeoffs were my favorite part of flying. It felt like being in a race car. You travelled faster and faster and then you were up in the air as the wheels left the ground. Grandpa was right. It was a perfect day for flying. There wasn't a cloud in the sky. It was bluer than I could ever remember. We flew low following the Gulf Coast shore line. Even the usual murky gulf waters looked clear today. Neither of us said a word. We were savoring the moment. The only thing that would have made it better would have been if I had been at the controls.

"What are you thinking about Bumble?"

"Nothing much Grandpa. Just about how much fun I'm having being with you, and how different my life's going to be."

"You'll have all sorts of new adventures. If I know you, you'll be at the controls of Air Force One before the summer is over."

"I doubt it. Nothing's ever going to be the same anymore, Grandpa. But I don't want to talk about it. I just want to enjoy today with you."

"Bumble, don't get discouraged. You've always been a fighter. You'll be on that softball field in a few months. I've already told your grandma that when we come to visit, we're flying *The Bee*, so you and I can get some flight time. I promise you you'll have your pilot's license by the time school starts next year."

"Thanks Grandpa, but I wanted it by my birthday. Now I may not even be able to get my driver's license with these stupid braces on my legs."

"I think you will. I'm just afraid the agents may not let you drive much. But that Landry fellow seems to be a pretty nice guy."

"He is. He understands me a lot better than most grownups."

"Look there's a school of sharks. Good thing there's no one swimming out this far in the water."

"They're following the fishing boats over there."

We followed the coastline until we reached Pensacola. Grandpa circled the airport a couple of times and brought *The Bee* in for landing. He taxied to a nearby hangar. As we exited the plane, a car drove up. Two agents got out and opened the car doors for us. We headed for Grandpa's favorite farmer's market located on the outskirts of Pensacola.

"Mr. Nettles, it's good to see you again. We were just talking about you the other day."

"This is my granddaughter Andie B. We flew down this morning to get some of those good tangerines you have; plus, my wife wants some grapefruit."

"We'll have your order ready in just a minute. Look around a little. We've got some fresh squeezed orange juice over on the far table. Help yourself to a glass."

"This is a neat place Grandpa. How did you find it?"

"Been coming here since before you were born Bumble. Your grandma and I found this place one time while driving home from a trip. Best citrus I've ever eaten. Not like that grocery store stuff we get."

"Mr. Nettles, we put your order in the car."

"Thanks. C'mon Bumble let's go find us some lunch."

We headed for a restaurant that advertised a pizza buffet. Grandpa had thought of everything. It dawned on me that this trip was not spontaneous. In order for everything to happen the way it did, Grandpa must have planned it. It was his special way of saying goodbye to me."

We flew back to New Orleans, and headed back to Grandpa's house. Both Grandmothers were in the kitchen. Cajun was curled up in the corner asleep.

"How was your trip?"

"Great. We had a lot of fun together. Even saw a school of sharks near Biloxi. Only thing missing was me not flying."

"Why don't go rest a little while Andie B? You look tired."

"Aw Gram. I'll compromise with you. I'll go in the den and watch the basketball game from the couch. I'm too old to be taking naps."

"Okay, but you forget Andie Beth that Elizabeth and I have been around you enough to tell when you're tired. You've been pushing yourself pretty hard these last two weeks."

"Yes ma'am. It's just that I'm almost sixteen, and I know when I'm tired too. Like last night I wanted to stay up, but I went to bed. But today was different. Grandpa and I had so much fun."

I went in the den and watched a basketball game on television. Later the four of us ate dinner. Mama and Daddy and Trey and Sam didn't come back until after we had all gone to bed.

Sunday morning we went to St. John's to church for the last time. Between us and all the agents we took up three pews. After church we drove to our house a few blocks away. Mama and Daddy held hands as they walked up to the front door one last time. The Grandparents and Trey and Sam followed them inside. I brought up the rear. The house seemed like a ghost house. Everyone walked around from room to room inspecting it.

As I hobbled around, I swore I was hearing, smelling, and seeing things. The smell of Grandma Josie's cinnamon buns baking; the sounds of a basketball game blaring from the den; Daddy running downstairs adjusting his tie as he ran out the door late for work as always; the smell of Mama's perfume when she came in my room to tuck me in; Trey dribbling a basketball through the house; Cajun barking at the cat next door; and me sitting on the steps.

I climbed the stairs to the third floor one last time, and went in my room. It was empty. In the doorway was the only indicator that I lived there. Daddy had carefully marked my height each year on the door frame. He stopped when I was eight years old, and he went to Washington. The cleaning team had scrubbed the door frame, but I could faintly make out the lines that marked my height through the years.

Sitting down on the window seat I lifted up the lid to the sweater chest. Carved in the bottom of the chest were the crudely carved initials A.N. + M.N. circled by a heart. I carved mine and Matt's initials when I was eight years old. I did it with Trey's Boy Scout knife that I took from his room. Then I cut my finger. Putting a Band Aid on it I lied to Mama when she asked me what happened. I told her that I cut it on a piece of glass at the softball field, and she believed me. I washed the blood off Trey's knife and snuck it back into his room before he noticed it was gone. I hated lying to Mama, but I wasn't supposed to touch knives. If she thought I was lying, she never called me on it. There is still a tiny scar on my forefinger.

I took one last look out the window. Greeting me was a sight I had witnessed millions of times before. A plane took off headed northeast. That was the direction we'd be flying in a few hours. I heard voices in the rest of the house.

"Well, Lynn this is it. Our house now belongs to Professor Rybolt and his family."

"I remember the first day we moved in. Prince Charming and his construction crew built me my castle."

"Only the best for my queen."

They both laugh.

"If I remember correctly, the paint wasn't even dry when you two moved in."

"That's right Dad. Lynn and I were so anxious to get settled we lived on the first floor while the crew took two more weeks to finish the upper two floors."

"Don't mind them Sam, they're reminiscing again. They do this all the time; talking about the good old days."

"I think it's sweet. Go on Mr. and Mrs. Nettles."

"Well I for one remember the day you brought Trey home from the hospital. That boy howled for three solid days. Thought he'd never stop crying."

"But look how lovable I turned out."

Everyone starts laughing. While they are standing in the living room talking I cut through the kitchen to the side steps outside. I've got to get to my special place one more time.

"Where's Andie B.?"

"Probably in her room. What did you do Mom, ground her again?"

"No, I bet she's sitting on the steps. Go look for her Gary."

"I don't get it what's the significance of the steps?"

"Sorry Sam, inside joke. Andie B. always heads for the side steps when she needs to think or wants to be alone. Been doing it since she was a toddler."

"How cute."

"Well, it always made it easy to find her. Nobody could get her to move from them but her Daddy. When he was in Washington and she'd get upset, Lynn would have to call him to talk to her."

"When she became a teenager, it got easier."

"Yeah, Mom would take the cordless phone to her and tell her to call him herself. That way if she couldn't get through to him she wouldn't blame Mom. There was a time when she didn't go out there much."

"She was still going out there Trey but a lot of times she would wait until the weekend when your dad was home."

"No one else could convince her to come in but him."

"But you knew she was there?"

"Yes, and I left her alone. We all did until it was time for dinner or bed. Then Gary would have a little talk with her and coax her inside. Sometimes she'd tell me what was bothering her, but a lot of times I found out from him."

"Guess she'll find a new spot at The White House. From the pictures I've seen there are plenty of steps.

"It will be interesting to see what she does."

Daddy came outside and sat down beside me.

"One last trip to the steps, huh, Buzzie?"

"Yes, Daddy, but you didn't have to come get me. I would have come in on my own."

"I know, but we looked around the living room, and you were missing. Your mama sent me to get you."

"Just like always. I can hear her now: Gary, go find your daughter. You ever notice Daddy, that I'm your daughter when I do something stupid and her daughter when I do something smart."

Daddy laughs.

"I've noticed that a few times over the years."

"You mean a few dozen times don't you?"

"You may be right. But let me ask you a question Buzzie."

"What's that Daddy?"

"When you do something stupid as you call it. What do you learn?"

"Not to get caught next time."

"Seriously, Andie B. What do you learn?"

"To observe the situation and to think before I speak or act. Grandma Elizabeth taught me that. But it's easier said than done."

"Well, if you remember that advice, you and your mama will get along a lot better."

"Yes, Daddy but it's hard. Sometimes Mama pushes all my wrong buttons."

"C'mon it's time. We have to get to the airport."

Daddy helped me up, and he and I went into the living room. We all walked outside and stood on the front porch. One of the agents brought a camera from the car and took a group picture of us. He locked the door, and we headed for the airport a few miles away.

We were driven to a special hangar away from the main terminal. The agents drove us to the stairs of the most awesome plane I had ever seen. Photographers were everywhere. Painted on the sides were the words: "Air Force One." The outgoing President had sent the official plane to fly us to Washington. I was anxious to see what the inside looked like, but realized that running up the stairs was not an option. Once again protocol was the grandparents boarded first followed by Sam, Trey, and I, then Mama and Daddy. When we entered the plane, the rest of the family was already on board including the aunts, uncles, and cousins.

Daddy had been on Air Force Once a few times before with the President, but for the rest of us it was the first time. An aide took us on a tour. One section of the plane has a bedroom with two beds, bathroom with shower, den, an office, and several meeting rooms for people traveling with the President such as reporters, aides, and agents. The kitchen is huge, and has every food you can imagine. The seats aren't in rows, but instead are in groups of five with a table in the middle. After the tour, I caught up with Lauren and Michelle and the other cousins.

"Wow. A.B. what do you think? From now on you'll be flying in style."

"I can't believe how huge it is. It's like a flying house."

"Kids fasten your seatbelts. We're taking off."

After taking off everyone walked around and talked. There were also people on the plane from the campaign. I remembered seeing them on election night at the house. Lauren, Michelle, and I stayed in one little cluster and talked. Occasionally someone would walk by and speak to us.

It was getting dark when we arrived in Washington. The lights in the city came on as if the entire town was on a timer. The plane landed at Andrews Air Force Base. When it finally came to a stop, there were the limousines lined up. Going down the steps everything was in reverse: first Mama and Daddy, then Trey and I, then Sam and the grandparents. We climbed into the cars, and it took thirty minutes to make the trip into the city.

We stayed at Daddy's townhouse. The rest of the family stayed at Blair House, the guest house across the street from the White House. As soon as we arrived Mama and Daddy hurried to change clothes. They had a dinner and parties to attend. Trey, Sam and I were staying in.

"Andie B. you and Trey try to get along. Sam, maybe with you here they won't kill each other."

"Yes, Mama."

"We'll be late tonight. The next few days are going to be hectic so get some rest."

"'Night Buzzie. We love you."

"Love you too Daddy."

Daddy's apartment was always well stocked with food. He and Mama had spent a lot of time thee over the last few months. One of Daddy's new staff members would be moving in it after we moved in the White House.

"What are we going to do tonight?"

"We've got to study Buzzard. I have tons of reading for my humanities class."

"Me too Andie B. You think you have homework in high school. Wait until you get to college."

"Well, for once I don't have any homework. But if I know Mama, I'll be in school the day after the inauguration. Brockton starts their new semester on Wednesday, and you know Mama she doesn't want me to get behind."

"We're going to study in the living room."

"I'll go in Daddy's office and play on his computer. See you guys later."

Monday morning. The day before the inauguration. When I woke up, it took me a few minutes to remember where I was. Although I had spent part of my summers here and occasional vacations over the last eight years, this room bore little resemblance to me. It had twin beds in case we had company. Sam had slept on the other bed last night; although I think she and Trey had stayed in the living room until Mama and Daddy came home. I watched some of the pre-inaugural festivities on television hoping to catch a glimpse of them. Mostly all I saw was celebrities talking about their latest movie or television show. Funny I never saw those people around during the campaign.

Sam was still asleep so I tried to be quiet when I got up. It's hard to do when you're clunking around on crutches. The growling in my stomach reminded me I was hungry. I threw on my robe and headed to the kitchen. Mama was sitting there reading the newspaper and drinking coffee.

"Morning Andie B."

"Morning Mama. Where's Daddy?"

"In his office making phone calls. What did you do last night?"

"Played computer games and watched television. I saw a bunch of celebrities. You never told me Adam Sandler supported Daddy. He was interviewed and talked about what a great President Daddy was going to be."

"Guess I didn't think about it."

"Have you met all those people Mama?"

"Not all of them. But when I was campaigning with your daddy I met quite a few. It takes a lot of money to get elected Andie B., and celebrities have money plus influence on other people who have money."

"Will I get to meet any celebrities?"

"Of course. There will be all sorts of famous people coming to the White House, and you'll get to meet plenty of them. An invitation to the White House is considered a pretty big honor."

"Can I invite someone famous myself?'

"Not unless you clear it with the President."

Mama laughs.

"Hi Daddy."

"Once we get settled in Buzzie you make a list of all the famous people you want to invite, and your mama and I will see what we can do."

"Awesome. I just can't believe all those people I saw on television last night. How many parties did you guys have to go to?"

"I lost count after the fifth one. Just a lot of smiling and handshakes. And there are more of them today."

"I guess that means I'm stuck here in the apartment."

"Not exactly. The congressional wives are hosting a mother-daughter luncheon in my honor, and I want you to go with me. Then we'll catch up with your daddy for a few appearances. Who knows Andie B? You may meet a celebrity or two."

When I went to get dressed for the luncheon, I looked in the closet and saw three new outfits. Of course, they were all skirts and tops. The skirts were long enough to cover my knee braces, so it wouldn't be obvious to the world what my legs looked like. About the time I discovered them, Mama came in the room.

"What do you think of your surprise? I thought you needed some new clothes. Do you like them?"

"Yes Mama, but now I'm confused."

"What do you mean?"

"Which one do I wear and when?"

"That's easy. The brown one today, the gray one tomorrow for the inauguration tomorrow morning, and keep the navy blue one in reserve."

"Glad you explained it. But what was wrong with my old clothes?"

"Nothing. I saw these one day when I was Christmas shopping here and decided to surprise you. I guess I forgot you're growing up and like to pick out your own clothes."

"Sorta. But it's okay Mama. I guess I won't be hanging out at the mall any more anyway."

"Oh, I think you'll still get some mall time. You're not going to prison Andie B. It's just that you will always have agents around you. You will be able to hang out with your friends. Now get dressed."

"Yes, Mama."

The luncheon turned out okay. I don't have to tell you about it though, because you were there. I wish I could have sat with you and your mom instead of at the dumb old head table. It felt like everyone was staring at us. I was stuck between Mrs. Bedford, the vice-president's wife and her daughter Claire, who is already married and has a baby.

Everyone around me was old. A couple of times I looked at your table and you were laughing and having a good time. Mrs. Bedford asked me the usual questions about how I felt about leaving Kenner, going to a new school, and how much longer I was going to be on crutches. I told her what she wanted to hear; about how excited I was to move to Washington, but that I would miss my friends. At least I had you here. I thought going to a new school would a fun experience. What a lie. I hoped to be off crutches by softball season. What a dream.

Mama's speech was pretty good. Does she ever regret dropping out of law school when she was pregnant with Trey? She could have gone back and finished after he was born. I mean who would want to be a guidance counselor when you could be a lawyer? Going to court and pros-ecuting criminals. Your honor I object. We have evidence to prove the accused was there on the night in question. It sounds like fun to me. Who knows? If I don't become a pilot, I could always become a lawyer. But, ugh, I don't know if I could handle three more years of college. After the luncheon was over, there were photographers everywhere taking our picture. I'm sorry I didn't get to talk to you anymore, but every time I started to walk toward you Mama called me back.

We caught up with Daddy at a Senior Citizens for Nettles reception. He was already there with the grandparents.

"Hey, Bumble, don't you look pretty today. I'm starting to like seeing you dressed up."

"Thanks Grandpa."

We sat on the stage. Trey wasn't here. Somehow he had managed to wrangle his way out of showing up. Every old person in the place must have had a camera. It seems like we stood up forever. My arms were getting tired from the weight of the crutches, but I didn't want to admit it. After what seemed like hours we sat down. Several people spoke, and then the audience asked Daddy questions about what he would do for senior citizens. One of the questions was how did he think he could relate to senior citizens when he was so young? Daddy reached in his back pocket and pulled his AARP card out of his wallet.

"See, I'm not as young as I look. I'll be 51 in May. Plus I am fortunate enough to have both my parents and my mother-in-law alive and well. I am concerned about their well being, and just as I supported legislation as a senator that assisted senior citizens, I will support future programs for senior citizens as your President."

The crowd cheered and applauded loudly. We made more stops during the afternoon. Each time it was the same drill; handshaking and pictures and Mama and Daddy introducing me to people. I have no idea who most of them were.

"Where to now Daddy?'

"Thought we'd swing by the apartment to pick up Trey and Sam and go to Chico's one last time."

"You mean we won't ever to get out again?"

"Not exactly. After tomorrow it will be a lot harder. Tonight I'm President Elect Nettles. Tomorrow night I'll be President Nettles."

"Did you have fun this afternoon Andie B.?"

"I guess. But it seemed like every person in Washington took our picture."

"Get used to it Buzzie. From now on every time we go anywhere, it's news."

"Don't you mean every time you go anywhere, Daddy?"

"No, that applies to all of us. After noon tomorrow, we're all a part of the First Family."

"Too weird."

"All you have to do Buzzie is follow our lead. The main thing to remember is don't talk to anyone if your mama or I aren't around. There are many reporters lurking around who would love to ask you questions."

"Your daddy wants to protect you, Andie B. The press has been told they're not allowed to interview you, but that may not stop some overzealous young reporter trying to make a name for himself. Some of them don't look much older than you so be careful."

"Yes, Mama."

I was relieved when we arrived at the apartment and Trey and Sam joined us. Maybe now the conversation would get away from the dos and don'ts of being the

President's kid. Little did I know what I had just experienced was only the tip of the iceberg. I thought they had told us everything when we had the big family meeting during Christmas vacation. That's when they explained to us about the agents who would be assigned to us. Now it seemed like every day a new rule was added.

"So big brother how did you and Sam avoid the public appearance scene all afternoon?"

"I made a few appearances. It's just I ran with a different crowd than you. Went to several rallies for student volunteers from around the country. Had to fight the babes off with a stick. I told them I was taken."

"No, I think I told them you were taken."

"I suppose you also told them you were a basketball superstar and a scholar."

"No, I think most of them already know."

"Funny, I never saw the word scholar in any newspaper articles I read. Did you Gary?"

"I make better grades than Trey. Mama you did tell Daddy I made straight A's on my final St. Martin's report card, didn't you?"

"She did Buzzie. I came up with the perfect reward for you. There's a room on the third floor near your room that has high ceilings. It has been used for storage. How would you like it for your own gym complete with a basketball goal?"

"You mean it Daddy?"

"Yes. It may take a few weeks to complete, but this way you won't have to go outside in the middle of the night to shoot baskets like you did in Kenner."

"Thanks Daddy."

"We may even install some padding on the walls so you can practice your pitching."

"I don't know if she's ready for all that Gary."

"Sure she is. It can be part of your physical therapy. Right Buzzie?"

"Right Daddy Maybe living in the White House won't be so bad after all."

"Yeah. All I'll have is my lonely old dorm room in Baton Rouge."

"And me. Poor Trey. The sad life of a superstar."

Everyone started laughing.

Our food arrived. We had been eating at Chico's forever. The first time I ever ate Mexican food was at Chico's. I was eight and Trey was eleven. When we had eaten out before in Kenner, it was usually at McDonalds ®. Sometimes Mama and Daddy went out to eat by themselves when he came home on weekends. When Daddy said he was taking us to a restaurant, Trey and I were excited. He tried to explain to us that tacos were just hamburgers in a shell. We both loved them and after that first trip, we always ate there every time we came to visit him. It was our favorite family restaurant. I'm sure Mama and Daddy went to fancier places when they were alone. It wasn't until I was a teenager that I realized there were other places just as good.

The spicy smell of the food made me realize how hungry I was. As we all stuffed our faces, conversation came to a dead stop. Since that first night I had learned to eat almost every item on the menu. Tonight I ate enchiladas and tacos. They were still my favorites. No one bothered us while we ate. I did see a few people point in our direction as if they recognized us, but no one approached us.

Tonight was the last time we would eat out as a family for a long time.

After dinner we returned to the apartment. Mama and Daddy had more parties to attend, and they changed clothes again.

"Andie Beth regular bed time tonight. No staying up late do you understand me? It's the honor system because Mama isn't here. Tomorrow is a big day."

"Yes ma'am."

"Good night Buzzie."

"Good night Daddy."

Trey and Sam studied. If they hadn't been stuck with me, they would have gone partying too. Grandma Josie was staying at Blair House with her sister, and Mama didn't want me to stay by myself or with just an agent. Trey and Sam didn't seem to mind. I think they just wanted to be somewhere together. They had more privacy in the apartment than they would have had out in public. I repeated my routine of the night before: playing computer games and watching television. I went to bed on time. I sort of expected Mama to call and check up on me, and I was surprised when she didn't.

Chapter 9

Inauguration Day Part 2

"Rachel are you out there?"

Inauguration Day was finally here. After two months of waiting and over two years of campaigning, today was the day Daddy would officially become the President of the United States. No longer would I be Senator Nettles' daughter, but instead I would be President Nettles' daughter. Tonight I would sleep in my new room in the White House. I laid in bed thinking about it. I was afraid to get up. Maybe it is all a dream, and I'm still in

Kenner. Nope, afraid not. This is definitely not my room in Kenner. I started to turn over and go back to sleep when I looked at the clock. It was almost 8:00 a.m. Mama said we had to leave by 10:00 a.m. so I'd better get up. Sam was still asleep. On the kitchen table was a note from Mama. It said: Andie B. your daddy and I are eating breakfast with President Heard and his wife. We will be back to pick up the three of you at 10:00 a.m. sharp. There's cereal on the counter. Make sure you eat something. It's going to be a hectic day. Love, Mama. P.S. If Trey and Sam aren't up by 9:00 a.m., wake them.

I grabbed the Rice Krispies® box, headed for the living room and turned on the television. All the networks were showing live Inauguration Day coverage. There was Mama and Daddy being greeted by President Heard and the First Lady, and walking in to the White House. There was a bunch of other people around who I assumed were cabinet members. This was my first glimpse of the inside of the White House other than what I had seen in pictures or newscasts.

Trey and Sam came in the living room just before 9:00 a.m. I was glad I didn't have to wake them, and I gave them Mama's message. While they were eating, I went in to my room and dressed. I'm still sort of self conscious about getting dressed in front of people. I'm embarrassed because I'm so flat chested. In gym class Heather would bounce down the court. I'm as flat chested as a nine year old. That's why Matt went crazy over her. Why would he want someone as flat chested as he is? Some of the girls even asked me why I bother to wear a bra at all when there is nothing to hold up. I don't even want boobs. They just get in the way of the basketball.

It dawned on me that Daddy was right. Everything I did from now on would be public. There are always going to be photographers and reporters around us. The spotlight was now on the whole family not just Daddy. I get goose bumps just thinking about the fact that someone is always watching me. It reminded me of those scary movies Trey and I used to watch late at night where someone suddenly jumps out of the bushes. I was starting to get used to having the agents around. Agent Landry and the others were pretty cool about giving me some space. But the idea that the world cared about what I did seemed dumb. I mean I'm just a fifteen year old whose Father happened to get elected President. What's the big deal?

Trey came in about the time they were talking about him on television.

"The President and First Lady have a nineteen year old son, Trey, who is a freshman at Louisiana State University in Baton Rouge on a basketball scholarship."

"That's you big brother. They're talking about you on television. They were showing me on crutches a little while ago."

"Yeah A.B., your knees are hot news."

He punched me in the arm, and I hit him back. It dawned on me that he called me A.B. instead of Buzzard. Great, now even he's changing. What's up with this family? Even Trey is acting nice to me.

"They're talking about you again A.B."

"The President and First Lady's daughter, fifteen year old Andie Beth, will live in the White House with them. First Lady Lynn Nettles has already enrolled her at Brockton Academy where many of the children of government officials attend. The school was chosen because of its excellent academic record as well as its security procedures. Andie Beth, an athlete like her brother, is expected to play basketball and softball when she recovers from her skiing accident which occurred during her Christmas vacation."

"There it is. My life in a nut shell."

We all laugh.

Agent Landry comes in the door.

"Your parents are waiting for you in the limousine outside. It's time for the inauguration."

I look around the apartment one last time. This is it Andie B. We grabbed our coats and walked out to the car. Mama and Daddy were waiting inside the limousine.

"Well, kids are you ready?"

"Nervous Daddy?"

"A little. Actually a lot. But the important thing is we're here together as a family."

"Did he practice his speech with you, Mom?"

"Bits and pieces Trey."

"We're here."

The car barely stopped when there were agents all around us opening doors. All the relatives and special guests were already seated. We had to wear these dumb lanyards around our necks with our names on an identification card. That seemed sort of ridiculous especially since everyone knew who we were. Sam sat on the second row beside Grandma Josie, and Daddy, Mama, Trey and I were on the first row. The entire ceremony took about an hour.

The neatest part was when Daddy was sworn in. Mama held a family Bible which had been in Daddy's family since before the Civil War. Trey and I stood with our hands on it too, and Daddy's muscular hand covered all three of ours. Even though he had been out of the construction business for a long time, his hands still looked more like a construction workers hands than a lawyers. Daddy and Mama looked straight into each other's eyes as he took the oath of office. It was evident they were in this together. When he finished, he hugged each of us. He hugged me so hard I dropped one of my crutches. Everyone laughed and that seemed to lighten up the situation. Even Mama laughed. I listened to his speech, but didn't pay much attention to it. I was too busy watching everyone watching him. Most of the crowd hung on his every word, and he was interrupted several times by loud applause.

Daddy, Mama, and the grandparents were whisked away to a luncheon in the Capitol Building. The rest of us went to the White House where the reviewing stand was set up for the Inaugural Parade. It wouldn't start for another hour so we would eat lunch there. It was my first time inside. Agent Landry walked beside me along with Trey and Sam.

When we arrived, there was Daddy's secretary, Mrs. Wiggins, waiting for us. Mrs. Wiggins has worked for Daddy his entire time in Washington. I had talked to her a lot on the phone when I would call Daddy from Kenner.

"Welcome to your new home Andie Beth and Trey. Come on in. I'll show you around."

There were so many people running around. The place reminded me of a maze. I could be lost in here for days before anyone would notice I was missing.

"There's a sandwich buffet set up for all of you in the family dining room upstairs. But first let me give you a quick tour of the downstairs rooms."

She took us through all of the public rooms that are open to tourists: the Red Room, the Blue Room, the Green Room, and the State Dining Room. It's all so huge. I was afraid to touch anything, and I noticed that my aunts were keeping a pretty tight hold on their kids. After that she showed us the East Wing where Mama will have an office. It's also the side of the White House where the cars drive up.

"Andie Beth this is the door where you will meet Agent Landry each morning to go to school. But don't worry. For the first few days we'll make sure someone points you in the right direction."

"Thanks."

Then we went in to the Oval Office. It's awesome. Trey immediately headed to Daddy's chair, picked up the phone, and leaned back.

"Do I look Presidential?"

"More like a poor imitation. Get up. I want to see what it feels like to sit in the President's chair. Who knows? I might just like it."

"Yeah right."

He punched me the arm as he got up, and I punched him back.

Everybody knows a female can't be President, Buzzard."

"And why not?"

"The country isn't ready for it."

"Maybe not now, but I've still got a few years before I meet the age requirement."

"Never happen."

"Just watch me big brother."

"Okay, you two. Now let's head upstairs so you can see the residence. All the President has to do is go out this door and around the corner, up an elevator, and he's home."

I know I'm going to be lost in this place. I hope there's a map around here somewhere. The way all these stairs and elevators are I may never find my way out. I feel like a little kid. I'm scared. I want to go back to Kenner. I hate this place. All the agents, doors and fences enclose me. I feel like an animal in the zoo. We're all trapped here, but everyone else can escape but me. People are staring at us. Most of them smile, but it seems like they are also sizing us up. Probably saying to themselves "So that's what his kids look like."

We entered another door and there was an agent sitting there. Mrs. Wiggins introduced him to us, and he punched several buttons and the elevator door opened. It took two trips for all of us to get to the second floor. There was another agent right by the elevator when we got off. Movers were still scurrying around bringing in boxes and arranging furniture. Mama and Daddy's room was at the end of the hall with a family room next to it. We peeked inside of it, and the suitcases from the apartment were already there. When I walked in the family room, there were the new recliners Mama bought at Christmas and the couch from home. In the back of the family room was a table and a small kitchen.

"This is where you'll have breakfast Andie Beth, and the dining room is next door."

"Where are our rooms?"

"On the third floor next to the solarium."

We headed up a ramp that led to the third floor. The solarium is a humongous room with tinted glass along the entire back side. It even has its own private balcony. There was a big screen television in it, a couch, and chairs. I didn't recognize any of the furniture. A hallway to the right led to three bedrooms. Mrs. Wiggins opened the door to the first room.

"Welcome home Andie Beth. This is your room."

As soon as she opened the door, Cajun came running at us. Since we had arrived in Washington, he had been in a kennel. A staff member had brought him to the White House that morning, and he had been sleeping on his rug. He almost knocked me over, and I sat on the bed and looked around. Cajun was so excited and kept licking my face. I tried to get him to calm down so I could take a better look at my new surroundings. Finally he jumped down and ran to one of my cousins. Everything was already in place as if my life had been magically transported from

Kenner to Washington without skipping a beat. My room was arranged exactly the same way it had been in Kenner. The desk and computer were against the wall. Derek Jeter and Harry Connick Jr. were in their spots so I could wake up to them each morning. I shuffled over to the closet and opened it. There were all my clothes complete with the new school uniforms I would have to wear to Brockton. Mama had thought of everything.

I didn't notice that everyone else had left. I guess they were giving me some time alone. Then I saw the window. But I can't see anything out it. The trees are too tall. I won't be able to watch any planes from here. Someone told me they don't let planes fly near the White House for security reasons. Just one more reason for me to hate this place. I stared at the mass of trees. I can't even see the sidewalk from here. The trees form a cocoon around this side of the

White House to protect it from public view. I feel trapped. I want to take a machete and cut out a hole so I can peek through and see what the rest of the world is doing. Life in the White House is going to be a life of isolation. No longer will I be in touch with the outside world. I get goose bumps thinking about it. Cajun runs back in the room and races around. He stops and looks up at me, cocking his head to the side and winking. It's like he has already discovered some secret about this place. Mrs. Wiggins comes back in the room.

"Andie Beth, you've got to go downstairs if you want anything to eat, it's going to be a long afternoon at the parade."

"Yes, ma'am. I'll be there in a minute."

"Okay, just follow the ramp down and the dining room is the second door on the right."

She scurries out. I've never seen her walk at regular speed. I pat Cajun on the head one last time and close the door. I walk out into the solarium and open one of the doors to the balcony. Looking around to make sure no one is watching me, I shuffle out. Looking up I see agents on the roof in gray coveralls, and looking down I see agents in suits walking around. This place is crawling with people, and everyone seems to know what they're doing except me. Hearing footsteps behind me, I turn around. It's Lauren and Michelle.

"We figured you might be hungry so we brought you a sandwich, chips and a Dr. Pepper®. Hope ham and cheese is okay. If not we can go back and get turkey."

"Thanks. Let's go sit on the couch. With these crutches I can't eat and stand up at the same time."

"A.B. can you believe you live here now?"

"Nope. It's freaking me out."

"I don't remember you guys having a big screen television. Where did that come from?"

"We didn't. Our old television is in the family room downstairs. None of this furniture is ours."

"Wow. It will be great for watching sports."

"For sure. Derek will look bigger and better. Trey might even look good on this television."

"How do you like your room?"

"Okay. It looks just like the one at home. I mean Kenner."

"It's bigger A.B. plus you have this room. It's like your own huge den. Can you imagine the parties you can have here? There's even room for dancing. I can see it now. A deejay over in the corner, and kids all over the place."

"One thing at a time. I'm having a hard time taking all this in. It's no big deal."

"It is a big deal A.B. It just hasn't sunk in yet. Wait until you really start looking around."

We are almost finished eating when Mrs. Wiggins returns.

"C'mon girls let's go. All the family has to be in the reviewing stand before the parade starts."

"Yes, ma'am."

The three of us head to the second floor where we catch up with the rest of the family. Once again Mrs. Wiggins guides us through the maze of elevators, doors, and hallways that make up the White House. We end up on a covered walkway leading to a reviewing stand in front it. She lines us up by families, and as each of us enters the reviewing stand our names are announced over a loudspeaker. People are lined up and down the street, and they applaud each of us as we enter. Trey and I enter last. Multiple agents surround me in case I trip. Can't have the President's Kid sprawled out on the concrete. We take our assigned seats on the second row. I sit on the end so I can stretch my legs. Because I will be doing a lot of getting up and down, I keep my crutches at my feet. The deep beat of a bass drum alerts us the first band is coming.

Soon we see Mama and Daddy walking in front of their limousine. They are holding hands and waving to the crowd. Everyone is cheering. There are signs in the crowd that say: Congratulations Mr. President and Nettles Is Our Man. Right behind them is the City of New Orleans float. The people on it are throwing out Mardi Gras beads and doubloons to the crowd. The float is divided in sections with each section representing a different part of New

Orleans. Matt and Heather are standing on the Metairie section which has a banner proclaiming: St. Martin's School – School of the First Kids: Trey and Andie Beth. The Kenner section at the end of the float says: Kenner: Home of The First Family Since 1980. Right behind the float is the St. Martin's Band. Trey and I stand and yell at all of them not realizing they can't hear us with the Plexiglas shield in front of us. After they pass Lauren and Michelle come stand beside me.

"Who was standing by Matt, A.B.?"

"Who do you think?"

"You mean that was Heather?"

"In the flesh."

After a few minutes Mama and Daddy come to the reviewing stand. We all stand when the loudspeaker announces their entrance. Daddy stops at my seat.

"What do you think of all this Buzzie?"

"It's something else Daddy. Did you see the New Orleans float?"

"Yes, before we jumped ahead in line, we talked with everyone on it. Oh, before I forget, Matt told me to give you this."

Daddy pulled a note out of his pocket. I recognized Matt's ragged handwriting. His writing wasn't much better than third graders. I carefully unfolded the note which read: *Congratulations A.B. Now it's official. You are now First Kid. So that's the end of us.* Congratulations A.B. After reading it I stuffed it down in my jacket pocket.

"Bad news Buzzie?"

"No, Daddy, just a final farewell. I'm going to sit by Grandpa for a while, okay?"

"Sure."

Daddy turned his attention back to Mama.

"Problem with Andie B., Gary?"

"Just something she will have to work out by herself. Matt gave me a note for her. She says it just says goodbye."

"And you think it says more."

"Don't have a clue. She's going to sit by Dad for awhile. Maybe he can help her sort it out. Let's watch the parade. There's the LSU band."

I plopped down in the seat beside Grandpa.

"Problem Bumble? I can tell by the look on your face that something or someone is bugging you."

"It's boys Grandpa. Stupid, stupid boys."

"Any one boy in particular? Trey? One of the cousins? Tell me who it is, and I will straighten them out."

"Matt."

"But he's history. You said so yourself. What has he gone and done now? I thought you two broke up on the ski trip?"

"We did sorta. But then we agreed it wouldn't be official until I moved. But since school started, he's been with Heather all the time. I mean most of the time he acted like I didn't even exist."

"So, what's the problem Bumble?"

"That is the problem Grandpa."

I pull the note out of my pocket and hand it to him. He reads it.

"A final farewell?"

"Like he's rubbing my nose in it. In other words, just in case you've forgotten, we've broken up. And there he was standing on the float with her."

"Well, it's his loss, and he's history. Believe me Bumble there will be plenty of boys at your new school."

"Yeah, but none of them will want to be within ten feet of me. Besides, who needs them? With all the agents around that's probably as close as they will be able to. I have more important things on my mind like dumping these stupid knee braces."

"I wouldn't worry about that. You will have your privacy. Concentrate on getting your knees in shape and keeping up your grades. I wouldn't be surprised if you don't meet another athlete."

"Thanks Grandpa. You always make me feel better."

"Look there's the Naval Academy midshipmen. We better clap loudly for them. That's where you'll be in another few years Bumble. Marching in formation."

"Think so Grandpa?"

"Know so Bumble."

We watched as a company from each of the military academies marched by. The midshipmen looked sharp in their navy blue dress uniforms. They looked the best of all. Grandpa was right. I would be there in two and a half years. All I had to do was keep my grades up, and recover from the accident. I had to pass a physical as part of the entrance requirements. If my knees didn't recover not only could I not play sports but I wouldn't be admitted to the academy.

After the parade all the family headed back inside the White House. Some of the adults walked around downstairs. I spotted Agent Landry.

"Agent Landry, can you point me in the direction to my room? I'm too embarrassed to ask anyone else."

"Sure, c'mon, I'll show you. Plus I've made you a map, complete with directions to the main places you have to go. I was going to wait and give it to you tomorrow, but if you girls want to go exploring, here it is."

"Thanks."

"And Miss Nettles?"

"Yes, sir?"

"Don't hesitate to ask anyone a question. It's easy to get lost in here. There's always someone around day or night. Remember, everyone here works for the President which means they all work for you."

"Thanks Agent Landry. I'll see you in the morning."

"You're welcome, Miss Nettles. Welcome to your new home."

"A.B. you have your own agent that you know by name?"

"Sure, Lauren. They assigned Agent Landry to me the day after the election. He even went on the ski trip with me."

"Yeah, about the ski trip?"

"We'll talk about it upstairs away from everybody else, okay?"

We went upstairs to the solarium. I really wanted to change clothes, but didn't just in case Mama came in and said there was somewhere else I had to go. Based on what she had told me yesterday, I thought the parade was the end of the festivities for me. Since I wasn't going to the inaugural balls, I was going to start the next semester of school tomorrow along with everyone else at Brockton. That meant no late night party as I had originally planned.

"If we're going to talk about the ski trip, we need to go in my room."

"Okay, we're here now. So what gives?"

"Yeah, was your accident part of your plan to skip the fancy balls or did it just happen?"

"Look, if I tell you guys this story you have to promise never to tell anyone. Rachel is the only person who knows, and she knows I will kill her if she tells."

I told them about what happened on the mountain. I had just finished my story when Mama poked her head in the door.

"I wondered where you were Andie B. We counted heads and realized you were missing. Girls, can you excuse us for a few minutes? I need to talk to Andie B. about a few things."

"Sure, Aunt Lynn. We'll catch up with you later A.B."

"Okay."

"Well, what do you think of your room? Sorry I missed seeing your first reaction to it, but Mrs. Wiggins said you were pleased."

"Yeah, it's alright. But you kicked Lauren and Michelle out of the room just to ask me that?"

"But don't you have somewhere to be? Some photographer to pose for?"

"Not until later tonight. Your daddy said Matt gave you a note. Something about a fond farewell?"

"Yeah, it's no big deal."

"Are you sure? You seemed pretty upset when you read it. Like you were going to cry."

"Like I said Mama. It's no big deal. Besides what difference does it make? I'm never going to see him again."

"It makes a difference if he hurt you."

"He's just a stupid immature boy. I'm giving up boys. I have more important things to do with my life. The first thing is getting out of this dress. Can I change now?"

"I don't see why not. You're home now, and you're not going anywhere else tonight."

"More like forever."

"Andie B. if you ever want to talk to me about boys, you can you know. Whether you believe it or not, I really was fifteen once."

"But things were different when you were a kid in the old days."

"Well, let me see. I changed schools in ninth grade when we moved to Corpus Christi, Texas, and your grandpa went to Viet Nam. Then he was back for my sophomore year and left again at the beginning of my junior year. He never came home alive."

"That's not what I meant Mama."

"Oh, you meant dating. Your grandma wouldn't let me date, but I had a boyfriend. I probably shouldn't tell you this, but I used to sneak out to one of my girlfriend's houses, one of the girls you're named after, Brenda, and I used to meet him there. If your grandma called and asked to speak to me, Brenda would tell her I was in the bathroom and couldn't talk. Kids didn't have cell phones then, so Mama couldn't call me directly."

"You lied to Grandma Josie?"

"For the entire three months I saw the guy. Then when I quit going to Brenda's house so much, your grandma started asking questions. I never did tell her what happened."

"But she figured it out."

"Probably. But she never told me, and I never admitted it. I don't want you to lie to me about boys Andie B."

352

"Well, there's nothing to lie about Mama. Matt and I have been friends all our lives. We were starting to move beyond that this fall. But now I'm here and he's in Kenner. End of story."

"And he'll always have a place in your heart Andie B. just like Nick will always have a place in mine."

"Did you ever tell Daddy about Nick?"

"Goodness no. Your father could care less about my old boyfriends. Nick is a part of my history, just like Matt will become a part of yours. Nothing but a story you can tell your daughter some day."

"No thanks. I'm not having any kids."

"Really, why not?"

"Because being a kid is the pits. Why would anyone want to have to go through this?"

Mama laughs.

"You will change your mind when you are older."

"Doubt it."

Mama laughs again.

"Now about tomorrow's schedule. Agent Landry will be with you in school like he was a St. Martins. Even though I want to go with you on your first day, your father has convinced me it isn't necessary. All your classes are with Rachel, and she'll meet you there. She has your locker number, and your books are in it. If you run into any problems, you tell Agent Landry."

"Yes, Mama."

"Any questions?"

"Just one."

"What's that?"

"Is it too late to back out?"

"Not unless you want to go to boarding school. Otherwise you're stuck."

"Can I change clothes now?"

"Yes, but not too sloppy. Jeans are fine but no sweats. Some of your daddy's staff members are around. From now on the only time you'll be able to wear sweats is when you are by yourself. Understood?"

"What a drag. Now I can't even dress comfortable up here."

"Too many staff members around Andie B. Here in your room or the second floor you can probably get by, but whenever you're out of the residence be careful."

"Yes Mama."

"Do you need help changing?"

"No Mama."

"Okay then. I'll see you in a little while."

Mama left the room closing the door behind her. I finally changed clothes. How lame. My guess is there wasn't even a guy named Nick. Mama made him up so I would think she went through some of the same things I go through. Yeah, right. I don't think she's clever enough to sneak out of the house especially for a boy. She had her nose buried in some book. I bet Nick is a character in a novel she read. Grandpa was off flying planes from an aircraft carrier, and Grandma Josie was running her antique store. Mama could do whatever she wanted. She was spoiled rotten. Grandma Josie told me so. Besides Matt and I were never girlfriend and boyfriend. We never made it that far. He never even kissed me. Oh well, if it made her feel better to tell that story then that's all that matters – at least to her.

Man, I was glad to be in jeans. I felt normal again. I went out to the solarium, and there was Grandma Josie. I started to ask her about what Mama had just told me but decided to wait

"Hi, Grandma Josie."

"Andie B. I wondered what happened to you. Why I've hardly seen you since we left Louisiana. It's been a big day for everybody, hasn't it?"

"Yes, Gram."

"That parade was something else, and your daddy's speech let the people know what he stands for."

"I know. I think it was his best speech ever."

"Well make sure you tell him that will you? He will appreciate hearing it from you. What do you think of your new home?"

"It's okay. I never realized how big it was."

"How's your room?"

"Like the one in Kenner only Lauren says it's bigger. I can't tell any difference."

"You better go sit down for a while Andie Beth or switch to a wheelchair. You've been standing for an awful long time today."

"Yes, ma'am."

I went to the doors to go outside to the balcony then changed my mind when I saw the rain blowing across it. At least it waited until after all the outside activities were finished. I stood there watching the rain beat against the windows not realizing Daddy had come up behind me until I felt his arm around my shoulder. I jumped when I felt his hand and almost lost my balance. He caught me before I fell.

"Sorry Buzzie, didn't mean to scare you. Wanted to see how you were doing. I've barely seen you all day."

"Daddy I didn't expect to see you. Figured you'd be too busy doing Presidential stuff."

"You better get used to seeing me from now on Buzzie. I've already told my staff I intend to eat supper each night at a reasonable hour with my family."

"That's going to be weird. Having you home for dinner each night."

"You know what's even weirder?"

"What?"

"That to get home I only have to walk part of the way around a building and up one flight of stairs. No commuting, no rush hour traffic."

"No real world."

"I wouldn't go that far. So what do think of this place?"

"I think if one more person asks me that question, I'm going to hit them."

"Well, don't let it be me. You could go to jail for hitting the President, and remember your mama and Trey fall into that category too."

"You mean I can't even hit Trey anymore?"

"Not when anyone is around."

"What a drag."

"Seriously, what do you think of your new home?"

"That it's big, and there are all these people around."

"Except up here. You won't have to worry about staff members. They have been told the third floor is off limits unless they're with your mama or me. So even though it may not seem like it, we will have privacy as a family. After today everything will settle down."

"That makes me feel better. Agent Landry made me a map so I wouldn't get lost. He's pretty cool Daddy. It's like he's always anticipating what I'm thinking."

"Sort of like a parent."

"Except he can't ground me, can he?"

"No, Buzzie he can't ground you. But he's here to protect you so if you do something careless he can tell your mama and she can ground you."

"Great. I can't win."

"Afraid not. But how long have you been standing? I think you need to sit for a while."

"That's what Grandma Josie said a while ago, but I was going out on the balcony when I saw the rain."

"Let's go down to the second floor family room. I think that's where your mama and the rest of the family are."

I turned around and there was a wheelchair.

"Hop in and I'll give you a ride."

"The wheelchair Daddy? I don't want to ride in the wheelchair. I hate it. I can walk."

"The wheelchair Buzzie."

"No Daddy. I can walk downstairs. There aren't even any steps. It's just a ramp. Don't make me ride in the chair.

"The wheelchair Andie B."

"Why Daddy? I hate this contraption."

"The wheelchair Andie Beth."

"Yes sir."

When Daddy pushed me in the family room, we were greeted by Mama, the grandparents, aunts, and uncles.

"Wondered where you wandered off to Gary? Thought maybe you were checking out your new office."

"No, I went looking for my daughter. Found her staring out the window at the rain."

"Supposed to turn to snow by morning. You may be stuck with us for a few more days."

"But how did you get her to ride in the wheelchair? All of us have all day to convince her to sit down, but I don't think she ever did."

"Why is everyone talking about me as if I'm not here?"

"Yes, everyone needs to quit picking on Andie B."

"I'm in the wheelchair because Daddy told me I had to be in it. It was either do as he said or risk getting grounded for talking back."

"Good choice Andie B."

"Thanks Mama."

"Andie B. gets that same determined look on her face that Gary gets when he's trying to prove a point."

"That look helped elect him. That look plus the voters of Texas and California."

"Well Bumble's look is going to have her on the softball field in April and marching with the Corps of Midshipmen in two and a half years. Right Bumble?"

"Right grandpa."

"I believe the part about the Corps of Midshipmen, but I'm not so sure about softball season this year. I think maybe she ought to sit out softball so her knees can fully recover."

"It doesn't matter what any of us think. If her therapy goes well, and the doctor gives her medical clearance, Andie B. will on the field on opening day."

"Now pitching for the Brockton Eagles, number 45 Andie Beth Nettles, otherwise known as First Kid."

"And all of us will be there to watch."

"Wouldn't miss it for the world."

"Mr. President dinner is served in the family dining room. The youngsters are eating in the solarium."

"Am I eating with the kids or you guys?"

"With us of course. You've been promoted to the grown up table Andie B."

Trey and Sam came in as we were heading to the dining room. I counted twenty-four chairs around it. While we were eating, I found out Trey and Sam spent the rest of the afternoon hanging out with some of the LSU students who came to the inauguration. I never even talked to the St. Martin's kids. They were heading home right after the parade. That figures. After dinner everyone scattered to dress for the balls. All the adults were going plus Trey and Sam. Mama even convinced Grandma Josie to go.

Once they left I grabbed my crutches and went back upstairs. No way was I staying in the wheelchair. The solarium was almost empty. The younger kids were already in bed. Some of the boy cousins were playing Madden Football ®on the television. It was weird watching the game on such a big screen. Lauren and Michelle were talking by themselves in a corner. I walked over to them.

I looked around and here came Mama, Daddy, and all the adults. For a minute or two I wished I was going with them. Then I remembered the turquoise dress and quickly changed my mind. The aunts and uncles were talking to their kids. I walked over to Mama and Daddy. Mama was wearing a sparkly royal blue dress.

"Mama you look beautiful. You sound like Mama, but you sure don't look like her."

"Why thank you Andie B. You would have looked beautiful in your dress too you know?"

"Not me, Mama. This is about as formal as I ever want to get."

The grandparents came over to say goodnight. I had never seen Grandma Josie so dressed up. I kept looking back and forth from her to Mama. Man, they look a lot alike. Mama and Daddy kissed me on the cheek.

"Lights out at 9:30 Andie B. School tomorrow."

"Aw, Mama. Bedtime isn't until 10:00. Besides I won't see Lauren and Michelle for a long time. Please Mama. I'm not a kid any more, you know?"

"No extensions, 9:30. Lauren and Michelle have an early flight so they are going to bed early too."

"Man, here we go. Haven't been here one day, and you're already changing the rules. Great."

"Just for that your night has ended. In your room now Andie B. And don't come out until morning."

"Ma Ma"

"I said now Andie Beth. Now move young lady."

"Yes ma'am. Good night everybody."

As I walked down the hall to my room, I heard the adults talking.

"Lynn, calm down it's over. She's gone to bed. We have a big night ahead of us. Don't let this ruin it."

"She pushes my buttons with her arguing and whining about every little detail. Just once I wish I could ask her to do something, and she would do it without questioning me."

"Lynn she's a teenager. That's what teenagers do. Relax. Take a deep breath. By morning it will have blown over."

"Mama, was I this bad?"

"I don't remember Lynn. I was practically raising you by myself while your Daddy was gone. But I remember we had our own war going on at home."

"Lynn what your mother is trying to say in a nice way is yes you were that bad, but she survived and so will you. Some day you and Buzzie will be as close as you and your mother are now."

"I don't think I'll live that long Gary."

"Now that I recall, I do remember saying that quite a few times while you were in high school, Lynn. There were quite a few times when I was glad there was only one of you."

"See Sweetie and look how you turned out. Buzzie is just going through a phase. Think of it like the terrible two's only this time you don't have to potty train her. I knew I could make you laugh. Now come on let's go kick up our heels."

"You're right. I'm ready for some fun."

When I made it into my room, Cajun jumped up from his rug and ran out the door. I slammed it behind him. There she goes again. Why did I have to have the bossiest mother in the universe? Why me? Lights out at 9:30? What does she think I am, nine years old? She's probably out there right now telling them how she doesn't understand why she got stuck with me. Well, it goes both ways lady. I dive on the bed and pound my fists on the pillow. There's not even a place around here where I can go by myself to think. Daddy talks about privacy. Yeah right. I bet my room is bugged. After I take off the knee braces, I take a shower. Everything was already set up in the bathroom including my favorite brand of shampoo. After my shower I turned on my laptop.

"Rachel, are you out there. Why aren't you on facebook®? Please talk to me. I could use a friend right now. You said you weren't going to the balls. Where are you? C'mon Rach answer me. Aw, forget it. I'm going to bed."

Cajun scratches at the door. I let him back in, find my copy of Sports Illustrated®, and climb in bed. It's almost 9:30, but I'm not turning out the light. Besides who's going to know? At 9:30 the light goes out. I don't believe it. She even went so far as to put a timer on my bedside lamp. She may have won this battle, but the war isn't over yet.

Chapter 10

First Day at Brockton Part I

"**R**achel, are you out there"?

I still haven't figured out the phone system, so I'm on the computer tonight for a little while. You didn't tell me this school gave so much homework. I've got a question about the biology homework.

"Where are you"?

This morning my alarm went off at 6:00. I have to get up a half hour earlier for school here, because of the long commute. Checking the lamp, I saw that it wasn't on a timer; the light bulb was just loose. Even after I turned it on, this room was still dark. I put on my knee braces and got dressed in my dorky school uniform: navy blue skirt and blazer with a white blouse. This is not what I am used to wearing to school. St. Martins didn't make us wear uniforms every day once we got out of the lower school. I pulled my hair back in a ponytail, but couldn't find a navy blue scrunchie. Oh well, a purple one will just have to do. I looked for my backpack, and couldn't find it. I could have sworn I saw it yesterday. There was a new one on the seat of the rocking chair with a note attached to it: A new backpack for your new school. Be careful using your crutches. Love Mama.

I opened the door, and Cajun went racing out. This dog seemed to know where he was going all the time. How did he figure this place out so quickly? I grabbed the crutches.

Hobbling into the den I saw Daddy sitting at the table with his cup of coffee just like we were still back in Kenner.

"Morning Buzzie. How was your first night in your new room?"

"Fine Daddy."

"Got some muffins here. They're blueberry, your favorite. Your mama told me to make sure you eat something. It will be a long time before lunch."

About that time Mama came in. She was dressed in a suit as if she was going off to work.

"You're not going to school with me are you Mama?"

"No, Andie B. I told you yesterday you're on your own."

"I just wondered. You're so dressed up."

"Well, I'll be dressed up every day. Your daddy and I have to make a lot of public appearances. Plus I have my own office and staff to run."

"Oh, okay."

"Did you look outside? It snowed last night. So be really careful on the sidewalks."

"Yes, Mama."

"It's time for you to head downstairs to meet Agent Landry. Let me check you out. Andie B. why a purple scrunchie? Navy blue would have looked much better."

"Couldn't find one Mama."

"Well make sure you find one before tomorrow. I know you have plenty of them."

"Have a good day Buzzie. Now you'd better get going."

"You, too, Mr. President."

"Andie B. come straight to my office and check in right after school. Agent Landry will point you in the right direction. You've got physical therapy this afternoon."

"Yes, Mama."

Two guys came in and Mama said they would help me navigate the White House during our first week here. Mama and Daddy continued their conversation after I left.

"I feel like I did the day I sent her off to kindergarten for the first time."

"She'll be fine. Besides, she's got Rachel to show her the ropes. She's been at Brockton as long as Andie B. was at St. Martins."

I passed lots of people on our way out of The White House. It was just a little after 7 a.m. and already the place was crawling. They all had these name tags on around their necks which also said what their jobs were. I tried to read a couple as I walked by but most of them didn't make sense. I did find out that the two guys helping me find my way around were interns assigned to Mama's staff.

Agent Landry met me at the entrance.

"Using the crutches full time now I see. I figured you'd find a way."

"How did you know I'd even try?"

"Because I've seen you in action."

"Well, she's not too thrilled about it. But I guess it would look bad if I went from using crutches at the inauguration to a wheelchair on the first day of school."

"She being the First Lady."

"You got it."

"And you don't think she'll change her mind tomorrow."

"Nope, she's too busy to be bothered with little old me."

"What about the President?"

"He told me whatever happens is on me. He's trying to understand, unlike her. Besides he's got a country to run. Where is this school? Out in the middle of nowhere?"

"The Virginia suburbs. There are a lot of government kids who go to it. It's only a couple of miles from the Pentagon."

"Can we ride by the Pentagon? I've never seen it."

"On the way home. If you're late for school on your first day, you'll be grounded, and I'll be fired. There will be other agents at school with you like it was in Kenner only more. But I'll still be the one sitting outside your classroom."

"Good. Take good notes will you? Especially in English and world history. Those classes are so boring."

"You're on your own in that department."

"Then what good are you?"

"To protect you. And don't you ever forget it."

"Who would want to do anything to me?"

"You might be surprised. There are a lot of evil people out there Miss Nettles who would love to hurt you."

"Yeah right."

"Just be careful. Make sure you can always see at least one of us."

"Great. So agents are going to be in the hallways all the time?"

"From now on you have your own entourage."

"Do we really have to do this? I'm not so sure I want to go to this school."

"Nervous, huh?"

"Nervous, me? More like scared out of my gourd. I think I'm in over my head. The First Lady has put me in this school with all these brainy kids and you and I both know that I'm a jock not a brain. She thinks I'm smart. I know I'm not. I do my best thinking while dribbling the basketball not while sitting in some boring classroom. Let's go back to the White House. I'll tell her I have cramps or something."

"Can't do that."

"Why not? I thought you said you worked for me. If I'm your boss, then why can't we go back? I am so not ready for this."

"I work for the President. He says you go to school. You go to school."

"Big help you are."

"Sorry, just following orders."

"I really don't want to do this."

The ride to Brockton took almost forty - five minutes. The school had a big gate around it complete with a security guard who waved us in. I felt like we were going to a top secret military base. Agent Landry drove the Blazer to the front entrance where Rachel was waiting. Several others opened the doors. They were trying to appear casual, but they didn't blend in with the crowd.

I hesitated. I really was scared. I looked around at my new surroundings. There was a banner strung across the hallway: *Welcome New Students*. Everywhere around me kids were standing in groups of three or four talking. They were all strangers to me. Little robots dressed in their identical school uniforms. Everyone had on nametags. The color of your nametag indicated what grade you were in. Sophomore tags were white. Most of the kids I saw had on white tags. I'd have to remember to ask Rachel what the colors were for freshmen, juniors and seniors. The floor smelled of fresh wax, as if it had just been buffed this morning. Already the shine was gone due to the tromping of snow laden shoes.

"So, how is it going with the crutches A.B.?"

"Easier. Fortunately I didn't have to walk through much snow with them.. By the way, where were you last night? I finally gave up when you didn't come on facebook®."

"Watching the inaugural balls on t.v. plus babysitting my little brothers. They wanted to switch to the Disney™ channel. Besides, what were you doing on facebook®? We have telephones you know? "

"I know. I just haven't figured out the system. I think I may have to go through an operator which means my parents will know every phone call I make. They took my cell away. Said it was for security reasons."

"Hadn't thought of that. Well here's your locker right next to mine. You owe me big time. I had to lay it on thick with the Dean of Girls to convince her to persuade the junior nerd who had this locker to move out. I told the dean your locker needed to be near mine due to your temporary disability. We couldn't have the President's daughter having to bend down to one of those low lockers now could we? Anyway, it worked and she bought it. Usually only juniors and seniors get the top row."

Rachel handed me the combination to the lock already on my locker. When I opened it, it smelled of disinfectant mixed with Lemon Pledge®. The smell gagged me. All six textbooks were lined up. Someone had even stuck a mirror on the inside of the door.

"So, how did you manage the top row before I got here?"

"Let's just say there's a certain junior football player who is passing geometry thanks to my mathematical genius."

"You cheated?"

"Ssh. Keep your voice down. Not exactly. I just assisted him with his homework which as you shall discover counts a lot at this school. He traded me his locker for "A" homework papers during football season. He passed geometry. I don't have to bend down on my knees to get a book out of my locker."

"I didn't think you were that clever."

"There's a lot about me that you don't know. You're on my turf now, Andie B. Welcome to the dog-eat-dog world of Washington. Our parents aren't the only politicians around."

"So what books do I need first?"

"Here's the drill. Mornings are geometry, English and world history. Afternoons are Latin, biology and phys ed. Just like you had in Metairie. Only difference is we eat lunch early after world history. Stick a candy bar in your backpack in the morning. After biology you'll be starving, and Coach Garvin won't let us eat in the gym."

"Lead on."

We headed slowly down the hallway. The crutches made for an awkward trip but fortunately Brockton is laid out like St. Martins. Some of the kids stared at me as we were walking. Rachel introduced me to several of her friends. There are separate wings for each major subject area. Overall the school is twice the size of St. Martins. We made it to geometry.

Agent Landry looked up and winked as we walked in the classroom, and I met the teacher Miss Frye. She didn't look much older than us. Once again Rach had come through and convinced the person sitting next to her to move so I could sit beside her. I'm not sure about all this togetherness. She had gone to an awful lot of trouble to clear people away from us. I was beginning to feel like a leper. Miss Frye welcomed me and several other new students. This was the first day of the new semester. I was relieved to discover that our class in Metairie had used the same book and was further along than they were here. At least for the first couple of weeks, I would be repeating material we had already gone over.

Sitting in class I found myself zoning out. I spent most of the hour looking around at everyone else. I guess Grandma Josie was right. These kids looked just like the kids in Metairie. The only difference was everyone was dressed alike. Rach had stuck a map of the school in my geometry book in case we managed to get separated so I studied it for awhile. Of course the agents had already visited the school, and with so many of them around my chances of getting lost were slim to none. Rach was eagerly answering questions. It was obvious to me that she was the one the teacher called on when everyone else was stumped. Although I am good in geometry, it is not my favorite subject. But I'm no competition for her. I looked up from the map, and Miss Frye had Rachel doing a problem on the board and explaining it to the class. This was different. Our teachers at St. Martins never made us go to the board. The teacher gave out the homework assignment just before the bell rang. If I just hadn't thrown away all my papers from St. Martins, all I would have had to do would be to copy it over.

We headed to English. It was right around the corner from geometry. Once again, Rach introduced me to the teacher, Miss Penrod. This school must get all their teachers right out of college.

"Welcome to Brockton, Andie Beth. Rachel told me your class in Louisiana was reading *Moby Dick* too, so you already have a copy of it. What chapter were you on?"

"Four ma'am. We started it right after Christmas."

"We're starting it today. So the first week or two may be a little repetitious for you. But if you have any questions, feel free to ask."

"Thank you ma'am. I will."

In this class I was the only newcomer. This school groups you by grades and aptitude. You may be with a different group in each class. St. Martins wasn't like that. I was with the same twenty kids all day except for fifth and sixth periods. English is not Rach's strongest subject.

I could tell by how quiet she was acting. Miss Penrod

called on me a couple of times, and I answered correctly.

If I'm ahead in every class, the next two weeks should be

a breeze. The teacher gave out the homework assignment:

read chapter one of *Moby Dick*. So far, batting 1000. This

school seems backward to me. I've been ahead in both

classes so far.

"Man, Rach you were right about the homework."

"I told you A.B. There's homework in every class every

night and weekends there's usually English and world his-

tory reading."

"So when do you geniuses socialize?"

"I thought you weren't interested in partying."

"It's not that I'm not interested. It's just that I hope you don't mind if I bring along ten or twenty extra people with me. Or perhaps you didn't notice the guys in the suits?"

"I noticed. But you forget we're used to that around here. The last President's son went here for his junior and senior year. Also, some of the foreign embassy kids usually have some sort of bodyguard hanging around."

"Well, it's weird to me."

"Not to us. Like I said welcome to Washington."

World History is my least favorite subject next to biology. But I was surprised to see a male teacher. All the teachers I had seen so far were women. Mr. Brown, who all the students called Colonel, was a retired Army officer. He passed out a detailed outline for the entire semester which included test dates, term paper dates, and book report dates. The Colonel required a book report each month plus three term papers. This guy must think we're college students. I was already lost five minutes into the class. My luck had run out.

"What grade did you get in this guy's class last semester, Rach?"

"An A of course."

"But the requirements are stricter this time right?"

"Nope, the same. I told you A.B. this school is hard. Everybody that graduates from here goes to college. That's why they call it Brockton Preparatory School. It prepares you for college. Get it?"

"I get it. But you know who you sound like?"

"Who?"

"My mother. She said practically the same thing."

"That's scary. Let's go to lunch. The cafeteria is on the other side of campus. First, we'll stop by our lockers and pick up our other three books."

"Okay."

I followed Rach as she maneuvered through the hallways. It was hard concentrating on not falling down as well as trying to remember where I was. The smell of spaghetti greeted us long before we made it to the cafeteria entrance. As we entered, Rachel gave me my student identification card.

"You show your i.d. card at the cash register A.B. It has a number on it, and your parents get a bill each month for how many lunches you eat. It beats having to worry about lunch money."

"So, is the food edible? St. Martin's food was dreadful."

"Well, you've got three choices: Italian, full meal, or sandwich. Most of the time I stick to the sandwich line except on Fridays when they have pizza in the Italian line."

"Sounds good to me."

We went through the sandwich line, and I grabbed a ham and cheese sandwich, Fritos®, and a Dr. Pepper®. St. Martins hadn't been this good. It was either the hot lunch or brown bag it. The lunchroom had picnic tables instead of regular ones. There were even some booths along one side, but you told me those were reserved for seniors. I couldn't believe that you made that freshman carry my tray.

"Hey kid. Carry this tray over to that third picnic table?"

"Rach."

"Kid, do you know who she is? She's the President's Kid. It'll make you a big shot with all your friends this afternoon. You can tell them you carried Andie Beth Nettles lunch tray to her table."

"Uh, sure. Whatever you say."

We both started laughing. Somehow, I think you've evolved from Indira Gandhi to General Patton the way you bark out orders. But what really blows my mind is the way people obey them. That kid didn't even blink an eye. He just did what you told him. I saw a side of you today I hadn't seen before. It was great meeting Carly, Jonas, Pia, Parker, and Eagan. But have you ever noticed that none of your friends have normal names? Back at St. Martins there were three Ashley's, two Lisa's, and four Katie's plus three Shawn's, two Jason's, and four Chad's. So far at Brockton I haven't seen two people with the same name.

"Hey guys, this is my best friend A.B."

"Glad to meet you."

"Same here."

"So what do think of Brockton so far?"

"Lots more homework than I'm used to and we've still got two classes to go."

"Get used to it. Besides some of the teachers give time in class to work on it. Just not today since it's the first day of the new semester."

"Aw, Jonas now you've gone and ruined it. I had her convinced that all we did was study around here."

"Yeah, right."

"A.B. don't let your best friend snow you. We have plenty of time for fun."

"That's a relief. At least we were ahead of you in geometry and English in Louisiana."

"Well, how was your first night at the White House? It must be weird living there."

"It was quiet Carly. Except my mom and I got into it right before she and Daddy headed to the inaugural balls. She thinks I should go to bed earlier here, because I have to get up a half hour earlier."

"Yeah, Rach told us about your ski trip and this cool guy named Ryan that she hung out with before you had your accident. How much longer on the crutches?"

"Until the middle of March. Is she still talking about that guy? That's all I've heard since the day she met him. But I'll be on the softball team in April."

"If you mom lets you play this season. From what my mom says, she may not let you."

"If the doctor gives me the okay, I'm playing. I don't care what she says. Do all you guys play sports?"

"Yes. Jonas and I play basketball and baseball; Parker plays football and baseball; Pia plays volleyball and soft-ball; and Carly plays basketball and softball."

"I play shortstop. Pia plays left field, and you know Rach will be your catcher. I hope your knees get okay. Our pitchers are lousy. The entire pitching staff graduated last year. The only senior on our team is the first baseman."

"Well, I want to play. I'm going to have physical therapy every day at the White House after school, and Daddy is fixing up a room where I can start throwing to a target."

"Awesome."

"Well, there's the bell. See you guys later in biology. We're off to the world of Latin translation."

"We'll see you in biology A.B. We all have bio and phys ed together."

"Great."

Before you could find another freshman, Eagan took my tray. I'm glad this is my last semester of Latin. Translating Caesar is so boring. Mama says I have to take French for the next two years. I guess I might as well get used to taking classes that I don't like. The Naval Academy only gives you one elective per semester. They dictate to you all your other classes.

Mrs. Heard was the oldest teacher I had seen so far. From what you told me she had been teaching at Brockton forever. Something about how she wanted to retire, but they couldn't find anyone to replace her. She's a lot older than our parents.

"Andie Beth, we are glad to have you joining us. Rachel has told us about her visits with you in Louisiana."

"Yes, ma'am. We've been friends ever since we were eight years old."

You were only a few pages farther along in the book than we were so it would be easy to stay caught up. She taught the class like my former teacher did. She called on someone to read a sentence, and then translate it. So, you're always reading ahead in case you are called on, but then if the original person messes up the translation, she calls on someone else. I constantly went back and forth. Fortunately, she didn't call on me. Guess she wanted to give me a break since it was my first day in class. When she gave the homework assignment out at the end of class, I finally figured out that you go over the homework each day as most of the day's lesson.

Biology was our last real class. It was way on the other side of campus. You explained this to me by saying they wanted to separate the science wing from the rest of the campus in case they blew up the chemistry lab. Before we arrived at class, I had already guessed that it would be a male teacher. You're right. Mr. Sewell does look like a mad scientist.

"Miss Nettles. Welcome to biology."

That's all he said. He's the only teacher that calls everyone Miss or Mr. He dances all over the room. Guess that's how he keeps everyone awake late in the day. I looked around and the crowd from lunch was there.

You looked bored throughout the whole class. I glanced over at your notes and you were writing Ryan, Ryan, Ryan all over a sheet of paper. Good grief. You're still hung up on the mystery guy.

In biology you used a different book than we did in Kenner. I was really lost. Some of the stuff Mr. Sewell went over made no sense at all. He passed out an outline with all the test dates, plus he wants a term paper too. Well, I can see what I'll be doing all semester.

I looked over and you were still writing. Then you suddenly snapped back into reality and raised your hand to answer a question. But I love all this science stuff. At least in science and math you have a problem and a solution. It's not like all the boring books we have to read in English. School is a drag. I just want to get out on the basketball court. Then I looked down and realized that wasn't going to happen. Not for awhile anyway.

After biology we headed to phys ed. I saw the gym ahead of us.

"A.B. you don't mind if I go on ahead since I've got to change do you?"

"No, go on. I just go straight ahead right?"

"Yeah, we'll all be together for a little while since it's the first day of the semester."

You ran ahead. It was the first time I had been on my own all day. It felt sort of weird, but free. Even though I appreciated all your help today, I realized I don't want to totally depend on you. I'm used to being independent, and I've got to stay that way. As I got closer to the entrance to the gym, a guy came up behind me and almost knocked me over.

"Sorry. I didn't see you. I'm late for class. I'm new here. Where's the gym?"

"It's straight ahead. I'm headed there too."

"I'm Ryan. You need any help with you books or anything?"

"I'm Andie Beth. Okay, but won't you be late?"

"Aw. Who cares? They can't do anything to me on my first day. You look awfully familiar."

"Yeah, like you really don't know who I am."

"Don't have a clue, but I've seen you somewhere before. Well gotta run. See you around. What did you say your name was?"

Before I could tell him, I was at the door where a teacher was standing.

"You must be Andie Beth. I'm Coach Shine, the softball coach."

"Glad to meet you ma'am. I'm your new pitcher."

"That's what Rachel tells me. You stats from last year speak for themselves, but what about your knees?"

"The orthopedists and physical therapists think I'll be ready. I'll have physical therapy every day after school at the White House, and the staff is renovating a room so I can start throwing from a chair to a target."

"That sounds great. As you may have heard, we desperately need you. I'm afraid last year's graduation took most of our team."

"Yes, ma'am. Rach and Carly were telling me about it at lunch."

"C'mon into my office. Coach Garvin and I have figured out your schedule for this class."

I went in Coach Shine's office. It was littered with softballs and papers and there was a trophy behind her desk of a golden bat. I couldn't read the plate on it, but figured it might be something she won in college.

"Coach Garvin and I were trying to figure out to grade you for the time you won't be available to participate in class. So we called your coach at St. Martins, and he said you kept statistics for him."

"Yes, ma'am. He also gave me credit for how many repetitions I did in physical therapy. The therapist gave him a report each week."

"Well, then that's what we'll do here. You'll keep the drill stats. At the basketball games you'll keep the individual stats on each player. That will free me up to pay more attention to the class and the games. Give these numbers to your physical therapist and have them contact me. That way I can keep track of your physical progress. Didn't I read somewhere that you have a dog?"

"Yes, ma'am. His name is Cajun. But what does that have to do with phys ed?"

"Find a place where you can throw his ball, and start throwing it at least ten times a day. It's never too early to start spring training. Your therapy will help your knees, but you don't want to lose the muscle tone in your arms. It's been a month since you've shot a basketball."

"Yes, ma'am and I miss it. I'm itching to get back on the court."

"Well, rehab takes a while. I hurt my acl during my junior year in college, but came back to win the batting title my senior year."

"Is that what the golden bat is for?"

"Yes."

"Where did you go to college?"

"San Diego State. Married a Marine and ended up here in D.C."

"Awesome."

"Well, we need to get out to the court. Welcome aboard Andie Beth."

"Thanks ma'am."

"Call me coach or Coach Shine."

"Only if you call me Andie B. Otherwise it has to be ma'am. Parents orders."

"Then Andie B. it is. For the rest of the week you can sit in the bleachers and watch practice until you start putting the numbers to the faces. Learn the players and their positions. I'll put you to work Monday afternoon."

"Yes, Coach Shine."

We left her office, and I went to the first row of the bleachers and sat down. Agent Landry was by the gym door with the wheelchair folded up beside him. The gym is bigger than St. Martins, and fancier. The guys were all in a group down by one basket, and the girls were at the opposite end. Basketball players had on their practice

uniforms while non - players had on shorts and tee shirts.
Coach Garvin, the head coach, moved to center court.

"Okay, people today we start a new semester. But for most of you it's just a continuation of the year. We've got four new students joining us. New students when I call out your name raise your hand so the rest of the class knows who you are: Nettles, Radiker, Gines, and Kessler. Make sure all you old people introduce yourselves to the new people. We're wasting time here. Let's practice."

I was the only new girl in the class.

My guess was right. Kessler was Ryan. I saw you looking at him. You have this funny way of cocking your head when you want to get someone's attention. It's sort of like come on over here - now. I figured after I left you went over and talked to him.

How many basketball games did you say you had won? Maybe it was because you had come off a long weekend, but your team looked sorry. Some of the players seemed to be just going through the motions. I wanted to get out there and start shooting some three pointers to liven up the place. You don't even communicate with each other. These stupid knees. I want to play. I want to light a fire under you guys.

Coach Shine told me I could leave when class ended. No sense in hanging around for the rest of practice since I couldn't play. Agent Landry met me at the door. We didn't talk. When we got to the main entrance of the school, there was the Blazer. It was the first time today that I realized how much it had been snowing. Two other agents helped me into the back seat while he got in the driver's seat.

"You look in pretty good shape after surviving your first day at the new school."

"I guess. But this place gives twice as much homework as St. Martins."

"You'll get used to it."

"Easy for you to say. Hey, don't forget you promised we'd drive by the Pentagon."

"We're on our way there now."

As we neared the Pentagon, I could see it looming in the distance. Agent Landry drove around the perimeter so I could see how big the building is. It's a lot larger than it looks in pictures. One of the other agents with us had worked there, and he quoted all sorts of statistics about how many offices were there and how different parts of the building house the different branches of the services. He also told me that when we're seniors our government class will probably take a tour of it. I don't know if I want to wait that long. Maybe I'll get Daddy to arrange a special tour for me. For some reason just thinking about all the decisions made there fascinates me. After circling the building, we headed back home to the White House. Somehow, saying home and White House in the same sentence just doesn't seem right. It's like I'm living out someone else's life.

Chapter 11

First Day at Brockton Part II

We drove up to the South Portico driveway where two agents rushed to open my door. One snatched my backpack, and one helped me with the crutches. It seemed like this took place in less than thirty seconds. It was like I was a football being passed from player to player. By this time someone else was behind the wheel of the Blazer, and Agent Landry was standing behind me. My backpack was on its way inside. People were rushing around just like they were this morning.

"The First Lady called to remind you to come straight to her office."

"Great idea, but I'm not sure where it is. Guess I need to know since this will be my daily ritual, right?"

"Just remember bear right to the First Lady and left to the President."

"What?"

"When you come in this entrance, if you are going to see the First Lady, follow the first hallway to the right. If you are going to see the President, follow the first hallway to the left. Right takes you to the East Wing and left takes you to the West Wing."

"And if I go straight?"

"Straight takes you to the elevator up to the residence."

"I got it. But most of the time I'll be going right. Mama, I mean the First Lady, has this dumb rule about me checking in with her right after school each day like I'm a little kid."

"Well, you had better get going. She knows you're in the building. If I know her, she's liable to come looking for you if you don't get there soon."

"Yeah, you're right. She's probably got me on a timer. I can hear her now. Andie B. why on earth does it take you so long to get from the entrance to my office? You know how busy I am. Now from now on you have exactly five minutes to get here or you're grounded."

"She wouldn't do that to you. Well, get going before you get in trouble. See you in the morning."

"Bye."

Following Agent Landry's instructions, I walked down the hallway to the right. People were scurrying by me. I came to a checkpoint where an agent was sitting. He was checking people's I.D. tags when they walked through. When I approached his desk, he waved me through without asking any questions or even speaking to me. I continued down the hallway past two more similar checkpoints. Again, the agents just waved me through. A few yards past the final one, I was greeted by a young woman whom I remembered seeing a few times at our house in Kenner.

"Andie Beth. Good you're here. It's me, Jamie Dyess. I'm the First Lady's personal assistant. Let me show you to her office."

"Thanks ma'am I was on my way. I just didn't realize how big this place is."

"Please, don't call me ma'am. It makes me feel old. I'm not even twenty five yet. You can call me Jamie or Ms. D."

"Then call me Andie B. because if you call me Andie Beth then Parent's Rules are I have to call you ma'am."

"Okay Andie B. You've got it. The First Lady has gathered all her staff in the conference room. She wants them all to meet you at one time. Then she said you've got physical therapy up the hall at the medical office. You passed it on your way here. But I'm the person you'll check in with every day after school. Some of the time you'll get a few minutes alone with the First Lady. She's pretty insistent about wanting this time set aside, but as you know it may not always work. If she's out of the White House when you come home from school, I'll phone ahead and let Agent Landry know so you don't have to waste a trip all the way down here. Physical therapy is five days a week. Your shorts and tee shirt are already at the medical office so you can change there. That way you don't have to go to the residence first. Am I going too fast? If so just let me know."

"No, I've got it. But do you ever stop to breathe?"

"Not if I can help it."

We both started laughing.

Mama's offices consist of a series of frosted glass walls dividing individual desks. No one was sitting at them. I guess they were already in the conference room in the back next to an office which I assumed was hers. The Conference Room door was closed. Ms. D. knocked, and then pushed it open. Twelve women and a couple of men sat around a long, highly polished table. Several others sat on couches and chairs scattered around the room.

As soon as we entered the room, I tried to stand up straighter and adjust my blazer and blouse. By now I was looking and feeling pretty wrinkled. Ms. D. motioned for me to go to the front of the room by Mama, and as I approached her I could see an empty chair on her right. Mama had been addressing the group, but stopped talking.

"Good job, Jamie. I see you found her."

"She was almost here ma'am. I didn't have to go far."

Now I see why Ms. D. didn't want me calling her ma'am. She had to reserve that expression for when she was reporting to Mama. Tuck this piece of information away in your brain, Andie B. If you want to make Jamie D. feel old, just ma'am her a few times. It will drive her nuts, and she'll start looking in the mirror as much as Mama does.

When I got to the table, Mama leaned over and kissed me on the cheek. She had never done that before. Our family only does that when we are saying goodbye or good night not as a greeting. Then the bell went off in my head again. She has to portray the image of the loving, caring Mother. It's part of her new role as First Lady. Looking around the table, I noticed that everyone had a cup of coffee or a soft drink can in front of them. Before I could think about it, someone handed me a can of Dr. Pepper®. Mama had that quirky smile on her face as if to say to me: See I thought of everything. If I hadn't been so thirsty, I would have gagged.

"Staff, this is my daughter Andie Beth or Andie B. as most people call her. I brought her here with us today for several reasons. First and foremost, so you could all meet her and recognize her. She will be checking in here every afternoon after school so get used to seeing her around. Second, I am putting out a strict directive that nothing about her goes to the media without being cleared through Jamie or myself. My daughter's life is off limits. I want her to be able to move around the White House without worrying that everything she says to someone will be in tomorrow's newspaper. So, if you ask her how her day at school was, and she says awful, I don't want to see that as a headline in the Washington Post™ tomorrow. Have I made myself clear on that point? This is especially true in regards to her rehabilitative therapy. Any leaks to the press are grounds for immediate dismissal. Last, I want you all to understand that my family comes first in my life. I was a wife and Mother for many years before I became First Lady. Even though I will be making a lot of demands on all of you, especially over these first few months, I expect you to take time to spend with your families. If you have a family problem and need time off to resolve it, I expect you to come forward and let Jamie know about it. Because on this side of the White House, that's what we're all about. If we can't take care of our own families, how do we expect to take care of a nation of families?"

Everyone clapped. There she was again making speeches. Everything she said sounded great to her audience, but in reality I doubted it. Of course, as long as I'm the perfect little angel she was making me out to be, we won't have any problems. Yeah right. Smile Andie B., smile. All these people are looking at you.

"Ladies and gentlemen I present to you my daughter, Andie B. If anyone has any questions for her, now is the time to ask them. When you do, tell her your name, and what you do."

I started to stand up, but Mama waved me back down. They asked me a whole lot of questions. One of them asked me what my favorite t.v. show was. I told her I only got to watch t.v. on weekends, and most of the time I just watched sports. Another one asked me what time I went to bed. This prompted another speech from Mama.

"The President and I are very strict with Andie B. On weeknights, including Sunday, she is allowed no t.v. after 7 p.m., and her bed time is 10 p.m. although sometimes we shorten it or lengthen it depending on the individual circumstances."

"Andie B. do you think of your parents as strict?"

"Yes."

"Are your friend's parents as strict as yours? I mean I know you kids talk about things like this."

"Some of them are. But I don't have a choice. Unless I want to hear the two words that every teenager dreads."

"I know what those two words are Andie B., but you tell them."

"You're grounded."

Everyone started laughing again. I glanced over and Ms. D. was tapping her watch as a signal that the meeting should end.

"Okay folks. Andie B. has to head to physical therapy, so we'll let her leave, and we'll finish our meeting."

Once again she pecked me on the cheek. I guess that was my signal to leave. I headed for the door where Ms. D. was waiting. At this point it dawned on me that this was all a show. Mama hadn't spoken to me directly during the entire time I was in that room.

"C'mon Andie B. I'll introduce you to your medical team."

"Thanks."

I walked down the hallway followed by Ms. D. We went past the first checkpoint, and came to a suite of offices. When we entered the reception area, there were four people standing there.

"Good, you are all here. Andie Beth I'd like to introduce to your treatment team. This is Dr. Hunter, the White House staff physician; Ms. Nichols, her nurse; Dr. Waddell , the orthopedist from Walter Reed who is taking over your case, and Ms. Brown, the physical therapist. I'm leaving you in their hands."

"Okay, thanks ma'am."

Ms. D. left, and the four of us started talking.

"I've got one important question for all of you. How much longer will I have to be on crutches?"

"Here's the deal, Ms. Nettles. Change clothes and let us examine your knees and test your mobility. I promise you you will have your answer before you leave today."

Ms. Nichols took me to the examination room where as promised my shorts, tee shirt, jacket and warm-up pants were in a chair. She told me not to put the knee braces on once I changed and to sit on the exam table. There were also a couple of hangers for me to hang my school uniform on. I had just finished changing when there was a knock on the door. Everyone came in. Dr. Waddell and Ms. Brown did a thorough exam. They poked and prodded every inch of both my knees, and moved them in just about every direction possible.

I was determined not to let them know that it hurt. A couple of times the pain cut through my knees like it did when I fell. I felt my face getting red hot, and I was glad I had on shorts instead of sweatpants because of the heat racing through my legs. I was determined that if they asked me to move my leg in a certain direction, that I would do it. After about fifteen minutes of this, they handed me my crutches and we went into the physical therapy room. It was as equipped as the one at Tulane was. All of the same machines were there.

For the next hour I went through a series of exercises which pushed me to my limits, especially since I hadn't therapy in almost a week. With all the excitement involved in moving, there just hadn't been time for it. I'm telling you Rach, this therapy stuff is harder than basketball practice. Especially, when your knees are stiff. Perspiration was dripping off my face. My eyes were stinging from the salt. I kept them shut during most of the exercises so I could concentrate. My legs throbbed from my thighs all the way down to the tips of my toes. I ached all over. Sweat drenched my shirt and it stuck to my back like glue. Every inch of my clothing and body were dripping wet as if I had just come out of the shower.

"Here's a towel Miss Nettles. We're finally finished for the day. We'll meet you in the front office in a few minutes."

I went back in the exam room and pulled on my sweatpants and clipped on the knee braces. I noticed that my school uniform was already gone. Someone had already taken it up to the residence. I grabbed my jacket, and went to the front office.

"You've still got a few months of therapy ahead of you, but if you continue to work as hard as you did today you'll be playing softball this season."

"You mean it Dr. Waddell?"

"Yes. You took quite a tumble down that mountain, but your comeback has been remarkable. Most people, including some athletes, don't bounce back the way you have."

"So, I'll be able to pitch opening day? I mean that's what my goal is."

"Miss Nettles somehow I think you can do anything you put your mind to. We'll get some free weights down here so you can work on your upper body strength too as part of your therapy."

"Would you please tell the President and First Lady?"

"That's already been taken care of."

"Thank you ma'am. Well, I guess I better get upstairs, take a shower and start my homework."

"Okay, Ms. Brown will see you here every day after school, and I'll check in with you once a week to monitor your progress."

"Yes ma'am. And Dr. Waddell. Thanks again."

"You're welcome Miss Nettles. Somehow I think you're right. Just be careful when you're walking outside. You don't want to fall again."

"Now, could someone point me in the direction to the elevator to take me upstairs to the residence?"

"Sure go right to the end of this hallway and take another right and there's the elevator."

Rach, it really seems weird having to ask directions around your own house. I took the elevator to the second floor where I was met by Cajun running around in circles. We both headed up the ramp to the third floor. All I wanted was to get out of these stinky clothes before anyone else got a whiff of me. When I entered my room I noticed that my backpack was on the chair, and my school uniform blazer and skirt were hung up in the closet. I took a shower, and decided to go exploring.

Tucking the map Agent Landry had given me in my jeans pocket I headed down the ramp to the elevator. When I arrived on the first floor, I went out a door that Agent Landry had labeled Family Entrance on his map. He had written a note beside it that said that this was the entrance Daddy would use if he was walking outside from the Oval Office to the residence. As I stood there, I looked over the South Lawn and could see the lights of the Oval Office. I couldn't make out faces just silhouettes of people. Across the lawn I saw the iron fence that surrounds the White House. I felt like a prisoner in my new home. Surrounded by an iron fence and all this security. It reminded me of the State Penitentiary we used to drive by on our way to Aunt Joan's house. Pulling my jacket closer around my neck and the hood of my sweatshirt over my damp hair, I eased myself down to the steps. I braced myself against one of the pillars, and surveyed the entire area. Realizing I had forgotten my gloves, I dug my hands deep into my jacket pockets. I had made it down okay, but trying to get up with the crutches could present a problem. To my left there was a basketball court and what looked like a patio. I remembered Mama telling me there was an outdoor pool. The snow began falling harder. I probably should go inside, but I liked being out in the fresh air even though I was freezing. I focused on the fence area again, and realized that there were people passing by. Some were even pointing toward the house. Then another strange thought hit me. I now live in a tourist attraction.

I remembered when Daddy was first elected to the Senate. He arranged for a special tour of the White House for Trey and I during our spring vacation. It was a tour just for senator's kids. It had been so long ago that I had totally forgotten about it. However, we didn't get to tour the residence. That President had grandchildren, and they would show this big playroom on television where the kids were playing with him and the First Lady. I had thought how neat it would be to have a room that big to spread out all your toys. It dawned on me now that that must have been the solarium. I was so caught up in my thoughts that I didn't hear the approaching footsteps.

"Well, Buzzie I see you found the steps."

"Daddy, I mean Mr. President. I didn't hear you coming."

"What are you doing out here? You must be freezing."

"Just thinking Daddy, and looking around."

"Caught up in your own little world."

It was then I noticed that Daddy was not alone. There was a young guy standing beside him whom I had never seen before.

"Sean, this is my daughter Andie Beth. Let's help her to her feet."

"Daddy, I can do it myself."

"I know you can Buzzie, but it's pretty icy out here, and I don't want you to risk falling again."

Daddy and Sean helped me get the crutches under my arms, and we headed inside. Sean opened the door for us, and when we got to the elevator he left.

"Goodnight Mr. President, Miss Nettles."

"Goodnight Sean. See you first thing in the morning."

"Bye Sean. Nice meeting you."

"Same here Miss Nettles."

When we were on the elevator, and the door was shut I asked Daddy who Sean was. He said he was his personal aide similar to Ms. D. who was Mamas. The elevator doors opened, and as we walked down the hall, here came Mama storming toward us.

"Lynn, look who I found sitting outside on the steps."

"Andie Beth, I've been looking all over for you. Your physical therapy was over an hour ago, and no one had seen you since. What have you got to say for yourself young lady?"

"I decided to go exploring, and I wanted some fresh air. Maybe you guys can stand being cooped up all day, but not me. It's no big deal. Two dozen people must have seen me between here and outside."

"Well next time tell someone like me or your grandma where you're going."

"You mean every time I walk outside I have to tell someone. C'mon Mama, Give me a break. It's not like I can just drive away."

"She's right Lynn. We want her to feel like this is her home. She has to have some freedom."

"Okay, just remember to look at your watch once in awhile. Dinner time is 6:30, and I expect you to be on time. Now go hang up your jacket, and wash up for dinner. Your daddy and I need to talk for a few minutes."

They were talking as I walked to my room.

"I almost started laughing when you said you found her on the steps. Some things never change. Took her less than twenty-four hours."

"Leaning against a pillar, and lost in her own little world. She didn't even hear Sean and I walk up beside her.

If you want to check on her, they're the steps heading to the South Lawn."

"Well, the orthopedist said her therapy is coming along."

"Bet she was daydreaming about softball season. She's determined to play."

"I bet you're right."

My hair was frozen. I picked up the hairdryer and tried to dry it. I couldn't show up at dinner with wet hair. Mama would have a fit. She'd give me some lecture about how I was going to catch pneumonia, and how I couldn't afford to miss school. After drying it, I decided not to pull it back. I headed back downstairs. It was almost 6:30.

I walked in the sitting room, and Mama, Daddy, and Grandma Josie were there. Mama and Daddy had changed clothes. They both had on jeans. I hadn't seen them in jeans in ages.

"Hi Gram. I haven't seen you all day."

"Well, I know. I'm used to seeing you right after school. Guess you're too important to come visit your old grandma now that you live here."

"I would never say that Gram. It's just I was pretty busy today."

Some guy came to the door.

"Mr. President, dinner is served."

The four of us went into the dining room. This was how it would be from now on. We would meet in the sitting room, and talk until someone told us it was time to eat. Definitely not like it was in the old days in Kenner when we would hang out in the kitchen until the timer on the stove went off. Dinner tonight was meatloaf with mashed potatoes which is Daddy's favorite meal. Guess Mama wanted our first meal as a family to be special. Only thing was the meatloaf wasn't as good as Gram's. She needs to give the White House chef her recipe. Already, I'm starting to miss her cooking, and eating in the kitchen.

"How was your first day of school Andie B.?"

"Fine."

"That's all you can say, fine?"

"Okay, really fine."

Everyone laughed.

"Your teachers seemed nice when we met them in December."

"They're okay. A couple of them are just out of college."

"Any cute boys, I mean hunks that I'm going to have to chase away from the White House gates, Buzzie?"

"Daddy."

"Look she's blushing Lynn. She must have seen at least one."

"Da-ddy, please. Besides, no guy will get near me. Too many agents around."

"Well, you will get a chance to meet a lot of guys on Friday night."

"What's Friday night?"

"There's a reception for your mother's and my staff and their families. Some of the kids go to your school."

"Does this include senators and representatives kids?"

"No, Rachel isn't included in this one Buzzie. Just the different cabinet members, their staffs, and the people who work at the White House. Your mother and I decided to include the families since we were having it on a Friday night."

"So, I really have to go. But all the kids will be little kids."

"Not necessarily. Not all our staff members are as young as Sean and Jamie. In fact a few are older than us."

"And yes, Andie Beth, you have to go. When the term family is included in an invitation, you are expected to attend. That's one reason your daddy scheduled this on Friday instead of a school night."

"But I'm not going to know anybody, and I'm going to feel stupid. I bet the next thing you're going to tell me is I have to wear a dress. Why can't I just stay upstairs?"

"Because I said so that's why. You are a part of this family. We don't expect you to be at every event, but some are mandatory, and this is one of them. Do I make myself clear young lady?"

"Yes ma'am. But it's just that. . ."

"No buts Andie Beth. It seems like every time I ask you to do something or ask you a question, it turns into an argument. You are a part of this family. Since Trey is away at college, you are considered the First Kid. People expect to see you. People want to get to know you. If we allow you to skip these events, then there are all sorts of questions to answer. I'm not making up excuses for you, just because you don't want to participate. Are you listening to me?"

"Yes, ma'am. I'll be there. In a dress."

"You bet you will, or you will spend the next month looking at those four walls of your room minus all the modern conveniences such as your telephone, television, c.d. player, and computer."

"May I please be excused? I'm not hungry anymore."

"Stay and finish your supper, Andie B. It's a long time to breakfast."

"No, Gram. I'm really not hungry. May I?"

"Go ahead Andie Beth."

"Thanks sir."

Daddy handed me my crutches. I went out of the room. I couldn't let him see me cry. She did it to me again. I could hear them talking as I walked away. I shuffled up the ramp to my room, and then realized I had left my biology book in the sitting room. I was going to show it to Daddy since it was the only book that was different from the ones we used in Louisiana. When I went by the dining room, I realized they were talking and the topic was me. I stopped and eavesdropped.

"Just one day. Just one day. I'd love to make it through just one day without having an argument with that child."

"You need to lighten up, Lynn."

"Fine. From now on I won't discipline her. I'll leave it all to you and Gary. We'll see how far that gets us."

"Maybe you need to take a different approach."

"Have you been reading Parents™ magazine again Mama?"

"No, I just mean the more you force your opinion on her, the more she rebels. Did you even stop to ask her why she didn't want to go to the reception?"

"I don't need to ask her. It's her obligation. We all have obligations and responsibilities now."

"She's a fifteen year old kid, Lynn."

"So."

"I had her convinced it might be a fun experience. She could meet some kids in an informal setting and just hang out for a while. It could be a chance to meet them away from school. And then you blew it."

"How? What do you mean?"

"You started putting restrictions on it. Telling her she had to wear a dress for instance. We called this event informal. Andie B. could wear jeans. No one is going to care what she looks like. Our daughter hates dresses. She's a jock. But you keep trying to turn her into a beauty queen. She's not a beauty queen. She could be, but she doesn't want to be. She's a jock who wants to fly fighter jets for the Navy. But you're trying to make her into Miss Teen USA™."

"So you're saying I should leave her alone to her own devices."

"I'm saying you should let her be a kid whose father happens to be the President. Buzzie didn't get elected. I did. We chose this lifestyle because we thought I could make a difference. Buzzie had it thrust upon her because she happens to be our child. Frankly, I think you owe her an apology. She didn't do anything wrong. She was just being herself."

"And there's nothing wrong with that Lynn. In fact up until last year, you two were close. But once you got caught up in the campaign, it's like you didn't want to be bothered with her."

"Because once I started leaving, she turned to you Mama, and to Gary. I was no longer her confidante."

"Bingo. Listen to what you said. You're jealous because of the relationship your mother and I have with Buzzie. The funny thing is you can get back your relationship with her if you will lighten up. I was hoping things would change once we moved here, but you're the one who has to change Lynn. Andie B. is the same kid she was a year ago, just a little taller. Her personality hasn't changed. Your attitude

toward her has."

"So, you both are saying I need to talk to her."

"Yes."

"I'll take her some dessert. It's lemon meringue pie,

her favorite."

"Forget the dessert she'll think it's a bribe. Just go

upstairs, tell Andie B. you're sorry, that we've talked it

over, and she doesn't have to wear a dress. Ask her if

she's still hungry, and if she says yes, she can come back

downstairs. Your mother and I will make sure there's some

meatloaf left for a sandwich and some pie. But don't force

it on her. Buzzie has a mind of her own. Just like you. Let

it be her decision. She's almost sixteen. She knows if she

is hungry or not."

I was doing my homework at my desk when there was a knock at the door. It was Mama. I didn't say anything.

"Got a lot of homework?"

"Yes Mama."

"Can you stop and talk for a few minutes?"

"I guess so, but if it's going to be another lecture I got your point the first time. Let's face it Mama I'm not the daughter you wish you had."

"You're not going to make this easy for me are you?"

"What are you talking about? From where I sit yelling at me has always come pretty easy for you."

"Your father, grandmother, and I had a talk after you left. They convinced me I was wrong to jump on you like I did."

"But you're not convinced?"

"It's hard for me to apologize to you, because I think I'm looking out for you. Andie B. when you continue to shut me out of your life, and don't talk to me, it comes across to me you don't care. But your father and grandmother told me tonight I'm the problem not you. You can bet I didn't want to hear that."

"And that's supposed to make me feel better?"

"Yes. Because I'm willing to make an effort to change. But that doesn't mean I'm going to let you disrespect me. It does mean that I'm going to lighten up on you a little, and let you take more responsibility for your own actions. You're almost sixteen. It's about time I started treating you that way."

"If you really mean what you say."

"All I'm asking for is a chance Andie Beth. I want to be your mother not your warden. Will you give me that chance and accept my apology."

"I guess so ma'am."

"You act like you're not sure."

"Well, it sounds good today, but what about tomorrow and the day after?"

"Have I ever broken a promise to you Andie B.?"

"No Mama."

"Well then there's your answer."

"Yeah, I guess so. Is that it? I've got a lot of homework."

"Yes, that's it. We saved you a meatloaf sandwich and some lemon meringue pie if you're still hungry."

"No thanks."

"Goodnight Andie B. I'll be back up later to tuck you in. Bedtime is 10 p.m."

"Yes Mama."

Then she came over and hugged me. I'm not sure I'm buying it.

Now about that biology homework. Are we supposed all the questions on page 100 or just the even numbered ones? C'mon Rach quit staring at the phone waiting for Ryan to call and answer me.

Chapter 12

Ryan

"Rachel, are you out there? I just came up to my room after supper. You're kidding about this Ryan guy right? The Ryan that's in our gym class is the guy you hung out with in Colorado? How did he end up in this school? C'mon Rach, give me the scoop."

"That's him all right A.B. Ryan Kessler in the flesh. When we were together in Colorado, he told me he was moving to D.C. He was going to a military school in Nebraska somewhere. Your dad appointed his dad to some government job. I think it's Undersecretary of State.

Anyway, it was something about his parents moving around

the world all the time so they stuck him in military school."

"But how did he end up in this school? Aren't there

tons of schools all over town?"

"A.B. everyone knows, except maybe you this school is

the best school of any of them. Plus it has the best security.

Half the kids in the school have some sort of bodyguard

or security with them."

"Did you know he was coming to this school when

you met him?"

"He didn't know the name of it. All he knew was that

he was flying from Colorado to D.C. The ski trip was a

last fling for him with his friends; just like it was for you."

"Rach, you have to go to work for the CIA when you graduate. They can use spies like you. Was he on the slopes the day I fell?"

"Yeah, I think so. I saw him at the bottom of the hill when they were loading you into the ambulance. Why?"

"Never mind."

It's just something about those eyes.

"He practically tripped over me on the way to gym class on Wednesday. Somehow the idea of this klutz being *the love of your life* just doesn't fit. I'm surprised he's not the one on crutches."

"A.B. you are so clueless when it comes to guys. Trust me this guy is a keeper. One night after you disappeared, we danced the night away. Even the slow dances."

"Mr. Two Left Feet can dance. That I've got to see."

"Don't worry you will. I guarantee you I'll be on his arm at the Valentine Dance."

"Yep. I can see it now. You are dancing the night away with Mr. Wonderful while I stay at home watching a basketball game and eating popcorn with Daddy."

"You'll have a date. Don't worry. I'll set you up with one of my friends."

"You mean one of your castoffs, don't you? Can't dance anyway with these stupid crutches."

"It's almost a month off A.B. You may be using a cane by then. Who knows?"

"Yeah right. It was great using the crutches at school the last few days. My arms sure get tired though. I want to start walking soon and putting some pressure on my feet, but Ms. Brown says that's still at least a month off. But at least everyone has quit staring at me."

It all started Thursday afternoon after school. There are too many people around telling me what to do.

"Ms. Nettles, you don't have to check in with the First Lady today."

"Why not?"

"Both she and the President are at Bethesda having their annual physicals."

"But, I've still got physical therapy, right?"

"Yes, and afterwards check in with your grandmother in the residence."

Physical therapy is really hard, Rach. My knees get stiff each day between times. I wish there was some sort of oil they could just shoot in them to make them move. At least today, I got to sit in the whirlpool. Did I tell you that Mama and Daddy have a Jacuzzi® tub in their bathroom? It seems the former President had arthritis and had it installed. Mama says I can use it sometimes. Sure wish she would put one in my bathroom.

"Okay, Miss Nettles that's all for today. You've made a lot of progress this week. What are your plans for the weekend? You can skip therapy tomorrow if you want to."

"No, ma'am. I'll be here. There's some sort of reception my parents are dragging me to tomorrow night, but it doesn't start until after dinner so I'll be here. I want to work out on the weights. My legs are getting stronger, but my shoulders get stiff with these crutches each day."

"Okay, I'll work on a series of exercises for your upper body, and we'll start those tomorrow."

"Thanks, Ms. Brown."

After therapy I went upstairs, took a shower, and then came downstairs to find Grandma Josie in the sitting room looking at a seed catalogue.

"Wondered if you and I were ever going to see each other again. I've hardly laid eyes on you for the last two days."

"Sorry, Gram. It's just the pace of this place. No one ever slows down. Can you believe there's a copy of Mama and Daddy's daily schedule on the breakfast table every morning?"

"What about you? Are you finding your way around okay?"

"Didn't get lost today if that's what you mean. Are you going to plant a garden? I see the catalogues."

"Thought I might see about asking for a little spot of my own back where no one could see it, or maybe a few plants on the balcony of the solarium."

"Are you kidding, Gram? You should be the White House gardener. I remember all those blue ribbons you used to win from the Kenner Garden Club."

"Pure luck, Andie B., pure luck. I just like experimenting. Most of those old women did the same old arrangements year after year."

"If Mama is as smart as she thinks she is, she'll ask for your advice when she decorates for her receptions instead of some high priced know-it-all. She's lucky to have you for a Mama."

"Thanks, Andie B. That's one of the things I'm going to miss from New Orleans. Don't get me wrong, I'm glad I'm here. You're not the only one making adjustments."

"I know Gram. I bet the ladies will miss you too. But we need you here with us, especially me. I sure miss your cooking. Can't you at least give the White House

Chef some of your recipes? They may be thinking they're cooking our favorite meals, but everything tastes so bland."

"Maybe your daddy needs to have a case of Tabasco Sauce flown in from McIlhenny."

"Sounds like a good idea to me. But what are you going to do all day without me or a house to take care of?"

"There's still plenty to do around here. Your mama wants me to help her with some of the redecorating here in the residence. Plus I'll go on some of the local trips with her. Why don't you take Cajun outside for a little while before it gets dark? No need for you to stay cooped up in here. Your parents will be home in time for dinner so make sure you're down here by 6:30."

"Okay, Gram see you in a little while. C'mon Cajun. Let's go toss your tennis ball around."

Cajun and I headed to the elevator to take us to the first floor. He was carrying his tennis ball in his mouth, and pranced around as if he owned the place. I went out to my spot on the steps, and threw his ball. My shoulder was really stiff. Cajun kept running back and forth with his ball, and eventually my shoulder started to loosen up. I see now what Coach Shine was talking about. I really do need to get ready for spring training.

I glanced up, and some of the interns were chasing Cajun around the South Lawn. They looked like a bunch of little kids playing keep away. They would grab his ball and toss it to each other. When Cajun did finally get a hold of it, they would chase him. Now I see why Caj liked it so much here. Wherever he went, people would play with him.

Hearing people scurrying around behind me, I looked at my watch. It was past 5 p.m. Most of the day staffers were taking advantage of Mama and Daddy's absence to leave work on time. I decided to wait here until some of the traffic slowed down in the central hallway. I'm still nervous around all these people. They all know me, but I don't have a clue who they are. Everyone stares at me.

Cajun finally came back to the steps followed by a cute intern who was tucking in his shirt and straightening his tie as he walked towards me.

"You must be the President's daughter, Ms. Nettles. I'm Brad Walker. I'm an intern on the President's staff."

"Glad to meet you Brad, but call me Andie B. please."

"Sure. Guess we wore Cajun out. He likes to come out here with us when we're on our breaks."

"I see. It's a good thing he has someone to play with. I'm not doing much in that department lately."

"Saw your accident on the news. You really crashed."

"In more ways than one."

"What?"

"Never mind. I was just muttering to myself. Brad, could I ask you a favor?"

"Anything. After all I do work for your father."

"Could you help me up? I can get down to the steps, but I'm still having problems getting back up."

"No problem."

He helped me back to my feet, and opened the door. Cajun ran in, and sat by the elevator door. Brad pushed the button.

"Nice meeting you Brad. I'll see you around."

"Same here."

Rach you would love this place. If all the interns look as good as this guy, then I should have some good views from the steps. The only problem is they are all in college or graduate school. You know Mama won't let me date anyone more than two years older than me. But I bet it gave him something to tell his intern buddies. You'll have to come over and guy watch with me.

I went to my room and grabbed my copy of *Moby Dick*^{TM}. Still not ready to be confined to my four walls, I decided to go to the solarium and read. This room is huge. The sitting area only takes up a small part of it. Daddy promised Trey a pool table and foosball table which should be delivered any day now. Even with that, there's still room for dancing. On Inauguration Day there must have been fifty people in here.

I stretched out on the couch with my head facing the doorway. That way no one could sneak up on me. The next thing I knew I woke up, and there was a blanket on top of me. I looked at my watch, and it was 8:30. Pulling myself to my feet, I was still sleepy. When I entered the sitting room, there was Mama, Daddy, and Grandma Josie.

"There's my girl."

"What happened?"

"Your Grandma came to get you for supper, and you were sound asleep. Figured if you were that tired, we wouldn't wake you."

"All I remember is lying on the couch reading. Then I woke up with a blanket on me."

"Saved you a plate. Let me go get it. Fried chicken and mashed potatoes. Crispy just the way you like it."

"I'm not that hungry. Think maybe I'll just have some cereal."

"Andie B. is everything all right? You haven't eaten much in the last few days."

"Don't worry Mama. I'm not anorexic or anything. I guess I'm just tired from all the physical therapy."

"You'd let me know if your ears were bothering you wouldn't you? Don't need to have you getting sick."

"Yes, Mama. I'd let you know. I'm fine."

"Buzzie, you know you don't have to push yourself so hard at the therapy. You still have almost three months before softball season starts."

"I know, Daddy. It's just that when I sit there in gym class, and see everyone running up and down the court; I want to be out there with them. You know how it feels Daddy."

"You're right. I do know. But give yourself a break. Don't be so hard on yourself."

"Here you go Andie B. I brought you a tray. The stewards stocked both pantries with Rice Krispies® and Sugar Pops®."

"Thanks Gram. Who told them to do that?"

"The President of course."

"You're not taking the credit this time Gary. I did Andie B. Some of our other favorite foods are in there too. Along with some fresh fruit and cut up vegetables. I wanted all of us, especially you, to have foods just like our old home. Your pantry upstairs has some snacks plus milk and orange juice."

"Thanks Mama. I've been eating breakfast there every morning, but I didn't know there was other food around."

"Do you have much homework left to do? Your nap cut into your study time."

"No, Mama. I got most of it done at school, and during the ride home. I was reviewing *Moby Dick*™ when I fell asleep. I'm ahead of the class in most subjects."

"Now that surprises me. I always figured these fancy D.C. schools were way ahead of ours."

"Maybe the public schools Mama, but you forget St. Martins had high standards."

"I'm glad about that. Means our girl can catch a little break anyway while she's adjusting to her new surroundings."

"Thanks Gram."

"Just saw the basketball score on t.v. Buzzie. LSU won again 83-58."

"Who'd they beat Daddy?"

"Auburn."

"I'll have to go text Trey, and see if he got in the game."

"Not tonight, Andie B. If you're finished eating, you need to get ready for bed and finish your homework."

"Aw. Mama. Please. It will only take me a couple of minutes."

"You know the rules. No computer after 9 p.m."

"But I couldn't help it. I didn't mean to fall asleep."

"That doesn't change the rules."

"Sometimes I think I'm in prison."

"Watch your mouth young lady."

"Tell you what Buzzie I'll call my friend at the Times-Picayune and get him to fax me the story, complete with box score. I'll have it for you at breakfast tomorrow morning."

"Thanks Daddy."

"Now, do what your Mama says and skedaddle."

"Yes, Daddy."

"Goodnight everybody."

"I'll be up later to check on you."

"Okay, Mama."

"Gary, you spoil that child rotten."

"Hey, somebody has to be the good guy here."

I went upstairs and got ready for bed. All the rest of my homework was reading so I went ahead and got in bed. I was still reading when Mama came in.

"Lights out Andie B."

"Okay, Mama. Oh I forgot. How was your and Daddy's physicals?"

"Pretty thorough."

"Are you guys okay? I mean there's nothing wrong is there?"

"Nothing for you to worry about."

"Are you sure Mama because you don't look too sure?"

"I'm sure. I'm just tired. It's been a busy week for all of us. Now lights out."

"Yes Mama, but I'm not sleepy now. Can't I stay up a little longer?"

"No exceptions. I'll get the overhead light; you turn off the one on your bedside lamp."

"Okay."

Friday after school I had therapy again. This time Ms. Brown had all the exercises for my shoulders and arms. After the session, I really felt loose. Instead of sitting in the whirlpool in therapy, I wandered down to Mama's office hoping that maybe I could convince her to let me use her Jacuzzi tub.

"Hi Ms. D. is Mama, I mean the First Lady around?"

"Well, hey there Andie B. She's on the phone but she shouldn't be long. Is there something I can help you with?"

"No, I just wanted to ask her a question, and it's kind of personal if you know what I mean?"

"I understand. But you know you can always ask me anything."

"I guess I'm just not used to Mama having a staff that I have to go through to see her. It's weird."

"Get used to it. But whenever you need to see or talk with the First Lady, I'll try to accommodate you. But there will probably be times. .."

"Yeah, probably times when she'll be too busy or she will be in a meeting. I know."

"You know it has nothing to do with you. It's just the nature of the job. The First Lady has a very important job here. At least in this office we like to think it is as important as the Presidents."

"Yeah right. Only the wars she fights are the mother-daughter wars."

As soon as I said it, I knew I shouldn't have. Mama picked that exact moment to walk out of her office. One thing Mama and Daddy always emphasized was that family business stayed at home. We were never to discuss our family problems with anyone else.

"Andie Beth in my office now."

"Yes, ma'am."

"What was that all about?"

"It was a joke, ma'am. You missed the earlier part. Ms. D. was saying that your staff thought their job was just as important as Daddy's. That's when I said what you heard. It was no big deal. I haven't forgotten the rule if that's what you're worried about."

"Just checking. So how was therapy today?"

"Tiring. But at least I don't feel so stiff now. That's why I came to see you."

"Oh."

"I wanted to know if I could take a bath in your Jacuzzi® tub. I forgot to bring my bathing suit down here so I couldn't use the whirlpool."

"I don't see why not. Why don't you go ahead and do it now. But don't forget to wash your hair. Even though tonight's reception is casual, it doesn't mean sloppy. What are you wearing?"

"Daddy said I could wear jeans, remember? I figured I'd wear the denim shirt with the Naval Academy on it that Grandma Elizabeth gave me."

"Okay, but wear the new jeans I bought you. Not those old faded ones with the holes. And make sure your shirt is tucked in, and wear a belt. And hair pulled back out of your eyes."

"Mama, are we going to go through this every time I have to make an appearance somewhere. I'm going to be sixteen in seven weeks. I've been dressing myself since I was four."

"'Fraid so. Everyone in the world is looking at us now. They're already making comments about how we dress. One reporter said my inaugural gown made me look fat; another said I should never wear royal blue."

"But what does have to do with me?"

"Your daddy and I can handle the criticism. But I don't want the press to criticize you. One way to avoid it is not to give them anything to criticize."

"I guess so. But it seems so dumb. Like who's going to care what I have on?"

"You'd be surprised. Thirty years ago there was a teen-ager who lived here who started wearing jeans around the White House, and when she and her parents left for trips. Finally the President stood up to all the criticism, and told the press to leave her alone."

"So, if it hadn't been for her, I'd have to wear a dress everywhere in public?"

"I think times may have changed by now, but all I'm saying is you're going to be in the spotlight for the next few years so get used to it."

"Yes, ma'am. Can I go now? I don't like talking to you in your office. You seem too, I don't know. You don't seem like Mama here. It makes me feel uncomfortable."

"Sure, go on and take your bath. Your daddy and I will be up in about an hour for supper, and then the reception starts at 8. Just remember to have all your clothes with you when you go to use the Jacuzzi®, because there are agents in the hallway. No streaking."

"Mother, please I know better than that. Besides how could I streak on crutches? It would be more like creaking."

"I know. You're almost sixteen, but you forget I remember the days when you would jump out of the bathtub; race around the house all soapy with your arms flapping in the air crying 'I'm an airplane, I'm an airplane.' I'd throw a towel to your daddy, and we'd corner you and throw towels over you and wrestle you to the floor."

"I don't remember that."

"You were only about three or four."

"How embarrassing. You don't have to worry about that now. That's one thing that gives me the creeps about this place; all these people constantly around even upstairs."

"The agents won't be near the third floor unless your daddy or I are up there, but once you come down that ramp you're fair game."

"I've noticed."

"Now get going. I still have some work to get done even if it is Friday afternoon."

"Yes ma'am."

I left Mama's office and headed for the elevator to the residence. I went into my room and grabbed my shampoo and clothes and came back downstairs. Grandma Josie was coming down the hall.

"Running away from home?"

"Not today. Mama said I could take a bath in her bathtub before supper."

"It's a nice Jacuzzi®. Just like all those fancy ones at those health spas I see advertised on television."

"So, you've already been in it?"

"Yesterday, but an agent almost walked in on me when he heard sounds coming from the President's bathroom. Lucky for me he knocked before he came in or that young man would have been in for a surprise."

"Hope that doesn't happen to me. Guess I'll drop off my clothes, and tell the agent I'll be in their room for a while."

"It might be a good idea."

I laid down my clothes on Mama's bed. The late afternoon sunlight shone brightly through the window. Hobbling over to it I noticed that the view from my parent's bedroom was not as good as the one from the solarium. Being one floor up definitely had its' advantages. There were several huge trees directly outside their bedroom window. They were probably planted years ago to give the

President's bedroom more privacy. There is also a window seat in front of the window like the one I had in my room in Kenner. If it weren't for these clunky knee braces, I would curl up here for awhile. Maybe I'll sneak down here and study sometime. Yeah right. Like I'm going to study in my parent's bedroom. I went out in the hallway, and stopped the first agent I saw.

"Is there something we can help you with Miss Nettles?"

"No, I just wanted you to know that I'm going to be in my parent's room for a while using their Jacuzzi® but I don't want to lock the bedroom door in case the First Lady comes upstairs."

"That's fine. Oh, your grandmother must have told you that we almost busted in on her."

"Yeah. I don't want it happening to me."

"Don't worry the First Lady called and told us. She was afraid we might embarrass you."

"Telling you was embarrassing enough."

As I walked away, I could feel my face getting redder by the minute. Leave it to Mama to think of everything. I don't know what to say to all these grownups that are around all the time. It's like everyone is always staring at me expecting me to do or say something.

I went in the bedroom and took off my clothes. This whole house seems so sterile. It's like dirt would be afraid to attach itself to anything. Looking around the bathroom I find Mama's Victoria Secret® bath salts I gave her for Christmas. Might as well enjoy my gift. I chose the pear scent because the lemon reminds me of Lemon Pledge®. Pouring some in the water the tub becomes an ocean of bubbles with just a tint of green. I eased myself into the tub enveloping my entire body in the light green ocean. As I inhaled it was as if I was lying on the floor of a pear orchard. Adjusting the jets on the Jacuzzi® sent a pulsating stream of water to my shoulders, back and knees. Gram was right. This felt awesome. I might never leave. It only felt like a few minutes, but it must have been longer because suddenly there was a knock on the door.

"Andie B. it's time to get out. Your mama and daddy will be coming upstairs in fifteen minutes. She said to remind you to wash your hair."

"Okay Gram."

Looking down at my fingers I saw that they were wrinkled like old prunes. I must have been in here longer than I thought but it felt so good I hated to stand up. I rinsed myself off in the shower and washed my hair. Sitting on Mama's bed I was buttoning my shirt when she came in.

"Need some help?"

"No, Mama I'm fine."

"Come sit at the vanity, and let me brush your hair."

I moved off the bed and to the bench in front of the vanity. Mama grabbed her brush, and gently stroked it through my hair. Every so often she would reach a tangle, and I would wince. Looking at my face in the mirror I realized I was making the same faces I did when I was a little girl.

"Mama, don't pull so hard. It hurts."

"Andie B. you want long hair, it's going to have to be neat."

"But Mama it hurts."

"Keep up the complaining and we'll go to the beauty parlor after school and get it all cut off."

"But Mama."

"Andie Beth hush your mouth this instant or you won't have either one."

"Yes ma'am."

Mama finally got the tangles out, and I handed her a scrunchie.

"You were deep in thought Andie B. What were you thinking about?"

"Nothing Mama. Nothing important."

"Take your dirty clothes upstairs to the hamper, and then wash up for supper. And try to stay clean until the reception."

"Mot-her. I'm not four years old, remember?"

"Sorry. Looking at you in the mirror just then I forgot that my little girl was all grown up. For a moment there I forgot where we were."

Too weird. She was remembering too. Good thing I didn't spill my guts to her about what I was thinking. It would have really freaked her out. No way would I ever have let her know I was thinking the same thing.

"Since you've still got some time before supper, why don't you read some of *Moby Dick*™?"

"Mama it's Friday. No respectable teenager in the universe is reading a book for school on a Friday afternoon."

"Except you."

"Ma-ma. You know I hate to read. Especially that boring old book."

"Doesn't matter. It still has to be done. Now go. And do what I say."

"Oh all right."

As I was opening the door Daddy came in. He reached down and kissed me on the forehead.

"Looking good Buzzie. Looking good."

"Tell that to your wife. She wants me to do homework on a Friday."

"What's this all about?"

"Never mind Daddy, never mind."

"You two at it again Lynn?"

"Never mind Gary, never mind."

I went upstairs, dumped my clothes in the hamper and went out in the solarium. These new jeans were stiff. Oh well, it didn't matter anyway. I can't do much bending. I stuck *Moby Dick*^{TM} on the couch where I could reach it if Mama came up, and turned on the television. I realized I hadn't watched t.v. since Inauguration Day. My life had been reduced to the White House and school. I flipped the channels until I found ESPN. Hopefully, they would say something about the Southeastern Conference or the Naval Academy.

Mama never did come upstairs so I managed to get away with not reading. English class is so boring. All that reading and writing book reports. Science and math are much more interesting. There you have a problem and a solution. Not same vague abstract idea like what did the author mean when he said this or that. Who cares? And all these books we have to read by these dead guys. Since Mama is a teacher, she loves to read. She can't understand why I'm not like her. The only books I like to read are the ones about flying. Grandpa Webb has taught me a lot about aviation history with the books he's given me. If I had been a pilot in World War II, the war would have ended a lot quicker. I would have been dodging enemy fire all over Europe and the Pacific. Just to have the wheel of one of those big bombers would be awesome. Imagine all that power in my hands. I can almost feel it.

I looked up and Daddy was coming up the ramp.

"Hey Daddy. She sent you to get me?"

"Not exactly. I volunteered."

"Uh oh. Here comes another lecture. What has she told you I've done this time?"

"Nothing. It's just that I'm noticing that you and your mother are arguing just about every time you're in the same room together, and it's got to stop."

"Did she put you up to this Daddy? Was this one of those 'Gary go talk to your daughter' conversations, and then she starts crying and telling you how disrespectful I am?"

"No."

"And then she tells you how I refuse to do what she says, and how you and Gram spoil me too much."

"No."

"Yeah right Daddy. That's exactly what she says, and you know it."

"Okay Buzzie. Let's say you're right. What are you going to do about the situation? I mean I give up. I have to live with both of you plus be President. When I leave the Oval Office at the end of the day, I like to think that my crises are over. Then I come upstairs and you're either arguing with your mother or she's sending you to bed early. Don't you get tired of all this?

"Doesn't she? You know it wouldn't hurt for her to give in once in a while."

"Like you do I suppose?"

"I don't have a choice. I'm the kid. No matter what I do it's not good enough for her. If I make a B+, she wants an A. If I read ten pages of *Moby Dick*™, she wants to know why I haven't read twenty. I can't win."

"Well, you had better learn how."

"Gram tells me to watch my mouth and my attitude with Mama. When I don't say anything, I get accused of pouting. When I talk, I get accused of talking back."

"That was good advice but something has to give in this relationship."

"And you're telling me it has to be me. I guess I had better plan on spending the next two and a half years up here, because the only time I seem to stay out of trouble is when I'm not around her."

"Buzzie tell me something. How long has it been this bad? I mean I know I haven't been around that much over the last few years. I thought this just started since November."

"Sorry, Daddy. You're wrong. It's been this way a while. Talk to Gram. She'll tell you. Only difference now is: you're standing up for me. Gram's been doing it for a long time."

"Why didn't I see it then?"

"Because you were a *weekend Daddy* or *geographical bachelor* is the term I think I heard Mama use one time. When you came home, everyone was on their best behavior. We all missed you. Trey and I were warned not to do anything to mess up our time together, or we'd be grounded. But you know what's so funny?"

"What's that?"

"Sometimes being grounded wasn't so bad because it meant I got to spend more time with you even if it meant her being around."

"Oh Buzzie."

"What Daddy?"

"Nothing. But promise me something."

"What's that Daddy?"

"That you'll try harder to get along with your Mama."

"Did she promise you the same thing?"

"No, I figured I'd ask you first."

"Why because I'm easier to convince?"

"No, because you're my kid, and you have to do what I tell you."

"Well, when you put it that way, I guess I'll try."

"That's all I ask. Now let me help you up, and let's go eat dinner."

Daddy and I walked downstairs just as Mama and Gram were heading for the dining room.

"Looks like they're going to eat without us."

"Can't win Daddy. Can't win."

Chapter 13

The Reception

"Rachel are you out there?"

Mama came in and saw me on the computer and promptly reminded me that I had the World History test tomorrow. Like I could have forgotten. So I studied for a while. She and Daddy are having dinner with the Vice President and his wife tonight so it will be just Gram and me. They just left. Figured you might want to hear the rest of the story so here goes.

Dinner was really quiet on Friday. It was like Daddy and Gram were trying to do everything to keep Mama and I from arguing with each other. Funny thing was I still say I did nothing wrong. I was just concentrating on not spilling food on my shirt or jeans. We had burgers and fries for supper. I was really surprised. That's been our Friday tradition since Trey and I were little kids. I didn't realize how hungry I was. I guess not eating much the last few days finally caught up with me.

After supper Daddy, Mama, and Gram headed for the sitting room. I headed back upstairs. We still had about an hour before the reception, and the thought of spending it in a room with Mama was worse than torture. Even though the reception was informal, we still had to make an entrance as a family down the stairs.

"Why don't you come in the sitting room with the rest of us Andie B.?"

"I'd rather go upstairs."

"You know you are a part of this family, and it would be nice if all four of us spent some time together."

"Do I have to? Are you gonna yell at me again?"

"No. Not unless you provoke me."

"C'mon Buzzie let's see what's on ESPN."

"Okay Daddy."

Mama buried her head in a book while Gram pulled out her crocheting. She was working on a throw for the couch in Mama's office. One of her theories was even their offices needed a touch of home. Daddy turned on the television, and he and I watched a sports news show. We noticed right away that the shows in this part of the country mentioned very little about the Southeastern Conference.

There were too many big basketball schools nearby such as George Washington and University of Maryland for them to mention any of the schools in the South. At least with all of us busy doing something there wasn't a need for conversation. The silence was interrupted by an aide coming in the room.

"Mr. President. Your guests are waiting for you."

Mama leaped to her feet, and rushed next door to their bedroom. Daddy stood up and for the first time that night I noticed he had taken off his tie, and also had on a denim shirt only his had the LSU logo on it. He straightened his shirt and pulled his comb through his hair. As I watched him do this, I saw the first hint of gray on the hair around his ears. That wasn't there three months ago. Already this job was getting to Daddy. Grandma Josie was not coming downstairs. According to her, there were some events meant only for the three of us and this was one of them. Daddy helped me up, and I tried to straighten my shirt and get my jeans leg to slide down but it wouldn't. I would have to ask for help. Mama walked in at that moment. Even in a pair of slacks she looked like she just walked out of a designer showcase.

"Could somebody help me please? My jean leg is messed up, and I can't reach it."

Daddy and Mama started towards me, and after a quick glance from Gram, Daddy backed off. Both of them were waiting to see how I would react to Mama's approach. Mama got down on her knees, and pulled the bottoms of my jeans down. Then she stood up and straightened my shirt and pulled a few stray hairs away from my face. Daddy came up beside her, and we all turned around to face Gram.

"Well, what do you think Mama? Does the First Family pass your inspection?"

"Very nice. I think I've got the best looking family in Washington. Now get going. Your guests are waiting for you."

"See you later Gram."

Cajun started to run out with us, but Gram called him back to her. He jumped in Daddy's new recliner as if he was claiming it as his new spot at least for the evening.

When we got to the staircase, an aide took one of my crutches, and I held on to the stair railing with one hand and balanced on one crutch. There were aides and agents behind and in front of us. If one of us tripped, we would land on someone. Since I was afraid of falling again, I was looking down at my feet the entire time we came down the stairs. Some music group was playing "Hail to the

Chief" as we came downstairs, and tons of people were milling around. At the bottom the aide handed me back my other crutch, and the three of us walked into the State Dining Room.

A receiving line was forming, and I recognized the Vice President and his wife. When we got to our place in line, one of Daddy's aides offered me a chair which I refused. As he walked away, he whispered in my ear "Just motion to me if you get tired. It's going to be a long night." He was right.

The line started with Daddy's staff. I recognized a few of them.

As each one came through, Daddy shook hands with them and introduced them to Mama and me. This included the kids too. This seemed to go on forever. About halfway,

Mama introduced me to Mr. and Mrs. Reece Kessler. Then Mrs. Kessler introduced me to Ryan.

"Andie Beth, this is our son, Ryan. I don't know if you have met or not. Since you go to the same school, you should get to know each other."

I looked up, and there was the same guy who had tripped over me on the way to gym class. Ryan Kessler. He was at this reception.

"Andie B. why don't you take a break from all this handshaking for a while. You and Ryan go mingle with the other teenagers."

"Are you sure Mr. President?"

"Sure. We can handle it from here out. Right Lynn?"

"That's fine. There are some refreshments on the other side of the room, Andie Beth. Maybe Ryan can help you maneuver through the crowds and find a place to sit down."

"Okay, M'aam."

As we walked away, Ryan was walking in front of me.

"You know, it's okay to walk beside me. It's not like I'm going to fall forward on top of you or anything."

"I know I just thought. . ."

"You just thought that when the First Lady gave an order that you had better obey it."

"I guess sort of."

"It's okay. I'm the one who is supposed to obey her orders only I don't most of the time so you don't have to."

"You know, I felt really dumb not knowing who you were the other day."

"You mean not knowing that I was the President's daughter?"

"Yeah, I kept thinking that I knew you, and all the time it was from seeing you on television, and at the Inauguration."

"No big deal. But you saw me at the Inauguration?"

"Yeah, when your father, I mean the President was taking his oath of office, and your family was standing there beside him. We were in the crowd."

"I was too nervous to see anybody. I kept telling myself 'don't fall down, don't fall down.'"

"You didn't look nervous to me. Just cold like the rest of us."

We arrived at the refreshment table where an assortment of cookies, brownies, and other snacks were displayed. Ryan grabbed a plate and put two of everything on it. At the end of the table was a steward dispensing

soft drinks from a soda machine like they have at fast food places.

"Miss Nettles if you'll find a seat we'll bring a Dr. Pepper® to you and what would your friend like?"

"Dr. Pepper® for me too."

We walked over to the side of the room where chairs were lined up along the wall. It was weird. As soon as we got close to the chairs, two people got out of them. Then I realized they were agents who had been sitting there until we arrived so we would have seats. I'm not used to being treated like a celebrity. As soon as we sat down, a steward brought us our drinks.

People were milling all around, going through the motions of talking with each other. Everyone seemed to know everybody else. I looked at the chairs around us,

and they were mostly filled by little kids whose parents had planted them there so they wouldn't spill their snacks.

"Either there aren't too many people with teenagers in your father's administration, or none of them came."

"They probably all had other plans. Most of the people I've met are either right out of college or have grandchildren."

"Well, I don't recognize anyone from our school. Being new I don't know a whole lot of people either."

"Me neither. Just my best friend Rachel and her crowd. But no one at that school talks much about their parents' jobs."

"Yeah, I noticed that. Everyone just sorta assumes you know who they are. Why isn't Rachel here? Her dad is on your dad's staff isn't he?"

"No, he's a senator. This reception isn't for members of Congress. That one won't be until a few weeks from now."

"Guess I figured she'd be here."

"She begged me to sneak her in, but my parents said no. Then I tried to get out of coming, and the President and First Lady insisted I show up, crutches and all."

"You have to call your parents the President and First Lady? That's awful formal isn't it?"

"Only in public. Then I do it sometimes when I'm mad at them. After the election, they gave me this thick book called: *Do's and Don'ts for Presidential Children and Protocol and Manners for Living in the White House.*"

"You're kidding right?"

"Nope. And the thing is there is always someone around watching me to make sure I don't make a mistake. If I do screw up, it gets corrected before anyone else notices."

"So, if you mess up what happens?"

"They throw me in the dungeon."

We both started laughing. I looked up, and people were looking at us. The crowd had thinned out some, and I could see across the room to where the last few people were going through the line.

"You want something else to drink?"

"Yeah, sure."

Ryan got out of the chair and ambled over to the steward who was dispensing drinks. He had that slow deliberate walk of an athlete, and someone who was confident enough not to care what other people thought about him. And he's easy on the eyes too. I can see why you're so hung up on him. But have no fear Rach, I know you saw him first.

"Why didn't you tell me I knew you from the ski trip in Breckenridge?"

"Because I don't remember seeing you there. I mean Rach talked about some guy she met. She kept hoping we would run into each other, but it never happened."

"How come you were never around when we were dancing at our lodge at night? Rachel would come over all the time."

"I was hanging out with my friends from my old school. Some of us had been together since kindergarten. Rach didn't like them very much, and to tell you the truth the feeling was mutual."

"Wow. I was never in a school that long."

"What were you doing at a school in Nebraska if your parents were in Washington?"

"That's because they were living in Beirut. My grandparents live in Nebraska so they sent me to a military school near them. That way I had family nearby for holidays and vacations."

"The President threatened to send me to boarding school right after the election."

"Why?"

"It's a long story, but let's just say I didn't want to move here."

"Why not? It seems like everyone waits on you hand and foot. I bet you don't have to do anything."

"Yeah right. The only reason they wait on me is because of the crutches."

"You know. We did meet at Breckenridge."

"No we didn't."

"Sure did. But you might have been too out of it to remember."

I looked up at Ryan's face, and his eyes. There was something about those eyes.

"Have you figured it out? Or do I need to tell you?"

"Your eyes look familiar. Did I see you on one of the lifts or someplace like that?"

"Close, but you still don't get it."

The entire ski trip raced quickly through my mind. Everything from the scent of the hot chocolate to the wind hitting my face as I raced down the slopes. Then I remembered the accident, and the out of control feeling I had as I tumbled down the mountain. It suddenly dawned on me. This was him.

"You're the guy. The one who tried to help me when I first fell."

"In the flesh. Man it took you long enough to figure that one out."

"You didn't figure it out either. What are you talking about?"

"Nope. All I knew was Rachel stood me up on New Year's Eve. Then some kid from your school said she was at the hospital with you."

"When did you figure it out?"

"The first day of school. After gym class Rachel and I were talking. She apologized to me for standing her up, and said it was your fault."

"But you didn't tell her you were coming here tonight?"

"I didn't know I was coming here tonight until after school today. At first my parents thought this was an adult's only reception. Then my mother looked closer at the invitation, and saw that the entire family was invited. So I tagged along."

"Listen Ryan. Let's not tell Rach we've already met. She's planning on introducing us on Monday. Let me wait and spring it on her then."

"Yeah, whatever you say. It doesn't matter to me. You girls are so strange."

We were so involved in talking we didn't see our parents walk up.

"Did you two spend the entire night talking to each other or did you mingle with the other guests?"

"I guess not ma'am. It was so crowded I haven't moved from this chair."

"Well, it's probably just as well. We really did have a great turnout."

"Mr. President, staff members don't usually turn down an invitation to the White House."

"I guess you're right Reece, now that you put it that way, everyone probably felt they had to show up."

"So what have you kids been talking about?"

"Ma' aaam."

"Whoops. Wrong thing to ask."

"Actually Mrs. Nettles, Beth and I were talking about the ski trip. It seems we met in Breckenridge during Christmas vacation."

"That's Andie Beth to you."

"You never told us about meeting the President's daughter on that trip Ryan."

"Sorry Mom. I didn't know who she was at the time. Actually, I didn't meet her until she had her accident."

"So Andie Beth is the injured girl you told us about?"

"Yes sir. Only I didn't know her name at the time."

"Interesting coincidence I'd say wouldn't you Mr. President?"

"Well, Ryan on behalf of the First Lady and me thank you for coming to her aid."

"No problem sir. But I didn't do much. These guys, I guess they were secret service agents, were there pretty quickly and shooed me away."

"Well thank you anyway. When it comes to my little girl, I'm very protective. You'll understand when you're a parent."

"You're welcome sir."

"Well Claire, Ryan, we'd better be going now. Mr. President, Lynn, it's always good to see you. And it was nice to finally meet Andie Beth."

An aide handed me my crutches, and helped me stand up. The six of us walked towards the entrance. By now there were only a few people left, and I couldn't tell if they were aides, agents, or guests since everyone seemed to be dressed alike.

"See you Monday Ryan."

"Yeah you too Beth. See you in gym class."

If I could have run after him, I would have and beaten him to a pulp. No jerk gets away with just calling me Beth. But don't worry I'll teach him a lesson.

"Seems like a nice young man Buzzie. Now aren't you glad you came?"

"Yes, Daddy. But he's Rachel's heart throb, and that means hands off."

"I wouldn't be so sure about that. If he's as smart as I think he is, I think he may choose the President's daughter over the senator's daughter. What do you think Lynn?"

"About what?"

"About this Kessler kid? We might just have to change our rule, and let Andie B. go on a real date before she's sixteen."

"There's plenty of fish in the sea. Good grief Gary our daughter talks with one boy, and already you've got her going steady with him."

"Your mother's tired, Buzzie, let's get her up to bed."

"As a matter of fact I am. Listen I'm going upstairs. Gary can you help Andie B.?"

"Sure, but in that case let's go raid the White House Mess, and see if they have any of those brownies left over, Buzzie. I saw everyone eating them, but never got my hands on one. That's the problem with these events. I never get to eat."

"Okay, Daddy. Sounds like fun to me. They were good, and I'll betcha they're all gone."

Daddy and I walked to the White House kitchen, otherwise known as the Mess. It was very noisy there as people scurried around clanging dishes and trays and putting away things. When Daddy entered the room, everything suddenly got very quiet.

"Is there something we can do for you Mr. President?"

"As a matter of fact there is. Are there any of those brownies left? My daughter and I thought we could have a late night snack."

"Yes, Mr. President. Would you like us to fix you a plate?"

"Thank you. I'll take it with us upstairs to the residence."

A steward brought over a plate filled with brownies and oatmeal raisin cookies which were Daddy's favorite. He and I walked back through the White House. It was so huge. This time we took the elevator upstairs, and went into the sitting room. Daddy went into the kitchen, and came back with two glasses of milk. Flipping through the channels I found a basketball game. Daddy and I watched for a while until it ended.

"Well, Buzzie guess you and I had better head for bed too. Can you make it upstairs okay? Be ready to leave at 9 a.m. sharp tomorrow morning for Camp David."

"Yes Daddy. And Daddy?"

"Yes, Buzzie?"

"Don't tell anyone, but I really did have fun tonight. Thanks for making me go."

"Your secret is safe with me."

As I went upstairs to my room, I saw Daddy talking with the agent in the hallway. Poor guy. He even had to tell the agents when he was going to bed.

I must have fallen asleep pretty quickly because the next thing I knew it was morning.

Chapter 14

Camp David

"**O**kay Rach maybe I can finally finish telling you about the weekend before I have to start studying again. That is if you hang around on facebook® long enough to hear the whole story."

"So, how was the reception last night, Andie B.? Did you have a good time?"

"It was okay Gram. Lots of people scurrying around. But the brownies were great."

Mama and Daddy came in. I couldn't really figure Mama's mood. I guess Gram must have picked up on it too.

"Lynn, are you okay? You don't look too good."

"I'm fine Mama. I've just got a bad headache."

"Buzzie, we have got to get the bakers to make us some more of those brownies. They were delicious. How many did we put away last night?"

"I don't know Daddy. I quit counting after four."

"How late did you two stay up? I didn't hear you come to bed."

"Beats me. I was just having a good time hanging out with my daughter, and see she still got up on time this morning."

"She's just like you. Anxious to see Camp David. Of course she won't be able to do much on the crutches."

"Is it Camp David she wants to see or the cockpit of Marine One? You know, Buzzie from what I've been told helicopters can be just as much fun to fly as jets."

"No way Daddy, not enough power."

"But they can go places jets can't."

"Forget it Daddy. I want to fly jets. You don't get g forces in helicopters. The best pilots are jet pilots."

"Don't say that aloud to the helicopter pilot or he may strand us at Camp David. It could be a long walk back."

"Mr. President, Marine One has landed."

We quickly put on our jackets, and Gram got Cajun's leash. After taking the elevator down to the first floor, we walked outside. There looming in the distance was Marine One, the President's helicopter. Daddy was right. It was awesome. It looked like a brand new car sitting on the showroom floor. The glare of the morning sun bounced off its sides. Two Marines were standing at the entrance. The bright blue of their dress uniforms was in sharp contrast to the gray overcast sky. A stiff wind cut through me with a biting cold which made me wish I had also worn a sweatshirt under my jacket instead of the running suit and tee shirt.

As we approached the helicopter, the Marines snapped to attention. Combined with their sharp salutes their actions were mechanical as if they were toy soldiers wound up to perform these specific actions. Watching Daddy salute was another story. It seemed unnatural to him. I had overheard a conversation during Christmas between him and Grandpa when he told him that his staff brought in a Drill Sergeant from Fort Benning, Georgia to teach him how to salute and how to recognize the different ranks in the military. They even made him a wallet sized chart of the different ranks for him to refer to. Daddy hasn't had much experience around the military. Grandpa got out of the Army before he was born, and Daddy managed to avoid the draft during Viet Nam when he hurt his knee playing football. The only time he's visited a military post was to campaign at Fort Polk or Barksdale Air Force Base.

We climbed aboard Marine One for the thirty minute ride to Camp David. After we were in the air for ten minutes, the co-pilot came back and asked me if I would like to see the cockpit. This is what I had been waiting for. Daddy nodded his head that it was okay, and Mama didn't notice. She and Gram were busy talking about decorating. Using only one crutch, I made my way to the front of the helicopter and sat down in the co-pilot's seat while he and the pilot explained the various gauges and dials to me. There were so many things you had to watch. They went through each one, and its' purpose. I can't imagine looking at all of them plus flying the 'copter at the same time. On Grandpa's plane there were only three that you had to watch once you took off. Even that was hard sometimes.

These guys seemed to think that flying helicopters was more challenging than flying jets because more could go wrong in a helicopter than a jet. I wasn't convinced yet I heeded Daddy's advice and didn't tell them my opinion. When we approached Camp David, I went back to my seat so the co-pilot could help land the aircraft. We landed in the middle of what appeared to be a baseball field complete with lights. With patches of snow around the infield, it looked in bad shape. Maybe Daddy will have it fixed up so he and I can have batting practice. He must have read my mind.

"Buzzie, this is going to be your field. By April it will be good as new."

"You mean it Daddy?"

"Complete with a pitching machine for batting practice. I'll even be out shagging fly balls with some of these young Marines. I figure we can have some games with you and the Marines versus me and the secret service agents."

"You sure you gonna have time Daddy?"

"I'll make time Buzzie. Once we leave the White House, it's relaxation time for all of us. No press or staff to bother us. It's family time Buzzie."

"Sounds great Daddy."

A van met us at Marine One. Normally everyone travels around Camp David in golf carts, but it was snowing harder so we rode in a van. We pulled up to a sprawling one story house with a sign out front reading: Aspen Lodge and a

smaller sign below reading: **Welcome President Nettles**.
As we entered the house, a huge fire was burning in the
fireplace in the spacious living room. Gram unleashed
Cajun, and he ran from room to room and then back to
me. Once again, the crazy little dog had already figured
everything out. The smell of coffee brewing mixed in with
the ever present Lemon Pledge® smell of furniture wax
was overpowering. We were greeted at the door by a young
aide who didn't look much older than me.

"Mr. President let me show you around Aspen, your
home away from the White House."

We followed her from room to room. At one end of
the living room was an open dining room which led to
the kitchen on one side and an office on the other. Yeah,
right. Daddy wasn't going to work here. To the left of the
entrance was a hallway which led to four bedrooms. Mama

and Daddy's was the biggest, and it was tucked away at the very end in a corner. They also had their own private porch. The one next to theirs was empty except for a bed and desk. It would be Trey's or used by guests. Gram's was across the hall from mine. The rooms were bare, and the colors were yucky and drab.

"Before you start protesting about the way your room looks Andie B., let me remind you that this is my first trip here too. It may take a few months to get this place looking like us."

"Okay, Mama."

"Your grandmother and I will be decorating the rooms, but you realize I now have two houses to decorate instead of just one so it may take a while."

"I get it Mama. You don't have to keep repeating it. But do I get any say so in how it looks?"

"A little bit once we get it narrowed down to two or three choices."

"For the time being, if you need to use a computer you can use the one in your daddy's office. Eventually we may get you one of your own for here."

"Don't know why she needs her own computer. Whatever happened to good old pencil and paper?"

"Nobody uses them any more Gram. Teachers want everything typed."

"What about my own t.v. Mama? Don't tell me I have to watch t.v. with you guys all the time?"

"We'll see but for the time being you can watch t.v. in your daddy's office if you don't want to hang out with us."

The three of us went into the kitchen where Daddy was sitting at the table drinking coffee. Mama poured one for her, Gram and me.

"What do you think of the house Buzzie?"

"At least it looks more like a home than the White House."

"It is a home. Our home away from home."

"Are we going to come here every weekend?"

"Not always. There will be receptions and events we'll have to go to in D.C., and there will be weekends we'll stay there because of your activities."

"Yeah, right."

"Some weekends we'll bring guests here, and I may have a meeting or two up here once in a while. But most of the time we'll be relaxing."

"It's a shame the weather is so nasty. I was hoping we could take a tour."

"Me too, Mama, but maybe tomorrow before we leave. You know Andie B. there are all sorts of activities here.

We had our old bicycles from Kenner shipped here so we can all go riding, jogging or walking."

"Me and my knee braces can hardly wait for that."

"Plus Buzzie, there's a bowling alley, tennis courts, swimming pool, and golf course. And you saw the softball field."

"Great. All these sports activities, and I'm on crutches."

"Buzzie, it's only for another month or so. Next thing I know you'll be racing me just like old times."

"Andie B. don't go feeling sorry for yourself. You'll be coming here for at least the next two and a half years before you go off to college. Camp David isn't going anywhere."

"Yes, Gram."

"Listen everyone. I'm going to lie down for a while. This headache just won't go away."

"Are you okay Lynn?"

"Yes Mama I think it's just my sinuses. The weather and I don't seem to be getting along the last couple of days."

Mama went into the bedroom, and Daddy went in to his office. Shuffling over to the window, I saw that it was snowing harder; this weather would be great for skiing. Once again I looked down at my knees, and realized I wouldn't be skiing this year. Gram came over and stood beside me.

"Andie B. I swear you've grown two inches since Christmas. Either that or I'm shrinking. What are you thinking about?"

"Just about the snow and skiing Gram. I'd love to be out there in it today. I mean we never had much snow in Kenner."

"No, it's too far south and close to the water. Speaking of which have you heard from any of your friends there?"

"Got a text from Lindsay. She said they won their game last night against St. Philip's and that Heather bounced down the court and made three, three point shots."

"No news from Matt though?"

"I don't expect to hear from him, Gram. He's history. It's time to move on."

"Did you meet any nice boys at the reception last night?"

"One, but he's already taken. Most of the kids there were young. Daddy and Mama have young staffs."

"C'mon Buzzie tell your grandmother the truth. You stayed huddled in the corner with that kid, Ryan all night long."

"Daddy, did you sneak up on me again?"

Daddy gave me his all too familiar wink which let me know that he knew I was interested in Ryan. But my problem was Rachel. She and I were best friends. Boys had never come between us because she lived in D.C., and I lived in Kenner. Matt got on her nerves sometimes when she came to visit, but it wasn't like she was attracted to him. And now we were after the same guy. I could wait a few weeks until she tired of him, and threw him back in the sea of girls just waiting to hook him, or I could fight for him.

I was treading on unfamiliar territory here. I wasn't used to fighting over guys. Until now I concentrated on sports. Once I heard Mama and Gram talking and Mama said she thought I was a late bloomer. Gram had reminded her that she was a late bloomer too. The only difference was Mama always had her nose stuck in a book or at the library. I was always shooting baskets or playing catch.

Gram told Mama it didn't make any difference. The results were still the same. Mama didn't meet Daddy until she was almost twenty-four.

I think that may be why Mama was so concerned. From her point of view, I was a lot like her in so many ways, yet I sure didn't see it. Her friend's daughters were the exact opposite of me. They loved to wear dresses, and I only wore them when Mama insisted. When they went to the mall, they hung out at shops like the Aeropostale® and American Eagle®. When I went to the mall, I hung out at the sporting goods stores and the video arcades. While they talked about eye shadow, I talked about shooting percentages and batting averages. Rach used to drive me nuts wanting to clothes shop every time she came to stay for a weekend. Guess we won't be doing much of that any more unless we want a bunch of agents tagging along.

"Buzzie, you want to take a little riding tour of Camp David?"

"Can we Daddy? I've felt locked up ever since we left Kenner."

"I don't see why not. It will be cold in the golf cart, but we've got our cold weather gear. Do you want to come Josie?"

"No thanks. I'll stay here in front of this warm fireplace. But I'll have some hot chocolate waiting for you when you get back. But don't stay out there too long. Lynn will kill both of you if one of you gets sick. And Andie B. make sure you wear a hat and gloves. You too Gary."

Daddy and I both laughed. We bundled up and went outside where a golf cart was parked by the front door. At Camp David we don't have agents in the lodge with us because no one but family and invited guests is allowed through the gates. However, there are staff members and crew members around. Daddy took the wheel, and we rode around. It reminded me of the old days when I would ride beside him in his construction company truck. Our first stop was the gym. There's exercise equipment like tread-mills and weight machines plus a full basketball court. Daddy held on to me while I shot a couple of baskets. I didn't make either of them. I was too afraid of falling. We stopped at the bowling alley. It's cool. There are two lanes so you can compete against each other. Down the road was the huge swimming pool. It's twice the size of our one in Kenner, and bigger than the one at the White House. The tennis courts are right behind it. Mama and Gram play tennis so there is some sport for each of us. Now Daddy can play golf without leaving home. I think we'll have lots of fun here during the summer. Maybe I can convince Mama to let you and some of the kids from school come up for a weekend sleepover.

"Well, what do you think of the place Buzzie?"

"I wish we could live here all the time Daddy. I mean there's a house, church and all this neat sports stuff. You could work in your office, and I could be homeschooled by Mama."

"I don't think the voters would like that Buzzie. They expect me to be in Washington."

"But you did say we could come up here a lot, right?"

"As often as we can. But you and your mama will have a say so about that. I'm sure there will be weekends when you'll have parties and dances to attend. We want your life to be as normal as possible."

"Daddy, my life will never be normal again for as long as I live."

"I wouldn't go quite that far. When you go to the academy, it should return to normal."

"But won't I have agents there?"

"Not like at the White House. The academy is a closed campus. It won't be like an agent will be sleeping next door to you in Bancroft Hall."

"Now that we're so close can we go visit it once I'm off crutches? I don't want the coaches there to see me while I'm still hobbling around."

"Well, I am scheduled to give a speech there to the first class midshipmen before school is out. But we have to make sure it doesn't count as one of your official visits. Otherwise, you'll mess up your recruiting chances. Talk to your basketball coach and see what she says."

"And you'll talk to Mama to convince her to let me go with you? Just the two of us?"

"I'll see Buzzie. Now let's head back to the lodge for some of that hot chocolate. I'm freezing."

We came into the lodge, and I could smell cookies baking. Gram was at it again. She always seemed to know exactly what to fix to hit the spot. Mama had told the staff that we would do our own cooking this weekend so the kitchen was fully stocked with all our favorites.

"How was your tour?"

"Awesome Gram. This place has every sport imaginable. I never knew Presidents were so into physical fitness."

"Buzzie, not every President played each sport. It's just that they keep up all the facilities in case we want to."

"It's really neat Gram. The pool is huge, and there's a gym with a regulation size court."

"Is Lynn still asleep?"

"I checked on her a few minutes ago. She must have taken some sinus medication because she's out."

"I'm going to go get out of this wet shirt. I'll try not to wake her."

"Daddy, stay in here. The LSU vs. Kentucky game is going to start in five minutes."

"I'll be back."

"What about you Andie B.? Is your sweatshirt soaked?"

"No, Gram I'm fine."

"Child no you're not. That shirt is dripping wet. Go to your room and put on some dry clothes before you catch pneumonia."

"Gram, I'm fine. Besides, by the time I get these braces on and off I'll miss the beginning of the game."

"I'll sit here and watch it while you're gone. Didn't you tell me Kentucky was first in the conference? They won't let a freshman like Trey start such an important game. Now go. We don't want to wake up your mama."

"Oh all right. I don't know what the big deal is. I'll eventually dry out."

"The big deal is I don't want you getting sick and missing school. Now go on before I have to get your daddy to make you."

"I'm going. I'm going. But watch the game, and see if you see Trey."

I went into my room and changed clothes. Since Mama was asleep, I decided to let my hair down. Nobody was going to see me out here. Daddy said there was no one at Camp David but the four of us. I put on my LSU sweatshirt and another pair of sweatpants. I didn't bother to put on shoes, just socks. Those chunky shoes I wear all the time really bug me. I can hardly wait to wear my old Nikes®

again. I went back in the living room, and Daddy wasn't there. That figured.

"What's the score Gram? Have you seen Trey yet?"

"8-2 Kentucky leading. I can see why they're number one. No sign of Trey yet."

"Aw. LSU always starts slow. I don't think they warm-up enough before the game starts. It's like they're in slow motion."

"Why don't you stretch out on the couch Andie B.? When your daddy comes out he can sit in the recliner. It will get the pressure off your knees."

"Yeah, Daddy probably isn't coming back out for a while. I bet he went back there and took a nap with Mama."

"You're probably right Andie B."

At half-time Kentucky was ahead by fifteen points. Daddy came into the living room.

"Sorry, Buzzie I laid down on the bed beside your Mama for just a minute, and the next thing I knew I was asleep."

"It's okay Daddy. I figured that's what happened. Besides, Trey hasn't gone in the game. I doubt if he gets in this one."

"Is Kentucky way ahead?"

"Yes, Daddy."

Daddy leaned back in his recliner. Gram went to her room, and it was just the two of us. Just like the old days. Today reminded me of when I was a little kid. It was the first time in ages that Daddy and I spent time together without other people around.

"There's Trey Daddy."

"I see him Buzzie."

As I looked at Trey, I saw him scratching his ankle where the scar from the fire was. It itched a lot. I noticed that whenever he was nervous during a close game, he would scratch that spot. I don't know whether sweat made it itch more, or whether his scratching was a reaction to being scared. If Daddy noticed it, he didn't say anything. No one ever talked about the fire. It was considered a family secret. Since Trey and his friends weren't seriously hurt, it was never brought up. Sometimes I really wanted to talk about it. Like when I noticed Trey scratching. But I was afraid to bring the subject up. The thought that I could have killed my brother scared me. Sometimes I still had nightmares about it. The look on Mama's face that day was permanently etched in my mind. I would have to live with this guilt forever. To escape the feeling, I started talking to Daddy.

"Are we going to get to go to a game this year? All the rest of the games are conference games. The closest he'll be to us will be Tennessee or Kentucky."

"I don't know Buzzie. Let me check my schedule. I'm not making any promises I can't keep. Plus there are all the security concerns."

"Just for a college basketball game? Who would want to mess with you there?"

"There are lots of crazy people Buzzie."

"Could I maybe fly to Mandeville and Grandpa and I go to a game? We could go to the game undercover. Just like two regular people."

"You mean incognito?"

"Yeah, that. I mean if you put Agent Landry in regular clothes instead of a suit he could pass as a regular guy. Do the agents always have to be dressed up?"

"Not necessarily. That might work. Let me talk to your Mama about it, and we'll see what we come up with."

"Daddy, it's not fair."

"What's not fair Buzzie?"

"Every time I ask you about doing something you say you have to talk it over with Mama. Can't you make any decisions on your own?"

"Not when they concern you and Trey. We're your parents Buzzie, and we make our decisions concerning you together."

"Yeah, but Mama treats me like I'm a baby. I'll be sixteen in seven weeks. I bet she won't even let me get my own car."

"We haven't talked about that since your last birthday when you got your learner's permit."

"I took Driver's Ed in summer school. All I have to do is take the road test on my birthday."

"But you know she's not going to let you drive in D.C."

"Why not? My friends do. Ryan's dad bought him a Mustang when they moved here and his birthday is after mine. He can't get his license until April. "

"A Mustang? They've been around since your mother and I were dating?"

"All the guys drive them Daddy. They customize them with fancy wheels and chrome everywhere. Rach and I have collected pictures of cars since we were little kids. Her parents are buying her a PT Cruiser. She saw the papers on it last week, and her birthday isn't until after school gets out."

"Now that you've brought the subject up, what kind of car do you want? That is if your mama and I decide to buy you one."

"See Daddy that goes to show you that you haven't been paying attention. It's the same car that I've wanted forever."

"Buzzie, I realize I haven't been around much the last year, but you're coming down pretty hard on me."

"It's just that no one in this family takes me seriously unless I do something wrong. During the times I'm not in trouble, you guys don't listen to me."

"You still didn't answer my question. If I took you to a car dealership today, what car would you pick out?"

"It's a no brainer Daddy. Just think about it."

"Okay, so what color?"

"Gray Daddy. Now what kind of car do I want?"

"Let's see. You're a beautiful girl so you want a Cadillac."

"Wrong Daddy. Guess again."

"You're an ugly girl so you want an old beat up Ford."

"Da-ddy, quit teasing me."

"I've got it. You're a jock so want something you can haul around your gear in."

"Finally. Now you're thinking."

"And since Ryan has a Mustang, and Rachel is getting a PT Cruiser, you want something in between. I've got it. You want a Jeep."

"That's it Daddy. I want a gray Jeep."

"Which your mama probably won't let you have."

"She will if you convince her. C'mon Daddy please."

Daddy put his recliner in the upright position, and I sat up on the couch. He came over and sat beside me, and I put my head on his shoulder and looked up into his eyes.

"Mama will say yes if you convince her Daddy. Just don't let her talk you out of it. Please Daddy."

Daddy put his arm around me, and pulled me close to him. He tilted his head down, and looked at me. I could feel his scratchy chin on my forehead. I knew then that the Jeep would be mine. I was Daddy's little girl, and somehow he would convince Mama that his little girl needed a Jeep to cruise around in. It would be a hard sell, but in the end Daddy would win over Mama and Gram's objections. The next hurdle would be to convince them I could keep it in D.C. instead of Mandeville or Maryland where I could only visit it occasionally.

The game ended with Kentucky winning by a land-slide. Trey never got off the bench. I could see the disap-pointment in his eyes as the team left the court. My big brother was used to being the star, and this team was full of stars. He would have to serve out his time on the bench until the juniors and seniors graduated.

Mama and Gram came in the room and sat at the table with a book of paint samples and wallpaper pat-terns. Daddy went in to his office to make some phone calls. I just sat there on the couch. I decided to go get my Playstation® from my room when Mama intercepted me.

"Andie B., if you don't have anything to do you need to be studying for your history test or reading your book for English."

"Mama. It's Saturday afternoon. I don't want to study. Besides *Moby Dick* is so boring and if I study for the history test now I'll forget it by Monday."

"And you've got a better idea of how to spend the rest of the afternoon?"

"Not really. But I don't want to study. Just because you like to read all the time doesn't mean that I like to."

"Well, do whatever you want to. I just don't want to see you moping around. So go on in your room. Your grandma and I can't concentrate with the television blasting."

"Good grief."

"Now Andie B."

"Do what your mama says Andie B. The quicker we get these colors figured out the quicker your room gets painted."

"Okay Gram."

I spent the rest of the afternoon in my room playing All Star Baseball on my Playstation®. There was no way I was studying on a Saturday. I had *Moby Dick* in my lap in case Mama came in. I figured I could tell her I was taking a break. I stayed in my room the rest of the afternoon.

The smell of fish frying lured me towards the kitchen. I could hear the grease splattering as Gram dropped the hushpuppies and fish into the frying pan.

"Come set the table Andie B. Your mama and daddy went for a walk."

"Okay, Gram. We haven't had a fish fry in ages. I sure like your cooking better than those White House chefs."

"Thanks Andie B. But you know when you get off those crutches; it will be your turn to cook."

"No thanks Gram. I'll leave that chore to you and Mama."

"Every young girl needs to know how to cook."

"Not in this day and age Gram. That's why they have restaurants. Besides I'll be eating in Mess Halls."

"Well, I'm still going to teach you. We'll start with something easy, like your favorite brownies. No young man will be able to resist you once you put a plate of my brownies in front of him."

"Gram."

"Just ask your daddy. Your mama would be an old maid schoolteacher if it weren't for those brownies."

About that time Mama and Daddy came in.

"Is that true Daddy?"

"What's that Buzzie?"

"Did you marry Mama because of Gram's brownies?"

"Watch what you say Gary."

"Well, let's say they were a contributing factor."

"Thanks a lot."

"Plus her eyes. Buzzie, your Mama has the most beautiful eyes."

"Yes, Andie B. and these eyes can tell you that your daddy is nervous. You've hit a touchy subject."

"What do you mean, Mama?"

"What she's trying to say Buzzie is I was attracted to her body, but it was your gram's brownies that won me over. I got a two for one deal."

"I think this discussion may be a little premature. You'll understand it better when you're older. What started it anyway?"

"Gram said she wanted to start teaching me to cook. And she said we'd start with the brownies."

"Good choice Buzzie. Can Rachel cook? Guys go for brownies."

"I don't know Daddy."

"Brownies are a good first step. Especially at your age. But I think he'll ask you out anyway."

"For the gazillionth time Daddy. He's Rachel's boyfriend. If he asks me out, it's the end of our friendship."

"She's right Gary."

"So what are you going to do?"

"Nothing. Daddy, quit teasing me."

"Yes, Gary. It seems like that's all you've talked about. When Andie B. is ready to date, she'll date. Besides she's not even sixteen yet."

"Seven more weeks Mama."

"But who's counting, right?"

"Me. I want my license. Even if I never get to use it because of all the agents. Since my birthday is on a

Thursday, I can go right after school. If you guys can't take me, Agent Landry can."

"Slow down Andie B. There are a lot of details that have to be worked out."

"Like what? It's simple. Agent Landry takes me to the office. I pass the test, and I have my license."

"It's a little more complicated than that."

"Well, you guys don't have to go with me if that's what you mean. Nobody expects the President or First Lady to show up with their kid just to take their driver's test."

"And suppose we want to go?"

"If I have to wait until you guys can fit it into your schedules, I'll be an old lady."

"No, I just meant that we'll have to make sure we have agents check out the Department of Motor Vehicles Office. I don't even know where it is."

"But Mama, that's why you and Daddy have such big staffs. Besides, you've got seven weeks."

"I get your point. But I do want to go with you."

"Aw Mama. It's not necessary. Let Gram go with me."

"Why do you want your grandmother instead of me?"

"She's calmer. Besides if you go, there will be reporters all over the place when the car drives up. If Gram and I and Agent Landry go, we can go in one Blazer."

"She's right Lynn. You've said you want to keep Andie B.'s life as normal as possible. If you show up at the DMV, both of you will be on the six o'clock news."

"Okay, I guess that makes sense. We're all going to have to make some adjustments including me."

Well, at least we finally got all the car stuff out in the open. It's weird Rach, it's like my parents are freaking out about my turning sixteen. I'm sure Daddy told Mama about the car I wanted. I'm still not sure if I'm getting it or not. She hasn't brought the subject up. But I don't understand what the big deal was about her going to the DMV with me. Why would she want to go? I just hope they let me keep my car here.

The rest of the weekend was pretty quiet. It quit snowing overnight. We went to church on Sunday. There's a chapel at Camp David which has services each week for guests and staff. It's really small though. Not like our big church in Kenner. Of course, Daddy and Mama spoke to everyone there while Gram and I stood around and waited in the background. The Chaplain is in the Navy, and he talked with me a little about the academy.

After lunch we came back to the White House. Mama told me if I wanted to the next time we came I could bring some extra clothes to leave at Camp David. That way I wouldn't have to pack a bag each time. I could just leave some jeans and sweats there. Makes sense to me.

"Rach, I gotta go. I hear Gram coming. She and I are having supper together tonight since Mama and Daddy are eating at the vice-president's house. Catch you at school tomorrow."

Chapter 15

The Introduction

"Rachel, are you out there? Today was one of the worst days of my life. Mama and Daddy are going to freak out when they see the grade I made on the history test. C'mon Rach, answer me. You're not mad because I already met Ryan are you? I tried to tell you over the weekend I thought the guy I met at the reception might be him, but you never answered me."

Sunday night I was having trouble studying for the history test. History and English are so boring. None of the names and dates made any sense, and the book is no help. It might as well be written in Greek. Since Mama and Daddy were out for the evening, I quit studying early. I logged back on the computer and Trey was on facebook® so we talked for a few minutes. Then I heard footsteps, and quickly turned it off. I don't need to be in any more trouble. It was only Gram coming to check on me.

"How's the studying coming?"

"It's not."

"What do you mean Andie B. Didn't you say you had a history test tomorrow?"

"Gram. I don't get it."

"Don't get what?"

"I don't understand why I have to study about all these old dead people who fought in wars hundreds of years ago."

"Because everyone has to take world history Andie B."

"But math and science are so much more interesting. In those classes you have a problem and a solution. In world history and English you just have tons of facts to memorize."

"Well, you still have to take the class."

"Can't I watch t.v. for a while? I've finished all my other homework. Please Gram."

"Your mama would kill me if I let you watch t.v. when you had a test to study for."

"She doesn't have to know."

"Sorry Andie B. but if you've finished studying you could always read a book."

"Gram."

"Why don't you go outside for a few minutes and get some fresh air. You've been cooped up here since we came back from Camp David this afternoon. Besides, Cajun needs to go out one more time."

About that time Caj came running into the room. I walked down to the second floor den and snatched his leash. Maybe Gram was right. A blast of cold air might do the trick. The White House was silent in a spooky sort of way. Sunday is the one day that the staff gets a break. Since Mama and Daddy were at the vice president's house, most of the agents and aides either had the night off or were with them. The lights in the corridors were dimmed lending an eerie sort of glow to the hallways. Usually, there were people constantly moving as if they were on some sort of secret mission that no one else knew about. It wasn't that way tonight. As Cajun and I left the building, I almost expected to see a **Closed** sign hanging from the door. I unhooked Cajun's leash, and he took off running.

I wandered over to my favorite spot in front of the pillar, and leaned against it. Cajun was racing around the South Lawn. It's hard to see very many stars from out here. There are still too many bright lights. Since no one is allowed to fly over the White House, I never see planes. I miss my old back yard. I wonder if the kids living in our old house appreciate what they have. I bet they don't even realize it.

Cajun came racing up to me with a dog biscuit hanging out of his mouth like a cigarette. Some agent out there in the dark must be giving him treats. He lay down beside me gnawing away as I petted him. Gram was right. I did need to come out here for a while. Sitting on the steps seemed to always clear my head. But it doesn't change my attitude. I still hate history. Cajun took off running again in search of another treat. I tried to run the names and dates for the test through my head, but I kept getting stuck. Maybe Trey was right. Next time I'll put all the questions and answers on flash cards. He says that's the way he still studies. He and his girlfriend run cards with each other. Sometimes they ask the questions. Other times they give the answers. Just like the t.v. show Jeopardy.

I looked at my watch. We had been out here for thirty minutes, and I was cold. Pulling my jacket tighter around me, I grabbed one crutch while resting my other hand on the pillar. Another hand handed me my other crutch. It was an agent who had been standing nearby in the shadows.

"Thanks. I didn't see you."

"That's good. Then I'm doing my job."

"What do you mean?"

"The President wants to make sure you have your privacy Miss Nettles. He doesn't want you to feel like you're always being watched."

"Even though I am."

"Right."

"Well, I should be off these things in the next few weeks. No more knee braces or crutches."

Caj came running up with another dog biscuit hanging from his mouth. I snapped the leash on to his collar, and headed back inside. Gram was where I had left her in the sitting room.

"Your cheeks are red. It must be cold outside. Did you clear some of the cobwebs out of your brain?"

"Yes, Gram. But I think Caj had the best time. He kept running up to me with dog biscuits hanging out of his mouth."

"It's the agents. They play hide and seek with him. When he finds them, they give him a treat."

"I wondered. He raced across the South Lawn like he was on fire."

"It's a game they play. Now you better get upstairs and get ready for bed and do some more studying."

"Aw, Gram. Do I have to? I'm on brain overload. I'll never understand this history stuff."

"Just concentrate and do your best."

"And if my best isn't good enough for Mama?"

"We'll cross that bridge when we come to it. Now scoot. I'll be up in a few minutes to tuck you in."

"Gram, it's still early. I'm the only almost sixteen year old that has to be in bed by 10 p.m. It's not fair."

"Andie Beth. Quit your whining and go."

"Yes, ma'am. Now you sound like Mama."

"Good. Your mama and daddy made these rules. You have to abide by them, and I have to enforce them. Otherwise, we're both in trouble."

When I came downstairs this morning, Daddy had already left for the Oval Office. Mama was reading a report as usual as she drank her coffee. She always had some report or folder in front of her. I grabbed a muffin from the basket in the middle of the table, and sat down. There was a glass of orange juice and a glass of milk already at my seat. I was halfway through my muffin before Mama even looked up.

"Ready for your test?"

"I guess so. It's so hard at this school Mama."

"You'll just have to apply yourself, and study harder. I know you're as smart as Rachel, and if she can do it so can you."

"Yeah, right."

"I won't be here after school today. I've got a doctor's appointment, and your grandmother is going with me. So go straight to therapy when you get home."

"Yes, Mama. I'm supposed to find out today when I can ditch these crutches."

"Well, you better concentrate on doing well on the history test, and forget about the crutches for now. That's your problem Andie B. You've got your priorities in the wrong order."

"But Mama, I miss playing sports. Actually I miss walking like a normal person."

"There's plenty of time for that. Right now you need to concentrate on your grades. Now go. Agent Landry is waiting for you."

"Yes, Mama."

When I arrived at school, you were waiting for me as usual. Agent Landry handed me my backpack, and helped me out of the Blazer. I hadn't seen you this excited about anything in a long time. You were all over this guy I could only see from the side. But even that view confirmed my worst fear. Your Ryan was the same guy I had met at the reception on Friday night.

"A.B. over here."

"Hi Rach."

"A.B. this is Ryan. Ryan, this is Andie B., my best friend in the whole wide world."

"We've met, Rachel."

"You have. Where?"

"I found Beth in the snow when she had her accident."

"You're the guy who stayed with her until the agents came."

"Yeah."

"A.B. did you know that?"

"Not until gym class the other day. Ryan sort of ran into me on his way to class."

"And then I had to go to that reception at the White House with my parents the other night and we saw each other again."

"So, you've seen my boyfriend twice in one week, and you haven't even told me. Some friend you are A.B."

"It's not that way at all Rach. I didn't have a clue who Ryan was even when he tripped over my chair on Tuesday. He recognized me, but I thought it was because I was the President's kid not because we had met before."

"And what about you? Were you going to tell me you had already met A.B. or were you going to act surprised?"

"I tried to tell you all weekend Rach, but you were so excited about our meeting each other. Besides, I didn't want to hurt your feelings. You were making such a big deal about me meeting Beth that I didn't want to burst your bubble."

"That's Andie Beth to you."

"Whatever."

"Besides, what difference does it make Rach? Now all of us know each other. I've got to get to my locker before first period. Are you coming Rach?"

"See ya in class A.B."

"Yeah. Later guys."

You two walked off holding hands. I'm happy for you Rach. He's a nice guy. And when you dump him, I'll be right here to catch him before he hits the ground. Another trophy for your trophy case in the den that will be tossed aside when the next guy comes along. And I your faithful companion will be waiting. Most of the guys you've dumped over the years haven't been worth the price of the Nike® emblem on their shirt, but there's something about this guy. Somehow, knowing you Rach, you don't see in him what I do. Ryan Kessler is way too deep for you. Eventually he will get tired of being led around by your leash. Who knows? For once in your life someone may actually dump you instead of the other way around.

Mama may be right. I may be a late bloomer. But even jocks get interested in guys. I can't explain the feeling I have every time I see him. I've never felt this way about a guy before. But for now he's yours. I'll stick to the friends creed, and I won't act interested. But if you guys break up, it's every woman for herself.

What am I doing daydreaming about some guy? This isn't me. A.B. doesn't gush over guys. Get your priorities straight Andie B. Concentrate on walking and playing sports. You've got to ditch these crutches. This afternoon your mission is to convince the doctor and physical therapist that your knees are healed enough to start putting pressure on them.

School was a blur today. You and I didn't talk much. I looked at your paper in English class, and you were writing Ryan's name all over it just like before. All I could think about was the history test. My gut feeling told me I wasn't prepared. When I saw the test paper, I knew I wasn't. Not only were there fifty multiple choice questions, but there were three essay questions. You had to answer two of the three. The only problem was I didn't know the answer to any of them.

Grades are no big deal to me, but they are to Mama and Daddy. As long as I keep a C average the school says I can play. Mama and Daddy say I have to have a B average or they'll make me quit. I can't quit now. The academy requires good grades, but athletes usually have a lower average. Plus I'm the President's kid. That ought to account for something.

The problem is you. When your best friend is a brain, it makes life hard on you. School comes natural to you. You don't study all the time like Mama thinks. Most of the time you're on the internet talking to boys in chat rooms. You love to read. You've already finished Moby. I'm struggling to keep up with each day's reading.

What makes it worse is that your mom and my mother are best friends. It's like they're always comparing notes. What Mama doesn't realize is that you could care less about sports. You play basketball and softball so you'll have extracurricular activities to put on your college applications. You're also in two or three clubs at school.

Most of what you do you do for attention. You have one older brother who's a senior, and three little brothers. You're surrounded by boys so your mom indulges your with anything you want. Your dad doesn't have much time for you, and sometimes I think you're jealous of the time I spend with Daddy.

I left school right after phys ed. Coach Shine said I didn't have to hang around for the rest of basketball practice. Physical therapy counts as my practice time. I could hardly wait to get home, and change. Agent Landry noticed something was on my mind.

"You're sure anxious this afternoon. Something happen at school that I need to know about?"

"Nothing other than the test. You could have least slipped me the answers under the door."

"That bad, huh?"

"Worse. Let's just say I might as well cancel any weekend plans until the end of school."

"When do you get the results?"

"Wednesday."

"Maybe you'll get some good news from the orthopedist today."

"Yeah, I may be grounded, but at least I'll be walking under my own power."

"Look at it this way. You'll be able to start your spring training."

"If Mama lets me come downstairs."

I went upstairs and changed into my bathing suit with sweats over it. That way I could use the whirlpool after therapy. When I entered the medical office all four of them were there: Dr. Hunter, Dr. Waddell, Ms. Nichols and Ms. Brown.

"Today's the day, right?"

"Day for what Ms. Nettles?"

They all started laughing.

"The First Lady said you were anxious to get the verdict about your knees."

"Yes, sir. It's been over a month since I had the accident. I'm tired of clanking around."

"Ms. Nettles, you do realize that you aren't going to be able to ditch the crutches one day, and run up and down the basketball court the next don't you?"

"Yes, Dr. Waddell sir. But for now I just want to put my feet on the ground like a normal person. I'm tired of always having help getting up and down like a little old lady."

"Let's get started then."

I went into the examining room. It smelled like alcohol.
I took off my shoes, the knee braces, and sweatpants. It was
freezing in there. Ms. Nichols wheeled in a portable x-ray
machine, and I lay back on the table. She x-rayed both of
my knees. Dr. Waddell and Dr. Hunter came in and poked
and prodded every inch of both knees. With Ms. Brown's
help they moved my knees in a bunch of different directions. Several times the pain shot through my whole leg as
if I was being stabbed with a sword. I never let on that it
hurt. I had to get off these crutches. Everyone left to talk,
and to look at the x-rays. I put my sweatpants back on, and
headed to the therapy room. Ms. Brown was there, and I
began my workout. After a few minutes, the doctors and
Ms. Nichols came in.

"Ms. Nettles, stand up."

"Sir?"

"I said stand up Ms. Nettles."

I reached down for my crutches.

"I didn't say anything about grab your crutches Miss Nettles. I just said stand up. Now do what you're told."

"Yes sir."

I stood up under my own power for the first time since December with both my feet on the ground. Ms. Nichols handed me a cane to help me balance.

"Miss Nettles, you are now ready to upgrade to a cane. We also have some smaller knee braces for you so you'll be able to wear regular shoes from now on. Let's get them fitted, and see you take a few steps."

I sat down. My legs felt rubbery after only standing for a few minutes. I couldn't believe it. I was standing on my own for the first time since right after Christmas. Ms.

Brown fitted the new knee braces, and I stood up again. Using the cane for balance, I took my first steps across the room. The floor was cold on my bare feet. My legs quivered like Jello® as I took baby steps across the room. It was as if I was learning to walk for the first time.

"How long will it take me to walk normal Dr. W.?"

"A few days. Try not to shuffle your feet. That could cause you to trip or fall."

"Great, now I've got something else to worry about."

"You've got to take it slow for the first few days. If you don't have confidence in what you're doing, then you'll need to keep using the crutches."

"No way, sir. I've come too far to go backwards. After today, no more crutches or wheelchairs for me. I've got to go forward not backwards. When can I start running?"

"Slow down, Ms. Nettles. You've got to get confident walking first. You'll be using the cane for a few weeks, and then walking on your own before you'll be able to run."

"I will be ready for softball practice though, right?"

"When does it start?"

"I think it's the end of February."

"Miss Nettles, knowing you and seeing the progress you have already made I think you'll be more than ready by the end of February. But for right now I think you need to concentrate on walking. The three of us are going to leave you and Ms. Brown alone so you can continue your therapy session."

"Dr. Waddell?"

"Yes, Ms. Nettles."

"Thanks."

"You're welcome, Ms. Nettles. But you and Ms. Brown deserve all the credit. You're the ones who have done the work."

I was so excited I felt like I could run across the room, but my knees were still wobbly. This was the most pressure I had put on them since the day of the accident. Finally, no crutches. I kept walking around the room. As I walked, I felt steadier on my feet.

"Miss Nettles, why don't you sit down? Take a break for a few minutes and work on the weights. You're making me dizzy."

"Ms. Brown. I'm just so excited. This is the first time I've been flat footed since December."

"Your face is as red as a beet. Take a break. You heard Dr. Waddell. Take your time to heal."

"Yes, ma'am."

When I did sit down, I realized how tired I was. Ms. Brown handed me a towel, and the sweat was dripping off my face and neck just like it did during a hard basketball practice. I was blinking to keep the saltiness out of my eyes. Reaching the back of my ponytail, I pulled the soggy scrunchies out of my hair. My hair stuck to my face and neck. My bathing suit felt glued to my body, and my sweatpants and sweatshirt stuck to it. It reminded me of my days following practice at St. Martins. I liked this feeling. It was a feeling of victory. I had reached a goal. Andie B. was back.

"I'm afraid you'll have to wear your chunky shoes upstairs one more time. We'd both be in trouble if I let you walk out of here barefooted."

"After I get upstairs, they're going in the trash can. I never want to see these ugly things again. Except for school, it's back to Nikes® for me."

"Just remember. Take your time walking. If you trip or fall, you risk injuring yourself again."

"Don't worry Ms. Brown. I never want to go through this again."

I pulled on a pair of socks and slid my feet into the chunky shoes one last time. Quickly tying the laces I was back on my feet. I walked out of the therapy room and into the outer office.

"Miss Nettles, slow down. There's a speed limit in this office."

"Sorry, Dr. Hunter."

"You mastered Walking 101 in less than an hour. Do you need any help going upstairs?"

"No, sir. In fact, I'm heading outside for a few minutes."

For the first time since we moved, I walked out the side entrance to the steps, and kept going. I wanted to see what Cajun had been seeing. My first stop was the patio. There was a high concrete wall all around it. It reminded me of a small house without a roof. At one corner was a barbecue pit, and the pool took up the middle. There was a cover on it, but the diving board was still there. The lawn furniture had been put up for the winter so I sat on the edge of the diving board. I couldn't see my room from here. It was obscured by trees. For the first time I noticed men on the roof of the White House. One of them was looking at me with binoculars. Yuck. I couldn't even walk in my own back yard without agents staring at me.

After catching my breath, I walked to the opposite end of the patio. Then I saw the basketball court complete with lights. There were two benches beside the court, and a basketball was on one of them. I sat down, dropped the cane, and took the basketball in my hand. Rolling it over I found the Wilson® trademark. This was a brand new ball. Lifting it to my nose I inhaled the scent of rubber mixed with ink. I dribbled it between my legs. It felt good to have my hand on a basketball. My palm recognized the familiar touch that I had grown up with. Scooting over to the end of the bench I began to dribble with my left hand. I was about to stand up and dribble when I heard a deep voice from behind me.

"Don't even think about it."

"Daddy, what are you doing here?"

"I was on my way upstairs for supper, and expected to find you on the steps. But one of the agents said you were roaming around out here. Thought I'd better come see what was going on, and it looks like I got here just in time. You weren't thinking about dribbling the ball to the basket and shooting were you?"

"Who, me? No way Daddy."

"Buzzie."

"Well, I was going to see if I could dribble with one hand while balancing with the cane in the other. Then if that worked."

"Then I did get here just in time. C'mon Buzzie toss me the basketball."

"Da-ddy."

"C'mon Buzzie. Now. You know you're not ready to play yet. You just got rid of the crutches less than two hours ago."

"But Daddy I had to try. I'm tired of sitting on the bench. I want to play. This court is awesome. The goals have cushions around them like the ones at school."

"Buzzie, toss me the basketball."

"Just one shot Daddy, please."

"Buzzie. Now."

"C'mon Daddy. You know you want to play too."

"Andie Beth, come over to this bench right now, and sit down beside me."

"Why sir? So you can ground me. If you're gonna do it, you might as well do it from there."

"No, so we can talk. C'mon Andie Beth."

I flopped down on the bench with my arms wrapped tightly around the basketball. The cane crashed to the ground. I wasn't going to give up the basketball. I had come exploring. When I left the White House after therapy,

I was on a high. Finally off crutches I felt free again. For the first time since we left Kenner, I was at home again - on the basketball court. Then Daddy had to ruin it. I didn't do anything wrong. All I wanted to do was to hang out at the basketball court in my back yard. It was just like the old days.

"Buzzie, why do you act this way?"

We were back to Buzzie. That's always a good sign. It means Daddy was cooling off. The vein in his neck wasn't bulging any more, and his face wasn't as red.

"Because sometimes you don't trust me Daddy. When I was at therapy today, the doctors and nurses told me the "do's and don'ts." I'm not going to do anything stupid, and get hurt again. Then you come out here all Presidential acting. I came out here to explore the rest of the yard.

Cajun has run all over the place. Before today, I hadn't been beyond the steps."

"Why didn't you just say so to start with?"

"Because you never gave me a chance. Sometimes you forget that I'm your daughter not some junior staff member."

"I guess I'm so used to barking out orders all day that when I see you about to make a mistake I want to protect you. Then Buzzie you were so defiant."

"I wasn't defying you Daddy. I wasn't doing anything wrong. All I was going to do was dribble the ball standing up. Then I was coming in."

"Buzzie, lately every conversation with you turns into an argument. Every time someone tries to tell you what to do, or how to do something you talk back to them."

"But, Daddy. It's just because you guys don't get it. On the one hand you tell me you respect the fact that I'm growing up, and on the other hand every time I go to do something you tell me to stop. I'm almost sixteen."

"I know, Buzzie. You remind me of that on a daily basis."

"Well, it must not be sinkin' in, because you and Mama treat me like I'm a baby."

"We're trying to protect you."

"You still don't get it. All I wanted to do was explore my own back yard like a normal kid who has moved into a new house. Only my house happens to be the President's house. I didn't bring the basketball out here. It was on the bench. I started dribbling it. That's all."

"So, you really weren't going to shoot?"

"Not until you challenged me. You didn't trust me to know right from wrong."

"Okay, well let's get inside. I'm ready for dinner. Your mother and grandmother should be back by now."

We walked back into the White House.

Chapter 16

Test Results

"Rachel, are you out there? Guess I'm grounded forever this time. Daddy even threatened to send me to boarding school."

I woke up today looking for any excuse not to go to school. I did not want to get the world history test back. Goodbye freedom. If I did as bad as I think I did, I may not even get to celebrate my sixteenth birthday. I thought about faking a sore throat or a cold, but one of the disadvantages to living in the White House is that there is a doctor's office on the first floor, and the doctor and nurse make house calls to the residence.

Fortunately, Mama was not in the kitchen when I went in for breakfast. Gram was the only one there.

"Still can't get used to seeing you using only a cane. How does it feel to be rid of the crutches?"

"Great, Gram."

"You'll be running down these halls before you know it. Now sit down and eat some breakfast."

"I'm not hungry Gram."

"You're not sick or anything are you? Because if you are you'd better tell me."

"No. I'm just not hungry."

"Well, at least drink some milk, and take a piece of toast with you to eat on the way to school."

I sat down, and drank a few sips of orange juice and a couple more of milk. Gram soon got involved in a morning news show, and I slipped out of the dining room leaving the toast behind. I was not in the mood for any conversation this morning. All I wanted to do was escape.

"You're early this morning. In a big hurry to get to school?"

"Not particularly. Just didn't feel like hanging out with the elders any longer than I had to."

"Makes sense. Especially at your age."

"Yeah, like you're so much older than I am."

"I've got at least twelve, okay eleven years on you once you have your birthday. Speaking of which, are you having a big party here at the White House, or going back to Kenner and celebrating there?"

"I haven't thought about it. I'm still waiting to see if Daddy is going to convince Mama to let me have my own car."

"The down side Miss Nettles is that even though you may be driving it, there will always be a Blazer full of agents in your rearview mirror."

"Great. Just what I need."

"And by the way, don't even think of trying to outrun them. Last teenager that tried that almost ended up in a bad car wreck."

"What happened?"

"It was a few years ago. But the stories I've heard about her was she was a *wild child*."

"What do you mean?"

"Always breaking the rules. Every time her parents were out of town, she got into trouble. She was always trying to dodge her agents. I don't want to tell you too much. Don't want to give you any ideas."

"Between my parents and grandmother there's not much chance of my getting in trouble. Someone's always watching me like a hawk."

"I don't know. Somehow I think you could figure out a way to accomplish anything you want."

For the first time since I've been at the new school, you weren't there when I arrived. I headed towards my locker, and dropped off my books for my afternoon classes. Then I saw Ryan walking towards me.

"Where's Rach? I figured you two were hanging out in the quad."

"She's sick. Said she left you a message on facebook®. Wants you to get her homework for her."

"No problem. I never turn on my comp in the morning. Not enough time."

"Now that you're using the cane does that mean you'll be playing softball this season."

"Keep your fingers crossed. I'll go nuts if I have to miss another season."

"What position do you play?"

"Pitcher and first base. What about you?"

"Pitcher and right field. That way I don't wear out my arm. Well, there's the bell. See you later Beth."

"Yeah, later Ryan."

Not only is he a jock, but he's also a pitcher. This guy is starting to look better and better. Guess I'd better quit talking about him to you. My thoughts on Ryan will have to stay my thoughts. Today I would be the one writing Ryan Kessler in the margin of my notes not you. I daydreamed my way through geometry and English. Then it was on to world history.

I could tell by the look on the Colonel's face that he was not in a good mood. He scowled at everyone as they walked in.

"Hurry up and take your seats everyone. It's going to be a long day."

No one paid him any attention. They kept on walking and talking. His face got redder. I have a feeling if he could have ordered us to get down and do pushups he would have. When the bell rang, people were still milling around. I looked up at him, and it looked like a cloud of steam was coming out of his ears like a bull getting ready to charge.

"I said seats everyone and I mean now."

Everyone sat down.

"Miss Nettles, where is your friend Miss LeBrun? She appears to be the only one missing today."

"She's sick sir. I told her I would get the homework assignment."

"Fine."

He took the stack of test papers, and slammed them on his desk several times. If I hadn't been watching him, I would have thought he was cracking a whip.

"What got into you people? Are your brains still on vacation? These are the worst test scores I have seen in ages. You're advanced placement sophomores, and you miss simple historical facts. All I can say is it's a good thing you have the rest of the semester to bring these grades up, because if this were the last test of the semester some of you would be joining me in summer school. Oh, and by the way, for those of you, who think you can get away without your parents knowing about this grade, forget it. The school secretary has called each of your parents this morning informing them of your grade."

Great. Just what I need. My only hope is the message gets lost in the massive tangle of phone lines in the White House. Somehow I don't think the President is going to take a phone call from a school secretary.

The Colonel handed out the test papers. When he came to me, he told me that you had made an A. Then he gave me my paper. A C-.

"Miss Nettles, you've got to pay more attention to the details. Otherwise you're doomed in this class."

"Yes, sir."

A C-. Great. When my parents hear about this I'm dead. If I don't get my grade up to a B by softball season, they won't let me play knees or no knees. There goes my car. And if by chance the secretary did get through to Daddy, he's probably got one of his staff members registering me at a boarding school. Making a C in Kenner wasn't so bad. I was thankful when I squeaked by with a B in world history. Even though my parents wouldn't admit it, I think they were relieved. They know that math and science are my best subjects. Even Gram will be on my case. She kept telling me I needed to study more on Sunday night, but all those facts were just a blur. Then he sprung the essay questions on us. I wasn't expecting them. It's the first time I've ever had essay questions in a history class. I'm not used to explaining history. Besides, why would I have to explain it to a teacher? Most teachers just give multiple choice or true-false tests. But not this guy, he's trying to make us into writers as well as historians.

The rest of the day went by in a blur. The only good thing that happened was that Ryan caught up with me when I was walking down the hall to gym.

"What's wrong, Beth? I figured you'd already be in the gym shooting hoops now that you're off the crutches."

"'Fraid not. First of all I've already been warned about playing basketball. I got in trouble with my dad because I was dribbling a basketball much less shooting one."

"Your parents are that strict?"

"Worse. Now when he sees the grade I made on the world history test I'm doomed. I may be the one going to boarding school."

"That bad, huh. He can't send you away just because you bombed one test. Did you flunk it?"

"Almost. A C-, which in my parent's book might as well be an F. And of course, your girlfriend made her usual A which won't help."

"What do Rach's grades have to do with yours?"

"Our mothers are best friends. My mom compares me to Rach like we were twins."

"Yeah, but you guys are so different. I mean like night and day."

"Thanks for noticing."

"I didn't mean it that way. You know, I mean well, you guys are just different."

"It's okay Ryan I know what you mean. You better get in there before coach makes you run laps for being late."

"Okay, see ya Beth."

"That's Andie Beth to you."

Coach Shine was glad to see me walking with a cane. She wants me to bring my glove and start throwing tomorrow. I can play catch from a chair to loosen my shoulder. She's also going to make a target for me to throw balls at.

Agent Landry was waiting for me after class.

"You look worse than you did this morning. Are you feeling okay, Miss Nettles?"

"Fine. Let's just go home. And Agent Landry, take the long way will you? I'm in no rush to get there."

"History test was that bad, huh?"

"Worse. At least if I had failed it, I could have used the excuse of not understanding the questions. But the Colonel wrote a note on my test paper telling me to pay more attention to details, and he wants both parents' signatures on it by tomorrow."

"That's bad."

"Yeah, it means both of them will come down on me not just her. Then my grandmother will join in. It's been nice knowing you Agent Landry."

"What do you mean, Miss Nettles?"

"After this afternoon, I'll probably be on the first plane to some isolated boarding school in Vermont where they send government kids who mess up."

"I don't think they would go that far, just for one test grade."

"All I can say is I've been practicing my defense in my head since third period, and I would still convict me."

"But a C- isn't that bad a grade. Especially for your first test in a new school."

"Thanks, but I'm afraid my parents won't see it that way. The school requires a C average to play sports. The President and First Lady require a B average."

"But you've always made a B average. So, what's the problem?"

"Agent Landry, get with it. Sometimes I barely make a B average which is good enough for me. But it's not good enough for them."

"Because?"

"My mom was an honor student. She loves all the classes I hate like English and history. Daddy wasn't the greatest student in the world, but he didn't have to be since he ran Grandpa's company before he and Mama went to law school."

"I didn't know your mother graduated from law school?"

"She didn't. She dropped out after her second year when Trey was born. But Daddy loved law school, and made good grades with Mama's help. Now they expect Trey and I to be as smart as them."

"Miss Nettles, you are smart. You didn't ask for my advice, but I'm going to give it to you anyway. Go in there and admit you screwed up, and I think you'll be okay."

"In other words, forget about my defense argument, and throw myself on the mercy of the court."

"Exactly. From what I hear through the grapevine, the President and First Lady have a lot of issues on their agendas right now. You tell them you screwed up; they ground you for a weekend or two, and it will be forgotten by your birthday."

"Thanks Agent Landry."

"We're here. Our twenty minute trip took almost an hour. I'll make sure your backpack gets upstairs. Take your test paper with you. The President is expecting you in the Oval Office. Hold your head high. A good lawyer always looks confident. See you in the morning."

I had not been in the Oval Office since Inauguration Day when Daddy's secretary, Mrs. Wiggins, gave us our first tour of downstairs at the White House. In my mind The West Wing was the official part of it, and I didn't feel comfortable with all those people scurrying around.

When Daddy was a senator, I never visited him at his office. Trey and I would always catch up with him at the apartment. He would walk in the door with his jacket in his hand, and his tie hanging loosely around his neck. Even when he worked at the construction company, he would come in the house and head for the shower. Taking a shower and changing clothes right after work seemed to be the way Daddy unwound at the end of the day. Of course, at the construction company he was always dirty. Mama made him clean up before dinner. I guess I never thought about him still doing it.

I was now at the offices surrounding Daddy's office. A girl who didn't look any older than me but must have been an intern approached me.

"Excuse me Miss, but you must be lost. The school tour group isn't allowed in this part of The White House."

Before I could say a word, I heard a familiar voice behind me laughing. I looked around, and it was Ethan one of the guys who had been on Daddy's staff when he was in the senate.

"It's okay Shannon. This tourist lives here."

"But sir?"

"Shannon meet Miss Nettles, otherwise known as first kid. Like I said she lives here."

"Sorry, Miss Nettles. It's just. . ."

"I know. I look like a tourist. Thanks Ethan. I'd hate to get kicked out of my own house."

"Shannon, weren't you on your way somewhere?"

"Yes, sir."

"Man, Ethan. You've got people calling you sir. How weird."

"I know. To tell you the truth, it freaks me out sometimes."

"She doesn't look any older than me."

"She isn't. Most interns are juniors or seniors in college. They come here for a semester then return to their school."

"No thanks. Once I leave here I'm not coming back."

"You might change your mind once you get away. By the way, what are you doing down here? I thought you hated being around your father's staff, or was it just me?"

"I was summoned here, and I'm lost. But I would have never admitted it to her. I figured if I pointed myself in the direction of the West Wing eventually I would see someone I recognized."

"And then I came up behind you."

"I would have recognized your laugh anywhere. I knew when I heard it I would be okay, but I was too embarrassed to admit I was lost."

"Summoned. Grades again?"

"World history. I hate it. The good news is if you don't know about it, maybe I'm not in as bad trouble as I thought. You used to always know when he was on a rampage about me."

"But now he's a lot busier. We don't get the chance to talk like we did when he was a senator. Most of my day is relaying messages, and blocking people from seeing him."

"You're welcome to block me."

"No, c'mon. Here comes Mrs. Wiggins."

"Ethan, where have you been? The President is looking for you, and his daughter. She was due in his office ten minutes ago."

"Sorry, Mrs. Wiggins. It's my fault. I saw Ethan, and we got to talking."

"Okay, Andie Beth, but come on. Here, let me straighten out your blouse and blazer. Get your hair out of your eyes, and pull it back tight. If I were you, I wouldn't say a word when you go in there. Let him do the talking, and make sure you say yes sir each time even if he calls you by a nickname."

"Yes, ma'am."

"And Andie Beth?"

"Ma'am?"

"Good luck."

"Thanks. I need it."

I knocked on the door.

"Come in."

I walked in the Oval Office, and it overpowered me. Daddy was sitting behind his desk, and several staff members were on the couches.

"I can come back later sir. I didn't realize anyone else was here. Mrs. Wiggins told me to just come on in."

"It's okay Andie Beth. We're finished with our meeting. I need an answer on the proposal before you leave today. Now, if you'll excuse us, my daughter and I have some business to attend to."

He walked his staff members to the door, and told Mrs. Wiggins to hold all calls. He walked over to his desk and picked up a stack of papers and slammed them down on his desk just like the Colonel had done in class.

"Let me see the test."

"Sir?"

"Let me see the test Andie Beth. Now."

I took the folded test paper out of my blazer pocket, unfolded it and handed it to him. His eyes were immediately drawn to the big red C- emblazoned on it with the note **Pay attention to the details** carefully printed underneath it. The vein in his head began to bulge as he quickly flipped through each page. When he came to the last page, his face became redder and redder. Both hands began to shake as he gripped the test paper and read the notes the

Colonel had written in the margin. He slammed the test paper on the corner of his desk and looked at it again.

"Totally unacceptable Andie Beth. What do you have to say for yourself?"

"Nothing sir."

"Nothing. You've always got something to say. What's your excuse this time?"

"No excuse sir. I screwed up."

"That's not good enough Andie Beth. I warned you when we moved here that if you screwed up, or did anything to embarrass your mother or me it would be boarding school. Is that what you want?"

"No sir."

The vein on Daddy's head was still bulging. He was looking for a fight, but for once in my life I took the advice of the two people who knew us best lately: Agent Landry and Mrs. Wiggins. Deep down I wanted to whine, and tell him how much I hated this school with all their homework. How I hated the White House and all the people constantly running around. As much as I wanted it, there was no going back to Kenner. My life as I knew it there was over. Now all I had to do was convince him how remorseful I was, and promise to do better. If I could do that, hopefully, I could avoid boarding school.

"Young lady I thought we had an understanding. You do well in school. You get along with your mother. We live happily as a family. Otherwise, I make arrangements for boarding school."

"Sir, it was just one test."

"But it was important enough for the school to call the parents and tell us the grades. Since your mother was at a speaking engagement, I had to take the call."

"I'm sorry sir. I never figured they'd call The White House, much less get through to you."

"And if they hadn't gotten through to your mother or me, would you have told us about the grade?"

"Yes sir."

"C'mon Andie Beth. Tell the truth."

"Sir, I would have told you for two reasons: number one, Mama would have asked me about the grade, and I know better than to lie to her; number two, the Colonel, I mean Mr. Brown, said that we had to have both parents' signatures on the test, and I don't forge signatures very well."

A slight smile crept across his face, and the vein began to go down. Daddy was starting to relax a little.

"Andie Beth, are you testing me?"

"Sir?"

"Are you testing me to see how far you can push me before I send you to boarding school?"

"No sir."

"Because if you are, let me show you something."

Daddy picked a school catalogue off his desk.

"I've had this catalogue since I made the decision to run for the Presidency. My friends told me sending you to boarding school would be the best thing to do for several reasons. First of all, your mother and I wouldn't have to worry about your safety. Secondly, you would have the discipline you need to keep your grades up. Lastly, it would be a more structured routine than you have here with both of us coming and going so much. Most of the time this catalogue stays in the bottom drawer of my desk. Give me one good reason to put it back there."

"Because you'd miss me sir."

"Explain."

"Ever since I was a little girl, you would come by the steps after work each day, and hug me and tell me how much you missed me. If I had had a good day, it was my special time to tell you the good things that had happened. If I had a lousy day, somehow seeing you made me realize Daddy was home now, and he could make it all better. But that ended when you moved here and became a senator. The phone just didn't cut it. That's when I started screwing up, because nobody cared. Mama was too busy with her life and responsibilities to be bothered with me. Sometimes, she didn't even make it to my basketball or softball games."

"But what does that have to do with now?"

"You said when we moved here that things would be different. All you have to do is walk out your back door fifty yards and come in the side entrance and you're home. I need you to still be there for me Daddy. Like yesterday when you came and found me on the basketball court. You immediately jumped to the conclusion I was doing something wrong. The only way I can get your attention is to screw up. You and Mama keep waiting for me to mess up all the time, so that's all I do."

"Andie Beth, what do you want from me?"

"I want it to be like it was when I was a little girl. I want you to come by the steps and ask me how my day was. I want to be able to share the good stuff that happened, and to be able to cry on your shoulder about the bad stuff that happened without worrying about being sent away. I want to be me, and I want my daddy back even if he is the President of the United States. But I don't think I can have what I want, so I guess you have to do what you have to do. And when Mama gets through with me, no telling what will happen."

"Don't you worry about your mama. She and I have already talked. You're right. I have neglected you. You are so grown up now I didn't realize you were pulling away. Most of it was my fault. I've never had a teenage daughter before, and I don't know how to react to your moods. So, the easiest thing for me to do was to pull away and let your mama handle things. Only you two are so much alike that you constantly butt heads, and I'm caught in the middle."

"Sir, what happens now?"

"First of all, I'm throwing away this catalogue which means we're in it for the long haul. You're right. Your mama and I do not want you to go to boarding school because even though you're driving us crazy, we would miss you. Secondly, you're grounded for two weekends which includes the Valentine's Dance. That means studying only: no phone, computer, t.v. or c.d. player. Any socializing will have to be with us old folks, and your mama is going to check your homework for the next month to make sure you're studying. Lastly, you're required to play catch with me each day for fifteen minutes. We've got to get that pitching arm of yours ready for the season, and who knows someone may ask me to throw out the first pitch at one of these stadiums. Any questions?"

"No sir."

"Good. Then don't make me have to call you in here again. Let me sign this test paper and I'll get your mama's signature on it and leave it on the breakfast table in the morning."

"You mean I don't have to talk to her about it?"

"No, we decided I would handle it."

"Daddy, I mean sir, thanks."

"Buzzie, come here."

I practically ran over to Daddy, and he hugged me tight. All the emotions from the day, the last few weeks, and even before the election came pouring out. I started crying. Daddy was back. Not only was he the President of the United States, but he was my daddy. I slipped out the back door across to the steps that led to the residence. None of the agents seemed to notice. I went upstairs to my room, and changed clothes. Might as well do my geometry homework before supper just in case Mama came to check on me.

Chapter 17

The Shopping Trip

"**R**achel, are you out there? It seems like forever since I've been on the computer. Even after the two week grounding, Mama decided that I was spending too much time on it so she cut my time way back."

It's been a rough month. I've spent most of it in my room studying. Even though I got three A's and three B's on my report card, Mama still makes me stay up here and study. Glad I didn't waste my time trying to convince her to let me go to the Valentine Dance. From what everyone at school told me, you and Ryan were practically the only sophomores there. It seems like all the juniors and seniors went to the dance as sort of a warm-up for the prom. Besides, I wouldn't have gone even if I could have. I couldn't have danced with a cane. I guess if anything good has come out of this whole mess it's been that I'm finally rid of it. For the first time since Christmas, I'm walking like a normal person - well, almost.

Well, it happened just like I predicted. You dumped Ryan for another guy. Maybe that's one reason we haven't talked much lately. You're with Caleb now. I sent out the invitations to my birthday party before you guys broke up, so Ryan may show up. I gave Caleb one at school today since I figured he would be coming with you.

I hope you're okay with the idea that Ryan may come. I guess I've been afraid to admit it to you before, but I kind of like him. He just never seemed right for you, but I didn't want to say anything as long as you guys were dating. But now that you're not, well I'm sort of interested in him. I guess I keep remembering he was the first one to my rescue after the accident. Besides, you have Caleb now. That guy adores you, and to think you guys have been in the same school forever and never even noticed each other. Well, gotta go. Talk to you soon.

"Andie B. I'm surprised you gave into this shopping trip so easily. Normally, getting you to try on clothes, especially dresses, is like pulling teeth."

"Aw, Mama. You didn't tell me we were shopping for dresses."

"Andie Beth."

"Just kidding, ma'am. This will be the first time I've been in a mall since we left Louisiana. Are you sure it's okay?"

"The agents have checked it out. Since it's out in the Virginia suburbs, we should be able to blend in pretty easily."

"They're not going to see me with these dresses on looking in a mirror. I mean you know."

"No, you'll have your privacy. Most of the agents inside the mall with us will be women. But c'mon Andie B., every other time I've suggested one of these trips you've thrown a tantrum. Why the change this time? Is it a boy or is it because you've got cabin fever from being cooped up in your room?"

"Gram told you didn't she?

"She mentioned something to me after your daddy and I got back from our trip about Ryan and Rachel breaking up. Does that mean you and he are you know, whatever you call it these days, an item?"

"No, we're still just friends. But I do like him. And besides Rach already has a new guy to boss around - Caleb."

"I never realized Rachel was so boy crazy Andie B. Why didn't you tell me? It seems like every time we talk you tell me she has a new boyfriend."

"That's just the way she is Mama. She's always been that way. I've been trying to tell you for years that the way Rach acts around grownups and the way she acts around kids are two different people."

"Sort of like Dr. Jekyll and Mr. Hyde."

"Who?"

"Never mind. They're characters in a book that I may put on your summer reading list."

"But anyway, back to Ryan. Did you invite him to your party?"

"Yes, when he was going with Rach. He may not come now that they've broken up, and she's with another guy."

"Why don't you invite him as your date? Unless there's someone else you haven't told me about."

"No, but when I invited people I didn't invite them as couples. It was just a group of us getting together for a movie and pizza. All the kids are either on sports teams or in one of my classes."

"Well, I know you don't like me giving you advice, and somehow I think if your daddy said this you would do it, but I think you ought to let Ryan know that you want him to come to your party. Don't ever tell your daddy this, but guys need to be pushed once in a while."

"You really think so?"

"I think so. Your daddy wasn't kidding that first weekend when he said he saw the looks you two were giving each other at the reception. Now that Rachel and Ryan are no longer a couple, I think it's time for you to make your move."

"Mama, I can't believe you said that."

"If I had waited for your daddy to make a move, I'd be an old maid school teacher in New Orleans instead of the First Lady."

We both laughed. By now we were at the mall which was nestled in the suburbs of Virginia. The agents gave us plenty of space as we entered. Mama looked like she was on an undercover mission. Instead of her usual power suit, she had on a sweater and jeans, and I was in a jogging suit and a baseball cap. We could have been any mother taking her daughter shopping after school. We had even made the trip in a Blazer instead of the limousine that usually chauffeured her.

"Okay, Andie B. I have my list but I have a feeling you have a list of your own, so what's first on your list?"

"We need to find a sporting goods store. I need a new pair of cleats for softball. My old ones from last year will work for practice, but I need a new pair for the games along with some socks."

"While we're at it, we might as well buy you some new Nikes®. You're still wearing that awful pair you were wearing on Election Day."

"Yeah, but I haven't been able to wear them since Christmas."

"True, but it's time they went in the trash."

At the sporting goods store I looked around to see if anyone noticed us. The stores weren't as crowded as they would have been on a weekend, but there were customers milling around. Several people looked at us; as if, they questioned whether we were who we looked like. I guess they got their answer when an agent went to the counter and paid the bill. Even then no one said a word. As we walked out of the store, one of the agents took the bags, and I didn't see them again until we were back at the White House.

"Okay, Andie B., my turn."

"Uh oh."

"You need four or five dresses plus a couple of pairs of dress shoes for the spring and summer."

"Ma-ma. I don't plan on dressing up that much. I figured I'd just hang out by the pool, and play softball."

"We'll talk about your schedule later, but for now indulge me. Who knows? You might enjoy being a girl."

I ended up trying on around ten outfits. By the time we got to the last one, I was starting to like the look in spite of myself. I even pulled the scrunchie out of my hair and let it fall free on my shoulders. Mama came up behind me.

"You look beautiful, and I can tell by the smile on your face that you like the look too."

"Yeah, sorta."

"Andie B. it's okay to change. You can be a jock by day and a woman at night. You don't have to be a tomboy twenty four hours a day. Look at Sue Bird and Monica Abbott. When you see them away from the gym, they're beautiful young women."

"Mama, Monica Abbott plays softball. She's not in the gym."

"Well, you know what I mean. You know what; your daddy may kill us both, but let's take all of them. I have a feeling you'll get plenty of wear out of them. Now is there anything else you need?"

"Just a new bathing suit, and jeans and shorts. I saw this one really cool pair of jeans and top over there that would be great to wear to my party."

"You're not wearing a dress?"

"Mother. Nobody wears a dress to the movies. Especially in their own house."

"Just kidding. Go get the outfit, and bring it over here while I round up the rest of these clothes."

I tried on the jeans and top. They are awesome Rach. I can hardly wait for you to see them, but you'll have to wait until the party. I wasn't sure if Mama would approve because they are cut kind of low, and the shirt does show some skin.

"Andie B. with that outfit on, Ryan would be crazy not to notice you. The only problem is; I'm not sure if it's appropriate for the daughter of the President."

"But Ma-ma, it's not like I'm going to wear it in public. I'll be in my own home at a well chaperoned party. I won't be in a bar downtown. Nothing is going to happen. Besides, all the girls dress like this. Just look around this mall. Please Mama. Normally I don't even ask for clothes. You're the one who came up with this shopping trip."

"Okay, just this once. But if I were you, I would keep this our little secret. Remember, if your daddy tells you to change clothes on the night of your party; I can only back you so far."

"This is too weird."

"What do you mean?"

"Because usually it is Daddy telling me the same thing. He'll tell me it's okay to do something, and then remind me that you can overrule him. Now you're saying the same thing. You guys are strange."

"Says the daughter to the Mother after she spent the national budget on clothes for her."

"It wasn't that bad was it?"

"Bad enough. C'mon we'd better get home before your father and grandmother come looking for us."

"I hate to admit it Mama, but I've had fun today."

"Me too, Andie B. me too. Now how much homework do you have tonight? Any tests tomorrow?"

"No tests. Just geometry and the usual world history and English reading. Guess we're back to reality."

Chapter 18

Happy Birthday

"Rachel are you out there? The last few days have been wild."

"Yeah, A.B., I'm here. Fill me in."

It all started Wednesday night at dinner. We hadn't talked much about my birthday party. All the plans were made. Ever since the shopping trip, Mama and I have gotten along better. She thinks I'm coming around to her way of thinking. I'm not so sure.

"Well, Buzzie, tomorrow is the big day. I can't believe you're going to be sixteen."

"I can. It's all she's talked about for months. Turning sixteen and getting her driver's license."

"Yeah, Gram, but Agent Landry said even if Mama and Daddy let me drive around here, there will always be a Blazer full of agents right behind me."

"And in front of you and beside you, and maybe in the car with you."

"Great, Daddy. Just what I didn't want to know."

"Can I still at least get my license tomorrow? Everybody else gets theirs on their birthday. Agent Landry can take me after school."

"We're one step ahead of you, Andie B. Since the Department of Motor Vehicles Office isn't too far from your school, I'm going to meet you at school, and we can ride over together."

"Mama, you don't have to take me like I'm some little baby. Why can't I just go with Agent Landry? I don't like riding in your entourage with the limousines and all the people. Besides, he's already let me practice driving the Blazer a couple of times."

"Andie Beth I will not embarrass you. In fact, I'm riding in a Blazer just like we did when we went on the shopping trip. This will be very low key. I promise."

"Okay, I guess."

"Rules are rules Andie Beth. We have to have the increased security. So, if you want your license, you'll have to play by our rules."

"Yes, ma'am but."

"No buts Andie B."

"At least I don't have any tests for the next week."

"Why not?"

"It's weird. The ninth graders are taking some sort of standardized test, and the juniors are taking their SAT's ® So, the sophomores and seniors don't have any regular tests since some of our classes have juniors and freshmen in them."

"That's a nice break for you."

"Yeah, Gram especially since it comes around my birthday. Only next year it means I'll be taking my SAT's® on my birthday. How gross. I don't even want to think about it."

"You'll do fine Andie B., besides you've got time to take an SAT prep class between now and then."

"Just what I need Mama, more school."

"Get used to it. Speaking of which, don't you have some homework to do?"

"Always."

"Then get to it Buzzie. You've got a busy few days in front of you, and you can't afford to get behind in your schoolwork."

"Yes, Daddy. C'mon Caj, maybe you can help me put some of these names and dates together."

Cajun didn't move.

"I think Cajun's saying you're on own, Andie B."

"Guess so Gram. See you guys later."

When I came in the kitchen for breakfast on Thursday, there was a candle stuck in a blueberry muffin on my plate. No one else was in the room. I know I wasn't late. Usually, it's just Gram and me. Daddy heads to the Oval Office early for a daily staff meeting, and Mama takes forever getting dressed so she's not up yet.

The morning newspaper was on the table, so I pulled out the sports section. It's time for all the basketball tournaments. Trey was in Atlanta for the Southeastern Conference tournament. LSU was expected to come out second or third in the conference, so he couldn't come to Washington for the weekend. But his spring break is in a couple of weeks, and he'll come here - at least for a couple of days. The rest of the time he will spend with his girlfriend. I like her, but there are times when I want him all to myself without her hanging all over him. For a big brother, he isn't such a bad guy. Every once in a while he gives me some good advice. I talk to him on facebook® sometimes about Ryan. That's one thing I really miss about Kenner. When I had a problem with Matt, I could talk to

Clay about it. I didn't find out until right before my accident that Clay was even interested in me. With Ryan it's a whole different story. The other guys I know like Caleb and Ethan, I don't feel comfortable around to even carry on a conversation about anything other than sports. That's one of the things I admire so much about you. You can talk to anybody whether they're six or sixty, and sound intelligent.

"It comes from years of practice A.B. You gotta remember that with three brothers I had to have a loud mouth or no one would hear me. Then when my parents needed to drag one of their kids to some fancy event, it was easier to leave the boys at home. Mom would dress me up, and I would be their perfect little angel. After a few years I got to liking it. Your parents kept you in the background. Mine put me on display. Half the people in D.C. didn't even know my parents had three other kids until last summer when they decided to take the entire family to the national convention where your dad was nominated."

"Yeah, I forgot about that."

No one ever came in the kitchen. I ate breakfast by myself, grabbed my backpack, and went downstairs to meet Agent Landry for the ride to school. I must have been early, because he was sitting at a table with the other agents drinking coffee.

"You're real early this morning Miss Nettles. Is there something going on before school that you forgot to tell me about?"

"No, I'm sorry. I guess I'm not used to walking fast, and none of the elders were upstairs for breakfast."

"Did you think they had deserted you on your birthday? Your grandmother is out in her garden, and your parents are at a breakfast meeting. You have to look at the appointment sheet on the breakfast table each morning, Miss Nettles. It tells you what your parent's schedule is each day."

"I know. I guess I don't think about it very much. They're always in meetings or appearances. As long as they don't drag me along."

"Sit down a few minutes and relax. That way we can finish our coffee."

"This is weird. I can go back upstairs. I guess I'm intruding."

"It's not often we get members of the First Family hanging out in the lounge with us, but you don't have to leave."

"Are you sure?"

"Stay. See, we even have the same muffins you do. Help yourself. You may need the extra energy today especially if you're going to pass your driver's test."

"Definitely. I just hope I can drive the Blazer. It's similar enough to our old van that I shouldn't have too much trouble."

"You'll be fine. Just relax."

"Easy for you to say."

"Miss Nettles, I think you have Landry pegged. Everything comes easy to him so he thinks it comes easy to the rest of us."

"Don't believe a word these people tell you about me."

"Deal. As long as they don't believe a word you tell them about me, we're even."

"Now I don't know about that. But we'd better go. Time for school."

When I opened my locker, there were several birthday cards and notes from kids. Walking to class, several kids stopped and said Happy Birthday to me. Man word gets around. Unfortunately, I didn't see the one person I wanted to see - Ryan. I didn't see you and Caleb until we got to class.

"Well A.B. you've gone and done it. Today starts the two month period each year where you're older than me."

"Yeah, Rach and it does feel good to reach this point every year."

"Have your parents said anything more about you getting a car?"

"Not a word. We talked about driving here in Washington, but not even a hint about when and if I'll get my own wheels. Daddy and I talked about it at Camp David one weekend when we first moved here, but not since."

"If my parents know, they sure aren't saying anything. But you know if I knew I couldn't keep it a secret from you."

"That's for sure."

"Shut up Caleb. Girls can keep secrets when it's necessary."

School was its' usual boring self. At least now I had phys ed to look forward to. I headed to the locker room with everyone else. Basketball season was over. Neither the boys nor the girls' teams made it to the playoffs. We started spring training for softball and baseball on Monday. I wasn't allowed to take fielding drills or run, so I spent the hour throwing to one of the catchers on the sidelines. I was allowed to take batting practice, and I could tell that working with the weights in physical therapy had helped me to gain strength in my arms and upper body.

"Andie Beth, you're really hitting the long ball."

"Yes, ma'am, but I guess I'll have to since I'm not sure how fast I can run."

"You keep hitting like you have the last couple of days, you won't have to worry about running. Once you start driving a little bit more with your thighs and legs, some of those balls will be going out of the park."

"I guess I'm still scared to follow through too much. I'm afraid I'll twist my knee."

"I don't think you have to worry about that as long as you have those supports on them. When's your next ortho appointment?"

"Monday I think."

"Ask the doctor then."

"Yes, ma'am I will."

We haven't started after school practices for softball. They won't start until April first with the season starting two weeks later. Because of all the congressional holidays here, school doesn't get out until the middle of June. If I was still in Kenner, I'd be getting out the end of May.

One rule that I hate at this school is that you have to wear your school uniform whenever you're on campus during school hours. This means after gym class you take a shower, and put back on the uniform you've worn all day to class. Yuck. I'm no clean freak, but it's like putting on dirty clothes again. I don't understand why we have to get all prim and proper just to walk to the car. Once we start having after school practices and games, we can wear whatever we want home. Of course they add a rule to that too. They say as long as it's decent.

The boys were still practicing when Coach Shine sent us to the showers. The only time I had seen Ryan all day, he was with a group of guys. He had his back to me, but I had seen enough of his blonde hair to recognize him from any angle. His cowlicks gave him away, and he had this habit of constantly rubbing his hand over the back of his head as if it contained some magic gel that would make his hair lie down. In the morning his cowlicks didn't stand up, which led me to believe that he did lacquer on some industrial strength gel before he left home each morning.

This locker room was different from the one in Kenner. Instead of the jocks getting the lockers closest to the showers, it was divided by classes. Juniors and seniors had the lockers closest to the showers and sinks and freshmen and sophomores had the ones closest to the door leading to the hallway. A lot of pranks were played on unsuspecting freshmen because of this. Doors would occasionally be held open a little bit longer than necessary causing outsiders to get a glimpse of a girl in the process of dressing or undressing. One of the advantages of having phys ed as last period is that the hallways on this part of the building are empty by the time we leave.

Rachel decided to hang around and wait for Caleb. They had agreed to meet in the quad. It was a gathering spot for students before and after school. The snack bar was open so students could grab a snack and hang out. That's another thing that made this school weird. Kids came from all over the area to attend. For some of them this was the only place they got to see each other.

"Guess I'd better get to the car, Rach. Mama insists on going with me to take my driver's test. If I'm late, she'll accuse me of messing up her schedule."

"Okay, see ya. But call me as soon as you get home."

"Will do."

Agent Landry gave me a look I had come to recognize as his *hurry up* look. Slinging my backpack over my shoulder, I headed for the front of the school. As I came out of the building, I was blown away at the sight of a Navy jet gray Jeep Wrangler parked where the Blazer usually was. There were two people sitting in it looking straight ahead. Guess somebody had managed to park in our space while I was in school. I stopped and looked around for the Blazer and Mama. The doors of the Jeep jerked open and Daddy got out from behind the wheel followed by Mama from the passenger side. They were both dressed in casual clothes. I mean clothes I'm not used to seeing them wear. Daddy had on an LSU sweatshirt and jeans, and even Mama had dressed down with a sweater and jeans. This was the first time I had seen Daddy look like a normal Dad since we had moved to D.C. Maybe Mama was starting to loosen up, because she looked the same way she did when we went on the shopping trip.

"Happy Birthday, Andie Beth. Your Mama and I thought we'd give your new Jeep a test drive before we turned it over to you."

I stood there in shock. I couldn't believe they were giving me my dream car even before I passed my driver's test.

"Gary, we've done it again."

"What do you mean Lynn?"

"We've surprised her again."

About that time you came up behind me.

"Rach, am I dreaming or are my parents standing in front of a gray Jeep?"

"That they are."

"Rach, did you just hear them say it was mine?"

"That I did."

"Then pinch me or something 'cause I've been having this dream for weeks, and how do I know it's real this time?"

"You really want me to pinch you?"

"Yeah."

You pinched me.

"Ouch."

"So you felt it A.B.?"

"Andie Beth, why don't you and Rachel come over and look at your Jeep?"

"You keep saying YOUR Jeep. So, it's not the family's Jeep. It's really mine?"

"Yes, Andie Beth it's yours. Complete with high insurance rates."

"C'mon Rach."

We walked over to the Jeep.

"Hurry up Andie Beth. You better sit in it, and take a quick lesson on how to work the turn signals and lights if you expect to take your driver's test using it."

"Okay Daddy."

I got in the driver's side, and you climbed in the passenger side. A.B. and Rach were ready to hit the road just like those people in that old movie, *Thelma and Louise®*. Daddy gave me a quick lesson in where everything was located.

"Andie Beth, if we're going to get to the DMV, we've got to go now."

"Yes, ma'am."

"See ya later A.B. I've got to catch a ride with my brother. He had a club meeting this afternoon."

"Yeah, Rach. Later. I guess I haven't thanked you guys, but I'm still in shock. Plus I never expected to see you, Daddy, this afternoon especially dressed the way you are."

"Buzzie, I've had this afternoon cleared on my calendar since the day after Election Day. I wouldn't have missed that expression on your face when you saw the Jeep for anything."

"Thanks Daddy. You too, Mama."

"You're welcome, Andie Beth. There are some rules we'll discuss later, but we've got to get to the DMV. Agent Landry will ride with you so you can practice your driving on the way over there, and your daddy and I will meet you there."

Agent Landry magically appeared beside me. We got in the Jeep.

"You knew, didn't you?"

"Of course."

"And you didn't tell me?"

"And ruin the surprise? I need this job. I told you in the beginning. There are some things I can tell you, and some things I can't. Plus, I've had too much fun listening to you speculate about whether you were going to get a car or not."

"And you let me ramble on."

"That's what I'm here for. But I will tell you this. You almost blew it when your grades and attitude went sour. If you hadn't straightened things out with the President, not only would you not have a car, but odds are you would have been spending today in Vermont."

I pulled up in the DMV parking lot. It was almost empty. Part of this may have been because it was late in the day, but somehow I knew that the people working there had been told that the President's daughter was coming to take her test. I recognized some of the people milling around as agents I had seen before. Mama met me at the door with my birth certificate and driver's Ed certificate. I had my learner's permit and school i.d. in my hand.

When we entered the building, it was obvious that they had cleared everyone else out. Since I was so nervous, this helped me to relax. Sometimes it makes me feel weird when I'm singled out for special treatment. Other times it's a relief. I filled out the paperwork, and signed it, and Mama signed it.

The examiner and I walked out to the Jeep, and he had me turn on the lights and signals. Instead of having to go out on the street like they do in some places, they had set up a road course complete with stop signs, a railroad crossing, and school zone. The only item missing was an expressway, but they did have an entrance ramp set up like one. I was glad I didn't have to drive on a real expressway. I had only done it twice in Louisiana, and that was on the causeway to Mandeville across Lake Ponchartrain where you don't have traffic merging. That's the one part of driving that scares me, but I wouldn't have to worry about it. No one is going to allow me to go barreling down the interstate. Not as long as I'm living in the White House.

"Congratulations, Miss Nettles you passed. But you might want to work a little on shifting gears so your movements aren't so jerky."

"Yes, sir. Thank you sir."

I went back in the DMV, and they took my picture, and gave me my license. I came outside, and there were Daddy and Mama.

"Congratulations, Buzzie."

"Thanks Daddy."

"We're proud of you Andie Beth."

"Thanks ma'am."

"But now for the bad news. Because it's rush hour, and you're still not familiar with the roads, Agent Landry is going to drive the Jeep back to the White House."

"Aw, Mama. I finally get my license, and now I can't even drive. C'mon Mama."

"'Fraid not. Like I told you there are some rules. Your daddy and I think there are still some situations where you're ready to drive yet."

"C'mon Daddy. I'm going to look like a baby if we pull into the White House, and I'm a passenger in my own new car."

"Hmm. You may have a point. Let's compromise. When you get two blocks away from the White House, you can get in the driver's seat. That way when you pull up to the gate, you'll be behind the wheel."

"Can I make Agent Landry get out and walk the last two blocks?

"Don't press your luck."

"Thanks Daddy."

I got in the passenger side with Agent Landry driving. Two blocks away I switched places with him, and took the wheel. I drove up to the gate, and was greeted by one of the guards.

"Good afternoon, Miss Nettles. Congratulations."

"Thanks."

I didn't know if I was supposed to park it, or where to park it until Agent Landry pointed me to a parking place with a sign in front of it that read: **Reserved for First Kid.** I eased the Jeep into the spot, and just sat there for a few seconds. It was mine, and I even had my own parking spot. Somehow, I wasn't ready to leave.

"Sorry, Miss Nettles, you can't sleep in it. Your parents are expecting you inside. By the way, here, I got you a little something for your birthday."

"Agent Landry, you didn't have to."

I opened the small box, and in it was a Naval Academy key chain.

"Thought you might need something to help you keep track of your new keys."

"Thanks a lot."

"See you in the morning."

I grabbed my backpack from the backseat, and headed inside. Instead of going straight upstairs, I went out to the steps and sat down. I pulled out my wallet and my new license and stared at it for a few minutes. I didn't even notice Daddy, Mama, and Gram watching me from the balcony above.

Chapter 19

The Party

"Rachel, are you out there?"

We're at Camp David again. Daddy wanted to bring Grandpa Webb and Grandma Elizabeth here. We came right after breakfast this morning. When I got back after taking my driver's test, they were upstairs with Gram. Of course, Grandpa wanted to see the Jeep right away, so he and I took a walk outside.

"How have you been, Bumble?" And don't give me any one word answers. I want the truth."

"Okay, Grandpa. I mean it's hard. Brockton is a gazillion times harder than St. Martins. There's lots more homework."

"But your daddy said you were keeping up your grades."

"Only after that big fight we had. It was 'shape up or ship out.'"

"What about you and your mama? You two staying civil to each other? You haven't mentioned much about her in your e-mails lately."

"She's still checking my homework. It was only supposed to be for a month, but since my grades improved once she started doing it, she's decided she's going to continue for the rest of the school year."

"And you're not fighting her?"

"Not all the time. Grandpa, am I giving in if I don't fight them all the time?"

"No, Bumble. You're just growing up. But there will be more fights. Your grandma and your aunts still get into squabbles once in a while and look how old they are."

"Really, Grandpa?"

"Really, Bumble."

"What do you think of my Jeep, Grandpa? It's the color of the jet I'm going to fly in a few years."

"That it is Bumble. That it is."

We walked around the South Lawn.

"I can see it in your eyes, Bumble. You're starting to like this place."

"Well, maybe a little."

"I saw in the newspaper the St. Martin's girls and boys lost in the region tournament. I think they missed you."

"Yeah, I know. Daddy's press secretary gets the New Orleans and Baton Rouge newspapers every day, and he saves the sports section. Daddy brings them when he comes upstairs for dinner."

"One of the perks of being President I guess."

"I guess."

"And were you going to get around to telling me about Ryan before I left to go home to Mandeville?"

"How do you know about Ryan?"

"Bumble, you forget your grandmas talk almost every day."

"But Daddy doesn't even know about Ryan."

"That's what you think Bumble."

"Okay, Grandpa. Now it's time for you to spill your guts. Tell me everything you know, or I'll leave you down here wandering the White House grounds by yourself."

"Just this is the guy from the ski trip who found you in the snow, and Rachel had a couple of dates with him, and moved on to someone else. Your parents and grandmother think he's your boyfriend."

"I wish. He's an awesome guy Grandpa. He's not as full of himself as Matt. Totally different. He's tall, has blonde hair, and is much better at sports. He aggravates me by calling me Beth all the time. He's a sophomore too and plays basketball and baseball. I just hope he shows up at the party."

"Why wouldn't he? You invited him didn't you?"

"Yep, that was when he was dating Rach. Now she's dating someone else, and I don't know if he'll still come."

"But you told him you still wanted him to come."

"In a roundabout sort of way."

"He'll be here. Wait and see. Now let's get upstairs. Your grandmothers are supposed to be cooking a special meal with some of the seafood we brought with us."

"But Grandpa, the White House has its' own chefs. Gram doesn't have to cook anymore."

"You don't think your grandmothers are going to let those fancy chefs mess with their shrimp and crawfish do you? Nobody knows their secret recipe, not even me."

"I can't believe you brought a cooler full of seafood all the way up here from Louisiana."

"That's one of the joys of flying your own plane, Bumble. No security checks to go through. The only thing I had to worry about is your grandma overloading the plane. I think she wanted to bring half the state to her boy and her grandbaby."

"Only her boy is now the President and is an old man, and her grandbaby is sixteen."

"Don't tell her. She still thinks he's sixteen."

"Oh Grandpa."

We went upstairs for dinner. Grandma Elizabeth and Grandma Josie had fixed all the family favorites: gumbo, crawfish pie, fried oysters, and boiled shrimp and crabs. It was a feast. The great thing about it was it was all fresh from the Gulf of Mexico. Grandpa even brought some Jax® beer for Daddy. Daddy can get about any food or beverage he wants by asking for it, but somehow knowing it's the real thing makes a difference.

I didn't think I'd have a birthday cake with the family since we were having one at the party. Plus, I don't think any of us had any room for it especially Daddy. I looked up and Grandma Elizabeth brought in a cake decorated with a car on it that looked like my new Jeep.

"Well, Bumble, I guess it's time to give you your present."

"I'm surprised he hasn't already given it to you, Andie B. It's been driving him crazy ever since we decided to do it. Give her the envelope Webb."

I opened the envelope and inside was a certificate to a flight school in Virginia.

"Figured you wanted to finish getting your pilot's license, so we found this flight school not too far from here. You'll have your license by the end of the summer."

"Thanks Grandpa, you too Grandma Elizabeth. Can I really do this Daddy?"

"We've already had the Secret Service check it out Buzzie. Only problem might be when you solo, you have

Agent Landry along as a passenger, but other than that and a little convincing by me to your mama, you can go."

"Wow, I figured the next time I'd get to fly would be after I graduated from the academy."

"No way Bumble. It means we'll have one more passenger with us when we're in the air."

"I guess I can deal with that. If I have to."

"I'm afraid my gift isn't quite that spectacular Andie B., but I think it's something you'll like."

I opened the box, and there was a photo album. Grandma Josie had put together a collection of photographs starting with me in the hospital, and ending with one recently of Daddy and I playing catch last weekend on the South Lawn. Leave it to her to come up with a sentimental gift.

"Grandma Josie, where did you get all these pictures?"

"Pulled them out of other albums, and some of the boxes your mama and I sorted through when we were moving. It's been fun looking at them, and seeing you grow up."

"Thanks Gram. I'll keep this forever. This has been a great birthday. Thanks everybody."

"Now, you better start heading toward bed. It's been a long day, and you still have school tomorrow. I hope you don't have any homework left to do."

"Aw, Mama. Come on. Can't I stay up a little longer? I haven't seen Grandpa and Grandma in a couple of months."

"You'll have the entire weekend. They're not going home until Monday."

"Please."

"Andie Beth. Do what your mama says."

"Okay."

"Now, Andie Beth."

"Yes, sir. Good night everybody."

Wow! What an awesome day. I can't believe I'm sixteen, and have my Jeep. Now, if I can get away with Mama not making a bunch of rules about me driving it, I'll be okay. Fat chance. She's probably already had them printed and handed out to the entire White House staff. Aw, who cares? The main thing is I have wheels, even if they are accompanied by agents.

Friday at school was a blur. I did see Ryan at gym, but once again he was with a group of guys so I still don't know if he's coming to the party. So far most of the kids I had invited had told me they'd be there.

One of the perks of Daddy being the President is he can get any movie as soon as it's made, and even before it hits the theater. He's getting us the latest Robert Pattinson movie. Now if he would invite him to the White House. I doubt if Daddy even knows who he is. He and Mama don't have much time to watch movies except once in a while at Camp David.

I couldn't wait to get home. Virtually flying down the hall with my backpack over my shoulder, I almost took out three or four people and an antique table on my way to the elevator.

"Miss Nettles, slow down."

"Sorry," I said over my shoulder to the unidentified person as I continued my quest.

By the time I reached the kitchen I had taken off my blazer and pulled the shirttail of my blouse out. It was Friday, and I was free. As I expected, the grandparents were sitting around the table. The location may have changed, but their habits hadn't."

"Slow down Bumble. You look like a hurricane flying in here."

"Sorry Grandpa."

"I hope you didn't run up the stairs. Your mama will kill you if you get hurt again."

"No, Grandma Josie."

"Have a piece of your birthday cake and a glass of milk with us. Nobody ate much of it last night after all that seafood."

"Cake sounds good, but I'm having a Dr. Pepper® instead of milk. I don't see how you guys drink milk all the time. Yuck."

"Okay. Well, sit down and tell us about school. Was everybody all excited about your Jeep and your license?"

"Yeah, except I wish I could drive it to school. But the dumb old school has a rule that says only juniors and seniors can drive their cars. Something about the student parking lot being too small for all the cars."

"You'll be there soon enough. Besides your mama and daddy aren't too fond of you driving in this Washington traffic. I was scared for you in New Orleans, and this place is 100 times worse."

"Bumble, you're growing up so fast. You have plenty of years of driving ahead of you."

"I know Grandpa. It's just. . ."

"I keep telling you Webb, this child wants to grow up now. She's not the little girl you knew in Kenner anymore."

"I've noticed it too Josie. Andie B. has aged since she moved. Our little tomboy is growing up."

"If you guys are going to talk about me like I'm not here, I'm leaving. Besides I want to catch the second half of Trey's game. I'm going upstairs to change and watch it on the big screen t.v."

"What time are your friends arriving?"

"Seven. We're having pizza in the solarium and then going downstairs to the theater."

"Wait until you see the solarium Andie B. Your mama went all out for your party."

I went upstairs. The solarium looked awesome. It was decorated in red and white the Brockton school colors, and there were balloons all over the place. I hurried up and changed out of my school uniform and put on sweats. It was way too early to start getting ready for the party. I flopped down on the couch and hit the remote. The second half of the game had just started and LSU was leading Vanderbilt by four. They had been lucky in their first two games, but if they won today they would have to play

Kentucky. The game was down to the final three minutes when Daddy walked in.

"Are they winning Buzzie?"

"Yes, Daddy by eight. But Vandy has one player who keeps hitting three pointers, so it's not in the bag yet."

"Scoot over."

Daddy flopped down on the couch beside me, and stretched his long legs on the coffee table. Somewhere on the way upstairs he had ditched his coat and tie. It was the weekend, and this was about as close to casual as a President could be. Sitting on the couch next to his daughter watching his son play basketball.

Glancing up we both saw Trey enter the game. One of the LSU seniors had fouled out. In an effort to get the ball back, a Vanderbilt player fouled Trey with only a few seconds left on the clock. I guess they figured a freshman would choke in a crucial situation like this. Little did they know Trey had spent hours perfecting his foul shooting in our back yard. He sank both of them sealing the victory for LSU. The buzzer sounded and the game was over.

"Wow, Daddy."

"That's my boy."

"All that time spent practicing paid off."

"That's what I keep telling you Buzzie. My guess is Trey didn't have a clue he was going to play in the game, but he went in and did what he had to do. Remember that."

"Yes, Daddy."

"Now what I have to do is go downstairs and grab some dinner with the rest of the family. Knowing you and your friends you won't let me have any pizza."

"Daddy."

"And you need to start getting ready unless you intend to wear sweats to your birthday party. If I know your mother and grandmothers, they'll be up here in a few minutes hovering over you."

"Everybody isn't going to come up here when my friends get here are they?"

"Just your mama and I."

"But you guys aren't going to hang around? I mean you'll say hello and then go away, right?"

"Wouldn't want your parents looking over your shoulder, would you?"

"Exactly."

"Well, to answer your question. No, we're not going to hang around, but there will be agents. I told the Service to put the youngest ones they have on duty tonight, so they wouldn't be so obvious."

"You mean in the movie, too?"

"Afraid so. But Buzzie quit worrying. They're there to protect you and your friends."

"Yeah, and to tell on me."

"You're wrong there. The only time the agents tell on you is when you break a house rule. Otherwise, they keep their mouths shut. I thought you knew that."

"Well, I know Agent Landry told me that, but I didn't know if it applied to the other ones."

"It does. So quit worrying and have a good time."

"Gary, so this is where you're hiding. Dinner is ready. Andie B. you had better change. Your guests will be here in an hour. I'll be back in a few minutes to check on you."

"Yes, Mama."

I took a shower, and put on my new jeans and top. Normally, I don't mess around with my hair. I pull it back in a ponytail. Tonight I wanted to look different. I decided to let it just fall. It's getting long, and now reaches below my shoulders. I was struggling to brush the tangles out when Mama walked in.

"Here, let me help you. You never have been very good at brushing your hair."

"Thanks, Mama. Ouch. It hurts."

"Are you sure you don't want to put it in a ponytail? That way it won't fall in your face."

"No, I want to wear it down."

"Now, stand up, and let me look at you, Andie B. You're not wearing your Nikes® with this outfit. What happened to those new flats we bought when we went shopping?"

"They're still in the box. I'm just not sure Mama."

"Not sure about what?"

"Not sure if this is the look I want. Maybe I ought to just put on an LSU tee shirt, my old cargo pants, and my hair back in a ponytail."

"You look great. The other day you were excited about wearing this outfit. Otherwise, I wouldn't have bought it. What's changed B.?"

"I'm sort of scared. Suppose I go to all this trouble, and he doesn't even show up?"

"Trust me B. He will be here."

"Mama, you haven't gone and done something stupid like call his mom have you?"

"Of course not. You may not remember her, but there was a girl named Jen that Trey had a crush on a few years ago. He spent the entire week debating whether he was going to her birthday party. I think this was the first major boy-girl party he went to. One minute he would tell me he was going. The next minute he would tell me to forget it. I

bought a present for him to take in case he decided to go."

"And your point Mama?"

"He went and they dated the rest of the year."

"So you think Ryan will show up?"

"Yes, I think Ryan will show up. I think Ryan was more

attracted to you than he was to Rachel in the first place,

and now he's available. Now, you find those shoes, while

I run downstairs for a minute. I have a necklace that will

go perfect with that top."

I dug the shoes out of the closet, and Mama returned

with a cool gold chain. For the third time in recent days,

she looked more like Mom like than First Lady. She had on

jeans, a turtleneck and blazer. We went downstairs where

Daddy and the grandparents were watching the local news.

"Gary, look at your daughter. Josie was right this afternoon when she said Bumble was growing up."

"She is. Let me see."

When I came in, Daddy had his back to me. He got off the couch, stood up and looked at me.

"Buzzie, seeing you dressed like that makes me realize my little tomboy has grown up. I'm not sure I'm ready for this."

Daddy ran his hand through his hair like he always does when he's thinking.

"I'm not sure about that top. With all those raging teenage male hormones, I'm afraid of what might happen. Lynn, you approved this outfit? I'm surprised."

"It's like you said Gary. We can't keep her a child forever. Our Baby B. is almost ready to leave the hive."

"It's no worse than what the two of you used to wear. In fact the jeans look like some you had Lynn I heard they were coming back in style."

"Okay, let's go upstairs and get this party started. Ready ladies?"

The three of us entered the solarium where a few of the kids were already milling around. Sometimes I forget everything in the White House is done in a big way. This wasn't your usual party in the family room with take-out pizza. There was every combination imaginable on a table against the wall. At the end of the table was a steward dispensing soft drinks from a dispenser like they have at restaurants. There was a huge round table in the center of the room so everyone could sit together.

"Mama, this is great. You thought of this all by yourself?"

"With a little help from my staff and your grandmother."

"Thanks. I love it. Especially the balloons. Here comes Rachel."

Then you came in dragging Caleb by the arm.

"Oh, darn. Thought I'd be the first one here, but I see some of the other kids beat me to it. Hi Mr. and Mrs. Nettles, I mean Mr. President."

"It's okay, Rachel. You can still call us Mr. and Mrs. Nettles. You don't have to be formal when you're hanging out with A.B."

"Thanks sir. Wow, A.B. this is awesome. It's not every kid that can say they had their sweet sixteen party at the White House."

"It is pretty cool, isn't it?"

I glanced up, and Mama and Daddy had moved away from us to the outer fringes of the room. It's one thing for me to be the President's kid, but even my parents know there are times that need to be reserved just for me. They had promised me they would only stay until the guests arrived, and then they would get lost. Of course, they would leave a few agents around as chaperones. Fortunately, most of the agents are young, and even though they try to blend in, it's sort of like having Trey or some of his crowd hanging out with me.

The funny thing is my Secret Service name is *Jazz* after the music of New Orleans, and because that's the kind of music I listen to when I'm studying. If I walk by an agent, it looks like they're talking into wrist; when they're actually just notifying other agents where I am. It has taken some getting used to over the last two months. I'm not used to having people hovering over me all the time.

I looked up as Ryan came in. He was with some of the other members of the basketball team. Deep inside I breathed a sigh of relief for two reasons: first of all he had shown up, and second he wasn't with another girl. None of the guys he was with had girls on their arms, so it was obvious they had all come together.

Kids began to stroll over to the pizza table, and soon most of them were sitting around the table. I looked at the door just in time to see Mama and Daddy leaving. Daddy winked at me, and Mama flashed her famous Lynn Nettles' smile which I had come to realize was her way of exiting every place.

I sat by Rach and Caleb or rather they had saved me a seat. I think Rach takes a certain sense of pride in being known as the best friend of the First Kid. She takes her role pretty seriously, and I'm glad to have her around. Rach is the kind of person who helps me get through the awkward times with people. She knows exactly what to say and when to say it. I can't talk to boys or grownups without stumbling. Rach talks to everyone like she's known them her entire life.

She'd be a lot better at this first kid stuff than I am. We talked about it once, but she said her mom convinced her dad he could do more for the country in the Senate than he could as President. Rach thinks it's because her mom didn't want to be in the spotlight. According to Rach, her mother would rather fill the society and soccer mom roles instead of having all the other obligations. And with four kids who could blame her. Instead of rebelling against it, that's what Rach wants too. Her goal is to marry a rich guy and be a jetsetter. Not me. I want a life and a career of my own with or without a guy. It will probably be without, because I can't see some guy following me around the world in the Navy. Unless he's in the Navy too, and then what would be the odds of us being stationed together.

One of the agents came to the table.

"Hey, everybody. Follow me. We're going downstairs to the theater on the first floor to watch the movie."

In the theater there are four big recliners on the front row which are reserved for the First Family. The rest of the seats are like normal movie seats. No way was I going to sit down there by myself. I sat in the back corner seat. When we came in the smell of hot popcorn overwhelmed me. On a cart by the door were bags of popcorn, cans of soft drinks, and bags of assorted candy. Looking around I saw Ryan was still hanging out with the guys he had come in with. Rach and Caleb had chosen seats in the middle off to one side, and everyone else had filled in various seats.

The theater seats fifty, so with the twenty of us and a few agents it was almost half full. No one seemed to notice I was sitting by myself. It was like I was standing outside an aquarium and all the kids were the fish inside. They noticed each other, but they didn't notice me. Once the theater got dark, and the movie started I saw a few more people come in and sit down. I figured they were some of Mama or Daddy's staff or interns who figured no one would notice them in the dark

There I was at my party sitting in a corner by myself. There were people all around, yet they were all caught up in their own little world. According to Rachel, I was the first President's kid in a long time to go to this school. The last President had served two terms in office, and when he was elected his youngest child was a junior in high school. She said she and some of the other kids had come to the White House for receptions with their parents, and to the South Lawn for the Easter Egg Roll, but never just to hang out.

The movie was great. Of course I think any movie with Robert Pattinson is good. I could look at him forever. I soon became so caught up in looking at him, and the story line of the movie that I forgot about being lonely.

When the movie was over, the lights came back on, and one of the agents stood up in the back of the theater.

"Ladies and gentlemen, if you will follow me, ice cream and cake will be served in the tent on the South Lawn."

I had forgotten about dessert. Gram had said something about having another birthday cake tonight, but it hadn't sunk in. But now I had something else on my mind. When

Ryan started to go out the theater door, I whispered in his ear: "Follow me."

"What?"

"Just follow me."

At first he looked surprised, but I grabbed his hand. This was probably the boldest move I had made in my entire life. I knew if I didn't make a move now, I'd probably never have the courage to do it. Moving quickly I led him down a dim hallway towards the Oval Office. There were one or two agents around, but since it was a Friday night Daddy's staff had gone home for the weekend. The few people who were around acted as if they didn't see us.

I told the agent outside of Daddy's office that I wanted to show my friend Ryan a picture on Daddy's desk. At first he was hesitant.

"Please Agent Waddell. We'll only be a minute, because we have to go join the rest of the party outside. If you let us, I'll even make sure someone brings you a big piece of my birthday cake."

"Okay Miss Nettles. You can have five minutes. Five minutes only."

"Yes, sir. Thank you sir."

Ryan and I walked in the office. I hadn't been here since the day I was summoned because of my world history test grade. The lights were dim, but the drapes shielding the rest of the office from the outside were partially opened. Just to make things legal, and to prove I wasn't lying, I led Ryan over to Daddy's desk and showed him my baby picture with my Naval Academy baseball hat, and LSU tee shirt and socks, and diaper. He started to laugh, and I quickly put my hand over his mouth.

"Am I the first guy you have dragged in here on the premise of showing them a picture?"

"Considering this is my first White House party, and guys aren't racing to hang out with me, when would I have had time over the last two months?"

"Well, if I'm your first then let's make it count."

We walked over to the window and he kissed me. My first kiss on my sixteenth birthday, in the room where I had almost been sent away to boarding school, by the guy who had given me his bandana three months earlier to stop the bleeding on my chin. Wow. Ryan Kessler had kissed me. My first kiss.

After what seemed like only seconds, there was a tap on the door. That was our clue to leave. On the way out I thanked Agent Waddell again, and we went outside a side door and blended in with the kids headed for the tent on the south lawn. Music was blaring from it, and I immediately recognized the group as the band, Allstar Weekend. Rachel turned around and started to walk towards me, and then she stopped. She saw Ryan and I holding hands and backed off.

"Beth, when you have a party, you really go all out. Did you plan all this yourself?"

"Not me. All I did was give Mama the guest list, and told her the name of the movie, and I wanted pizza."

"What about the band? How did you get them to come here?"

"I have no clue. I'm as surprised as you are."

We walked in the tent, and the band was at the front playing. On the side was a table with a birthday cake formed in the number 16. There was also the same steward dispensing soft drinks. I looked around for my parents but didn't see them. The band stopped playing. Out of nowhere came Trey, and he strolled up to the front.

"For those of who don't know me, I'm Trey. I'm Buzzard's, I mean Andie B.'s big brother. I had to get special permission from my basketball coach to fly up here tonight to help her party down on her birthday. I wanted to give her a special present. So, with the help of my parents, I arranged for the band behind me, which you know as Allstar Weekend, to play for this celebration. I'll shut up now, but before I do I think we ought to call the birthday girl up here so we can embarrass her by singing *Happy Birthday* to her."

Ryan let go of my hand and pushed me forward into the crowd. Kids continued to push me forward until I reached the front. I could feel my face turning red. I do not like being the center of attention. It was awful looking out into the sea of kids. I thought it would be better if I looked at the back of the room, but it was worse because there were Mama, Daddy, and the grandparents smiling away. Mama's usual pasted on smile had been replaced with a look like a mischievous little kid. It was her *I got ya* look. It was the same look she gives me when she catches me doing something I'm not supposed to do.

Everyone sang *Happy Birthday* and my face turned redder and redder. It felt like it took them an hour to sing it. Afterwards, Trey handed me the microphone and told me to say something. I hate to give speeches and to speak in public.

"All I can say is this is the best birthday ever, and the biggest surprise I've ever received. Thanks everybody."

I dropped the microphone on the ground and walked back towards Ryan. Trey followed me and grabbed my shoulder before I reached Ryan.

"Gotcha Buzzard, didn't I?"

I punched him on his arm.

"You dog, why didn't you tell me about this? You said you weren't coming up until Spring Break."

"It was just an idea I had one night while I was studying. I mean what do you give the kid who lives in the White House. So I called Dad to see if he could arrange for the band."

"And you didn't tell me. I hate surprises. I ought to kill you for this."

I hit him again.

"Watch it. I need these arms for the next game. Anyway, as it happened the band was starting a tour, and they were going to be in Baltimore tomorrow night, so Dad arranged

for them to be here tonight."

"If I wasn't so mad at you for surprising me, I'd say

thanks."

"Hey, I take what I can get. Anyway it's good to see

you walking like a human again."

"Yep. Is your girlfriend lurking around in the shadows

somewhere? Don't tell me she let you come by yourself."

"She didn't make the trip. I have to fly back tomorrow

morning. We'll talk later. Go hang out with your friends.

I'm heading for the cake."

"Big brother?"

"Yeah."

"Thanks."

I hit him again.

"Okay, that's three times. Mom said never to hit a girl, but I'm doing it anyway. Just wait until you get upstairs."

"I'm going to get some cake. Are you coming?"

"No, I'd better go spend some time with Mom and Dad and the grandparents."

"Okay, I'll see you later."

I walked over toward the refreshment table, but before I could get there someone tapped me on the shoulder. It was Ryan."

"Wanna dance?"

" Sure."

Chapter 20

Mama's Crisis

"Rachel, are you out there? I guess you've heard about Mama. I'm scared Rach."

"Yeah, my mom told me when I came home from school. It sure happened quickly. Are you okay? When is she scheduled to have the surgery?"

"I'm okay. I think the surgery is scheduled in a couple of weeks. She should only have to stay in the hospital overnight."

Mama and Daddy told me about Mama's problem over the weekend while we were at Camp David. They wanted to tell me first, before I heard it on the news or from someone else. Grandma Josie wasn't with us. She had flown to Texas to spend some time with her sister. She hadn't seen her since the inauguration. It was weird not having her around. I guess I hadn't realized how much I had come to depend on her. Neither had Mama.

I knew Mama had had several doctor's appointments over the last few months, but I didn't think much about it. After all adults were always doing strange things. One thing about my parents; they keep their adult business to themselves. They never talked about personal stuff to me. Part of it was due to their over protectiveness, and part of it was, well I guess because most of the time when I was them we were talking about me.

Grandma Josie served as the middle man in the whole situation. Especially when Mama and I didn't get along. Several times I overheard conversations where she would tell Mama how much I was like her. This only made Mama madder. Grandma Josie would remind Mama about how she acted when she was a teenager. Even Daddy occasionally got into the act. Of course, he didn't say too much on the subject. He had been the victim of Mama's ranting, and although he has a temper of his own, he often defends me around her.

Unless we have guests with us, Mama and Daddy make sure weekends at Camp David are family time. It is the only place they can relax. Sometimes, though, Gram and I watch a movie in her room, or I watch t.v. or play games on the computer by myself on Friday nights. Then when I walk in to say goodnight to them, they're usually stretched out on the couch, and Daddy has his arm around her. I notice they've been doing that a lot more lately, but I figured it's just because they hadn't had a chance to spend much time with each other.

The day started off like most of our Saturdays. Daddy and I went jogging, and then he pitched batting practice to me. Some of the agents and Cajun chased balls in the outfield. Cajun wouldn't give up the ball once he got it, and it took several agents to catch him. One ball I hit would have been out of the park at the field at school.

We came back to the lodge, and Mama was sitting at the kitchen table drinking coffee. Daddy started to hug her around her neck, and she brushed him off.

"Oh, not you don't. Don't put your sweaty arms around me."

I started laughing and pulled out a chair to sit down.

"And you too. Both of you hit the showers before you come in here."

"Ma-ma, I'm hungry."

"Lynn, I'm starved."

"You heard me. Now. Both of you. This food will still be waiting for you when you're done. It's not going anywhere."

When I came back in the kitchen after showering, they were both there. Mama had changed from her robe to jeans. Even that was unusual since she was normally dressed when she came in the kitchen first thing in the morning. They flashed each other serious looks, and for a minute I thought I was in trouble. I ran a list through my head of things I might have done wrong and couldn't come up with anything. My grades were okay, and I hadn't talked back to either of them lately. No one had questioned me about going into Daddy's office the night of the party, so I guess the agent hadn't mentioned it to anyone. The most they could have gotten me for was whining about coming to Camp David this weekend. I really wanted to go to the *Lady Antebellum®* concert with you and the gang. But they're both insistent about hard security is at concerts. I think that's one reason why they brought *Allstar Weekend®* to the White House instead of me going to their concert. Guess I won't be having much of a social life as long as Daddy is President, and if Daddy runs for a second term, I'll graduate from the Naval Academy, and he'll still have another year and a half in office.

We ate breakfast, but they were still acting all serious. I stood up to go to my room, and they called me back.

"Andie Beth stay here. We've got to talk about something."

"Aw, sir, what have I done wrong now? I'm really trying to stay out of trouble. What is it this time?"

"Be quiet a minute and listen."

I hadn't heard Daddy talk to me that way in a long time. Whatever this was, it must have been important.

"Andie B. what your father is trying to say is this isn't about you. You haven't done anything wrong, at least nothing that we've found out about."

"What is it then? Has Trey been in an accident or is something wrong with one of the grandparents?"

"No Buzzie, nothing like that."

"Then what gives? 'Cause you guys look awful serious if this is about nothing."

"Andie B. it's about me."

"What do you mean, Mama?"

"You know I had a physical recently."

"Yeah."

"And I've had to go back to the doctor a few times since then."

"Yeah, I thought that was because they messed up some of your tests or something."

"Not exactly. It's because they wanted to run more detailed tests."

"Mama, you're scaring me. What's wrong?"

"Andie Beth."

"Yes, sir."

"What your mama is trying to say is that. . ."

"Andie B. what I'm trying to say is that the doctors found a lump in my breast that has to come out."

At that point Mama broke down. All that cool collected Lynn Nettles composure melted right before my eyes. It's awful when you see your parents go into meltdown. It's bad enough when I get frustrated enough to cry in front of them, but to see Mama acting this way was too much for me. Daddy went over and hugged Mama tight. I ran out of the room.

I ran outside and down the street as fast as I could. I stopped, caught my breath and ran some more. Looking over my shoulder I realized no one was running after me. Mama and Daddy were probably still back in the lodge consoling each other. I could turn around and go back in. In fact, I probably should do it. But I couldn't. All sorts of thoughts were flashing through my mind. Was she going to die? Who else knows about this? If Mama died would Daddy still be President? I mean they had been together like forever. What about Grandma Josie? Is this why she went to visit her sister? How long had everyone known? What about Trey? Did he know, and was he keeping it a secret from me? What would happen to me? Would this be a reason for Daddy to ship me off to boarding school? After all, he might not think Grandma Josie could handle raising a teenager. Why was I thinking so much?

I looked up and saw the steeple from the Camp David Chapel rising through the clouds. I ran over to the door, and tried to jerk it open. It was locked. Of course. It was Saturday. I sat down on the front steps and cried. Then I just stared into space for awhile. I wasn't sure whether I was ready to return to the lodge or not. What would I say when I arrived there? Part of me wanted to put my hands over my ears, close my eyes tight, and shut out the world. But deep inside I knew I could never get away with it.

I ran back to the lodge, flung open the door, and looked around. Mama and Daddy were standing at the sliding glass door, holding hands and looking out into the back yard. Once again I was dripping wet with sweat, but I didn't care. I ran to Mama, and this time she didn't push me away. I'm taller than her now, and I held on to her tight, as if I let go of her I would lose her. We stood there for awhile. Finally, I spoke.

"You're not gonna die, are you?"

"Not if I can help it B. I plan on being around for a long time."

Daddy silently left the room.

Mama spent the next thirty minutes explaining what had happened and the procedure she was going to undergo. It's called a lumpectomy, and if they get the lump and the bad tissue out, she won't have to have a mastectomy. There are all sorts of other details about whether she might have to have radiation and chemotherapy. She answered my questions, and told me she and Daddy called Trey last night to tell him. They wanted to tell us both together, but didn't want Trey to miss any classes to tell him. In fact Mama didn't want either one of us to miss school when she had the surgery. She would only be in the hospital overnight if everything came out all right. Otherwise, they would start chemotherapy right away. They were telling us this weekend, because Mama's condition would be announced to the public on Monday.

We sat on the couch for a long time. Mama had her arm tight around mine. She brushed my hair out of my eyes.

"Mama are you scared? Truth."

"Yes, a little. But I trust what the doctors tell me B. The best doctors in the world are at Bethesda, and they've called in some other experts from Walter Reed and Columbia Presbyterian."

"And they say you're gonna be okay?"

"They say the odds are in my favor, and if I'm not okay in round one, they'll know what to do in round two or three if necessary."

"I guess being the First Lady means you get the best service."

"It helps. But if we were still living in Kenner, I'd be treated as well at Tulane or LSU if I needed it."

"Yeah, I guess so."

"But B. I have a question for you."

"Okay."

"Are you scared?"

"I'm not sure yet. I mean I just found out about this. You guys have known about it for a while. Why didn't you tell me sooner?"

"We didn't want to upset you. You've gone through so many adjustments of your own, and I didn't want you worrying about me on top of everything else."

"I guess I just never thought. . ."

"That something might happen to me. Me neither. The doctors tell me these lumps are quite common in women of my age, and some of them are benign. So we have to have faith."

"But if it isn't?"

"We'll cross that bridge when we come to it. I plan on being around for a long time."

Mama lifted up my chin.

"Look B. you and I have had a rough year with a lot of ups and downs. But we're going to make it. Just like we always have before."

At that point Cajun ran in and jumped in our laps.

She squeezed my arm really tight, and Cajun led the way to the back yard. Mama and I sat in the swing while Cajun chased squirrels. Neither of us said anything. I think we were letting it all sink in.

We didn't talk about it for the rest of the weekend although it was obvious to all three of us it was on our minds. Daddy and I watched the Yankees play the White Sox on television Saturday afternoon, and Saturday night I watched t.v. in my room.

When we went to church on Sunday it seemed to mean a little bit more to all of us than it normally did. Since we're at Camp David so often, the chapel there has become our home church. I like it better than St. Andrews in Washington. When we go there, I feel like we're worshipping in some gigantic cathedral. There it's like everyone is aware the President is in the building. At Camp David it's like we're the Nettles' family from around the corner. All of the worshippers are people and their families who live and work there. It reminds me of the church in Kenner.

Monday night at dinner Mama's surgery made the evening news. Her press secretary announced it at a morning news conference. It was only a couple of minutes, and then there was some medical correspondent talking about all the possible outcomes. I was glad when it was over.

The next two weeks flew by. On the day of Mama's surgery, she had to be at Bethesda at 7 a.m. I set my alarm extra early so I could say goodbye to her. Daddy and Gram would go with her, and they would leave the White House at 6 a.m. I managed to drag myself downstairs by 5:30. The three of them were sitting in their usual spot around the kitchen table.

"Andie B. you didn't have to get up so early. I was going to come check on you right before we left."

"I know Mama, but I wanted to be fully awake when you left. Besides, I need to study some more for my world history test. I wish the Colonel would quit giving us so many."

"Well, in that case you'll have some extra time before you go to school. Just try to go to bed a little earlier tonight."

"How long do you think you'll have to be in the hospital?"

"A day or two depending on the pathology report."

"Buzzie, I'll let Agent Landry know when the surgery is over, and he can bring you to the hospital after school."

"I don't see why I can't skip school today."

"Because there's nothing you can do at the hospital but sit around and wait. At school you'll be busy. You know how your daddy and I feel about you having to take make-up tests."

"I know it's just that. . ."

"Andie B. I know you want to be with your mama, but I promise you your daddy and I will take good care of her. After you visit her this afternoon, I'll come back with you so you don't have to spend the night here alone."

"Thanks Gram."

About that time one of the aides came in the room.

"Mr. President, it's time to go."

We all stood up, and I started to follow them downstairs. Mama stopped me and hugged me tight. Then she let go."

"Stay here and study B. I'll be fine."

About that time Cajun ran in the room and jumped in my arms. Mama patted him on the head.

"Cajun takes care of my girl for a few days, okay?"

Cajun wagged his tail furiously as if he understood completely.

After everyone left, one of the stewards brought in muffins. I ate one feeding part of it to Cajun while reading over my world history notes for the umpteenth time. This class is as dry as dust, and nothing I do can make it more interesting. Thank goodness there's only six more weeks of school. I cinched my B average on my last report card by making an A in English. It was the first time in a long time. The reason was the teacher finally assigned an interesting book to read, *Catcher in the Rye.*® Holden Caulfield sure beats those boring people we've been reading about all year.

I finished breakfast and headed downstairs to meet Agent Landry.

"Good morning Andie Beth. Did you wake up in time to see the First Lady before she left for the hospital?"

"Yes, sir. But is it just me, or are you a bit cheerier than normal this morning?"

"No, it's not just you. My wife and I found out yesterday afternoon we're going to be parents. So I guess that yes I am a bit cheerier than normal."

"I figured something must have happened. I mean congratulations. So, there's going to be a little Landry on the scene. How awesome."

"Does that mean you'll babysit for us?"

"Real cute. I'm babysitting your kid while some agent babysits me. I wouldn't wish that on anybody. Besides changing poopy diapers is not my style, and by the time the kid gets housetrained I'll be at the academy."

"True.

"But I'll tell you what. When she gets old enough to play sports, I'll teach her how to shoot a fade away jump shot and throw a fastball."

"Fair enough. But how do you know it's a she?"

"Just a wild guess."

"Ready for your history test?"

"As ready as I'll ever be."

"Then let's go."

I hate taking a test when I have other problems on my mind. First it was the midterm in Kenner on Election Day. Then my term paper was due on my birthday and now this. What's scary is I think I did okay on it. Don't fool yourself though Rach. Even though I may be doing better in history, it doesn't mean I like it. If I never see another world history book after June 10, it will be too soon. I hope it's not a requirement at the academy.

On the way to biology class, Agent Landry rushed up behind me. I jumped. He sort of scared me.

"Sorry, Miss Nettles. Just wanted to catch you before you entered the classroom. The First Lady is out of surgery."

"Is she going to be okay? Did they get the entire lump? Is it cancer?"

"Yes, she's fine. The doctors won't receive the pathology report until late tomorrow afternoon. Now, you better go to class before the bell rings."

Today in gym we did warm up drills in preparation for the opening game tomorrow. I still wasn't sure if I was going to pitch or not. Finally, Coach Shine came over.

"Andie Beth, how are your knees holding up? Are the support braces working all right?"

"Yes, ma'am. I've been running interval drills and going after ground balls."

"What about bending when you pitch? Do you think your knees can take seven innings?"

"They aren't sore any more after practice. Sometimes when I go home, I sit in the whirlpool in the physical therapy room or my parents' Jacuzzi® tub. It helps."

"Okay, we'll see how you look tomorrow. I still haven't decided between you and Marti. One of you will be at first base, and the other will pitch. You aren't having any problems stretching to catch the ball at first are you?"

"No, ma'am."

"Good, okay everyone. Hit the showers."

After class I realized I had left my warm up jacket in the dugout. I headed back outside just as the baseball team was coming in from practice. Ryan had my jacket in his hand.

"Forget something?"

"Yeah, I didn't realize it until I was in the locker room."

"Can't lose this. You want to look good warming up for your first game tomorrow. I heard the President is throwing out the first pitch."

"Yep. To Rachel. How funny is it that my father is throwing out the first pitch to my best friend? He's a pretty good pitcher."

"Did Coach Shine decide who the starting pitcher is?"

"No all she said was it was either Marti or me."

"Have you heard how your mom is doing?"

"Just she's out of surgery. After I run an errand, I'm heading over there."

"You run errands? I thought you had your own staff to do those sorts of things."

"I don't have a staff. My parents have staffs. All I have is agents lurking everywhere."

"Yeah, I noticed. You gonna be online later?"

Chapter 21

The Haircut

"Maybe. Depends on what time I get back from Bethesda.

"I'll catch you later. I sure wish they'd let sophomores drive to school. Lucky for me Nick lives down the street from me so I can catch rides home after practice."

I wandered over to the Blazer where Agent Landry was standing. Now was the time for me to put my plan into action. When I first found out Mama had a lump, I began to do research on the internet. One of the first bits of information I discovered was people on chemotherapy lost their hair. Mama's hair is beautiful. There is never a hair out of place. The idea of her not having any hair freaked me out, so I can imagine what it was doing to her. She and I have the same hair color: brown with a pinch of blond scattered in it. If Mama has any gray hair, I sure don't know about it.

In my research, I discovered an organization called *Pantene Beautiful Lengths®*. They accept donations of hair from people to make wigs for patients undergoing chemotherapy. Mama was always complaining about my hair getting in my eyes, and my ponytail was starting to bug me. Especially after gym class or playing in a game. Plus it takes forever to dry. I found out all about the organization, and discovered they are legal. On their website they gave instructions on how to donate hair, and different beauty salons that knew how to cut the hair just right and how to bag it.

This was my plan. I would have Agent Landry take me to one, and I would get my hair cut. If Mama needed a wig, *Pantene Beautiful Lengths®* could make her one out of my hair. If she didn't need one, my hair would be donated to someone else who did.

The only problem was convincing Agent Landry. I hadn't told anyone about my plan. I wanted it to be a total surprise. If we lived in Kenner, it wouldn't have been a problem. I could have driven myself. But I wasn't sure whether I could get the agents to go along with me. Every little thing I do at the White House takes planning.

"Ready to go to Bethesda Miss Nettles?"

"Not yet Agent Landry."

"Do you want to stop at the White House and change clothes? I know how you hate being seen in your school uniform."

"Actually, I had somewhere else in mind. We need to stop at *Hair Today* in the Arlington Mall. I have an appointment there in about twenty minutes."

"An appointment. Your parents didn't say anything about you having a hair appointment after school."

"I guess they forgot. You know with everything happening. I mean let's face it Agent Landry, they have more important things on their minds today than reminding some junior staff member to remind you to remind me I have an appointment at a beauty salon after school."

"Are you sure about this? Maybe I need to call someone and verify it."

"C'mon Agent Landry. My parents and grandmother are at Bethesda. If you call one of their staff members, all it will do is get someone in trouble for not telling you. I'm paying for this out of my allowance, so it's no big deal. Can we just go now?"

"If you say so."

We got in the Blazer, and I gave the agent who was driving the address. It's the same place you and I went to at the mall a few Saturdays ago. Only that time all I had done was get my bangs trimmed. This time I was going for the works. Agent Landry did call back to the White House to let them know where we were going, and by the time we arrived at the mall there were several other agents inside. I grabbed my purse out of my backpack. Once inside the mall I headed straight for *Hair Today*. There was a woman who didn't look any older than me standing behind the counter.

"Hi. I have an appointment at 4 p.m. for a haircut."

"Nettles, right?"

"Yes."

I sat down in the chair, and before the stylist started she asked me how much I wanted cut off. It came as a surprise to her when I told her all of it, or at least most of it. I told her I was donating my hair to *Pantene Beautiful Lengths®*. Agent Landry was seated in a chair facing the entrance to the salon. I could see his back in the mirror, and noticed agents walking around and talking into their wrists.

"How short do want it?"

"Really short. Softball season starts tomorrow, so I want a wash and go haircut."

"I've seen you on t.v. I knew your name sounded familiar. You're the President's Kid aren't you?"

"In the flesh."

"Wow. What's it like living in the White House with all those people around all the time?"

"It's okay."

Mama and Daddy had warned me before we moved to Washington to always be careful about what I said around strangers. What they really meant was if you were in a bad mood, and said what you honestly felt, it could get you in trouble.

"Are you sure your parents are okay with you getting your hair cut this short? I remember reading in some magazine you have had long hair all your life."

"Yeah, they're cool with it. Besides my old hair is going to a good cause."

"We receive a lot of donations for *Pantene Beautiful Lengths®*. Okay, are you ready to look?"

She handed me a mirror, and I couldn't believe it. Not only was my hair above my ears on the sides, but in the back too. I kept rubbing the back of my neck where my ponytail used to be and running my fingers through the hair there. Then I turned my head from side to side and realized my hair wasn't going anywhere. Mama wouldn't have to worry about telling me to get my hair out of my eyes, because where there used to be bangs only short sprigs remained. Sort of like leftover twigs after a big tree has been cut down. Normally I don't look at myself in the mirror, but I couldn't stop looking because I looked so different. I really liked it, but in the back of my mind I was wondering what my parents would think. I thanked her and paid her making sure I gave her a good tip. Agent

Landry got up from his chair, and we headed towards the mall entrance. There was a flower kiosk by the door, and I bought a bouquet of flowers to take to Mama. That way if I was in trouble for getting a haircut at least I would have flowers as a peace offering. I was also carrying a plastic bag with my ponytail in it so I could send it off to get it made into a wig.

"You sure look different. I'm not sure if your parents will recognize you. How does it feel not to have any hair?

"Weird. But I like it."

"Guess I'll have to alert the other agents. Especially the new ones. I'll have to let them know who they're looking after."

"It's an awesome change. Totally extreme. If it weren't for all you guys hanging around all the time, I bet no one would recognize me."

"Don't even think about ditching us."

"Never entered my mind. But now that you mention it. I mean all the photographers are looking for a kid with a ponytail and a baseball cap. Now, if I wear a baseball cap, it will cover up all my hair. Now if we could just ditch this black Blazer."

"Why do you want to ditch the Blazer?"

"Because it's like a signal we're arriving. The family either travels by limousine or Blazer. Don't you think we could switch vehicles once in a while?"

"Your Jeep, perhaps?"

I thought so. Agent Cox called from Bethesda. Said the First Lady is awake and asking for you. So just get in the car."

"Yes, Agent Landry sir."

It took another thirty minutes to get to Bethesda. When we arrived, I jumped out of the car and realized I had no idea where I was going. I tucked my blouse in, and adjusted my blazer. Grabbing the flowers, I headed for the hospital entrance. At that point Agent Landry said goodbye, and one of Mama's agents took over guiding me through the maze of hallways to the Presidential Suite. This place reminded me of the White House with all these people scurrying around, each on their own personal mission.

The Presidential Suite is more than just a hospital room. There is a separate living room and bedroom off to the side of the patient's room. There are no windows, and it reminds me of a cave. Based on how long it took us to walk there, I figured it must be deep in the back of the hospital somewhere. There were agents all over the place, and two standing outside the door to Mama's room.

At first they looked at me like they didn't recognize me. Agent Landry was right. One of them, an older guy who I recognized from accompanying my parents to one of Daddy's speeches, opened the door for me.

There lying on a hospital bed was Mama. It was the first time I had ever seen her in a situation like this. Even from across the room, she looked tired and pale. Gram was sitting in a chair on one side of the bed, and Daddy was sitting in one on the other side. He was holding her hand, and talking softly to her. Gram saw me first and motioned me over to the bed.

"About time you made it here. What did you do? Walk from school?"

At that exact moment she noticed my hair. A shocked look flitted across her face for a second, but she didn't say anything. Daddy looked up, and I walked around to his side of the bed. Mama was lying very still with her eyes closed.

"Is she okay? Is Mama going to be all right?"

"I'm fine B. Just fine."

"Does it hurt Mama? Are you sure you're okay?"

I started to bend down to hug her, but I was scared to touch her. Daddy stopped me.

"No hugs on this side for a few days Buzzie. Your mama is pretty sore."

"Oh, yeah. I almost forgot."

By now Mama was fully awake. She kept staring at my hair and then she started laughing.

"Andie B. what happened to your hair?"

"I had it cut."

"This afternoon?"

"So that's why you're so late."

"Yes, Gram."

Only Gram knew what time it was. Mama and Daddy were so caught up in themselves, and the fact Mama was lying in a hospital bed I doubt if they even knew what day it was.

"Why did you cut off all your beautiful hair?"

"Because Mama might need it Gram. I even saved it. I read all about this place on the internet called *Pantene Beautiful Lengths®*. They make wigs for people who might need them if you know, they have cancer."

"You did that for me Andie Beth."

"Yes, ma'am. It's all in a plastic bag. If you need a wig, you can have one made out of my hair. And if you don't need it, then someone else who does can have it."

Mama started to cry.

"Mama don't cry. I've been thinking about having my hair cut for a while. It gets too hot when I play softball or basketball. When you became sick, and I started reading about what might happen, I figured now was the right time."

"That was generous on your part Buzzie."

"You look so different. Do you like it?"

"Yes Mama. It's going to take some getting used to. I didn't do it to be generous Daddy. I did it because sometimes a person just feels like they have to do something. Like it's the right thing to do."

"How did you get away with it without any of us knowing about it?"

Uh oh. Now I was in trouble. Okay, Andie B. it's time to explain your way out of getting grounded.

"Well, I sort of told Agent Landry you guys said it was okay. At first he wanted to check with someone to make sure, but I told him one of your or Mama's staff members was supposed to tell him, and with everything going on they probably forgot ."

"In other words Andie Beth you lied."

"Yes sir, but it was for a good cause. Besides by the time we got to the mall, he had called other agents so it was okay."

"But you still lied. Agent Landry is there to protect you, and he trusts you. I want you to tell him tomorrow morning that you lied, and to apologize to him for doing it."

"Do I have to? I mean sir it's embarrassing."

"Yes, you have to. And even though you did it for a good reason doesn't mean you're not getting punished. You're grounded for two weeks."

"Sir, isn't that kind of harsh? I did it for Mama, doesn't that count for anything? She's been threatening to make me get my hair cut for a long time. In fact, every time she sees it in my eyes. Look Mama, no bangs to worry about any more. Mama help me."

"Sorry Andie B. I'm too weak. Besides you know better than to play us against each other."

"Gram?"

"Oh no, child. You're not dragging me into this one. I told you a long time ago what your mama and daddy says goes. They make the rules. I just have to enforce them."

"Well, it's not fair. I thought I was doing a good thing, and I wanted to surprise Mama with a special gift in case she needed it. Now I get in trouble."

"Andie Beth, you're not in trouble for getting your hair cut. Your gift to your mama is special. Hopefully, she won't need it, but the compassion you're showing is first rate. Even if it was only Agent Landry, you should have told someone ahead of time. You put him on the spot by lying to him. Because of all the security precautions, you have to tell someone your plans before you act on them. Do you understand? End of discussion."

"Yes, sir."

"Fine, now let's move on to a more pleasant subject. Like what are the three of us going to have for supper?"

One thing about being the President, even when the First Lady is in the hospital, you receive first class service. A small table was brought into Mama's room, and Daddy, Gram and I ate dinner. While we were eating, Mama fell back asleep. After dinner, Gram decided she and I had better head back to the White House. I had managed to do most of my homework at school and on the way to Bethesda. As we were preparing to leave, Mama woke up.

"Good night Mama. I didn't want to wake you, but Gram says we have to go."

"Good night B."

I kissed Mama on the forehead.

"Get better."

"Will do."

Daddy and I walked outside for a minute so Mama and Gram could have a few minutes alone.

"Still mad at me Buzzie?"

"A little, Daddy."

"You'll get over it."

"Do I have to?"

"Remember what I always tell you. Examine your options."

"Yes, Daddy."

About that time Gram came out, and she and I headed to the hospital entrance guided by a band of agents. We didn't talk until we got in the car.

"Is she going to be okay, Gram?"

"I think so. But the doctors won't have the pathology results until tomorrow afternoon. They think they got it all. She'll be sore for a few weeks."

"That's good."

"Don't you worry about a thing, Andie B.? I have a feeling everything is going to be all right with her. You, on the other hand, I'm not so sure about."

"Oh, Gram."

"You've got to stop arguing with them Andie Beth. If your mama had been feeling better today, I have a feeling you might have been grounded until school is out. Not so much for the lying but for arguing with your daddy.

They're your parents. You have to resist the urge to argue with them all the time."

"But they have so many dumb rules."

"Andie B. the rules are in place to protect you. You have to understand that."

"I know Gram, but I just want us to be a normal family."

"You're way past that. Your daddy is the most powerful man in the United States. Some people would say he is the most powerful man in the world, and because you are his daughter all the rules go out the window. Right now he's also worrying about your mama. You need to be on your best behavior."

"Okay, Gram. When you put it that way. But it's not fair."

"Never said it was."

We rode the rest of the way in silence. When we arrived at residence, I went upstairs and got ready for bed. I was in bed reading *To Kill a Mockingbird®* when Gram came in to say goodnight. She sat down on the side of the bed like Mama always does.

"I called the hospital, and said your mama and daddy had both gone to bed."

"Okay, Gram."

"I guess that means we ought to turn in too. Andie B. I know it's been a rough day, and you think everyone has come down on you pretty hard. I want to tell you how proud I am for what you did today about donating your hair."

"Even if I did get grounded."

"You were grounded for other things you did, not for your sacrifice."

"It was worth it Gram."

The next day I headed for school. When I met up with Agent Landry in the morning, I did as Daddy had said and apologized to him. He said he figured all along I was lying, but he knew I must have had a good reason.

It was hard concentrating at school. All I could think about was the first game of the season. Even kids who normally weren't interested in sports were talking about it. It was the prime topic at lunch. I sat down with you and Caleb.

"Quit giving her a hard time Caleb. She's not going to drop the ball."

"I can see the headlines now: *Senator's Daughter Drops First Pitch of the Season.*"

"Are you kidding? Our game won't make the papers."

"It will with your dad throwing out the first pitch. I bet there will be photographers all over the place."

"Get real. This is Brockton Prep vs. Arlington Christian, not the world series."

"Are you pitching?"

"Don't know yet. Coach Shine said she'd tell us at gym class. It's either Marti or me."

"You're a better pitcher than Marti. Besides I've been waiting eight years to be your catcher."

"Yeah right. The only reason you're a catcher Rach is because you hate to run."

"That's for sure."

"Yeah, all you have to do is sit there and watch the game."

"Aw, Caleb you are so naïve. When A.B. throws heat, I do more than watch the game, I cry."

"And all the time I thought that was sweat rolling down your cheeks."

"Those were tears of pain. I had to convince my mom to buy me a new glove."

"You probably told her you needed a new one in order to catch the President's kid."

"You got that right."

"You really told her that."

"Yep, told her if my picture was going to be in the paper, I needed a new glove and cleats. Didn't want some reporter talking about poor Senator LeBrun, and the fact he couldn't afford the best for his only daughter while his three sons look like something out of *Sports Illustrated's Best Dressed Players.*

"How funny."

Lunch ended, and we went to our afternoon classes. As soon as I changed into my uniform in gym class, I strolled toward the diamond. Caleb was right. The school had brought in extra bleachers, and a security fence had hastily been installed around the field. There were extra agents wandering around, although their suits had been exchanged for golf shirts and khaki slacks. They were still very visible by their earpieces, and their constant talking into their wrists. One tried to stop me as I entered, but when he saw Agent Landry in his usual shadowing spot, he backed off.

I walked towards the pitcher's mound and looked towards home plate. This was part of my pregame ritual. I imagined the best hitter on the opposing team staring me down, and I stared back. I threw several imaginary pitches toward the plate, as I talked to myself. Then I went to home plate and stood in the batter's box. I gazed at each field to see the angle of the sun, and took a few imaginary swings of the bat. Then I made a slow trot around the bases as if

I had just hit a ball over the fence. Wandering back to the locker room, Rach ran up to me out of breath.

"Hurry up. We're having a team meeting. I looked around and couldn't find you. Then I remembered."

"Remembered what?"

"Remembered how you told me you always liked to go out to the field before the game. C'mon."

"There they are. Was wondering what happened to you two?"

"As I was saying, the decision for the starting pitcher today was a hard one. I didn't choose this player because her father is throwing out the first pitch. I chose her because of her determination to come back from an injury. If anyone has a problem with that, you can see me after we beat Arlington Christian. Our battery will be Rachel catching and Andie Beth pitching. If Andie Beth gets into any trouble, we'll switch her and Marti from first base to pitcher. Let's go ladies."

By the time I made it to the field the second time, the stands were beginning to fill up. As Rach and I warmed up on the sidelines, the Arlington team was taking fielding practice. Then a hush came over the crowd. I looked up and saw Daddy walking in. Rach and I paused, and then continued throwing. There was someone with Daddy, but with the glare of the sun, I couldn't recognize him. They were both shaking hands with the principal, Coach Shine and other officials. Coach Shine motioned to Rach it was time to begin, and she headed for home plate. I walked towards the dugout, and there was Ryan leaning over the fence.

"Beth, did you see who's here?"

"Yeah, my dad. But we knew he was coming."

"No, the guy with him."

"I couldn't tell who he was because of the glare. The sun was in my eyes."

"It's Derek Jeter. Agent Landry told me the President brought him here as a surprise for you. The Yankees are playing the Orioles in Baltimore tonight. Your dad convinced him to come to your game this afternoon."

"You're kidding."

"Nope. I got it straight from Agent Landry."

Now I was really nervous. Not only was I starting the first game of the season with Daddy watching, but my favorite player would also see me play. Stay cool Andie B. The public address announcer came on.

"Now ladies and gentlemen, the President will throw the first pitch of the season to the Lady Tigers' catcher, Rachel Le Brun, daughter of Senator and Mrs. Anton Le Brun of Louisiana. And the umpire calls it a strike. Rachel tosses the ball back to the President, and now he turns the ball over to our starting pitcher for the day, his own daughter, Andie Beth."

I ran out to the mound. Daddy handed me the ball.

"Your mama is going to be okay Buzzie. They got all the cancer. She'll have to have radiation only and no chemotherapy. Now go win this game."

"Yes sir, Mr. President."

Daddy pecked me on the forehead, and I could feel my face getting red.

"That ladies and gentlemen may be the first time a President has ever kissed a pitcher on the mound. Bet C.C. Sabathia won't let him get away with that."

The rest of the game was a blur. Gram had stayed with Mama at the hospital. All I knew was she was going to be okay, and I was on the top of the world playing softball again. I forgot about Derek sitting over there with Daddy.

Rach and I played the best game of our lives. Marti hit

a two run home run, and J.J. had a base clearing double

which was all we needed. We won the game 5-1 due to

an error in the outfield. Daddy and his entourage left the

stadium as the final out was made at first base.

I headed towards the locker room with the team, and

Ryan came running up beside me.

"Want to go celebrate?"

"Can't."

"Why not? Because of all the security. Hey, I know

Agent Landry has to tag along. I'm cool with that."

"Grounded. For two weeks."

"Beth, you stay grounded. What did you do now?"

"Lied to Agent Landry. Told him my parents said it was okay for me to stop and get my hair cut yesterday. Plus I talked back to the President. So no computer. No phone."

"Good grief."

"So, if you want to talk to me it will have to be at school. Or maybe I can sneak you in one of the back gates of the White House."

"Yeah, and get us both shot."

"True. Half the agents don't recognize me with my short hair."

"I almost didn't recognize you. But I like it. It's fun to run my fingers through it."

"Watch it. There are agents all around."

We were now at the gym.

"See ya Beth. If you ever get ungrounded, maybe we can go out sometime."

"Yeah, I'd like that."

I hurried through my shower, and met Agent Landry at the Blazer for the ride home. Home. weird. For the first time since we moved, I thought of the White House as home. The ride seemed quicker this time. I wasn't ready to go upstairs, and Agent Landry had told me Daddy was on his way to check Mama out of the hospital, so no one would be there anyway.

Cajun greeted me as I entered the building. I dropped my backpack by the elevator and headed towards the South Lawn Entrance. Cajun raced out to find some treats, and I sat on the steps, leaning against the pillar, my chin resting against my doubled fists. Here I was. Once again on the steps thinking about life.

THE END

*A*ndie Beth Steps *is a work of fiction. However, it deals with problems and situations faced by modern families. It can be adapted for use in book clubs, parent-teen workshops, weekend seminars, and Vacation Bible School. To learn more about Andie Beth Steps and how to use it in your church or organization, contact the author at: AndieBeth1@yahoo.com or on facebook at Andie Beth Nettles.*

LaVergne, TN USA
06 April 2011
222936LV00002B/2/P